BONE
DEEP
BONDS

BONE DEEP BONDS

A NOVEL

B.G. ARNOLD

atmosphere press

© 2022 B.G. Arnold

Published by Atmosphere Press

Cover design by Matthew Fielder

No part of this book may be reproduced without permission from the author except in brief quotations and in reviews. This is a work of fiction, and any resemblance to real places, persons, or events is entirely coincidental.

atmospherepress.com

Chapter 1
Phillip and Brian
Monday, April 1, 2002

Slowing down, Phillip drummed his fingers on the car's leather console, then once again combed them through the black mustache he'd attached before leaving his home in Maryland. If there was one thing he couldn't stand, it was boredom. It set him to thinking about worrisome things outside of his control. Like this search. Looking for the perfect boy, he'd been traveling the back roads of Ohio for two days. He knew if he were successful in his mission, photos of his selected youth would be nailed to telephone poles with detailed physical and geographic information, along with the boldface contact number of the Missing Children Hotline: 1-800-843-5678.

Picturing the photos called to mind one startling occurrence from over a decade ago, when Phillip had picked up his morning milk carton to witness the waxy image of the current boy he'd installed in his underground apartment. Testing his recall, he was quite certain it had been Ted, or "Teddy Bear," as he had named him. Indeed he'd been like a warm cuddly toy. That is, until his sweetness became cloying.

The point was, the whole panic reaction of society toward a missing child demonstrated their ignorance. Or at least in his case. If only they could comprehend the incredible opportunities he presented his chosen ones, they would realize he was more like a Renaissance patron than a common kidnapper. For after his lads had learned their lessons well, he returned them to their social order as sprouting young men, enlightened and able to spread the fruits of his teaching.

No criminal, he. For at a propitious time and place, his captives reappeared near their homes, heavily drugged, though quite intact, much like the magician's assistant who had been sawed in half in full view of the audience. And all of his boys had acquired the benefits of higher education. All except that *dummkopf* - God, what was his name? The one who had escaped through an oversight, when Phillip had been laden with grief after the death of Cerberus the First, his favorite guard-dog companion. Well, he'd undoubtedly blocked the boy's name from his memory, because he wanted to erase that whole sorry chapter. The rest of his lads had reaped the benefits of free tuition, luxurious room and board, plus indescribable bonuses. Phillip sighed. He knew that the farmers and blue-collar workers couldn't begin to understand his mission, which was exactly why he had to keep it covert.

The car's display read Monday, April 1, 2002. *All Fool's Day*. The road was straight and untraveled, so Phillip clicked on his cell phone appointments, noting he was due back by Thursday, at the latest, for an important *KOCS* meeting on Friday. The first order of business was to change the absurd acronym. He'd heard people snicker about it. And rightly so, even though the community knew it meant *Keep Our Children*

Safe. Phillip would straighten that out. This would be his second time to oversee the monthly meetings as their new Chairman of the Board, making it critical that he return in a timely fashion.

Oh, hell, he'd give this search a couple more hours, and then head east for home. Feeling parched, Phillip drank deeply from the bottled water he'd bought at the last gas station, some hundred miles earlier. Although the neighborhood stations often proved to be sources of useful conversational information, for anonymity's sake, he disliked stopping in small towns for gas. His BMW always stood out among the mud-splattered utility trucks and vehicles. To offset the riffraff's upper-class image his car created, he purposely dressed in casual attire when he went hunting. This time, along with his nondescript sweatshirt and jeans, a brown canvas jacket and black athletic shoes, he'd added a *Cincinnati Reds* baseball cap, pulling it low over his forehead to hide his distinctive widow's peak.

Long ago, he'd scuffed up the gym shoes, then rubbed grease and rust into his outer clothes, repeatedly washing them until they appeared old and grungy. He kept his hunting costume in a trunk at the back of his bedroom closet, bringing it out for these special trips. Few men his age could still fit into clothes that were purchased nearly two decades ago, he mused. And then there were his thespian skills. Although it had been over twenty years since he'd graduated, during his college days, Phillip had had plenty of practice on-stage in Harvard's *Hasty Pudding* troupe, pulling off far more challenging roles than that of an average Joe in an above-average car.

It was a shame he had to use his favorite car for this activity, but it was necessary. Whichever car he took, careful driving was about all that was needed to avoid being stopped by a state cruiser. As an additional safety measure, after he'd driven a decent distance from home, he always stopped for a quick dirt-lane switch of his registered Maryland license plate, to a non-registered one, for the eyes of the surveillance cameras that speckled the freeways and cities these days. In eighteen...no, nineteen years, he had never been stopped. Thank God, because that would most likely mean end-game. Although he'd tried numerous computer programs, he'd been unable to produce an ersatz driver's registration that matched his alternative plate. As a result, if he were stopped, even with his utmost conversational ingenuity, his true identity would undoubtedly surface.

At the last gas station, there had been the usual inquiries about his "fine ride" and Maryland license plate. He told them that he'd borrowed the car from his wealthy brother-in-law, in order to make this vacation trip to check out the region where he'd been born. "And," he had added, "even though I was a toddler when my family moved east, the Ohio countryside is still in my blood."

"Where in Ohio?" one of them had asked.

He'd replied that he couldn't remember the name of the place, because he'd been so young, and his parents had passed, but he thought he remembered them saying that it was somewhere on the outskirts of Columbus. After his family had moved away, long ago, the city limits had expanded, obliterating the town. "Eaten up by the suburbs," he had said, wrinkling his nose in disgust. They had nodded in sympathy.

An older man inquired where he was from in Maryland. He had given his usual response of "Mannasas." It was one of his litmus tests.

"Oh, I've heard of that," the man said.

He'd never encountered one who knew Manassas was in Virginia. They were gullible. Ignorant, really. And that was the reason Phillip sought red-neck country boys. He took great pride in helping them transcend their backward environment.

Ahead of the car, a shaft of sunlight shone on a lone runner. Even though Phillip was approaching the runner from the rear, the stride and musculature were telling. It was a male. Whether a preteen or early adolescent, he wasn't certain. As he drew closer, he noted the springiness of the runner's steps and the loose flow of his carriage. This one looked to be a youth. He'd observed that about the time joggers entered their teens, they tended to tighten up, believing it conserved energy. Which it didn't.

Slowing down, he saw the boy glance over his left shoulder, then ease onto the gravel at the side of the road, without breaking his stride. His sideways movement was graceful and his turned face had a strong profile, the chiseled chin bearing the mark of a master sculptor. Phillip judged him to be around twelve, which was his maximum cut-off age, for he'd found out the hard way that once testosterone fully kicked in, his boys became much harder to control.

From the back, the snugness of this one's gray sweatpants revealed alluring mounds of flesh that flexed and rippled, setting off corresponding pulsations between Phillip's legs. He willed himself to concentrate on non-arousing points of safety. Outside of the runner, he hadn't seen a person or a car on Conley Road since he'd turned onto it, over a mile ago. Just tedious farmland, dotted with cows in barren pastures, set out with occasional bales of hay.

On the back of the boy's blue sweatshirt appeared the raised yellow lettering of what was, most likely, a high school athletic team, although he hoped the lad wasn't already past the eighth grade. The lettering spelled *Cougars* in script, with the tail of the 'g' underlining the *Cou*... Probably a developing track runner or soccer player. Passing him, Phillip flashed a smile.

The boy waved his left hand, then immediately looked down at the road for his return to the asphalt. Slowing down even more, while watching the runner in his rear-view mirror,

Phillip couldn't tell what color the runner's hair was, because the boy wore an obnoxious green woolen hat with a fuzzy blue ball on top, the sides pulled down over his ears. Most likely his mother had knit it for him, cautioning him to wear it today, to protect his ears from the biting wind.

The runner's eyebrows were a light color. Some shade of blond. By his age, most of the blond boys were darkening to brown. He'd never had a fair-haired boy before. More important than the color of his hair, this one's complexion looked clear. Once, he'd picked up a youth when the sun had slanted into his eyes, and he'd been unable to see clearly until his passenger was in the car. The boy's face had been covered with acne. Finding it repulsive, Phillip had let him out at the next corner, on the pretext that he had suddenly noticed the time, realizing he was due somewhere in the opposite direction within ten minutes.

Braking, he put the car in reverse, slowly backing up until he was abreast of the runner, who hesitated, and then slowed down. Phillip pushed a button, rolling down the passenger window, feeling a blast of chilly air.

"Hi there. Seems like pretty harsh weather to be running. Building up a sweat like that, you're liable to catch cold. Need a ride?" He addressed this to the boy's chest, as the runner had yet to lean down and look in the car.

Finally the boy lowered his head, as he settled his forearm on the open window frame. "Thanks for the offer, but I set out to run to a friend's house. I need to get in shape."

"In shape for what?" Phillip said, taking in the boy's visage, particularly his wide-set brown eyes under light eyebrows. With his fair complexion, he'd expected some shade of blue.

"Well, mainly for track, although I won't start competing until fall," the boy said, almost apologetic.

"I thought you were a track runner. Even from the back. I guess it's your musculature. Long, lean and sleek. I'm a soccer coach," he said, adding a pitch of pride to his voice. He sometimes surprised himself at just how good he was at this game.

"Really? Back in Maryland? I noticed your license plates."

'That was good. The boy was observant.' "Yes, I'm just here for a short time, visiting some relatives in Milton." Milton was a small town he'd passed through some fifty miles ago.

The boy stroked the ridge along the rolled down window with his middle finger. "What kind of car is this?" he asked.

"It's a BMW."

"I thought so, but it's even cooler than they look on TV. Yours is like the ones in the James Bond movies. My dad has all his videos, back to *Goldfinger*. What model is yours?"

"It's a 760i, with all the bells and whistles."

"That's cool. I never thought I'd get this close to a real BMW."

"Hey, how 'bout if you had a chance to drive one? I assume you're of the age to be practicing for your driver's permit," he said, knowing the lad wasn't, but purposely flattering him with the addition of two or three years on his age.

The boy scuffed his foot backward in the roadside gravel. "No, not really. I'm not even thirteen. Driving's a ways off. Thanks anyway, but I need to get back to jogging."

"Hey, it's good to see such a well-disciplined young athlete. But if you'd really like to see how high tech the new models are, you can try out the passenger seat just to the end of this road, and then I'll loop back and drop you off here. So you can continue your run." That way if they saw anyone on the road, he would indeed drop him off.

Phillip could read the internal struggle on the boy's face. A smile tugged at his mouth, then slid into a frown. He'd undoubtedly been warned never to accept a ride from a stranger. But he couldn't be too far from home, which always made people feel more secure. And Phillip knew he didn't create the image of a pervert, or a psycho. Still, he didn't flatter himself. He knew that above all, no matter how he appeared, or what the boy had been told, there was the allure of the BMW and its sex quotient for budding young males.

As for himself, he liked the road-handling, safety features and luxury of his favorite model. Once, he'd tried the hunt in his run-about Toyota, knowing it stood out less in terms of identification, but as he'd suspected, it had severely limited lure-appeal, culminating in a dry run.

With his hand still on the window-frame, the boy said, "I don't get it. Are you a salesman or somethin'? 'Cause if you are, you're in the wrong part of the country."

"Au contraire...I wouldn't sell this baby to anyone. I just picked up on our mutual admiration of a beautiful product, and thought you might like a short spin it it. I'll drop you off wherever you want to go. In town?" That was always convincing, as in any small town there would be the safety factor of many bystanders who could see and identify the boy.

"OK. Why not?" The boy entered with a swagger, swinging the passenger door open so wide that its hinges groaned. The black leather seat made a whooshing sound as it compressed under his weight.

He settled his long legs awkwardly in the passenger space, compelling Phillip to say, "The seat adjusters are located to the right of your seat. Play around with them 'til you're comfortable." He watched the boy quickly figure out the icons. He'd come to expect this with country boys, who seemed to have mechanical aptitudes surpassing those of their city cousins.

As the youth settled in, Phillip extended his right hand. "Hi, I'm Phillip. And whom do I have the pleasure of meeting?"

The kid looked startled at the formality, but adjusted quickly, shaking his hand firmly and responding, "My name is Brian. Brian Brefort. I live down the road you probably turned off of, before this one."

That was a lot of valuable information he hadn't expected

to come by so easily. "Brian...Brian Brefort. I like the sound of your name. It's alliterative."

"Alliterative? Sounds familiar, but I don't remember what it means."

Good. He now knew Brian was a boy who was willing to inquire about things he didn't know, rather than trying to cover up his ignorance. That meant he was teachable.

"Alliteration is the sound your name makes. Br-ian Br-efort. The initial sound repeats and kind of rolls off your tongue. You know what I mean?"

"Yeah...like *Mama's Macaroni*....I just made that up."

"You catch on real quick, Brian. *Brainy Brian*."

They both laughed, clearing the tension. The car started forward as Phillip said, "Be sure and fasten your seatbelt."

Brian reached down and pulled it across his lap. Phillip heard it click in place at the same time that he triggered the automatic door lock. He saw a shadow of fear cross the kid's face. Anticipating his reaction, he said in an even tone, "Just a safety precaution I take with every passenger." He smiled reassuringly, and the boy's countenance cleared. "So what'll it be? A spin into town?"

"Sounds good."

"I'll continue down this road 'til I find a good turn-around. And then take a left at the corner, toward town?"

"Left. That's right." Brian grinned at his small tease, seeing that Phillip responded to wit. As he relaxed into the ride, Brian turned his attention to the man and the interior of the car. Phillip looked to be at least ten years older than his dad, so he figured he must be around fifty. He had a trim black mustache, kind of like the old-time images he'd seen of some goofy silent-screen actor named Charlie Chaplin. Or Adolph Hitler. The mustache was so black it looked like he'd taken boot polish to it. It matched both the outside and the interior of the car.

Brian found himself drifting into the feeling soft leather gave him. He remembered a pair of soft kid gloves Aunt Louise had when he was younger, and how he'd picked them up when no one was looking, rubbing them along his cheek. He didn't want anyone to catch him doing it, because it was the closest thing he'd ever felt to human flesh. It had made him think of the time he'd caught a glimpse of his older sister's naked, budding breasts, and he'd wondered if they were as soft as the gloves.

Brian looked at the dashboard. It was so filled with gauges that it reminded him of the control panel of airplanes he'd seen at the Air Force Museum in Dayton. The only things he could identify for sure were the speedometer and the tachometer. Phillip was going 30 mph.

"Hey, how come you're going so slow? I thought anyone who drives a BMW likes to go fast."

"Oh, I like to go fast alright, but we're not on the Autobahn. What's down this road? I seem to have meandered off course."

"This road leads to the town dump. It's closed on Mondays, so I run along it to stay away from traffic. Ordinarily I'd still be in school, but there was an early dismissal today. Some teacher's meeting."

"Good for you. Using your time well. And good strategy for a running road. But about how far to the dump…and are there any houses between here and there? I mean, anyone you know? Like your friend for instance?"

Somehow the question seemed oddly stated, but it was no big thing, so Brian let the little feeling that was starting to scratch at him, fade away.

"There aren't any houses on this road, except the ones you passed at the corner. You must have seen them. There's the McCammon farm and the Fowler's place." There, he'd told this guy, Phillip, that anywhere they drove around here, everyone would recognize him. "And hey, you mentioned you were visiting relatives in Milton. Whose family is that? We play them in football."

The guy hesitated a moment and then said, "The

Kowalskis. I doubt if you've ever heard of them. They don't have kids in the high school."

Brian shook his head, and the man continued. "Say, this is a beautiful part of Ohio. Must really be something when all these deciduous trees turn their fall colors."

The word *deciduous* didn't throw Brian. He'd skipped fourth grade, and almost always made the honor roll. Plus he'd studied the broad-leaf and evergreen trees in an extra-credit assignment.

"Yeah, it's something alright. My favorite season of the year. Football weather. I thought about trying out for the football team, 'cause I'd probably be the fastest running back Digby's ever had, but then I decided I could get hurt bad playing football, and that track's much safer." He didn't know what made him want to brag to this man. Maybe it was because he drove a spiffy BMW. Or maybe because Digby was such a small town that he wasn't used to having people ignorant about his academic records and athleticism.

"Well, that's cool, Brian. Congratulations," the man said, looking down the road. "Is that sign coming up, for the dump?"

"Yeah, that's it. The road dead-ends at the dump, so we'll have to turn around to head to my friend's house." He looked out at the familiar fields they were passing. "Sometimes my old man and me come down here and shoot up tin cans, plastic junk. Once we even shot up an old TV. Dad said Elvis used to do that in his living room when he didn't like what the DJ said about his new album."

"See," Brian pointed across to the driver's side, "I was going to cut across to a lane in that field over there. It's a shortcut to my friend's house. But you can't drive a nice car like this, down there. I'll show you the way by the road."

"You're right. I didn't intend to drive across a field," said Phillip, stopping under a giant oak. Using his valet key to unlock a compartment in the console, he removed something from it. It was a stainless steel handgun. "Maybe you and I can pop off a few rounds before we head to your friend's house."

Phillip hated to start off with a gun in his hand, startling his young innocents, but he knew there was no better way to bring them under his control. He saw a flash of panic as the kid's eyes widened, and then the boy bolstered himself, managing to maintain his cool. He was already beginning to like this lad. In spite of fear, he was capable of reining in his emotions.

As Brian took a deep breath, he could see the kid's developing Adam's apple bob up and down. At first his voice came out in a squeak, but then he lowered its register. "Hey, that's a nice pistol you've got there. My dad's got one just about like it. A *Ruger*. Right?"

"So, you not only know your trees, you know your guns, too. You have any experience shooting… beside tin cans?"

"Sure." Brian cleared his throat noisily. "My dad and I shoot clay pigeons nearly every weekend. He used to hunt, but he says he doesn't have the heart for it anymore."

Phillip could tell the kid was pushing hard to think of something natural to say.

Brian's words came out in a heated rush. "I only shot one animal myself – a porcupine. But I know how my dad feels about killing wildlife. It's just that the deer population has exploded in the past couple of years. They're getting to be a real nuisance. A neighbor lady got injured bad last fall when she hit one crossing the road. Late at night. It slid up her hood and came crashing through her windshield. The crazy buggers come right up in our yard, eat our vegetables. We had to fence the garden in."

His captive was fast running out of talk about anything other than the gun in his hand, that he kept pointed at the kid's chest. He'd bring him around so he could no longer pretend to ignore it. "So you know enough about guns to know I'm cocking this now," Phillip said, as he pulled back the hammer.

"And you undoubtedly know that all I have to do is pull the trigger, in order to shoot you."

Brian got a faraway feeling like he was viewing the whole scene on a movie screen. It took a minute for him to reclaim reality, and then he spoke from a place in the middle of his brain that felt as though it was melting. "Why are you fooling around like this? What do you want from me?" He could hear his voice break, as though he was about to cry. Swallowing hard, he said, "I don't have any money on me. What do you want?"

"I'll tell you exactly what I want. And if you do as I say, there will be no need to use this."

"OK," Brian said, thinking desperately about making a break for it, until he remembered that this insane man had control of the door locks. Besides that, someone he'd originally judged to be an ordinary guy, except for the car, now appeared quite crazed, and would probably shoot him in the back the first chance he got. A blur of images floated in front of him. First he turned toward the man and begged for mercy, then his body was riddled with bullets, blood spurting from all the wounds. Then his mom and dad were shoveling dirt on his casket, while his sister, Lauren, dropped his raggedy old stuffed bunny that he'd given her as a joke, into a dark hole in the ground where he soon would be.

"OK," Brian said, the repetition echoing in his head. Was he really going to give in that easily? Yes, there was the gun, the difference between life and death. The image of the dying porcupine flashed across his mind. One minute it was running, the next, it was instantly still. "What do you want me to do?"

"It's really very simple. Especially for a jock like you. I want you to lie down on the seat, curl up on it as best you can, with your feet toward the door, your legs hanging down and your head right here," Phillip said, thumping his corner of the console. "I want your face looking toward the dashboard and your arms held behind your back, as though they were handcuffed. And I want you to stay that way until I give you different directions. Now that's pretty simple, isn't it?"

"Yes sir," Brian said in a meeker voice, deciding his best chance of staying alive was to act as though he was following directions given by his new high school track coach, who oddly enough, asked that his runners address him as 'Sir.'

"I have some rope within reach. Do I have to bind your hands and feet?"

"No sir," Brian responded.

"OK then."

Brian struggled to get into position, wincing as he thrust his arms in back of him.

"Hold on a minute. I want you to sit up...very slowly. No funny stuff."

Brian did as he was told, relishing the release of his left shoulder. "Is it OK if I take off my hat? My head is starting to sweat."

"Sure."

He saw the look of surprise that crossed the man's face as his red curls sprang out from under their cover. They were Brian's top ID. He was the only redhead in town. His dad had told him that he got it from his grandfather, but he'd never known him, because 'Pop' had died in the Korean War, long before Brian was born.

"Put your hat back on, and pull it down so it covers your hair." He obeyed. "That's good. Now I want you to reach into the glove compartment and get out the brown bottle."

Alarm buzzers sounding in his head, Brian suddenly realized that *Phillip* might not be his captor's real name. The bottle was right on top. There was a label that he turned toward him, hoping to spot a name. All the information had been blackened out.

The two of them were sitting at the dead end of the road, with the motor idling. Brian noticed that the guy kept glancing in his rear-view mirror, checking for any approaching cars. Maybe Brian could stall and somebody would drive up. Then, even if the man sped away, that person would surely remember the car. But no one was likely to come here at this time of day, especially on a Monday. Sometimes he'd seen guys parked down here, making out with their girlfriends. But that was in the evening.

Phillip raised the barrel of the gun slightly. "Turn the label away from you and pop off the cap, being careful not to spill the pills." The snub-nosed barrel twitched. "How much do you weigh?"

On a deep in-breath, Brian answered, "About one-forty." He wondered why the guy wanted to know. Maybe it had something to do with weight leverage, if Brian decided to fight him.

"About one-forty," mused Phillip. "How tall are you?"

"Almost five-foot-ten."

"Hmm," the man said, eying him up and down. It reminded Brian of a farmer's eyes measuring livestock at a county auction.

"Well then, I want you to take two of those pills. You can wash them down with the bottle of spring water, right here." He pointed the barrel of the gun to the cup holder on the console. "I'm not trying to poison you. They're perfectly safe. In fact, they'll make you feel good. Warm and drowsy. You should fall asleep in about twenty minutes. Which is what I want. You're a little too smart to count on you not figuring out where we're going, just because you can't see."

"Where *are* we going?" Brian asked as he reached for the water bottle.

Phillip laughed again, this time with a mocking edge to it. "Maybe you aren't as smart as I gave you credit for. Didn't I just tell you I don't want you to know where we're going."

"OK then, why are you taking me there?" Brian was feeling less shaky now that he was sitting up and could see familiar territory, along with his captor's half-smiling face. "It's not going to do you any good if you're kidnapping me, because my folks aren't well off. If you ask for much money, they couldn't begin to come up with it."

The guy looked at him sharply, and then down at the pills in his hand. Brian looked at them too. Each of the capsules was half-yellow, half-brown. He tossed them into his mouth, trying hard to swallow. They wouldn't go down, and he began choking.

Phillip shoved the water bottle back in his hand. "Here, take a big gulp and swallow hard."

Brian barely got them down, when Phillip barked, "Now open your mouth, real wide." He did. "Stick out your tongue, then curl it up to the roof of your mouth." Again he followed directions, not really sure why they'd been given. Nothing made much sense anymore.

"Good," Phillip said. "Now get back the way you were, relax, and leave everything up to me. No wait, one more thing. Toss me your hat." Phillip let it drop into his lap, then with one hand still holding the gun, he removed a small pair of scissors from the console, snipping off the blue ball from the top of the hat. It rolled off of the seat, dropping to the floor, followed by the sound of the scissors hitting the rubber mat at Phillip's feet. "There, that's much better," he said. "Fuzzy balls are for girls."

After Brian managed to put his hands behind his back again, Phillip reached into the back seat, grabbed a blanket, and threw it over his body. He pulled it up until it covered Brian's head. Although Phillip had left him a small open space to breathe, Brian could hear the short, raspy breaths his fear brought on. He tried calming himself, imagining he was sitting next to his dad in their church pew.

When Phillip turned the key in the ignition, Brian noticed the starter didn't growl like his dad's. It purred. And his shoulder didn't hurt as much this time. That scared him.

Maybe his head and body could get used to anything this strange man ordered. He felt the car make a U-turn at the entrance to the dump, turning back down the road. Brian knew that what he needed to do was to think straight and concentrate on where the car was going. He could tell from the turns and sounds, that they were going around the north end of Digby, which seemed like a risky move on the guy's part. But he didn't dare sit up, even if he could. Counting two STOP signs, he noticed which way his body shifted, so he'd know which way they'd turned.

Soon the count and directions faded from his mind, like a fog had rolled in and wrapped around everything he tried to think. It wasn't an ordinary fog, cold and damp, penetrating his bones. It felt good. Pleasant and warm, like the down comforter his mother used to pull up to his chin on cold winter nights, when he was just a kid. He tried to hold on to the feeling of home and family, but it too slowly faded away.

Chapter 2
Owen and Jane
Monday, April 1

A man emerged from the second floor of a row house on the west side of inner-city Baltimore. Facing the door, he pulled it shut slowly, as though he were afraid of waking someone. Above all, he hoped the closed door would cage the nightmare he was trying to escape.

When he'd awakened, groggy and sodden from fear, he'd looked around the drape-dimmed room at the disarray of glasses, beer bottles and ashtrays littered with remnants of joints and cigarettes. The scene was all too familiar. The room was not. He'd wrestled tattered jeans over his graying briefs, pushed his hood down to his eyebrows, and exited into a plywood-paneled hallway. As he turned toward the staircase, he saw someone approaching and jerked his arms up to cover his face, nearly running into a young woman.

"Sorry, I didn't mean to startle you," she said, "but this is my apartment you're leaving."

He dropped his arms and scanned her face. She didn't appear angry, as he would have been in her shoes.

"Some guy named Danny invited me here last night," he offered.

"That would be my boyfriend. But I doubt he invited you to stay overnight."

"Maybe not," he mumbled. "I don't remember."

"Where are you going?" she asked him, trying to see his eyes.

"I don't know. Where am I?"

"Right here in front of me," Jane replied, a smile right behind her laughter. She remembered wondering about him last night. He was the silent one, while her boyfriend, Danny, and two other men had come up from the corner tavern, since it closed early on Sunday evenings. They'd continued to smoke, drink and hang out. Retreating to her bedroom, she had abstained, knowing she'd be leaving before ten for the night shift at The Women's Shelter. Danny had assured her he would straighten things up and see that the apartment was locked when he left. This was the second time he'd been irresponsible about partying in her place. Rather than taking it out on this apparently homeless guy, she would speak to Danny about nixing these spontaneous get-togethers in the future.

She tried again. "You're just down the street from Chino's, and you must have slept over after the gathering last night. It's my apartment. I had to leave and go to work. Are you the last one out?"

He pulled back his hood and appraised her. She was pretty. Sky blue eyes like his baby sister, Tina. He hadn't seen Tina for so long. "Yeah, I guess I am. I didn't see anyone else in there."

"Well," she said, "I'm just coming home from work, and I'm about to heat up a strong cup of coffee. Would you like to stay for one yourself, before you start off to the place where you don't know you're going? Maybe you'll remember then."

As she spoke, Jane recognized her compulsion to reach out to derelicts was once again spinning into motion. Although it didn't make much sense, in spite of their coarseness, there was an element of little-boy pathos about them that made her feel like she should rescue them. At the same time, they seemed to be a life-saving log floating by, holding the promise of refuge for her. Refuge from what, she wasn't sure.

"No thanks, I'll pass on the coffee," said the man, "but it's a decent offer."

"Then take me up on it. I think you need to sober up from whatever it was you were smoking? Snorting? Drinking? Do you know what you were using?" Jane had learned to be direct with characters like this haunted man in her hallway. They didn't respond to pretense.

His head was beginning to clear. It was almost as though her insistence made it impossible for anything else. "I think it was all three. Smoking herb, snorting coke, drinking beer. Maybe even shooting up, but I don't think so. Don't remember the rush." He hadn't shot up anything, hadn't used a needle in years. He was just testing this broad's limits. Seeing what she could handle.

Jane knew he hadn't shot up, because that was the one line she was sure Danny would not risk crossing. Not in her apartment. At the start of their relationship, Danny had developed hepatitis C from shooting up heroin, making her vulnerable. His *Interferon* treatment had been successful, he was in remission and no longer using, while Jane had periodic checkups, assuring her that she hadn't contracted it from sex with him. Thus, no use of needles had become her cardinal rule.

"I sure hope you didn't shoot up with a dirty needle," she said, taking his hand and leading him to the kitchen. "You could get hepatitis."

"I already have it," the man said, testing her again by not

removing his hand, although it felt strange.

It had been so many years since a woman had held his hand. He felt her hesitation when she heard that, but damn, she didn't even pull away. Instead, she sat him down at the kitchen table, pulling a red ribbon tied to a chain that dangled from a naked lightbulb.

She glanced about, saying, "My whoever stayed after I left, sure did make one hell of a mess."

"It wasn't me. I nodded off early," he said, "but I'll help you clean up. If you want." He was surprised at what this welcoming woman pulled out of him, without his even thinking about it. He hadn't offered domestic help to anyone in ages. It was enough to try and keep his own shit together, even though it wasn't much more than a carload, as he'd moved from room to room over the years.

"No, I don't need your help. But I think you need some strong coffee." Jane pulled out a wooden chair. "You can drink it slowly and sober up while I pick up some of this stuff. Do you like yours straight up, or on the rocks?" She grinned, displaying dimples.

"Black is good. Even though caffeine gives me the shakes after a night like last night. It'll feel like magnitude 7 on the Richter scale."

"Richter scale? Sounds like you know some things, outside of drugs." She poured two cups of coffee from a glass pot and put them in the microwave.

"Yeah, some stuff filters through the haze. What's your name, anyway?"

"My name's Jane. 'Just Plain Jane,' they call me."

"There's nothing plain about you. You could light up a Christmas tree."

"Why thanks. That's the nicest thing anyone I've met coming out of my apartment has ever said to me. Now...let me see your palm. Then I can tell you what your name is."

As though hypnotized, the man uncurled his fingertips,

while she laid the back of his right hand on the cold enamel of the kitchen table. Then, placing her warm palm under his opened hand, she brought it closer to her face. A wisp of blond hair fell from her ponytail, tickling his nose.

"Now, let's see. Oh, looky here," she said tracing her fingernail across his palm. "You have a deep interesting lifeline, and I can see something emerging. It's an *O*, then a *w*, then an *e,* followed by *n*. It's your name – *Owen*."

"Hey, what's with you? Are you a psychic or something?"

Jane laughed. "No, silly. I remember it from last night. I was at your party for a short time myself, before I retreated to my bedroom. But you were too high to remember me. Right?"

"Right. Shame on me. Missing out on the good things in life. Doing drugs."

"For how long?" The microwave beeped and she removed two steaming cups of coffee, placing Owen's in front of him. "Let it sit a minute. I got it too hot."

It felt good to have someone warn him that he might hurt himself. The last person who had done that was Tina. Odd that this woman he'd just met seemed to care.

"Doing drugs? About as long as I can remember. Haven't been sober since – can't recall. Wait, I cannot tell a lie. I do remember when I started using whatever drugs came my way. It's been ever since I started having this recurring nightmare. The one I had last night. Which is why I was sneaking out of here, trying to leave it behind. Scares the bejesus out of me."

"Tell me about it. I really dig dreams. Maybe I can unravel it for you."

'Why not? What do I have to lose? She won't be able to tell who *The Lizard* is. Only I know his name is Phillip.'

"I know what it's about…it's him. Only he's a giant lizard that keeps sticking me with his poisonous tongue, that looks like a pitchfork…backing me up against a rock wall until I have nowhere to go. I keep dodging it, but finally, he gets me. I can feel his tongue piercing me, and then I can feel the poison slowly travel through my bloodstream, and I know when it hits my brain, I'm gonna die. It's almost there when I wake up screaming. I'm always afraid if I don't wake up, it'll reach my brain. That's why I do drugs. They protect me."

Owen couldn't believe he'd finally told someone his nightmare. It must be because he'd never see her again. He'd make sure he didn't.

"God, that sounds real scary," Jane said. "But I don't get the part about the drugs protecting you. I mean, you'd just done drugs, and it seems like they brought the dream on."

"It's hard to explain. But I know the drugs coat my brain. Or something like that. So he can't ever kill me."

"You keep saying *he*. Who is *he*?"

Nobody had ever asked him that before. He was not about to disclose something she could hold him to. But then again, it would be a relief to partially tip the lid off his secret, without releasing vital information. Maybe it would help to have somebody know part of his story.

"*The Lizard* lives here in Baltimore." There, in just six words, he'd shared more private information than he had in so many guarded years. Then suddenly, as though it was separated from his control, he banged his clenched fist on the table so hard that his coffee cup jumped up, tipping over, its dark chocolate stream pooling on the table.

Jane grabbed a bunch of napkins, soaking it up.

"I'm sorry," Owen said, as she threw the soggy paper in the trash.

"Don't be. It's OK. I'm the one who's sorry. Sorry you have a real-live monster chasing you in your dreams. Sorry you have reason to fear someone so much. I'd probably be using hard drugs myself if I had to contend with that."

Jane was looking straight into his eyes, which was a bit unnerving. Then she looked beyond him at a spot over his shoulder. "Do you mind if I make a suggestion about that nightmare?"

He nodded.

"I used to have them, too. And did heavier drugs at the time. Now I'm just a recreational dabbler."

"Yeah, so fire away," said Owen.

"Well, like I said, I used to have nightmares too. They diagnosed me as PTSD. *Post-Traumatic Stress Disorder.* I did some self-education and found out about 'lucid dreaming.' It's like auto-suggestion. Before I go to sleep, I tell myself if a scary monster turns up in my dreams, I'm not going to run away from him. I'm going to turn around and face him, and tell him to bug off. Like 'I'm not afraid of you. You're just a figment of my imagination.' It works. So help me. The monster collapses. Just like letting air out of a balloon."

Owen looked deep into her eyes and felt like he was floating on the surface of a still lake. Then he blinked and his skepticism returned. "Yeah, I get the point. But this is different. *The Lizard* really exists in the waking world. Probably not too far from here." No more facts. He didn't want her to have any knowledge that might lead to him. Even if she could, no one else must find him. *The Lizard* was for Owen, and Owen alone.

"You mean you still have contact with him?"

"No, but I will. Keep him from doing more of his evil deeds. Then I'll let the air out of his balloon. You better believe I will."

"Oh, I believe you. You're too intense, not to. But your approach sounds kind of…oh, let's just call it 'radical.' They say two heads can think better than one. Maybe I can help you figure out a practical way to deflate him. I'm offering my services. I'm pretty good at detective work, but I'll need to know more about him."

Owen could tell she was sincere in her motivation to help him, though he wasn't sure why. The mystery made him pull back. Hard. "No, I can't talk about it. I gotta go home." He rose from the table feeling wobbly, but knowing it probably didn't show, because he'd made an art of covering up his drug tremors, along with his fears.

"Let me drive you. I'm not sure how you wound up at Chino's, but apparently it's pretty far from where you live. I know the streets of Baltimore, like...like the palm of your hand. Please. Let me."

"No, I need to get out in the open air. Let it smack me in the face. Walk this one off." Owen pulled his hood up again, lowering it to his eyes, where he could barely see her blues anymore. He walked toward the door, hearing her follow him.

"Look, Owen..." He turned, seeing her reach into her slacks pocket, bringing out a small card. "Here, take my business card. From where I work. And if you think you could use some help, call me there."

He hesitated only a moment. "No, I don't want your card. But thanks for letting me stay the night. Maybe I'll see you around some time." He turned the inner doorknob and walked out toward the staircase, not even looking back.

"Bye, Owen."

Even though she'd shut the door behind him softly, its sound magnified in Owen's head with each step he took down to the street. By the time he stood at her corner, the sound of the shutting door vibrated through his body like the striking of a Chinese gong. Maybe he'd made a mistake in leaving so soon. He glanced over his shoulder to see Jane pull back a drape, watching him from an upstairs window.

Jane dropped the worn swag of drapery from her hand, as Owen disappeared around the corner. She doubted she'd ever see him again. He was so alienated, so mistrustful. She knew the vulnerable state he was in after an evening of drugs, followed by the nightmare, and that he had never intended to give her a glimpse of his secret rage and shame. There were those few precious moments when he'd opened up, but her timing had been off. Once again, she'd been too maternal, her habitual response to derelict souls, be they animals or people. When she'd rushed in, it had turned him off. She'd scared him, and he was gone.

'Good God, will I ever give up trying to save lost souls?' But what was to become of Owen if he didn't accept a hand up? Hopefully someone could reach him, and he wouldn't be relegated to the psychic dumpster of humanity. Witnessing tormented beings like Owen, Jane wanted to believe in reincarnation. If she could choose, she would return in animal form. Preferably a bird, soaring above the horrific mess man had made of Earth. She knew that all animals were wired to feel pain, but with the exception of the survival trait of avoiding painful stimuli, she saw no proof that any animal, other than humans, carried pain forward in their minds, reshaping it into obsessive monsters that prolonged their suffering. Like Owen had done with his nightmares, his hatred, and his plans to gain revenge.

Enough rubbing of her worry beads. Just Plain Jane had many chores to tend to, thanks to Owen and the likes of him. But at least they possessed their addictions as lame excuses for irresponsibility. Danny had no excuse for his. He'd definitely cleaned up his act, and outside of an occasional drink and toke or two of marijuana, he'd been straight for over a year. What was he thinking, allowing Owen to stay overnight?

Jane followed her nose through her three small rooms, until she found a pool of vomit next to the toilet. At least someone had tried. Earlier, when she'd entered the apartment with Owen, she'd smelled it, but she didn't want to offend him by going straight to it in an accusatory manner.

As she gathered her cleaning supplies to address the matter, she began laughing out loud. It was preposterous to be concerned about offending someone who had slept here uninvited, and could be the one who had barfed in her bathroom. "The hostess with the mostess," she admonished herself.

The phone interrupted her thoughts. It was Danny.

"Hi, Kitten."

"Hi, Danny. Where'd you come up with that name?"

"I thought of it the other day. You were positively purring in bed."

"Perhaps I was, but that was before I came home this morning to find Owen had slept overnight on the couch, and the apartment was a mess. You didn't stay to see that it was cleaned up, and everyone was gone. As we discussed. And as you promised. You aren't backsliding with your rehab, are you?"

"No-oo," he said, "but I can see where you might think so. I'm sorry I didn't stay until everyone was gone, but I suddenly remembered I'd left my back door unlocked, and had to dash. Owen said he'd pick up on his way out."

"And you don't know any better than to take the word of a homeless druggie about such things? Aside from the fact that when he left, there was no way for him to lock up my place. Meaning your security is more important than mine."

"You're right. My actions were thoughtless. Maybe I had one too many beers, in which case I would be backsliding a bit... but maybe Owen stayed to protect your unlocked apartment."

"Nice try, but that was hardly his motivation, since he was exiting the apartment when I came up the stairs. But like most vagrants, he needed some help to get on his way, so I made him a cup of coffee. And we talked a bit. Owen's a tormented soul, as you must know. He offered to help clean up, but I preferred to handle it myself." Jane winced at hearing her self-proclaimed martyrdom. She knew she was hoping to create the illusion that she had dismissed Owen, and not the other way around.

"Oh, come on, Kitten. I'm sorry. I'm at work now, but as soon as I can get away, I'll be by to clean up. Leave it for me. Go to bed and get your beauty rest, and I'll be along about the time you're waking up. Please."

"No, Danny. You know me. I can't rest until my apartment is set in order. And for another thing, there's a pool of barf in the bathroom that reeks. I was about to get to it when you called."

"Damn. I'm sorry. I know you won't rest until order is restored. But let me make it up to you. Flowers? Dinner out? A movie? What'll it be?"

"Just promise you won't let it happen again. I'd be happy with that."

"Done. Absolutely. But beyond that, Kitten, you really should give more consideration to moving in with me, or at least moving out of that drug ghetto. My barista earnings may be slim compared to yours, but if you'd room with me, your half would be even cheaper than the low rent you're paying."

"Come on, Danny, you know it's more than the rent. I started out here when it was all I could afford. And after all these years, it's home. Especially since Domino and his Vice Squad consider me their good luck charm, and offer me gang protection. Where else can I get that kind of security for a pittance?"

"OK, you win. As usual. I won't bring it up again. But do I have your permission to call you 'Kitten'? I'd like that."

"Well, I do like the way it sounds. And you know I'm nuts about kittens. You're the second person today who's objected to my 'Just Plain Jane' name. The other one said there was nothing plain about me. That I could light up a Christmas tree."

There was silence at the other end, acknowledging that Danny knew he was being baited. Finally he said, "My great powers of deductive reasoning tell me that person must have been Owen. And that, as you can see, he's not such a bad guy. In fact, he's the kind that if you got to know him, you could probably straighten him up. Like you did me."

He took the bait alright. But why did Danny keep bringing

these men around, when he knew how easily she was taken in.

"Yes, I probably could help him if I wanted, but I'm resigning that role. Reserving it for the people I get paid to help."

"Straight thinking. Reserve your energy for things that benefit you. Like the children at The Shelter. And me, of course."

Funny he should add that. Jane had just been thinking that maybe she was getting tired of helping him. "Yes, of course. Well, I need to get busy and clean the apartment. If anything, it needs a hosing down."

"OK. But don't tire yourself out. I haven't forgotten that you have to catch the night train again this evening. Keep in touch, Kitten. And remember, I love you."

"I love you too, Danny. Goodbye."

Somehow the 'I love you' felt obligatory. As she hung up, Jane found herself thinking of what Danny had said, and wondering if she really could help Owen.

Outside of eating and catching up on her emails, Jane spent a good part of the afternoon cleaning. Shaking out scatter rugs, sweeping floors and refreshing the bed with clean sheets. No matter. She wasn't due at work until ten. It still amazed her that they were now paying her more to work nights, when most of the Shelter's women and children were asleep. And that outside of minimal record-keeping, she could do anything she wanted with her down time. Lately, she'd been reading more, and writing in her journal.

Of course, night shift meant she didn't see as much of Danny, or much daylight, either. He often arrived home from work barely two hours before she had to leave for her job. And even though the Shelter had scheduled her for three consecutive twelve-hour work-nights, so that she now had off

Wednesdays through Saturdays, she slept a good portion of the extra day she'd gained, trying to adjust her internal clock to the next three days of staying awake in the world of light.

After a short shrift of sleep, grabbing a sandwich and getting ready for work, Jane folded her arms on the kitchen table, resting her head in the little hollow space they made, while sitting in the chair where Owen had been. She thought she could smell him. Why was she so obsessed with him? He was a down-and-out dirty druggie. Beyond the realm of redemption, no doubt. He even smelled raunchy. Probably had never even tried rehab.

What was it about him? Ah, yes…the old 'Savior' mantra on its endless tape loop. Maybe she could save him. That was the reason she picked up stray animals and found homes for them, the reason she'd majored in psychology in undergraduate school and earned her master's in social work, and the reason she now chose to work in a woman's shelter, trying to help victims climb out of their hidey-holes.

Ditto for the reasons she'd hooked up with Danny. Another victim par excellence. His father had committed suicide when he was only eight, his mother had never remarried, and since he was the only child, his mother had then gone about schooling Danny to fill his father's shoes. Which of course was a master script for failure.

While Danny's father wasn't there for him, Jane's father had been 'too-much-there' for her own good. His pathetic alcoholism and recurrent bouts of rage, when he would assault her mother, leaving her to Jane's care, made Danny's father appear heroic to have decided that his family was better off without him. Instead, Jane and her mother had cringed in the corners of their lives for nearly twenty years, trying to escape her father's notice, only to have the tyrant die a slow death from cirrhosis of the liver, soon after she had left home for good. Jane swore that every time she returned to visit her mother in Philly, the whole house still smelled like alcohol, even though her mother didn't drink. Her father's odor even permeated Jane's dreams, as though his essence was sprinkled on her pillowcase.

Danny wanted to marry and have a family, but she didn't trust enough in the safeness of the world to protect a child, her child. She preferred to work with other people's wounded children, building a nest for them, where they could retreat and find nurturing, guidance and protection.

Working at The Shelter as the Children's Specialist, she was awed by the kids who were drawn to her cubicle at all times of the day, and now, the night. When they couldn't sleep, they'd sneak out of their rooms, startling her as they quietly appeared at her elbow, while she was writing about one of them in her journal. They'd ask her to read to them, or crawl up in her lap, playing with a lock of her hair while they sucked their thumb.

Last week, one of them had asked if Jane would 'dop' her.

"How do I 'dop' you?" Jane had asked.

"Oh, you know. Change mommys, change names."

She had laughed and said, "I think you mean 'adopt' you."

"Yeah, you know. Like a 'dop-tion.'"

"Oh, sweetheart," Jane had said, nuzzling her face in the girl's frizzy crown of brown curls. "How do you even know about adoption? I mean, I'd love to adopt you, I really would. But your Mommy would never let me take you away from her. She loves you too much. Besides," she added, "it's against the rules. My boss wouldn't let me."

Tonight would be more boring than usual. The girl with the brown curls was gone. In fact there were only a couple of young boys and their mothers in the shelter, and they sought each other's company exclusively. What to do? Maybe she should start writing in earnest. Not just about the day's events and her interior thoughts that bubbled to the surface like an underground hot spring, but something more durable. Like a story about...hmm. Maybe a novel about a man like Owen.

She didn't have to think twice to know what *The Lizard* had done to him. It was painted all over the canvas of who Owen was, and how he had reacted to her. Beginning with his exaggerated startle response and ending with his abrupt departure, Jane knew that *The Lizard* had deeply penetrated and exploited him in ways that Owen could not abide, leading him to believe that the only solution was to eradicate the enemy from his life.

Jane sometimes wished her antenna didn't receive such signals, but her receptor buds seemed to have cloned themselves over the years, leaving her more highly sensitized, for better or for worse. She had only to be in the presence of someone like Owen for a short while to know if they were either the victim or the perpetrator of sexual abuse. Or both.

The supreme trick was to walk the high wire over the chasm of fear and maintain one's balance, conquering the dizzying heights by tipping neither one way nor the other. Like her childhood hero, Karl Wallenda. He'd done it over and over again in his courageous high-wire career. His acts were the embodiment of mind over matter, although gravity eventually won, snatching him from the sky, into the giant chasm between two San Juan skyscrapers.

Well, Owen may choose to reject her help by never seeing her again, but she would write her way into his life. If he fell into the swift currents that swirled below him, he could either choose to drown or catch the life preserver she tossed him. Jane's bet lie in her reading that Owen was a hardened survivor.

Just Plain Jane thought he couldn't find his way home, but he'd fooled her there. He didn't have a home to find. That was the true meaning of freedom. No home, no job, no possessions, no one to be responsible to, or for. Let freedom ring.

It was a good day. Sunny and brisk, but not so cold that he

needed more than his hoodie. Owen could wander the streets of Baltimore all day, walking off the drugs. He had five dollars left in his pocket, and he probably wouldn't get real hungry until evening. Then he could hit the fast food dumpsters, if need be. Or maybe he'd hole up with a flush street buddy, flop in someone's house like he did last night, or as a last resort stay at *St. Vincent's* homeless shelter, although he hated to accept charity, defining him as someone who couldn't forage for himself. He hadn't been there in over a year, but it would feel good to take a shower, have warm pellets of water sluicing over his tired body, and wash out his underwear.

The grinding of wheels on concrete, and a young voice shouting, "Look out," jolted Owen from his reverie, as he quickly stepped to the left. 'Wrong way.' The skateboarder swerved just in time to avoid running into him, full force, calling, "Look out, Dude." He then appeared ahead of Owen, swooshing his hands like a giant bird in flight, regaining his balance.

This must be his lucky day. He could have wound up in a tangled web of bruised and bleeding flesh with that young boy. Owen turned and looked in back of him, making sure there wasn't a gang of them. Like migrating birds, they often traveled together. No, he didn't see any more skateboarders, but there were a number of school-age kids on the street. What day was this? Monday or Tuesday? Maybe it was some obscure federal holiday, or one of those indeterminate dismissal days when teachers were attending some in-school training program.

Whatever brought about the children's presence was gratuitous. Their flashing smiles, buzzing activities and bright colors, reminded him of prayer flags snapping in the breeze outside the Buddhist temple. Carefree children had a way of bursting through smog, misspent years, and the dark convoluted corridors of his veins and brain. He traveled on, buoyed with an energy he hadn't felt in months.

The afternoon was waning before Owen realized that the streets he'd unconsciously taken, led back to the large one-room apartment he'd previously rented. To get there, he'd scored on a good drug deal, making enough for the security deposit and the first month's rent, with some left over. After that cash had dried up, he'd supplemented his income with some S&M and MSM. Through a drug lord that he'd dallied with, he'd been introduced to some of the big players, the big payers in the world of 'Men having Sex with Men.' They came from the ranks of the right-wingers, the religious and the righteous CEOs who had images to maintain, and were willing to insure their secrets.

During flush periods, Owen toned and cleansed his body, procuring uppers like Ritalin, Adderall and cocaine for the revitalizing energy they brought. He stayed away from meth. He'd known too many burnt-out light bulbs from that wattage. But his most important boundary was that he only played the roles he chose. When it was S&M, he would administer the pain, knowing that what would normally be called severe punishment, was exactly what his clients begged for. He could do that, as long as they asked him for it. And in MSM, he was always the top man, never the bottom. Again, he only gave his customers what they wanted. They came to know him, then called on him for his specialties.

"Protect thyself" was Owen's primary motto and code of ethics. He used the best quality condoms in the rare instances they weren't supplied by his client, and so far he hadn't contracted any dire venereal diseases. The way he checked that out was to clean himself up, then go to the nearest blood bank giving blood, at least biannually. They screened the donors scrupulously for AIDS and hepatitis, not wanting to add to worldwide epidemics. He'd never been rejected. And he never used needles to inject his drugs of choice. He either took them orally, pulverizing the pills, or emptied the capsules, snorting their powder.

Another firewall he chose for security reasons, was that he did not possess a cell phone or a personal computer. His clients could never reach him. That way they knew they were very special when he contacted them, much like a lover would. Often many months would pass before he began moving through his short list. His customers reserved private lines and personal sites for him. He could sometimes use a pay phone, although he'd found they were getting mighty scarce these days. Better still, he communicated on a library computer, meeting his clients in some out-of-town location, or, on occasion, a yacht. They generally sent a cab or limo to pick him up, and always supplied their own pleasure tools. That way their safety and hygiene were assured.

The one thing he always kept in his possession was a list of the names and numbers of his clients, along with his drug contacts. He placed them in a small index book in his jeans pocket, all of the information encrypted in a memorized code. So far, no matter how blasted he became, he had never lost it, nor had he ever forgotten the code, which he kept only in his head.

There was a down-side to not being able to be contacted by others. He hadn't connected with his mother or his younger sister, Tina, in over ten years. Maybe his mother was dead. He didn't know, and didn't particularly care. She'd always been a hypochondriac, and he didn't want to be responsible for her in her failing years, which would be expected of him if he were in her life. He was the only son.

Right before Owen had started kindergarten and Tina had just begun to stand up, his dad had walked away from them, never to be seen again. He remembered that his dad had yelled something about not being the father of his baby sister.

The only part of the equation he didn't want, was losing contact with Tina. He had been her protector. She'd be almost twenty-two now. Her birthday was near Easter, his near

Christmas. She must be beautiful as a full-grown woman. He hoped she didn't draw men to her for that reason alone. Owen remembered her as sweet-natured, capable and confident. He prayed down-trodden people hadn't beaten those qualities out of her, simply because they envied her natural beauty and brains.

Looking up, Owen saw that he was at the corner of the street where he'd rented an apartment before his landlord had kicked him out. He'd coasted for several months, taking a break, not paying his rent, but finally the owner caught up with him, changing the locks. Owen was well-experienced in the renter realm, and had used up his tricks of not paying for a month so that his landlord would resort to using his security deposit. Then he'd stretched his stay out for another month, because, even though he knew he would be served an eviction notice, he also knew from experience that it took the civil courts months before they acted on it. But this time his landlord had trumped him by changing the locks and moving his belongings outdoors, most of it water-logged and useless by the time he'd found it.

Owen knew it wasn't entirely an accident that he'd wound up where he was. He was hoping some painters or maintenance men might be working on the place, getting it ready for a new renter. If so, they might get careless, take a break or lunch, leaving the place open. He didn't care that much about any of his belongings left behind. All, that is, except the bricks of hashish he'd recently procured and stored in the freezer of the refrigerator. The total amount had a street value of around $20,000. But he'd sell it to the touts wholesale, so his cut would be more like $15,000. Owen had chosen that position in the drug chain, because he was less at risk than those at the top or the bottom. Plus there was the perk of being able to pinch a small supply of it for himself.

Pushing hash was a rarity these days. Nearly all the buyers wanted hard drugs or pot. But there were still the discerning few who knowingly preferred the opium-like aura of hashish, its sweet paste of secretions from the female flowers containing four times the THC of marijuana. And he seemed to have a corner on the street market. Someone would be waiting for deliverance.

He wondered if the landlord or a cleanup person had found the box he'd stored them in, and if so, what they'd done with it. Maybe they wouldn't know what it was and toss it. No, that was highly unlikely. They were grown men and this was still a street-drug neighborhood, though a far lesser one, compared to Jane's. Well, he could hope. There was something about this day that painted a streak of optimism in him.

Sure enough, as hoped for, when he got to the back door, he saw nothing that aroused his suspicions. He looked around to see if there were any trucks or vehicles parked nearby that he recognized, or that had maintenance company logos on them. He didn't see any. Trying the door that entered into the kitchen area, he found it opened effortlessly.

Owen called out, "Anybody here?" There was no answer.

The place was bare except for some painter's drop cloths and rinsed-out rollers and brushes in the kitchen sink. He checked out the bathroom, the only part of the spacious room that had a closed door. No one there. Owen hurried back to the refrigerator, jerking open the door. It had been cleared of the beer, condiments, and the crusty bread he'd kept there, although it contained some soft drinks and Saran-wrapped half-sandwiches, undoubtedly the workmen's. Not much hope, but at least it was still plugged in and working. He slowly opened the freezer, and there beyond all expectation, was the unopened box he'd stored. 'Unfucking-believable!'

A moment of shock, and then Owen began wondering how he was going to carry it away, undetected. It was way too cold, and would give him freezer burn if he put it next to his skin for any prolonged period. He had to find some hard container to carry it in, and fast. The workers would undoubtedly return from their break soon.

Owen dashed out the back door and nearly collided with the solution. A blue wheelbarrow had been left in the back yard. It would look odd on city sidewalks, but it was a workable solution. Rushing back to the freezer, Owen removed the frozen bricks of hash from the box, tucking them under his arms, inside his hoodie, carrying them to the wheelbarrow, scarcely noticing the cold fire they created. He dropped them into the metal bucket, and then ran back to the apartment, where he grabbed a painter's drop cloth to conceal the contents. Looking around, he saw the coast was clear, so he picked up the wheelbarrow's wooden handles and set out, walking nonchalantly down the sidewalk, as though he was accomplishing some necessary work task.

He'd gone barely two blocks, when a maintenance vehicle with two men in the cab, came around the corner. The driver gave Owen a double-take. It probably was the apartment workers. He smiled and nodded his head toward them, continuing on his way as though there were nothing in the world that concerned him. Even if they recognized the wheelbarrow as theirs, they didn't stop, most likely deciding it wasn't worth their time or effort to give chase.

Still, Owen didn't operate on chance. He ducked down a narrow alleyway, racing, until he spotted an aging metal, back-yard storage shed, its door askew on the one remaining hinge. Peering inside, he could make out some splattered paint cans and a broken ladder. There was still ample unused space.

The wheelbarrow was scarcely ten feet away in the alley. Wheeling it into the shed, he then placed the hash bricks inside the drop cloth. Grabbing its corners, Owen ducked around to the inner-yard side of the shed, leaning his back against it. He needed to catch his breath, think of a plan and allow some time to pass, in case the workmen came looking for him. He was pretty sure he knew where he was. If he calculated right, he should be able to walk about a block and a half down the alley, take a left, and there would be a thrift store. He'd bought his hoodie there.

Owen waited about ten minutes, and neither saw nor heard any movement from the garbage-littered backyards, except for some furtive rats that scurried away when he moved. He knew it might look strange to enter the thrift shop toting his stash in the painter's canvas, but he couldn't conceal the freezing bricks comfortably anywhere else, while he looked to buy a large backpack for them. Besides, anything goes in thrift stores.

He remembered the old woman he'd once seen there. The one who was looking for some plastic bananas to stick in the top of a long, gaudy scarf she'd wrapped around her head, forming a turban. She'd told him she wanted to look like "*Chiquita Banana*," whoever the hell that was.

Noticing Owen's skeptical look, she'd offered, "Oh, you're too young to remember her. She was on TV, and used to sing and dance." And then she'd launched into a ridiculous song, singing in a cracked voice and stiffly swaying her hips, trying to appear like a woman forty years her junior. The only part of the song he remembered was the ending, since he knew it to be true: "You should never put bananas in the re-frig-er-ator."

He was right. The thrift store was where he remembered it was, and they had a large frayed backpack for $3.50, plus tax. No one even glanced twice at his bunched drop cloth. He scooted around the corner, into the alley again, unwrapping the hash and placing it in the backpack that he'd insulated with some thick cardboard he'd found, stacked against a store shelf. Hoisting it to his shoulders, he folded the canvas cloth, leaving it in the alley. There was nothing incriminating about it, unless someone got down on the ground and sniffed the odor of thawing hashish, but even then, nothing linked it to him.

He was pleased to have pulled the whole thing off without a hitch, and began what felt like a triumphant march down the alley, onto Sears Avenue. Then it occurred to him that he didn't know where he was going with his precious heist. Well, not really a heist. He'd paid for it up front, which is why he'd been so broke that he couldn't pay his rent until he found a buyer. Or resort to S&M, but somehow he wasn't in the right state of mind for that, nor was he left with any decent clothes. He was getting close to selling his stash and nearly doubling his money when the landlord had changed the locks.

Owen slowed his pace, thinking of possibilities where he could store his treasure for safekeeping. Of his tenuous friendships that remained, the lot of them were druggies. If he stayed with any of them, they would expect a cut. No, he couldn't afford that now. He needed to get back on top.

Suddenly, Jane's face floated in front of him. She had invited him. She wanted him. He knew that. And what did she want from him? Ah, of course. She wanted to help him, and by God, she could. Owen's pace quickened as he thought of the possibilities of warmth, a place to sleep, decent food, and a freezer to store the hash, until he could forge a bridge to a buyer. He was pretty sure Jane would go for his hard luck story and want to help him. But how to present it? She'd said that Danny was her boyfriend, but they didn't live together. Still, she might not be open to having a short-term male roommate. The apartment had only one bedroom. Though he could easily sleep on her couch, as he had last night, be gone most of the day, and then leave whenever she wanted. Just until he made a cash contact. Although he knew she wouldn't lie about him to her boyfriend. She wasn't the type.

Maybe he could continue his street life, simply renting her freezer until he was able to get rid of the dope, and then...well, he'd be flush again and could go his own way, paying her something for the favor. Still, it made him uncomfortable to think of being separated from his stash. Hopefully she'd let him flop for a few days.

Thinking of Jane, a lot of good things seemed within the

realm of possibility. Again, it was tied to his sister, Tina. Jane's blue eyes, the penetrating knowledge she seemed to have about him, without judging him, down to holding his hand when he'd told her it had been in some pretty dirty places.

Owen thought he'd been walking aimlessly again, and was surprised when he looked up at the crosswalk and saw that he was only blocks away from Jane's apartment. He found himself hoping like hell that she'd be there. It was such a long-ago feeling that it seemed unreal, as though it was an actor's part he was playing. But what the fuck. He'd give it a whirl. If she didn't go for it, nothing gained, nothing lost.

Chapter 3
Dave
Monday evening

Dave Brefort was flooded with facts that led him to the terrifying conclusion that his son had been kidnapped. On his way to the police station, its shock waves swept through every cell in his body, though above all, he was aware that he didn't want to be accused of emotional overreach by Chief Compton. In order to trigger a thorough search and investigation, he must be taken seriously, because this was the most serious event of his thirty-eight years. Dave was working so hard to tamp down his fear that he felt himself breaking a sweat, despite the fact that the cab of his truck was chilly.

Waiting for the green light at Limestone Street, Dave replayed the most significant clue. Running out of work earlier than usual, he'd decided to call it a day, go home and relax. He'd crossed the grassy sward between his welding shop and the house, only to find a distraught Peggy. She did not respond to his calm reassurances.

"My God, Dave, he came home around noon. An unannounced early dismissal day. Or maybe he cut school. I don't know. He never gave me the reason. He said he'd go for a jog along Conley Road...that's what he told me. He left wearing his *Cougars* sweatshirt, and that new wool hat I knit for him. I insisted he wear it because it's so nippy out. But that was over three hours ago, and I've found no trace of him. I didn't want to upset you and interrupt your workday, so I toured the neighborhood, with no results. Then I called both Roger's and Heather's house, but they said they never saw nor heard from him after he left school." Trembling, Peggy repeated that Brian had probably been dismissed from school early, and that he'd taken an after-school jog along Conley Road, over three hours ago. She was about to call Dave, when he'd appeared.

Dave got in his work truck and went about questioning neighbors that were along Brian's usual jogging route. He'd struck pay dirt with his good friend, Forrest McCammon. Forrest may not have finished high school, nor use the best grammar, but he knew how to squeeze the last kernel out of a field of corn, and was the shrewdest poker player in town. His savvy was respected by all, and Dave knew Chief Compton would agree.

As he waited for the light, he recalled his conversation with Forrest. His friend had taken off his *John Deere* cap, scratching the top of his head where a bald spot was forming. "Well now, I seen Brian jog past, around, say, two-ish. Figured he was getting back into his running routine." He cleared his throat and spit in the weeds beside his driveway. Dave remembered looking at its glisten in the fading light of early evening.

"I thought to myself," Forrest continued, "...it's too damn early for the kid to start that pounding-the-pavement stuff. He'll wear himself out 'fore he's a man, and then have to pay for it. Flat feet, aching joints..." He glanced at Dave, sensing his neighbor's new-found impatience. "Anyways, a while later, when I left the barn to bring a straggler in for milking, I was mighty surprised to see a spiffy black car driving slow, in that direction," he pointed, "...away from the dump. You know I'm keen on most every car model that goes down my road, but I'm not for sure the make of that one...but I'm sure it was foreign. From Europe, I reckon."

Forrest scratched his head again, and as though that revealed the answer, he said, "But I think most likely it was a BMW. It looked like the kind James Bond drove in that video our families watched together last New Year's Eve. And it had an out-of-state license plate. That I'm sure of."

"Did you get a good look at the driver? Was he alone?" Dave heard his rushed speech, and tried to slow his thoughts down.

"Well, now," Forrest said, "not a real good look 'cause he was a bit far off for that. But I know'd it was a man. The guy reached up and settled his baseball cap. Struck me a bit odd. I mean, a baseball cap and a classy car? And then he looked my way, and I'm pretty sure he had a black mustache. Struck me it was the same color as his car, and I wondered if you had that kind of money, if you'd do somethin' like that on purpose."

Forrest looked down at his feet, and Dave could tell he was embarrassed for thinking of things like matching colors. 'Damn him. Why didn't he just stick to the point?'

Once again, Forrest cleared his throat and continued. He wasn't used to having Dave's rapt attention. "But there was no one else in the car. Leastwise, not that I could make out."

"You didn't catch the license plate by any chance, did you?" Forrest was known throughout town for his remarkable recall of license plate numbers... 'but with the way things were going....'

He scratched his memory spot again. "Well, I do recall thinkin' it was an out-of-state plate, like I said. It had a real light background with dark numbers on it, a little like ours, but then there was somethin' way different 'bout it. Some kind of somethin' squarish in the middle of the numbers…but it was too far off to make out the numbers."

Forrest stopped and stared straight into Dave's eyes. "You don't reckon that guy picked our Brian up, do you, Dave?"

Someone Dave didn't recognize laid on the horn in back of his pickup. He'd lost track of present time. Apparently the light had turned green a while ago, as it was now yellow. No one was approaching on the cross street, so Dave went through, the car behind him roaring past as the light turned red.

The guy gave him the finger, as he gunned his souped-up Corvette. "Quickest way to hell," Dave muttered.

'Well, at least the guy woke me up,' he thought as he pulled into the Community Center parking lot. The back of the building was as dark as the skateboard park that lay beyond it. The town council had voted to stop lighting the skate park at night, as it attracted too many drug dealers and vandals. Today's criminals were audacious. The location of the Police Department, a stone's throw away, had done nothing to deter them. In fact, it seemed to have presented an enticing challenge.

Now only two streetlights glowed at the edge of the parking lot, lighting up Forrest's Camry parked near the back entrance. Thank God he was here, as promised. Forrest was the definition of a good neighbor. And Chief Compton had responded to Dave's call, even though he'd locked up shop and gone home a couple of hours early, leaving the dispatcher to alert him, if needed.

Thoughts of his girls swirled in his head as Dave opened the back entrance and walked down the dimly-lit corridor to the Chief's quarters. His sweet Peggy, ordinarily calm in crisis, had been unusually shaken when she'd hugged him as he'd departed for the police station. He had retreated so far into himself, he'd scarcely felt her embrace.

"I think you're wrong, dear. I think he'll show up before the evening's out," she had said. Her quivering bottom lip belied her reassurance. She had kept her voice to a whisper, not wanting to transmit more fear to Lauren, who had retreated to her room. At seventeen, Lauren had moods that rose and fell like a riptide, sometimes pulling the whole family under their spell. It never ceased to amaze Dave that she was the polar opposite of her brother, who could always be counted on for unwavering stability.

Lauren's voice had come from her bedroom. "Dad, I'm almost ready. Please take me with you. I can tell the police things about Brian that could help. Things you and Mom don't even know."

'Always the know-it-all,' Dave thought. His response was unusually harsh. "No, Lauren. Absolutely not. You stay here and keep your mother company. And don't answer the door to anyone except me or the police." As he left, the last thing he'd heard was her whimper.

Inside the Community Center, the brown-tiled hall he followed had been flanked by dingy metal lockers during his school days. That was before the tax levy had passed, surprising even those who had voted for it, bringing in enough revenue to build a new high school around the inner shell of the old one. The major remnant of the old school's bygone days was the community gym, whose steel doors stood open. Dave heard the iron rattle of the basketball hoop, followed by grunts of approval from a boys' pick-up game. Someone had slam-dunked the ball, hanging on the rim for a split second, sending out his vibrations. Macho stuff. Boys stretching and yearning to become men. If only they understood the responsibilities and sorrows of manhood, they wouldn't be so eager to cross its threshold. Until such time, the heady distractions of rushing hormones, cheap-thrill stimulants and an avalanche of brassy, eye-popping experiences became theirs for the choosing. In spite of its dangers, Dave silently prayed that

Brian's freedom to make those choices would occur.

He turned the rattly knob of the police office door. Above it was a large, frosted glass window, the old-fashioned kind that had been on the entrance to the school's restrooms. Across the window, in thick lettering, arced a black rainbow, spelling out *Chief of Police*. Not even Compton's name under it. Someone saving an ounce of labor, knowing someday Compton would be replaced. 'As we all will,' thought Dave.

Inside sat Brenda Bowlby, the only female officer on the force, substituting as dispatcher on the evening shift. 'Class of '81,' Dave noted automatically. She raised her head from the paperwork fanned out across her desktop, the florescent light above her, gleaming on henna-rinsed hair. The color reminded Dave of a cocky bantam rooster that had brought him a 4H blue ribbon at the county fair, almost thirty-five years ago.

'Damn! Why did he keep thinking of irrelevant details when the task at hand needed every ounce of attention he could muster. Come on, be easy on yourself, Dave,' he thought. 'Distractions serve a purpose at times like this. Most likely they're here to keep my boat afloat in deep waters that would drown me if I allowed their surge to wash over me.'

"Hi, Dave," said Brenda. "The Chief's expecting you. Forrest showed up about ten minutes ago."

She gave him a sad smile, saying, "Go on in. Hope everything goes well for you."

He didn't even give her the courtesy of looking directly at her, as he strode into the Chief's office. Compton and Forrest both rose when he entered, like he was some sort of dignitary. Strange that adverse conditions brought about respect, but he'd take it. Cooperation is what he came for.

"Have a seat," Compton said, gesturing toward a leatherette swivel chair whose burgundy cushion was split, a small froth of yellow innards spilling out.

Dave nearly threw himself into the chair, giving a quick nod to both men. "Catch me up on what you've talked about so far. Sorry I'm late, but I had to talk to Peg and Lauren, try to calm them down."

Compton leaned back in his matching swivel chair, which had been reupholstered, demonstrating some acknowledgement of rank. Forrest sat forward on the edge of a folding chair. They looked like the two gray boulders at the end of Dave's driveway.

"OK, let's start from square one," the Chief said. "First of all, we don't know that Brian has disappeared in some *nefarious* manner." He paused, his unusual word choice suspended in the air. "I mean, it's not outside the realm of possibility that he cut through the woods and got lost after dusk."

Compton glanced at Dave, who looked as though he was about to explode. "You know I'm just saying that as a remote possibility because at this point, I...I can't think of any others. We know that Brian's a home boy and would never get lost in our woods, but what I meant was..."

"What you meant was, you don't know jack-shit about where he is, or what's happened to him," said Dave. He was instantly aware that he'd responded just as he'd warned himself not to do. And that it arose from his frustration in Compton's lack of knowledge.

"Cut the crap, Dave. We came here to help you," said the Chief.

Dave looked at Forrest, who looked away. "Sorry. Every nerve in my body is jangled and I can't think straight."

"Understood," Compton cleared his throat. "Now...let's start with what Forrest saw. A man he's pretty sure was in a black BMW from out-of-state. The obvious thing is to find out what state that car is from. Forrest says he saw a shield, or crest, in the middle of the number and letter series. And they were dark, on a light background. Right, Forrest?"

"Yep, you got me the word to describe that thing in the middle, Chief. And you know I always notice license plates.

Probably know the numbers on half the cars in town."

"OK, Forrest, then take a look at this," said Compton. He flopped a green loose-leaf binder on the desk, thumping the cover. "Here you go. All fifty states' license plates, illustrated and arranged in alphabetical order. Start at the beginning and see if you can identify the kind you saw."

"Damned, if that ain't something," Forrest said. "Didn't know such a thing existed." He opened the book timidly, starting slowly through the pages, becoming bolder and more rapid, as he saw none that matched his recollection. The silence of Compton and the rigidity of Dave declared their tension.

Finally Forrest came to a dead halt. "There, that's it," he said, jabbing his finger at a page. "It's Maryland. Looks like the license plate I saw. Unless there's another one after this that's just about the same."

Compton turned the book toward himself, and inspected the color plate. "Just as I thought. Black figures on a white background, with that shield in the middle." He expelled his breath sharply, as though he'd been holding it in. "No, there's no others that resemble that license plate closely. So now we know it's likely to be a black BMW from the state of Maryland. That narrows it down considerably, and yet, where can we go from there? If that's all we've got to go on, it's kind of like the old 'needle in the haystack.' We'd have to sift through every black BMW sold or leased in the state of Maryland, or the D.C. metropolitan area. In fact, it could have been bought or leased most anywhere, then the guy moved to Maryland. Or maybe he doesn't even live in Maryland, and those are counterfeit plates."

He glanced at Dave, seeing that he was about to explode. "Hey, I'm not trying to discourage you. It's just that I don't want you getting muddled up with false hopes."

Dave stood up with a sudden jerk, sending his wheeled chair clattering across the wooden floor. "Never mind, Chief. I don't need your help. I can do it myself."

Compton slammed the palms of his hands on top of his desk, pulling his chair forward. "Now just a damn minute. What do you mean, you can do it yourself? What I'm telling you is that it's going to be hard to do, even with the cooperation of two state police forces. There's a logical order to follow here. What do you propose to do yourself? You're sure as hell going to need our help, Dave."

"I'm going after him."

"Going after who?"

"The man who kidnapped Brian in the BMW. He's from Maryland. I know he is. And I'm going to Maryland to find my son."

"Hold your horses, Dave. Give us some time to check our surveillance cameras at some strategic intersections, and then check our database for identified child molesters in the state of Maryland."

"Child molesters! So that's what you've been thinking. Why didn't you say so?"

"I just did. Sit down, Dave, and calm down. Let me sum this up one more time. We're not sure if the man driving the BMW picked Brian up. But if he did, what other reason would he have for kidnapping him? The guy's obviously well-off, so why would he pick up a poor country boy – relatively speaking –unless he planned to do something like that?"

Dave's face was still flushed. "All the more reason for finding him ASAP. I don't think you guys can move fast enough. I'm not blaming you. The bureaucracy slows you down. But not me. He's my son and I already have the scent of his trail. You guys will be shuffling through papers while I'm out there following footprints. I know I can find him. Call it a sixth sense…intuition. I call it faith in the Almighty. And I believe in His power to guide me to Brian."

"I'm glad you feel that way. But give us at least twenty-four hours so we can check out some things that you can't. Slow the fuck down, Dave. I don't want to see you going off half-cocked."

Dave sat back in his retrieved chair, but still felt as though he was coiled to spring out of it at any moment. He looked piercingly at Chief Compton and Forrest. "OK, Chief. I'm willing to give you twenty-four hours, but if you haven't found him by then, I'll head out there myself. In the meantime, phone me any time, night or day, if you come up with something. And I'll check with you before I leave."

Dave paused, running his hands down the outside of his thighs, then cupping his knees as he leaned forward. "I'm counting on you, Chief, to help with the crime stuff when I head out. And when I do, Forrest, if you and Sarah could keep an eye on Peggy and Lauren. You know Peg's dad's got Alzheimer's bad, and her mom's consumed with taking care of him. I know my girls are made of pretty strong stuff. It's just that if you could stay in touch...stop by, cheer them up a little, it would help immensely. If I leave, I know it's going to be hard for them. On top of their not knowing what's happened to Brian." He heard his voice crack when he said *Brian*, and he knew he was close to tears, in spite of the terror.

The two men rose and Forrest said, "If you have to go, Dave, we'll see to the girls. Don't you worry."

On the drive home, a portion of the afternoon newscast flickered through Dave's mind. He'd gone back to the house around noon to grab a sandwich, and caught an image on the TV as he'd crossed the empty living room. He'd stopped to see what it was about. Excited throngs were gathered in Stockholm, cheering Sweden's legalization of same-sex marriage. Somehow the news threatened him. Not in an abstract way that news from another country halfway around the world usually did. Homosexual marriage felt personal. And ominous. Just last Sunday, the deterioration of the traditional

Christian family had been the topic of Pastor Jackson's sermon. Dave wasn't sure, but he thought the majority of Swedes were Christians. How could they morally uphold legislation that flat-out denied the word of the Gospel?

Arriving home from the police station, again, the focus was the T.V. Dave found his girls somberly watching a newscast. Peg clicked it off so fast he couldn't catch what the content was. It didn't matter. He knew it was too soon for Brian's disappearance to air on the local news. Even if it had been phoned in by someone, the city newscasters would assume it was just another case of country bumpkins over-reacting. Teenagers could go missing for days in Dayton or Columbus, before they were reported. Some parents were embarrassed to report it, assuming their bad boy was drugging it up with friends, and they didn't want to be cited for negligence. Others were actually relieved that their errant child had struck out on his own, believing they would hear from him soon.

Peggy jumped up off the couch, rushing to hug him again. And again, he felt like a statue, his arms remaining at his sides. Her hug was immediately followed by an anxious, "What did Chief have to say?"

Dave led her back to the couch, sitting down beside her. Lauren was perched at the other end, her eyes so wide and unblinking, she looked like a bullfrog. He needed to choose his words carefully, not wanting to add to the growing volcano of panic. Placing his wife's delicate hand on his broad calloused palm, he said, "The Chief had a lot to say – about nothing. They don't begin to know…even as much as I do. Fortunately, Forrest was there, and Compton had a license reference book. You know…kind of like a bird identification book, but showing state license plates. Forrest ID'ed the plate he saw on a black BMW as a Maryland license. Like I told you, I knew he'd be the one to cast light on matters. Originally I intended to leave for

Maryland in the morning, but Chief talked me into remaining here for twenty-four hours. Which means I'll leave on Wednesday morning. Give them some time to check into some stuff, and see what support we can set up for the two of you, here at home. As Compton put it, he doesn't want me going off "half-cocked."

Peggy withdrew her hand from his as though she'd received an electric shock. "What do you mean, leave for Maryland? How do you know where to go in Maryland? Or if that car even picked Brian up?" She swallowed hard. "Oh, darling, please don't go."

Dave saw her jaw thrust forward. There it was, her usual resistance to sudden change. "You sound like the Chief, Peg. Lots of reasons why I shouldn't go. I just know in my bones that the man in the black BMW from Maryland kidnapped Brian. And I can cut through a lot of crazy red-tape and be on his trail much faster than two state police forces, God-knows-what agencies, and scores of employees who don't give a damn about our Brian. I have a strong sense of how to go about this. And most important, I have faith that our Lord will guide me."

He watched Peggy's face as he spoke, and he could see her lips begin to twitch before she once again set her jaw, tight as a vice. Grinding her teeth together, she sat forward, then straightened her spine, saying, "To go to Maryland to track down some ghost of a man is crazy. It makes far more sense for you to stay home and keep in touch with all the incoming information that can be passed on to you...through Compton, and...and the state police. You might even make it worse for Brian by going out there."

"Oh, please, Dad, we need you," whimpered Lauren.

"Yes, we do," said Peggy in her strongest voice. "For God's sake, listen to us...to Compton...to reason."

"Peggy, you listen to me. For Brian's sake, I'm listening to God."

Chapter 4
Phillip and Brian
Late Monday evening

Lady Luck hadn't stroked Phillip like this since he'd followed a hot inside tip, betting on Royal Queen to win the Preakness in '88. Twenty thousand, at five to one odds. Not bad for a day's work.

This kid was a big winner too. Because of Brian's cramped position on the passenger seat, not allowing him movement of his limbs, Phillip witnessed the boy's fight with the drugs play out on his face. He kept batting his eyelids, opening and shutting his mouth, flaring his nostrils, trying to stay alert, until the pills finally did their job, severing the last thread of his consciousness. The boy succumbed to their torpor within fifteen minutes. Phillip smiled when he observed his stillness. He savored conquering boys with heightened sensibilities.

When the boy was inert, Phillip pictured Brian's reaction to the gun, watching his eyebrows raise and his eyes dart to the door, but unlike Jimmy, Brian didn't follow his impulse, trying to escape. With Jimmy, Phillip had pointed the muzzle a little to the right of him and shot, just to let him know he meant business. That had been the gun loaded with blanks, so he wouldn't damage his car. He kept his lethal pistol in a floor-level open recess on the driver's door. Just in case.

The kid was in a deep sleep. Phillip reached over to touch-taste him, squeezing the kid's biceps between his thumb and forefingers. Brian's muscles were in a resting state, yet following the softness of skin, Phillip hit a bulk that meant only one thing - body discipline. He knew he had no part in bringing that about; nevertheless, he felt he'd earned this boy. The year since Jimmy was gone had peaked his appetite. Searching numerous states for a replacement, he hadn't found one. He'd picked up a number of young boys he thought might meet his standards, but once they were in the car, he discovered they were dull and uninviting, dropping them off where they wanted to go.

Phillip knew what was best for him, and what was best for his boys. It angered him that if people knew about his activities, they would call him a pervert. His father had been the real pervert. He'd practiced incest, knowing full well, as every father must, the reasons for its deep social taboo.

Still, there had been family compensations. Early on, Phillip had seized the power his father offered by choosing his son as his desired sexual object. The culmination came when his father died and left his fortune entirely to him. The only proviso was that he support his mother until such time as she remarried. There were no siblings, and his mother didn't contest the will, saying that as long as Phillip supported her, she would move out of his domain.

He turned his GPS off, as he approached Pennsylvania's western border. 'Myra,' his pet name for his reliable GPS, kept directing him to Route 70, while he wanted to stay on the side-roads that paralleled it. He shut off her insistent, "Make a U turn." Following the scarcely traveled two-lane roads, he had allowed his mind to drift back to the days when his father would lecture him, hoping to prepare his only son for the adult world he must enter. His oft-repeated adage had been: "Nothing in this world is free. We have to earn every penny of it."

Phillip couldn't get over the irony of that proclamation. As the CEO of a large Savings and Loan corporation, found to be fraudulent years after he'd died, his father's fortune had been far from earned. Whereas his son had, indeed, worked to earn his share. In fact, he'd developed his role into a talented art form. When Phillip was preparing to leave for Harvard, his father had died from a brain tumor. Between packing and driving there in his father's Ferrari, Phillip had attended the funeral, shifting his feet a lot, and looking down, as though he were hiding tears. Six years later, he'd graduated *Summa Cum Laude* with three Master's degrees in what he considered to be the three castles of knowledge: physics, philosophy and psychology.

When he'd liquidated his father's holdings, keeping only the blue chip stocks, he'd found he could live quite comfortably off the bank interest and stock dividends. With a portion of his inheritance, Phillip bought what he assessed was a generous amount of municipal bonds to produce monthly income for his mother. He thought of it as alimony, since his father had, in essence, divorced her for him, long ago.

Because of the invisible barrier his father had erected between them, once he could navigate on his own, Phillip and his mother no longer needed to pretend to like each other. She had fled soon after her husband's funeral, living in a small town in upstate New York. For all he knew, she might have remarried, although he considered it only fair that he continue to pay her a monthly income for the remainder of her life.

Phillip checked the clock. He'd been driving for over three hours and his bladder was full. Brian was as still as a rock.

Pulling to the side of a wooded road, he relieved himself in the remaining snow, boring a hole and sending up a puff of steam. It pleased him to see that even his piss was mighty.

Settling back in the car, he accidentally jostled the boy's head, causing him to stir. Phillip patted his head, and rubbed his hand down the length of the arm that had worked its way out from under him. That was fine. He wanted him to be relaxed for as long as possible. A soft groan escaped Brian when the car started up, but as soon as they were moving, he fell back into a deep sleep.

Giving into his desire to feel the boy's hair, Phillip fingered its texture between his right thumb and forefinger. It was silken, like he'd heard baby's hair described. Originally it had shocked Phillip that the boy's hair was red, but he liked it now that they were out of his home territory, and the threat of identification had subsided. He'd never had a redhead before. Plus intelligent and athletic to boot.

Phillip reached down to Brian's cheek, and stroked that too. Like the texture of the hair on his head, his cheeks were as soft and smooth as a baby's. He was tempted to reach between Brian's thighs, but decided to savor the wait. Just the thought of doing so brought on an erection. Making sure the safety was on, he cradled the gun between his thighs. Reaching down, he stroked both barrels.

Suddenly, like an unexpected orgasm, bright blue and red flashing lights appeared behind him. Phillip fought to keep from braking abruptly. What the hell was a police cruiser doing out on this godforsaken road to nowhere? Clearly he wanted him to pull over, although there was no more than a foot of gravel shoulder on his right, before a ditch dropped off into the woods. Phillip coasted to a stop in his lane, then pulled the blanket up to obscure Brian's head, as he fished his wallet with his driver's license, out of his back pocket. That was always the first thing they wanted.

The policeman exited his car, leaving the revolving lights

on. Phillip could scarcely see beyond the lights, but there didn't appear to be any houses nearby. Just ongoing woods on both sides of the road. As the policeman approached, he saw him press his hand down on the trunk lid, checking for an open lid, a sign of ambush. With the cop's attention diverted, Phillip swiftly removed the gun from between his thighs, releasing the safety and resting it on the seat next to his left leg, where it was concealed from highway view, yet easy for him to reach. He knew the cop wouldn't stick his head in an open window.

From outside the car, the officer glanced in the backseat to make sure there was no hostage, illegal drugs or weapons, just as the police procedures manual had said. It paid to be prepared. Phillip pressed a button with his left hand, lowering the driver's window, then put both hands on the steering wheel, as he knew it would be asked of him.

He looked the policeman directly in the face. By God, it was a woman in a deputy sheriff's uniform!

"Sir," she said, you're driving with unregistered license plates. You'll need to step out of the car." She held a flashlight in her left hand, while her right hand rested on the security holster over her right hip, but she made no move to draw her gun. Flashing her light over the heap that was Brian, she said sternly, "What's under the blanket?"

Now Phillip was in familiar territory, knowing he could outwit his opponent. It was like a good game of chess. "Officer, that's my errant nephew that I was sent on this mercy mission to bring back to Maryland, where my brother – his father – is waiting for him. He loaned me his car for the occasion. I'm afraid, Kevin...that's my nephew, was having too much fun at his cousin's, and didn't want to return home. He's still sleeping off his intemperate drinking from earlier in the evening."

"Using your right hand, pull the blanket back, so I can see him," she directed Phillip. He did as bid, hoping the bright light didn't arouse Brian. Clearly this was the penultimate move in the chess game. She might already have information about a missing redhead from Ohio. More than likely that's why she'd pulled him over, and in checking with the dispatcher, found out that his plates were unregistered.

After shining it on Brian's head, the officer dropped the beam of her flashlight from the car's interior, commanding: "Alright now, you need to get out of the car with both your hands in the air. Don't touch the door. I will open it for you." She had moved her right hand to the gun's butt as Phillip raised his hands, but then switched its action to reaching for the outer handle. It was locked.

Realizing her vulnerability if she reached into the car, she said in a clipped voice, "Move to your right. Now!" Phillip slid to his right, giving her clearance from him grasping her hand.

That's all Phillip needed. A common error from a common cop. As she unlocked the door with her right hand, it was left unavailable for any other action in the split second it took Phillip to reach to his left, grasp and fire his gun, discharging the bullet into her chest.

She stood only a foot or so from the end of the blunt barrel. He saw a quick, red spark, heard the lightning crack of gunfire, followed quickly by a sibilant sound, and then the slower clunk of the flashlight on the road. The smell of gunpowder sharpened all of Phillip's senses. He looked up to see the deputy's eyes widen, then flutter, as she reached toward her chest. Blood began oozing between her fingers. The officer staggered backward, her mouth forming a silent *Oh*. Phillip shot again, this time about six inches higher than the first shot. She continued her fall backward, reeling, as she hit the asphalt.

Nothing was coming on the road. He jumped out of the car, just as Brian began twisting and moaning. Phillip couldn't tell if she was dead, but he had to make sure. He fired one more shot at closer range, this one between her eyes. A mercy shot. Wanting to shoot out the cruiser's flashing lights, he realized he couldn't afford any more time, and the explosive sound it would make. It could very well be that the dispatcher had already heard the gunshots, or if not, she surely would begin to wonder why she couldn't contact the deputy. In any event, other cruisers would soon be dispatched.

As Phillip opened the driver's door, he glanced at the road to see if his shoe imprint or the tire's tread marked the snow. No, the remaining snow had receded into the shade of the woods. He entered the car, dropping the pistol into the door recess. Starting up the engine, he reached over to calm Brian. His eyes were barely open, but he was struggling to say something. Phillip leaned over, asking, "What did you say, son?'

"Are you okay? I thought I heard a gunshot," Brian said.

This was good. The boy didn't know what had happened, but he was already worrying about Phillip. He patted him on the shoulder, saying, "Don't worry, young man, I'm taking care of you."

Phillip saw Brian blink his eyes and look up at him beseechingly, as though he was the only person in the world he could depend on. If that's what he was thinking, he was right. Phillip would bring him safely home to his own little apartment.

The first step was to find some dark turn-off to change the license plates. He had procured a Pennsylvania plate and stored a magnetized screwdriver under the back seat for just such an event, although Phillip had to admit that he never thought he'd need them. Was he getting sloppy about darting under the radar, or was it just a matter of luck? He'd have to think his whole operation through, before ever heading out again. Still he felt confident he could beat this one. No need to panic. That was the prime rule to follow when things didn't go the way he'd expected. Just reason it through. He would have to change his license plate, get back on Route 70 and merge with the late night traffic.

Oh, and the fake mustache had to go. It was the most

recognizable feature of his physical identity.

Gingerly, he peeled back one corner. At home, he'd always loosened it with hot compresses. 'Oh hell, I can't fuss around with it.' Better to tear it off in one bold move, rather than trying to remove it in small steps, prolonging his suffering. Time was of the essence. Phillip grabbed the partially peeled corner and yanked it down across his upper lip. It was all he could do to stifle a scream. He checked his lighted visor mirror to see if the removal had caused bleeding. No, but it left a splotchy reddened band of skin above his lips, as though he'd shaved with a dull blade. No time to minister to it. He tucked the costume mustache inside the Reds cap, and pushed them under the front seat, noting there were some short black hairs sticking to the adhesive.

Phillip drove for several miles before he spotted an unlighted country lane with woods on either side. Using a special flashlight that clipped to his jeans, he pulled in and performed the license plate change with the speed of a garage mechanic, then began to wend his way back to Route 70, with the help of Myra. What would he do without her? With his instruction, she'd even located the nearest highway patrol and the closest community police station from the location of the shooting. He'd breathed a sigh of relief, seeing that both of them were at least twelve miles from the shooting. It must have been ten minutes before Phillip heard the distant sound of emergency sirens.

The interruption was unfortunate, but things were falling into place. Phillip never saw another car the whole way back to the entrance for 70 East. Brian fell asleep as soon as the car resumed its ongoing speed. From then on the whole operation went so smoothly, Phillip had to admit that he couldn't have planned it any better.

Apparently it was meant to be. It must have been that deputy's time to go. Being a woman certainly hadn't increased her chances of staying alive. Why the police had opened their ranks to females confounded Phillip. Their place was in the home, and even there, they were short-sighted, his mother being a prime example. And this one, further proof. She should have known better than to approach a car in the dead of night, on a lone country road, without any assistance or witnesses, and not have her firearm drawn. It irritated him that the deputy's short-sightedness now made it necessary for him to flee like a fugitive, when he was the deliverer of so many young men's elevated futures.

Phillip kept his radio on the news station, waiting to hear about the shooting. It was more than an hour before he heard the report of a deputy sheriff shot and killed around the town of Hillsdale. There was no description of Phillip, the make of his car, or a red-headed boy riding along with him. Instead, there was a description of several acts of bravery on the part of the deputy that had been shot, and some laudatory comments from her Chief.

Some of the sentiments expressed were enough to make a common man cry. These Midwesterners were long on feeling, though crucially short on logic and reason. Something he would relish teaching Brian. Thank God he hadn't been captured. Lucky Brian. Phillip must continue a cautious route home, insuring his companion's safety and security. The stupidity of the deputy sheriff had nearly ruined that, but in the end righteousness prevailed. Phillip chuckled to himself at his twist on religious terminology, even though it was entirely true.

Chapter 5
Jane and Owen
Monday late afternoon

After the apartment was tidied up, Jane's mood changed. She felt more organized and light-hearted. Her friends knew she couldn't stand living in the midst of clutter. A cluttered room, a cluttered mind, she'd often told them, trying to rationalize why her cleanliness teetered on the brink of compulsion.

Jane knew she wasn't alone in her kingdom of trying to create order out of chaos. In her work at The Shelter, one of the questions she frequently asked the women was, what they did right after the abuse they periodically suffered. The answer should have been that they called the police to report the assault, but Jane had stopped expecting that, as they most frequently talked about "cleaning up."

As one of the women had put it: "If I can still stand up and walk around, I clean up the mess he made when he took out after me. It's kind of like petting a tiger's ruffled fur. Soothes the savage beast."

"Who's the beast you're soothing?" Jane asked in an innocent voice.

The woman looked surprised, then answered, "Well, I guess I always thought of 'the beast,' as him, but come to think of it, he's taken off and I'm all alone with the rage that roars up in me. So I spray it, dust it, mop it...until it's all settled down in its cage. And then I take a nap, or eat a candy bar. I've gained a lot of weight that way," she said, pinching the roll on her belly, "but we sure as hell have a clean apartment." She laughed at her insight, and Jane gave her an understanding smile, making a mental note to be sure to advise the daytime staff to once again go over the ways of reporting and documenting abuse at their next group meeting.

Jane settled herself in the denim-upholstered chair by the window overlooking Lexington. The same one she'd retreated to minutes after seeing Owen vanish from view around the corner that morning. Like a shawl, the late afternoon sun warmed her shoulders as she picked up her journal and read the scrawling entry she'd begun that morning. "He's a down-and-outer, but not a whiner or a complainer. He's rough and scrappy, and fights hard to remain a survivor. If only his rage toward his abuser doesn't cancel out his good qualities. I doubt if he'll return. I was too motherly, suffocated him. He needs lots of breathing space."

Jane picked up the ballpoint pen on top of the opened page and began writing again. She'd barely begun the next sentence, when there was a sharp rapping on her door. Startled, she rose from the chair, calling out, "Who is it?" No answer. She moved toward the door, wondering who would knock that forcefully at this time in the evening. It sounded like the law. If Danny came by unexpectedly, he would tap lightly, followed by a two-note whistle. Her friends generally tapped out a light rhythm, or called out to her.

Jane hesitated, settling the brass ball at the end of the door chain in its runner, opening the door a crack. She was startled to see a slice of Owen's darkness through the two-inch opening. Whatever possessed him to return?

"What do you want?" she asked, sounding sterner than she intended.

"Well, shoot, I returned because you invited me. Remember?"

"Yes, but I never really thought you'd take me up on it. Did you forget something?" Jane asked, removing the chain and peering at him, but not opening the door any wider.

"No, I don't have anything to forget except the clothes on my back," Owen grinned disarmingly. "Can I come in?"

"Well, okay, but I have to warn you that I'll be going out on a date in an hour or so. And then to work," Jane said, as she opened the door. She was surprised at how hesitant she'd been, and how easily she'd lied about going out on a date. It was a protective measure, although when she'd been thinking about Owen before he showed up, protection had never entered her mind. Maybe her brain radar was telling her she'd been too naive.

Stepping in, Owen said, "Oh, I won't take that much of your time. Just want to ask you a few questions, and then I'll be on my way."

"If it's counseling you're seeking, I charge sixty dollars an hour, or thirty-five for a half hour." Jane said, finally smiling at him to let him know she wasn't entirely serious.

"Oh, I thought you were a palm reader. I didn't realize you're a licensed fortune-teller. But no, that's not why I came. Like I said, I just want to ask you a few questions."

"OK, let's hear them. But before you start, I prefer to sit. I've spent the afternoon cleaning. We can sit over there, next to the windows," Jane gestured toward the sunny spot she'd just left. "Take your backpack off. It looks heavy," she said, as she settled in her chair.

From her tone, Owen could tell that although Jane didn't issue orders often, she expected compliance. He slid the straps over his shoulders, letting the pack slide down his leg to a resting place on the living room rug. As he did that, he once again realized the hash bricks were thawing. He needed to work fast, get some answers, or move on to other alternatives, like an open place to lay them, so they could dry out. He followed Jane, warily sitting on the edge of the chair she pointed toward.

"Sit back and relax," she said. "It makes me nervous just to look at you. You're like the proverbial 'cat on a hot tin roof.' Can I get you a cooling glass of water?"

"Thanks, that would be great. I've walked over half the city."

"How come?" Jane said, walking into the kitchen, her back to him as she removed a glass from the kitchen cupboard, then turned on the faucet.

Spotting an opportunity, Owen walked up behind her, making her jerk as she turned around, spilling some water on her t-shirt.

"Oops, sorry. I guess I'm not the only one who startles easily," he said.

Jane picked up a dishtowel and dabbed self-consciously at the wet spot over her breast. He could see she wasn't wearing a bra, as the spill made her nipple stand out.

There was pregnant pause, and then Owen said, "Sorry. I came over for some ice cubes for my drink. You're right. I need to cool down."

"Help yourself. There's some in the freezer. Haven't used any for a long time, so they might be kind of hard to crack out of the tray."

Owen opened the freezer door. Its inner walls were coated with frosted ice nearly an inch thick. There were two ice-cube trays, and a box of what looked like macaroni and cheese. It was a compact space, but large enough for the bags containing the bricks of hash. "Looks like you don't use your freezer much."

"Oh, you know, winter and all. Don't find much need for frozen foods. I'm a vegetarian, so I buy a lot of fresh produce."

"Good for you. I don't eat much meat myself, but I'd have a hard time passing up a juicy T-bone steak if someone offered me one." He cracked open a tray and dropped several ice cubes in his glass, then followed Jane back to the chairs near the front window. It was hard making small talk with a woman. He was rusty, but it was worth it if it paid off as he wanted.

Jane sat down rather primly, her hands folded in her lap. "So what brings you my way so soon after you said you wouldn't return?"

"Well," said Owen, circling the glass in his hands, watching the miniature whirlpool he'd created, hearing the clink of the ice cubes as they settled. "Well, I know you have a date, and then to work, but ...didn't you tell me you're on the night shift or something?"

Jane nodded affirmatively.

"Oh, so you counsel the night people. The ones who prowl the streets and are probably looking for a warm place this time of year."

"Not exactly. I'm the Children's Specialist at a Battered Women's Shelter."

"Hey, bully for you. The hell with the pimps, prostitutes and night scum. You put your energies where they can do some good. I'm all for 'Save the Children.' They're the only ones we can save. If it's not too late. So listen, I won't waste your time. I'll cut to the chase."

"Good," said Jane. "I like a man of few words and maximum action."

"Just so happens you have a man of action dangling on your line, but he needs a little help to carry it off. Now, if I tell you something somewhat illegal, you'll treat it as a confidence, won't you?"

"Yes, just as I'm sworn to at my job. The prohibitive clause being that I'm required by law to disclose any threats you make to harm yourself or others."

"No problem there. Unless you think what I'm about to ask you might put you in harm's way."

"Don't tease. Tell me straight up what risks you're talking about. The psychic in me says it's about drugs."

"The psychic in you is right. But the druggie in me says it's no riskier than having a bunch of thugs hanging out in your apartment, doing God knows what drugs and deals. Like last night for example..." He stopped, looking at the floor. "OK, what I'm asking you to do," Owen said, pushing his backpack forward with the toe of his shoe, "is to store the bricks of hash in here," he jabbed at the backpack, "for a couple of days until I make a contact that will get them off my hands. And out of your freezer. I'll make it worth your while. The psychic in me says you're a fair person, so the offer of you setting the rental price is on the table."

"Ah, so that's why you asked for the ice cubes in the freezer. I should have known. You seek profit around every corner, in everything you ask for. You really are an opportunist."

"Yes, primarily, you're right. But I'm offering you profit too. Tit for tat." Unconsciously, he looked at the wet spot on her t-shirt. Jane leaned forward, covering it up.

"Before I commit to anything, tell me this. Why can't you store it in your own freezer, or a friend's? You just met me and hardly know me. Speaking of risks." Jane sat back, leveling her eyes with his.

"Although I may have led you to believe otherwise this morning, I don't have a freezer. Or a room to sleep in presently. Secondly, I don't have any 'friends' I feel I can trust. I sense you're fair and square, and my initial take on people and the level of trust I can place in them has been 99 percent accurate for quite some time. I haven't been burned for at least a decade. I learned the hard way from someone who gave me third degree burns."

"You mean the bad guy. *The Lizard,* right?"

"Good connective memory. You're batting one thousand."

Jane thought a minute. "I'll allow you to do it on one condition."

"Name it."

"I'm not interested in money nearly as much as I am in *The Lizard.* You talk to me about him, and I'll consider the use of my freezer a fair exchange."

Owen hadn't expected that, and looked down at a spot on the rug for at least a minute before looking up. "OK, that's a fair enough deal. Let me get these in the freezer right away, before we go any further."

Jane followed him to the refrigerator, opening the freezer door while he reached in to feel the contents of the backpack with both hands, pulling the bags of hashish out of their boxes by their drawstrings. He didn't open them, but she knew what the bricks looked like. They would be about the size of a concrete brick, but flattened, thinner. It wasn't the first time she'd had hash bricks in her freezer, but she was not about to tell him that.

"Hey," Owen said. "the ice is awful thick. Do you mind if I chip some away, so it allows more room and cools more efficiently?"

"No, that's fine. What do you need to do the job?"

"If you have a spatula, that should work fine. Just need to run hot water over it for a few minutes."

"I do have one. Just be careful you don't poke a hole in the freezer wall, or we're in big trouble."

"Good thinking," said Owen, respect reflected in his voice. He took the spatula from her, swiveling it under the hot water faucet.

As he began scraping the ice, Jane retreated to the living room again, thinking about the situation. She wanted Owen to be indebted to her, knowing it meant he would be more amenable to her suggestions and counsel. His revealing what he could about this man, Phillip, would deepen if she could offer him more in the exchange. Jane was convinced cracking that chapter open was the key to Owen's salvation. He'd admitted he had nowhere to stay. He could flop on her couch while she was at work for the next couple of nights, and be gone by the time she returned, around noon. By then he should have found a drug contact and have enough cash to find his own sleeping quarters. She didn't trust him enough to leave her valuables behind, but she'd take her banking papers, her few gold pieces of jewelry, and her laptop with her to work, storing them in the Shelter's safe.

Explaining it to Danny wasn't an obstacle. At this point, he could take it or lump it. After all he's the one who got her this involved with the likes of Owen.

Tuesday morning

Owen made himself awaken before Jane let herself in. He was sitting in the denim chair reading a Sarte novel he'd taken from her bookcase, when she came through the door. Owen mumbled "Hello," and continued to read, feeling her eyes on him, aware of her advance.

Jane bent down and glanced at the cover, showing some amusement when she straightened and said, "You chose Sarte? Have you ever read him before?

"No, but I must say, he's a bit of a bummer. I take it he's a nihilist."

"My, what big words you use. But no, he's not. Nearly the opposite. He's an existentialist."

"Whatever he is, he's a bummer." Owen tossed the book on the couch, looking up at her. "How was your day at work? Or rather, your night?"

"Pretty uneventful. Which is what I like about working night hours. I have plenty of time to do what I want. Read, write in my journal, whatever. How about you? Did you sleep well?"

"Like a rock. Your couch is damn comfortable. A hell of a lot better than sleeping in a cardboard box."

"Really?" Jane arched her eyebrows. "You really have slept like that?"

"Only a few times. I try to avoid it. But I've done it on rare occasions. In better times I sleep in my own place, or flop at a friend's. Like I did last night."

"Glad to hear you consider me a friend, and not just a flophouse. You're welcome to stay here one more night, or until I need to inhabit my apartment during the day. What about your drug contacts? Will you have some money by the time you have to leave?

For the first time since she'd met him, Owen looked chagrined. She knew there was a dent in his ego. "Don't tell me. You're having trouble with your contacts."

Owen looked down at the floor, which Jane knew was a 'yes.'

"I was afraid that might happen. It just so happens I have a back-up plan," she said, not able to disguise the note of triumph in her voice. "Would you like to hear it?"

He nodded.

"Well, believe it or not, I have a friend from my personal 'Vice Squad,' who can facilitate such matters. Quickly, no doubt. All I have to do is say the word."

"That doesn't feel right. Putting it off on you, and someone I don't even know. Or trust."

"Oh, believe me, he's one hundred percent truth-proof. He considers himself deeply in debt to me, and will conduct the whole thing through me, never even needing to know my source of the drugs. He'll pay cash on the barrel within twenty-four hours, no questions asked. How much do you figure the bricks are worth?"

"Upwards of fifteen thousand to a middleman."

"Since he's on top and will make a profit, he might even pay more. At least, to me."

"Never encountered such a deal. Who is this 'Wonder-Man?'"

"His name is Domino. They tagged him that as a kid growing up in this neighborhood. Because his mother was white and his dad black. They're long gone, but Domino has a son, his only child, who graduated from law school not long ago. His son lives out-of-state. No one knows exactly where, but he's rumored to have supplied Domino with some grandchildren, who the old man wants to leave wealthy."

"So where do you get your edge with him?"

"It just so happens that I saved his son's life. Literally. I was on the scene when his boy, about sixteen at the time, snorted some coke with something that he was terribly allergic to, mixed in. He went into anaphylactic shock. I gave him CPR, called the medics, and saved his life. And then I followed up with some counseling that turned the kid around, and he remained straight, went on to college and law school. Brilliant kid, really. Domino credits his son's life and turn-around to me. And he's forever grateful. Practically kisses the ground I walk on.

"So you really do save people."

"Yes, I do, and I'll save your sorry-ass from having to sleep in cardboard boxes again, if you just say 'yes.'"

"I thought it was 'Just say 'No.'"

"You should have said that ten years ago. Is it a deal?"

"Sure. What do I have to lose?"

"Well, let me remind you that you still owe me the rent."

Owen nodded in acknowledgment.

"OK, coffee coming up. And I bought some croissants on the way home," Jane said, shaking a white paper bag speckled with grease spots. "They're pretty rich. 'Cause they're basically slabs of cream cheese wrapped in pastry."

"I thought you were a vegetarian."

"I am. Vegetarians allow milk products in their diet. It's vegans that don't eat any milk products."

"Geez, you guys are really choosy."

"Yeah, I guess you could say so. But mainly about ingredients. Kind of like the difference between uppers and downers."

Owen put his index finger to the tip of his tongue, swiping a downward motion in the air. "Score another point for you. I should keep in mind that you've lived on both sides of the track. What I didn't understand is why, since you'd quit drugs, you'd want to live in a drug haven like this." He nodded his head toward the window. "But I begin to understand."

Jane bristled. "First of all, I haven't completely quit drugs. I smoke what I want, when I want, and the same with drinking. It's just that I have control of my appetites. I don't just do it because I crave it, or everyone around me is doing it. And as to why I haven't moved from this neighborhood, aside from Domino and his friends who have my back..." She hesitated for a long moment, looking out the window. "I have a lot of compassion for addicts, and I want, I want..."

"You want to save them," Owen finished her sentence.

"Gosh, you don't give a person a place to retreat. You really barrel in," Jane said, realizing her face was flushed.

"Oh, come on now, I'm not the psychic. It's as plain as the nose on my face. Otherwise, why would you have invited me back, why would I be standing here now, getting ready to talk to you about my crazed nightmares. Let's level with each other. I may be an addict, but I haven't lost my instinct for what motivates people. Besides drugs, that is." He grinned.

"OK," said Jane, aware of the exasperation in her voice. "I won't play games with you. I do want to help you out of the hole you've dug for yourself. Give you a hand up. But will you accept it, is what I want to know."

"If I've learned anything in this world, it's that nothing's certain. I'm willing to talk to you, bare my ragged soul if you insist, but that doesn't mean I'll do what you say. In spite of addictions, at heart I'm a pretty pragmatic guy. If you tell me something that makes sense, that I haven't tried before, I'm willing to give it a shot." He'd let her off the hook.

"Understood," Jane said. "But before we start on the heavy stuff, would you like a bowl of Cheerios with milk?"

"That would be great. Haven't had Cheerios in a long time. Do you have any sugar to top it off? I crave the stuff."

"Sure do." Jane brought the box of cereal, a pitcher of milk and the sugar bowl. Outside of slurping and chewing, there was silence, until Jane picked up the last crumbs of her croissant, when she looked up and said, "Where did you grow up?"

"In Gary, Indiana. Next to the steel mills. There's a song about it in *The Music Man*. Ever heard it?"

Jane nodded.

"Well, it's nothing to sing about, believe me. It's the armpit of the Midwest."

"So how did you wind up in Baltimore?"

Owen didn't have to think long to know that she'd be more likely to help him if he told her his story. "Fool that I was, as a teenager, one sunny weekend I was out on the Calumet Expressway, thumb out, hitchhiking to I didn't know where. Just anyplace away from Gary. And this guy in a cool Ferrari stops and offers me a ride. Says he'll drop me wherever I want to go. After about an hour's drive, he pulls into this state park, drives down some remote road like he knows where he's going, and then parks. I'm about to get out and run for it, when he whips out a pistol that definitely gets my attention. He threatens to shoot me if I don't swallow these pills, he orders me to take. Whatever they were, I figured they were better than a shot in the head, so I do it."

"Is this what you want to hear? Am I boring you?"

"Don't tease, Owen. You know I want to hear the story that led you here. And you know it's not boring."

"No, I honestly don't know that. I've never told anyone before, and I'm not much of a storyteller. No one's ever asked before." That part was true.

"Please continue. I'm truly interested in knowing all the ingredients that make up the Owen in front of me now."

"OK. I'm convinced of that, although I don't understand it." Yes, he did.

"So the next thing I know, it's night, and I'm stumbling out of his car into his fancy-dancy house where he locks me up in this room in his basement, where he fed me good, taught me all kinds of things, from Aristotle to Einstein. For…I don't know how long. Except that it was summer when he picked me up, and it was winter before I busted my way out of there. He slipped up one day, took his guard-dog with him, left things unlocked, and was gone a long time. Probably had to take his dog to the vet or something. Something unusual. Boy, I'll never forget that dog and his growl. Cerberus. A German Shepherd. He's probably dead by now."

"Cerberus," Jane mused. "Did you know that's the name of the dog in Greek mythology that guarded the gates to Hades."

"Figures. Phillip was always telling me about mythological heroes, but he failed to tell me that one."

"God, the whole thing sounds so awful. Particularly the part about not being able to get out of that confined space for so long. But at least you finally escaped. Did you go to a police station to get help?"

"Hell no. I barely got a mile down the road before I keeled over. Had convulsions, I was told later. Maybe from drug withdrawal. Maybe from the drugs themselves. I don't know. The doctors never told me the reason. The next thing I remember, I was waking up in a hospital."

"So you waited until you were released from the hospital,

and then reported it?"

Owen shook his head sadly. "You don't understand. I was considered a homeless drug addict. No ID on me, or anything. Phillip was a rich, well-established dude in Baltimore. I couldn't even remember where he lived, because after I escaped, I had a window of amnesia from the period of the night before I escaped, until I came around in the hospital. I now know it was probably because he was feeding me a cocktail of drugs. I often wondered where he got them. They were good drugs."

He had Jane's rapt attention. Anyone that he'd kept company with before had heard so many bad-luck stories, they didn't care to hear any more variations on the theme. They were just looking for their next fix to obliterate another bummer like him. It felt so strange to unwrap his story and discover that it contained elements of something approaching adventure.

"Anyway, the doctors didn't believe me, couldn't understand who the hell Phillip was from the description I gave them. I know I was still terribly confused. I don't know. Could be that Phillip wasn't even his name, but it's what he always called himself. It doesn't matter. Anyway, early on I decided not to pursue those matters with the police. Instead I concentrated on getting better and finding him myself."

He looked up. Jane was still enthralled. "The first step was getting medically stable so I'd be released from the hospital. Then drug rehab, then a halfway house. It was there I met a group of guys who invited me to stick with them when we got out, and we moved to this neighborhood. Originally. But since then, there's been so many moves, I can't count them. And most of the guys are gone. OD'ed, in prison, wandered off to God knows where. You know the scenario."

"Unfortunately, I do. But you fail to recognize you're not one of them. Let's try this - what about the family you came from, in Gary. Didn't you attempt to locate them? I know I would have."

"No, they weren't anyone I wanted to locate. My dad abandoned us when I was – oh, before I was even in first grade. My mother prostituted herself to supplement her ADC income, when she wanted something special for herself. Aunts and uncles were bums, winos. The only one I wish I could see is Tina, my younger sister. She was like an orchid growing in a weed patch. She had – actually, as I remember her, you remind me of her. But it's been nearly ten years ago, and I don't know what changes have come down on her. Orchids can be choked out by weeds you know."

"Yes, but she must miss you terribly. I bet she feels totally abandoned. Seems to me she's the one bright spot in your life. Worth looking toward the light. Do you know if she's tried to find you?"

"She can't. I made sure my past didn't catch up with me. Since my identity was buried, I did an underground search of guys around my age that had disappeared like me, and assumed the identity of one of them, right down to his social security number. My name used to be Tommy, but his was Owen. I thought that was pretty ironic."

"How's that?"

"Owe-n. Like somebody owes me something."

"My God, I've never heard such an incredible story. You amaze me. Like the complexity of taking another man's identity. Down to your understanding of words like 'ironic.' Believe me, I'm not insulting your native intelligence. It's just the high level of sophistication you've acquired since you didn't finish high school, and haven't had opportunities for what they call 'higher education.' You're pretty amazing."

"I hate to admit it, but it's largely due to that fucker, Phillip. He spent the major part of his day tutoring me in history, philosophy, geography – you name it, he knew everything about it. He was a walking encyclopedia. When he wasn't teaching me, he was cooking upstairs and bringing gourmet meals to me. He didn't feed me the drugs until after dinner, when he slowly and methodically sexually conditioned me."

Owen could see the topic of sex made Jane visibly uncomfortable. She kept looking at her watch. "Listen, I need to get moving. But tell me one more thing before I leave. What is it you plan to do about this guy, Phillip?"

"I plan to hunt him down and see that justice is done. It's that simple, and so far, that difficult."

"Well, what even makes you think he still lives in Baltimore?" Seems to me, smart as you make him out to be, he'd have fled after you escaped."

"No, not the case. I've even seen him twice since I escaped. He passed by me on the sidewalk once, while he was in his car. Last time I saw him he was in a BMW. But I wasn't fast enough to memorize the license plate."

Owen began to feel heated up by his memories. "Hey, I even had a short 'clearing zone,' put some things together, months after I'd escaped, and found my way back to his house. At least I thought it was his house. But a dotty old lady came to the door, and didn't even know who I was talking about. She said her brother had bought the house for her, and she had a live-in aide to help her out. End of the line. Or that line anyway. But when I have my shit together, get some wheels, I plan to search for him in the swankiest neighborhoods of the city. It's my life goal to once again meet *The Lizard Man*. Face to face."

"And when you do?"

"Well, I'll leave that one up to the Super Psychic to figure out. You've already demonstrated your amazing powers to penetrate my blasted mind."

Chapter 6
Peggy and Dave
Late Monday evening into Tuesday morning

Engaging the emergency brake on her own anxieties, Peggy spent a good half hour comforting Lauren in her daughter's newly redecorated purple bedroom. It was already well past midnight before they landed there. She sat on the edge of her daughter's bed, under the posters of a forlorn-looking Frances Bean, the love-child of the suicidal Kurt Cobain and Courtney Love, next to a large photo-copy of a fluffy golden puppy licking the face of a Goth teenage girl with coal-black hair and a stud in her nostril.

Reaching deep to block out the sinister vibrations of her surroundings, in spite of what Lauren defensively stated to the contrary about "Nirvana's spirituality," Peg stroked her daughter's hair, smoothed her forehead and massaged her hands, all the while murmuring to her, until she finally found the key to unlock her serenity. Remembering how she sang

Jesus Loves Me to her as a young child, she sang it over and over, like a lullaby, watching Lauren slowly surrender to sleep.

Tiptoeing out of the room, Peg returned to another hellish landscape where she and Dave had been dumped less than five hours ago. There, lying in bed, both of them on their backs, they held hands, their eyes wide open, rehashing the few options that appeared possible for them.

Dave was confident that he was being perfectly reasonable about driving to Maryland to pick up the trail of Brian, but Peggy held onto her belief that the whole family would be safer if he made their home his headquarters. She prodded him, until he once again resorted to his ace in the hole.

"We both know that I should head out there as soon as possible. I trust God is on my side. He'll guide and protect both Brian and me."

Peggy looked at him out of the corner of her eye. "Well, I wouldn't count on it, since *He* seemed to be asleep at the wheel, when *He* allowed Brian to be kidnapped in the first place."

"Oh please. Peg, spare me your cynicism. It cuts deep."

With that she rolled over, flinging her arm across his shoulder and burrowing her head in the clean white t-shirt he'd donned, after tossing the one musky with fear into the clothes hamper. Within seconds, Dave could feel her shoulders shaking, and sensed a growing wet spot on his shirt. He held her even closer, then tipped her chin up to look into her eyes.

"What else is going on? Come on, out with it."

Peg swallowed hard, saying, "I hate to bring this up. I promised myself I wouldn't...but, but...the news from the imaging center where I was this afternoon, is not good." She knew she was playing the 'pity card,' and she felt shallow about manipulating his feelings, although she was willing to forsake her independent spirit, if it would keep him at home. At least she wouldn't be lying about her circumstances and her need to lean on him.

"What do you mean, 'Not good?' This morning you told me you were going for an ultrasound and the doctor would reveal the results of that later this week. Surely they can't tell if a tumor is malignant or not, just from the image."

"Not often. But the tech left the screen exposed to my view, and I saw a dark image in my left breast. It looked like a starburst. I commented on its shape, and she called it a "speculated tumor," but she wouldn't tell me any more than that. When I got home, I looked it up on the medical website, and it basically said that tumors taking that shape are almost always malignant. From what I gathered, that means I'll have to have a surgical biopsy, undoubtedly followed by removing the tumor and any malignant lymph nodes they might find. And some course of treatment – either chemo, or radiation. Maybe both."

Although Dave counted himself lucky for having been "unfit for service" during the Viet Nam War, due to 'fallen arches,' the war had raged around his vulnerable youth, making him feel at that moment, as though he were deep in its combat zone, trying to dodge bullets at supersonic speed. Like battleground bravery, he knew he needed to stay strong and hold a steadfast course. Rolling over toward her, he brought Peg's slim torso into an enveloping body hug, whispering in her ear, "Oh my God, I'm so sorry."

They both clung to silence for a moment, then Dave took a deep breath and continued, "The last thing we need is to oppose each other. How do you think we can handle this one? I mean, in terms of..."

Releasing his grip, Peg sat up, looking at him full-face. She knew from experience that it was to her advantage to remain stoical about her dilemma, thereby standing a better chance of winning him over. But she'd definitely gained his awareness with her breakdown.

"I've been thinking about this in fits and jerks between reports about Brian, and it shouldn't make any difference in the short run. I can handle the surgical biopsy on my own. That is, a friend can transport me to and from the hospital, which I'm sure Sara, or someone else can do. Outside of that, I'm pretty sure they shouldn't have to proceed with any surgery or treatment for weeks. From what I read, the tumor's been growing for years, so its removal is not a matter of life or death…at this stage."

Suddenly, Dave was no longer with her. He sat up, swinging his legs around to his side of the bed. "Why didn't I think of it before?"

"Think of what?"

"The CB."

"The CB?"

"Of course. I can listen in on the police band. Find out if they're tracking the kidnapper. Chief should have relayed information we have to the state police by now. Maybe they have a lead. That could determine my course of action."

"How does that help with what we just talking about?"

"It will determine priorities. If they have a lead I can follow, speed will be of the essence. But not before making sure that a support team is set up for you. Don't you see?"

What Peggy saw was that he already had his slippers on, and was heading toward his bathrobe on the closet hook. If she could just slow things down, maybe it would begin to make sense. It felt as though she were in a movie, playing the part of a wounded woman in a war zone, left alongside the road, while everyone else was running away. At that moment, she felt a sharp, piercing connection to Brian.

"Hold tight. I should be back within five, ten minutes," said Dave. And with that, he was gone.

Tying his bathrobe shut to ward off the night chill, Dave opened the cab door of his pickup, and turned on his ham radio. It had been awhile since he'd listened to it. Newer electronic gadgets captured his interest now, although occasionally he still tuned into it on the highway, getting a kick out of the trucker's lingo, particularly when he was on a longer trip and they forewarned him of upcoming traffic snarls. And he hadn't forgotten his handle. He'd been dubbed, *Iron Man,* because of his welder's shop. He hoped he could live up to it.

Scanning for the police band, he thought he'd found it, but there was a lot of static and jabber he couldn't understand. He was about to give up, when he got out of the cab and struck the antenna in disgust. Responding like an errant student, suddenly a voice came in clearly. Dave remained stock-still, afraid any movement would disturb the clear reception he was suddenly receiving.

"Repeat: Urgent. Probable downed officer needs help at coordinates F-5 and D-11, All units in range, please report. Possible dead body of downed officer. Ambulance on its way. Barricades needed. Officer dispatched to stop black BMW with unregistered Maryland plates. Suspect kidnapper of twelve-year-old male from earlier report. Danger. Caution still needed...."

Dave started running toward the house, but he tripped and nearly fell. Kicking off his slippers, he ran the rest of the way barefoot, not even feeling the cold, rough ground. Rushing into the bedroom, he found Peg sitting upright against plumped pillows, studying a road map. She looked up, startled. "What is it? What's happened?"

"I got the CB to work, and the police are on the trail of the kidnapper."

"How? In his car, or what? Where is Brian?"

"They haven't caught up with the kidnapper yet, but Brian's still obviously in the car."

"My God, Dave, slow down. I can't keep up with your thinking. I still can't even believe that Brian's been kidnapped. Please. Start from the beginning of what you heard, and break it down for me."

"Don't you see, Peg. They're calling all cars to the scene of a murder. The kidnapper shot and killed a deputy sheriff who apparently stopped him. Somewhere near Hillsdale."

Peggy squealed, then clapped her hand over her mouth, stifling it, remembering Lauren. She removed it, speaking in a hoarse whisper, "Oh my God, he's a cold-blooded murderer. What are you thinking?"

"Don't you get it, Peg. If he didn't have Brian in the car, alive, he would have no reason to kill the deputy. If he had killed Brian – stop and think – what reason would he have to do that, when he kidnapped him for some purpose? And if he had murdered him, he would have ditched his body somewhere along the road. He sure as hell wouldn't keep a dead body in his car. Brian was in that car alive, which is why the guy killed the cop that stopped him, so he wouldn't have to face serious charges. And he's on his way back to Maryland, some way or another. It's possible he ditched his car and stole another one... no, that doesn't make sense, as he'd have to leave the BMW behind and it would provide all kinds of evidence. Now..."

"Please, please, Dave, stop with your reasoning." Peggy held her hands over her ears. "I don't understand why you think this is hopeful. To me it means that Brian's life hangs by a thread in the hands of a madman."

"Peg, this provides hope, not doubt. God is telling us Brian's alive. And that I can pick up on the trail. As swiftly as possible. This decides everything. I'll need to leave tomorrow morning. It's already 1:30. I'll pack, and then we can try and catch a few hours sleep before I leave. I'll call the Chief from the car, and let him know I'm headed out. I'm sure he knows about the murder, as he had to be the one who called in the kidnapping that ignited this chain reaction."

Dave stopped and listened to Peg's moaning. "Oh my God, Oh my God." She was still sitting up in bed, but her crossed arms were holding her hunched shoulders, her head hung down, her chin nearly touching her chest, as she rocked her upper body. Clearly she needed more than words.

Dave shrugged out of his bathrobe, quickly sliding over next to her, pulling her down to once again rest her head against his chest. "There my darling. Be still a minute. Ssh...ssh. There, there...that's it. Now what do you hear?"

"Your heart beating," she murmured.

"Yes, and it's beating in rhythm with yours and Brian's. And Lauren's. He's telling us that if we believe in Him and all the miracles that He creates, He will reunite us as the strong family we are. The most important thing that we can do is to maintain our faith. The rest is up to Him." Though his mind was on fast-forward, Dave continued to hold her until a half-hour had passed, and he heard Peggy's soft, comforting snore. Her envied her temporary state of grace, yet began to make ready for his departure in the morning.

Checking off a mental list, he packed his underwear, t-shirts, pajama bottoms, casual clothes, shaving kit and his Bible. Last, but not least, he added a family photo, showing him with one arm around Brian, the other around Peg, with Lauren, as usual, squeezing in, trying to get closer to him. It struck him that it wasn't just for his sake that he'd packed it, but for identification purposes, too. It was a good likeness of Brian.

Finding a large cardboard box, he put in a good pair of shoes and some gym shoes. He retrieved his cold slippers from the yard, and added those. Then, on a whim, he tossed in a paperback crime novel that was beginning to collect dust. Maybe he could learn something from it. Lastly, he threw in some stretch-for-strength exercise bands that he hadn't used yet. Looking through his side of the closet, he removed his best suit, the only one that still fit him since he'd begun a weight-lifting regime. He retrieved his trench coat from the hall closet for inclement weather, and hung the two of them in the mudroom near the back door, where he would grab them on his way out. His *Cincinnati Reds* jacket for cool weather should be the last item he needed, in the way of outerwear.

Good God, it looked like he was preparing to be gone for some time. How long? He didn't know, but it stopped him in his tracks. Kneeling, he prayed to Jesus, asking him to help find Brian, so the two of them could safely return to the family, where they would continue worshiping him in thanksgiving.

Slipping quietly into bed beside Peggy's still form, he glanced at the clock, surprised to see it was past three in the morning. He'd get a few hours shut-eye, get up by six, and make breakfast for the four of them – no, three, he corrected himself – before heading out on the hardest journey he'd ever taken.

As he fell asleep, he drifted into a dream of swimming in a dark underwater cave, and he was amazed that even though he didn't have breathing equipment, he swam effortlessly, deeper and deeper, into the grotto that opened onto a labyrinth of halls and doorways. He kept wondering if he would have enough air to last until he opened the door that mattered.

Even though he hadn't set his alarm, Dave awoke with a start at six o'clock. Just as he'd planned. He didn't want to jar Peggy awake with his preparations for leaving, knowing full well that she would retake her resistive stance, if he didn't go about things smoothly. Slipping quietly out of bed, he picked up the sweatshirt and Levi's he'd dropped on a chair, carrying them to the kitchen, where he dressed.

Checking to see that his luggage, plus odds and ends, were in readiness by the back door, he set about cooking a hearty breakfast for the girls, knowing it was an understated token of his caring, when what they wanted was for him to stay home.

Thinking his way down the road to the stops, precautions and communication that he would need to tend to as he made his way toward Maryland, Dave suddenly smelled burning oatmeal. Skimming the top two-thirds out of the pan into a microwave bowl, he fried some bacon and made the coffee. He set out nuts for Lauren and raisins for Peggy, their favorite things to mix in hot cereal. It wasn't until he started to put the bacon on the table that he noticed he'd cooked twice as much of it as the three of them would eat. Bacon was Brian's favorite breakfast food.

Dave was at the sink, trying to scrape the remains from the bottom of the cereal pan, when Peggy approached him from behind, wrapping her arms tightly around his waist and pressing her cheek against his back. "I couldn't sleep either. Are you still going to do this?" she asked in a defeated tone.

"Yes, I really am," he said, not turning, his voice terse. She was at it again, still playing the guilt card. Didn't she understand that it wasn't easy for him to take the warrior role, leaving what remained of his family to chase after a killer, possibly having to confront him in order to save his son? Yes, God was on his side, but He wouldn't supply any earthly magic shields. Didn't Peg know that, in spite of his faith, he was scared shitless.

He'd always been known as the wimp in his family. His older brother had habitually proven that he was made of sterner stuff by protecting Dave from schoolyard bullies. His mother had continually complimented Dave on his "soft, sweet heart," making matters worse. And his dad had never seemed to back him, urging him to use his brother as a model.

Still, he needed to be kind to Peg. She was under a tremendous amount of stress. In some ways, more than he was. He knew it was difficult for her to take the passive role, as she always approached problems aggressively. At least he could put his coiled, nervous energy into motion.

'You've got to be more understanding,' Dave admonished himself, feeling a surge of warmth flush his cheeks as he turned toward Peg, saying, "I promise I'll keep you informed every step of the way. I know how hard it is for you to stay behind."

"Thank you for that, Love," she said, caressing his cheek. "And I'll do the same for you. I know I can't stop you. I'll let you know about the course of my doctoring. And who I set up to help me with that. Along with how Lauren's handling matters. We both know that she's 'Daddy's Girl,' even if she's not the same girl who signed up for that. And that it won't be easy for her. I expect some occasional kicks from her. I might have to refer her to 'da Boss,' and you can try keeping her in line from afar."

Lauren's slippers scudded across the floor behind them. "Did I hear my name mentioned in vain? Oh good, Dad, you burnt the oatmeal. I hope you didn't throw out the top part 'cause I like it when that happens. It gives it a nutty flavor." She looked at the full meal already laid out and waiting on the table. "Uh, oh...you guys can't fool me," she said, placing her hands assertively on her hips. "Dad's cooking us his farewell, on-the-road breakfast. That's what's happening, isn't it?"

"I'm afraid so, Sweetheart," said Peg. "Looks like we'll have to try our darnedest to be a strong home team. And that means you'll have to try extra hard in school, and..."

"Oh, no...No! I shouldn't have to go to school! I'm sure that Principal Canon will excuse me to help Dad search for Brian. He might even consider it my civic duty, and give me extra credit in Social Studies for it. Don't you think so, Dad?" she said, giving him her most beguiling smile.

"I'd like to have you along as a companion, but it's far more important that you stay home and tend to your responsibilities here, Lauren. In fact, your mother will be calling on you for help soon, herself, as it appears she might be needing some surgery." There, that should head off any arguments about where Lauren is needed, and why she should stay at home.

"Oh, you mean that silly mole on her face that she's been talking about having removed. She won't need my help for that."

"No. Lauren, it's about having a malignant tumor removed from my breast. Surgery, then treatment following that." Much to her chagrin, Peg found she nearly enjoyed the shock value of what she imparted, after being accused of surgery for the sake of vanity.

"Oh god, Mom, I didn't know," said Lauren, *squelched* written all over her face.

With little left to say, the three of them sat down at the breakfast table, concentrating on their eating, until Peggy asked, "About how long do you figure it will take you to Maryland? That's where you're headed, isn't it?"

Dave knew she was purposely keeping her words to logistics. "Yes, the Baltimore area. At least to begin with. If traffic flows smoothly, probably ten hours, including stops. Once I get on the super-slab, it should be a breeze."

"So you'll make it a long day's drive?" Peggy said. Lauren was looking down and no longer speaking. He heard her sniffle.

"Sure. Doesn't make any sense to break it up. My biggest goal is to save time and money." He cleared his throat. "Besides finding Brian, of course." As if they didn't know that. Dave wet his index finger, sweeping the remaining bacon crumbs into his mouth. Looking down at the empty plate, he realized that he had not only cooked, but had eaten the major portion that was intended for Brian. Something about it felt sinful.

"Listen, you two, I'd better get on the road and hopefully beat some of the morning commuters. I'll take my cell phone and try to tie up some of the loose ends from the road. Like inform Chief Compton, call Forrest and Sarah about overseeing your surgical procedure, Peg. And whatever else comes up.

"No need to take on my health issues, dear. I'm perfectly capable of handling whatever comes up on the home front. And I'll make contact with Chief Compton this morning during his office hours. At least this once, to help you remain calm and focus on what's ahead. I want to make personal contact with him, anyway. I can always convey any important news back to you. Because you need to concentrate on the immediate road ahead of you. Nothing's more important than that, right now."

"Thanks. Oh and Peg, there's three orders in the shop. They're on the books. Claghorn, Reimer, and... oh, I don't remember. Call them and arrange for a pick-up. Then refer them to that new young guy in Clifton. They'll understand."

"Of course, dear. I'll take care of it."

They pushed back from the breakfast table simultaneously, Dave making his way to the back door. After several trips to the car to stow his belongings, he returned to the back porch for farewells. He stooped to give Peg a long embrace, feeling the dampness of tears on his cheek, but not acknowledging them for fear of a meltdown.

Next he chucked Lauren's downcast chin, lifting her face and kissing her lightly on the tip of her nose. "Now you be 'Daddy's Girl,' and don't give your mother any gray hairs." He gave her an exaggerated wink, like he used to when she was a little girl. "I'll be sure to call tonight, before your bedtime. Do your best at school today. Promise?"

"Promise," Lauren said, reaching out with her little finger, linking it with her dad's, both of them giving a strong tug. He could tell she was trying her best. Not even a tear this time. He wondered what her mother had said to keep up her flagging spirits. Leave it to Peg to uphold the family morale, as only she could do, over and over throughout the tests that life had brought them. But none so big as this.

As he stepped across the back threshold, Peggy and Lauren called out in unison, "May God be with you."

"And with our Brian," Peggy added, a catch in her voice.

Dave turned toward his girls, uplifted by their contagious spirit. "And may He reunite us as a family to continue to worship in His name." There was a small but fervent chorus of "Amens."

He was glad he'd already made the trips out to the car, stashing everything he'd packed, so they didn't need to come out, making his physical leave-taking even harder. They seemed to be of the same mind, as they hung back on the porch. He honked and waved as he pulled out of the gravel drive, watching his home recede in the rear view mirror, until it became only a speck in a distant field.

The sun was just rising above the horizon, creating a dazzling but hazardous glow. Dave angled off on a road, heading north, knowing it would eventually connect to Route 70. The sun now rose on the passenger side, so he flipped the visor in that direction. Warmth crept around its edge, in contrast to the cold stone that had begun sinking in his chest. He turned on the radio, dialing in the morning news, settling into the drive. One of the first news items was the murder of a female deputy sheriff outside of Hillsdale, Pennsylvania, late last night.

Wanting to make certain where Hillsdale was, Dave pulled off on the highway shoulder, leaving his blinkers on. He was surprised he hadn't looked it up last night. 'Too overwhelmed. I needed to focus more on facts.' Getting out his Road Atlas to confirm his suspicions, he spotted Hillsdale as a small town with a road that ran parallel to Interstate 70, which was the major artery toward Baltimore. 'Of course the killer would keep off the Interstates whenever possible.'

Dave watched his rear view mirror as he reentered the highway. After that, he turned the radio off and drove as though on automatic pilot, not even noticing where he was, yet knowing he was headed in the right direction.

Something kept digging at him, underground, like the moles that mounded up his summer lawn. It was a male voice, but he couldn't recognize whose it was, or just what it was saying. Something about not telling. "Don't tell anyone, or..." Or what? He saw an outlet billboard zoom by as the voice began coughing. There was a familiar raspy quality about it. It was his Uncle Harry, his father's older brother, who had died of TB when Dave was in sixth grade. He remembered feeling guilty because he was glad when Uncle Harry died. He'd prayed for years that God would forgive him for feeling that way.

Why should he have felt that way? Especially since Uncle Harry didn't disguise the fact that Dave was his favorite nephew, and was the only relative who gave him Indian Head nickels to add to his collection.

Dave was edging up on a semi going slowly in front of him, when a car came up from behind, then moved to the passing lane, staying abreast of him. Yet another car moved up on his rear, fast approaching him. He was on the outer lane, with only a narrow shoulder on his right. He was boxed in, feeling the panic of claustrophobia. It felt like he was suffocating. When he went to turn off his cruise control, he became aware that he had to remove his right hand from his groin. His fingers were so rigid, he had trouble straightening them.

It was then that his body remembered. It remembered the creeping of his uncle's fingers, and his own small fingers stretching to encircle his uncle's huge pink shaft, trying to push it away. Then the probing in his butt, the steady thump, thump, like the iron arms of steel derricks he'd seen, drilling for oil. And the pressure that traveled up his spine, making it difficult to breath, making it feel like his head would crack into a thousand pieces. And finally, the hollow, searing pain when his uncle withdrew.

Uncle Harry had always ended by saying, "There now, wasn't that fun?" Then he would place three cool Indian Head nickels in his palm, and add, "Now don't forget. This is our special secret. Don't tell anyone, or your mom and dad will really be mad at you. They won't love you anymore."

There it was, after all these years of itching in a place he couldn't scratch. He wanted to speed away from it, but he was still trapped by the cars. Stomping on the brakes flashed through his mind, but he realized it would spell instant disaster. His heart was beating so fast, he felt it would surely hammer its way out of his chest. Sweat burst from all his pores, as though he was overheated, but he felt cold and clammy.

"You're losing it, Dave. Calm down," he said out loud, and then began repeating, 'Calm down,' over and over, making it a monotonous mantra. The sound of his own voice steadied him, and soon the car on his left began pulling ahead, allowing him to scoot out behind it, before the car in back usurped that position.

Here he was on a desperate search to locate some godless, evil man who had kidnapped his innocent son, and planned to commit unspeakable acts of violence upon him. He was as certain of this as he was of the long repressed memories of his uncle. There must be some invisible web connecting his uncle's treatment of him, and this terrible man who had captured Brian. History was repeating itself, but that wasn't all bad. Because now Dave could get inside of the mind of this evil man, and that would allow him to find his lair. Dave instinctively knew all of his masks. He would look under the rich man's trappings, in the churches, and in the 'do-gooders' social clubs. He had been too young to know how to stop his uncle, but he knew he could stop this man. If only he could reach him before he harmed Brian so deeply that the scars would never heal. Dave's mission was defined. When he saved Brian, he would have saved himself. He did not allow himself to think about the alternative.

Chapter 7
Phillip and Brian
Tuesday – Early AM

"Wake up, we're here," Phillip said, shaking Brian's shoulder.

Startled out of a deep sleep, Brian looked up to see Phillip's scowling face in the blue-white shadows of a full moon. Barely awakened, Brian wondered if *here* was part of a dream-scape, or the real world.

Phillip dragged him into reality by shaking his shoulder again, extending his other hand across Brian's body, urging him to grasp it. "Here, take hold and swing your legs out. You'll get your mooring once your feet are on the ground."

Brian kept his hands in his lap, fearful of touching Phillip.

With considerable force, Phillip reached into the passenger well and swung Brian's feet out to touch the ground. Because his legs were numb, Brian hesitated to try standing.

"Come on, boy. You're not crippled, just sleepy. Stand up."

Brian tapped his right foot on the ground and finding it

solid, tried getting out of the car. His knees wobbled, but Phillip tugged on him until he found himself upright, 'pins and needles' prickling his calves. The tingling sensation reminded him of how he'd purposely sat on the lower half of his legs when he was younger, trying to induce that weird but funny feeling. Now it was scary, a reminder that he was not in full control of his body.

Phillip stood back from him, watching him totter. "You can do it, son. Walk out ahead of me." He gestured with his right hand, allowing Brian to see the glint of a gun he was holding.

That did it. He almost choked trying to hold back the tears, as a giant shudder passed through his body. The last thing he wanted to do was show Phillip his fear. Displaying courage was the only thing he had going for him. Brian already knew from before he took the pills, that his captor would treat him with more respect if he didn't act like a crybaby.

'Don't look at the gun and Phillip's face,' he told himself. Brian looked beyond him, seeing the shadow of a mansion. He took a few halting steps, setting off a motion detector. Floodlights crackled, lighting it up. It felt as though he'd walked onto the movie set of some grand manor. Like the kind in the video, *Jane Eyre,* an old-fashioned movie his mom coaxed him into watching with her, one long winter's evening. There were things he remembered his mother naming, like turrets and widow's walks, along with mammoth stone urns that sat on the arms of concrete-tiered porch stairs, leading up to an elaborately carved front door.

He stumbled toward the front porch as Phillip said, "No, not that way. Head to the right of the house and follow the brick path."

Bordering on terror, he felt a hysterical urge to laugh. Like Phillip was the Wizard of Oz and Brian was to "Follow the Yellow Brick Road." He even heard the music playing in a corner of his mind.

As they rounded the corner of the house, more floodlights

came on, lighting up the backyard with the winter remains of formal gardens, backed by dense woods. If only Phillip weren't holding the gun, he would have tried to make a break for it. He wasn't sure what lie beyond the woods, but it showed some possibilities for the future. If he had one.

Brian thought he'd heard a dog whimpering. As the lights came on, it began barking and lunging at the cyclone fence of its cage, which must have stood nearly ten feet high. He quickly grasped why the fence was so tall, because the dog leaped at least five feet, and then tried to climb the fence, at times hanging by its toenails, then falling back. It was the most massive dog Brian had ever seen, startling all that remained of the dulling effects of the drugs, out of him.

He hung back as Phillip moved toward the cage, saying, "I'd like you to meet Cerberus."

"Thanks," said Brian, "but I'd just as soon skip it."

"No, I insist. I doubt if you'll ever have another opportunity to meet a dog like this. He's a full-blooded Italian Mastiff, with papers to prove it. A real rarity. His line almost went extinct, but some aficionados managed to breed them back. I brought him home from a trip to Italy." 'That was after I'd been forced to kill Kevin, and sorely needed a vacation,' Phillip thought. "He weighs one hundred and thirty pounds – all muscle and bone – and he's trained as an attack dog."

Brian sensed his eyes widening.

"Don't worry," Phillip said. "He won't attack you. Unless I give the command."

Phillip unlocked the cage and Cerberus came barreling out, ignoring his master, advancing on Brian. The dog was growling and slobbering at the mouth. Brian stood as rigid as a ship's mast while the dog circled his legs, head down, sniffing and snuffling at his shoes and pant legs. He felt the dog's wet nose and instantly clenched his groin muscles, afraid he was going to lose control of his full bladder. After several riveting minutes, he must have passed inspection, as the dog quit circling him, turning to his master.

Phillip patted his dense, dark head, saying, "Good boy, good boy. Looks like you've stayed fit. Ate all your kibbles did you? Hope it wasn't all on the first day."

Cerberus licked Phillip's hand, and then dropped behind the two of them as they formed a small procession to a door at the back of the house. Phillip reached into his pocket and took out a pronged key, fitting it in a small steel device beside the door. They entered the house on the basement level.

Phillip turned on some lights in an entryway that reminded Brian of their mudroom at home, only much grander. It had marble counter-tops with walnut cabinets hung above them. There were gold faucets at the sink, although Brian realized they probably were brass. But he could tell it was all top-of-the-line stuff. His dad always took him along when he shopped for fixtures for customers, pointing out how you could tell quality when you saw it.

On one level Phillip's wealth dazzled Brian, on another, it deepened his fear. How could he protect himself against a man who had so much money? There was no limit to what Phillip could acquire to protect himself.

He was led into another room, as Phillip turned off the entrance lights. Cerberus was still with them, and it appeared that he was going to be staying on his heels. Like cars approaching from the rear when he was jogging, dangerous things he could sense but not see, made Brian anxious. He felt his body trembling, and he tightened his muscles, making him shake even more.

Phillip turned and gave him a slick smile, saying, "Cerberus make you nervous? You'll get used to him." Passing through another doorway, he announced, "This is the gym, and when you graduate, you can play around in it."

Brian didn't know what he meant by 'graduate,' but he definitely got the impression it meant he'd be staying here for some time. That was both hopeful and scary. At least it appeared that Phillip wanted him to remain alive, but for how long and for what purpose, Brian wasn't sure. Although he was becoming more and more certain that Phillip intended him to be there for his own pleasure, and Brian could think of only one pleasure that might be. At that thought, he tightened his buttocks, feeling as though he might crap in his pants. Everything Phillip did seemed aimed at reducing him to an infantile state.

Even though Brian's mind was riddled with fear, he was able to look around and almost admire the gym. It was about a quarter the size of the high school's, yet somehow it contained every piece of exercise equipment found in large gyms. The centerpiece was a Universal machine, along with a weight bench and free weights, a vaulting horse, rings, a punching bag, a small trampoline, a stationary bike, and on the back wall, there were evenly spaced holes and pegs for climbing.

The trampoline and wall climbing didn't make sense to Brian because the ceilings couldn't have been more than ten feet high. If he were to build up much bounce on the trampoline, he'd crack his head, and he knew he couldn't climb any more than about three feet up the wall. It felt good to be figuring things out, even if they didn't make much sense.

There were a couple of other odd things about the gym. One was that it didn't have any long horizontal windows up high, like the ones Brian had seen in his friends' basements. In fact, it was basically buried underground, like a tomb. That meant he was cut off from another potential avenue of escape. The other thing that puzzled him was, from the looks of Phillip's body as he removed his coat, tossing it on a vault, it didn't appear he made good use of his equipment. Although he was not overweight, neither was he particularly muscular.

'Stay on your toes, Brian,' he reminded himself. 'Phillip needs to be fed admiration.'

"This is a really cool gym. Who..." when Phillip interrupted him to say, "Follow me. I have something else to show you. This will knock your socks off." He proceeded to walk toward the climbing wall, turned another key in a receptacle, and pulled out a large section of the wall by one of the climbing pegs that acted as a doorknob.

It was too dark to see anything on the other side of the door until Phillip clicked a switch, and a double row of can lights came on. They reflected on a large swimming pool, whose waters were a glacial aquamarine from the colored tiles lining it.

"Wow," Brian said, giving Phillip his due, letting his eyes glide along the smooth surface. He could hear the bubbling of water entering the pool.

For the first time, Cerberus came out from behind Brian, going to the edge of the pool and looking down on it. Phillip patted his broad head, saying, "I think I should change his name to Narcissus. He's always captivated by his own reflection. Aren't you Cerb?"

The effects of the drugs had definitely worn off. Brian began feeling hyper-alert, taking everything in, storing it in some deep recess of his mind. It reminded him of the accident he'd been in with his mother. She had skidded into a guardrail on an icy bridge, and pieces of the car's trim flew up and hit the window like exploding shrapnel. One of them had blasted through the back passenger window, a shard of fractured glass leaving a triangular scar where Brian's jawbone joined his neck. He had watched it hurl toward him, and the split second before it hit had seemed eternal. Like the accident, time seemed to have slowed to a snail's pace. He touched the bumpy scar on his jaw just to remind himself that there had been another time and place before Phillip.

The guided tour continued. He'd never seen anything like Phillip's basement. It must have been constructed for Hollywood stars, sheiks, or some grand person. Certainly not for the likes of him. The next thing he knew, Phillip opened another camouflaged door that didn't appear to be there. This last door led through a short dark hallway to a room that Phillip announced would be Brian's.

Like the car, the gym, and the swimming pool, Brian realized that without the fear factor, he would be totally enraptured with the skills it took to construct the room he entered. The walls were craggy limestone rocks, put together like pieces of a puzzle. There was even a fireplace with a raised hearth at one end of the room, although the place where the logs would ordinarily go, was covered with wrought iron fretwork, black andirons standing like guards at either end. His dad would have admired the craftsmanship that went into its construction. Thinking of his dad, so far away and unable to help him, made Brian want to cry. He clenched his shivering jaw, telling himself that he needed to concentrate on the room.

Above the closed fireplace a large oil painting hung, done in swirls of black and brown with some white streaks mixed in. It wasn't clearly drawn, but Brian thought he saw horse's heads in it.

"What do you see in that painting?" Phillip asked.

Brian was afraid it was some sort of trick question, but decided it was probably best to say what he thought. Phillip seemed to respond best to honesty. "It looks like two, maybe three horse's heads to me."

"Good boy," said Phillip, in the same manner he had addressed Cerberus. He clapped Brian lightly on the back. "That's the same thing I said when I first saw it, and the artist insisted that's not what he intended it to be. But he wasn't sure what he did intend. So-oo, since perception is in the eye of the beholder, and you and I see the same thing, that means we're compatible. It's like a giant Rorschach, and our minds project similar interpretations. Do you like horses? I do."

What did it mean to agree with him again? "Yes," Brian said, letting his eyes roam the walls at the same height, to another picture hanging over the bed. It was an enlarged black and white photo of a draft horse standing in show position, his stupendous equipment ready for mating. Brian looked away as quickly as he saw it, his eyes dropping to the floor in embarrassment.

"Well, what do you think of that horse?"

Brian kept staring at the floor, seeing a thick red patterned rug covering most of the room, the borders around it displaying a wood surface that was the color of the ebony keys on a piano.

"I say, what do you think of that picture, son?" Cerberus emitted a low growl in the background.

"Well, sir," Brian hesitated, searching for language like the farmers around home might use. "Right off hand, I'd say that's quite a dangler."

"A dangler," Phillip mused. "I like that." Again he clapped Brian on the back. "On top of everything else, you have quite a sense of humor," he said, stroking his chin. Brian noticed that his mustache was gone. It must have been a disguise, as he couldn't have had an opportunity to shave, unless he'd done it in the car. Which seemed unlikely.

"A dangler," Phillip repeated, chuckling. "I'll have to remember that one."

Phillip's eyes guided Brian's to the bed that was the dominant feature of the room. Again, Brian had never seen anything like it. He couldn't tell if it was perfectly round, but it was far from the rectangular shape of other beds he'd seen in people's homes. It looked like a photograph he'd seen in his dad's *Playboy* magazines that he kept hidden in a box, in the back of his bedroom closet. Once, Brian had been instructed to look for some dress pants there, leading him to think that maybe his dad had purposely given him a glimpse of what it meant to be a man. He remembered being shocked at the nearly naked, provocative women in the magazines, because they seemed in direct contradiction to his dad's religious views. It was even harder for Brian to imagine that his mother tolerated them.

There had been an article about the guy who owned *Playboy*, and photos of his "Home Headquarters." This bed was the same shape as the bed of that guy. The bedspread on it was rich, red velvet, with a black crest in the middle, and black borders around the edges. A headboard that curved along the top was padded with the same red and black material. Brian thought it was beautiful, at the same time that he feared its lushness. It seemed like so much of what Phillip said and possessed, brought up internal conflict in Brian. He said, "Red and black. Aren't those the colors of Satan?"

"I really wouldn't know," Phillip said. "He's just some clown to me. But I suppose so. Red for the fires of Hades, black for the evil shadows of his heart. It so happens it's my favorite color combination. Maybe that means Satan and I have something in common." He chuckled again. "But what I want to know is, how do you like your bed?"

'Mine, again.' Brian didn't answer.

"Hey Brian, don't be afraid of it. 'A bed is a bed, is a bed.' Gertrude Stein used to say things like that, and her expatriate groupies thought she was a profound poet."

Phillip pushed his three middle fingers down on the mattress, and after making a slight indentation, the mattress sprang back to form. "It's made of the same material they use for the astronauts' beds. Here, try it out," he said, sweeping his hand toward its broad expanse.

Once more, Brian hesitated, and then sat down tentatively, nearly sliding off its curved edge.

"No," said Phillip. "Lie down on it and see how it feels."

Brian stretched out on it stiffly, his arms held to his sides. Lying on his back made him feel unprotected. But the mattress supported him firmly, and Phillip didn't move a muscle, so he quit tensing up, and when he relaxed, the bed did feel comfortable. Somehow it was soft and firm at the same time. "It feels great," he finally managed to say.

"Good, because it's going to be your bed for as long as you're here."

"How long will that be?" Brian asked quickly, knowing he probably wouldn't get an answer to his question.

"As long as it takes," Phillip answered in his usual enigmatic way.

'Takes to do what,' Brian wondered. "Is there any chance I can call my parents, just to let them know I'm safe. Nothing else."

Phillip stared at him for a few moments, and then said, "You know the answer to that, don't you?"

"Yes sir," he said.

"You know, I like you addressing me as 'Sir'. Continue to do so until I tell you otherwise." He stared at Brian again.

"Yes sir. I'll do that, sir." Brian felt like he should click his heels together and salute him, and would have, if he thought that's what was expected of him. Yet he hated being obedient to this strange man he scarcely knew, and didn't trust.

"So what do you think of your video screen?" Phillip asked, sweeping his eyes across to the wall near the foot of the bed. Brian hadn't even glanced there, because he had kept his eyes locked on Phillip, and what he was instructed to look at. When he looked at the wall, he was surprised to see a mammoth screen. A person could appear life-size on it.

"People appear life-size on there," Phillip said, as though he was reading his thoughts. It was eerie how that kept happening, making Brian feel like he had no privacy.

"Wait until you see some of the videos I have in store for you," he said. Brian felt uncomfortable with the way he said it. It sounded oozy.

"Would you like to see your bathroom?"

"Sure," said Brian, trying to act normal, and then changed it to "Yes sir."

"You don't have to call me 'Sir' every time you address me, Brian. Every once in a while will be sufficient."

"OK sir," he said, feeling stupid for responding in the same way. It confused Brian that he felt like a servant toward Phillip.

'It must be the fear' he thought, because although he was ordinarily polite to his elders, he didn't put up with people pushing him around.

Phillip showed him to the bathroom. It was like something straight out of pictures Brian had seen of Hawaii. The walls were made of limestone rocks too, and the shower wall looked like a waterfall, with a small stream pouring off the top rock and running down, splashing and spraying on the porcelain bottom of the tub. There was no shower curtain. Instead, up high, there were lots of lush plants placed on wall ledges, while some grew in planters built around the outer edge of a tub. Mounted in the ceiling was a grow light that Phillip told him was on a timer, and should never be turned off. Inside the tub there were molded seats in the corners, and around its interior, he saw round, gold-rimmed holes.

Brian pointed to them. "Are those to water the plants?"

"Obviously you've never seen a whirlpool before. You're in for a delicious surprise. Those little holes are where jets of water come from when you're in the tub. You can back up against them, and it feels like a thousand tiny fingers massaging aching muscles. Or for that matter, any other body parts that like to be massaged."

Phillip grinned for the first time, and it transformed his face, making him appear younger. Then he reached up and triggered a concealed button that brought forth a fine spray of water from the back shower wall. Puffs of steam rolled up from the porcelain bottom as the water splashed on its surface.

"As you can see," Phillip said, "as soon as you turn the shower on, it's immediately hot. The water heater is right behind the wall, so you don't have to wait for the deliverance of heat. Isn't that what we're all waiting for...the deliverance of warmth?" He chuckled.

Although he didn't understand Phillip's attempts at humor, he knew there was a religious reference in the word *deliverance,* but he didn't see anything funny about it.

Brian's thoughts drifted, until he was brought back to the present with a smack on his buttocks. His coach did that sometimes when he came in off the track after a particularly good run, but Phillip's smack didn't feel the same. Coach Brown's felt like it was part of the workout, but Phillip's felt more like it was done for his own pleasure.

Suddenly Brian became aware of the urgent need that he had somehow staved off. "Excuse me sir, but I need to relieve myself."

"Of course," said Phillip, leaving the bathroom until he heard the toilet flush.

"Say, aside from not being able to relieve yourself, you must be getting awfully hungry by now. You haven't done either for at least ten hours." He reflected on the fact that ordinarily he would have covered the distance in under eight hours, but that he'd lost nearly two hours with the deputy sheriff business, and then changing the license plates.

Brian's ears perked up. So that meant they were about ten hours from his home. If he kept listening, maybe he could figure out what direction they'd gone in, and begin to get a fix on his present location. Although what good that would do him, he didn't know. Unless he could get to a phone or a computer.

"So...would you like a Reuben sandwich?" Phillip asked.

"What's a Reuben sandwich?"

"Oh, I forgot. You probably don't have delis in your part of the country. Do you like sauerkraut? Have you ever had it before?"

"Oh sure," Brian said, glad Phillip had finally mentioned something familiar to him. "My mom's side of the family is mostly German. We eat sauerkraut."

"Well, this is a sandwich made with Kosher corn beef, sauerkraut and Swiss cheese. The cheese melts into the – well, let's just say it's delicious. Want one?"

"Sure. I'll try it." Phillip scowled at him, so he added, "Sir."

"OK, I'll be back in about fifteen minutes with sandwiches for both of us. Though I must admit that it's an odd time of the night to be eating. But I'm starved. In the meantime Cerberus will stand guard outside your door. Won't you, Cerberus?"

The dog stood up, wagged his tail and barked, as though answering yes, following Phillip out of the room. The door was left open a crack, and Brian could hear Phillip going up the stairs, while the dog remained outside, snuffling through his fur, no doubt chasing a flea. Brian wanted to close the door, but he didn't dare, since he feared provoking Cerberus with even the smallest of movements.

He sank down on the edge of the bed as quietly as he could, and looked uneasily around *his* room. There were things he hadn't noticed before. On the entrance wall was an ebony chest with stainless steel drawer pulls. He rose and quietly risked opening the drawers, finding them filled with various t-shirts, socks, pajamas and underwear. Between the fireplace and the bed there was a closet door. That and the bathroom door looked like they were oak. In the hollowed out curve of his headboard there were other items. There was a CD player, and a set of plastic glasses that he wondered about, because they didn't match the class of the room.

Brian laid back down as carefully as he could, hoping he wouldn't disturb Cerberus. He tried thinking his way out of the room, but he couldn't picture any other reality. It was as though he'd been born here and would die in this room. In his mind, he tried pushing the door, but it wouldn't open. Exhausted with his effort to regain the world he once knew, he fell asleep before Phillip returned with the Reuben sandwiches.

When Phillip returned, he found his boy much as he'd

appeared in his drugged state. Witnessing his inertia, Phillip removed Brian's shoes and socks, trying to pull the covers down, but the boy's dead weight wouldn't allow for movement. OK, he was probably out for the night, so he'd take the sandwiches back upstairs, eat his, and then bring a coverlet down for Brian.

When he'd returned, Brian hadn't stirred an inch. Phillip laid down beside him to make sure he was still breathing. He was. Being so close to him, he could feel the boy's body warmth, and within a minute it created a companion warmth in his groin that couldn't be ignored. He placed his hand lightly over the lump in Brian's sweatpants, gently rubbing it until it knotted in response. Placing his other hand inside his robe, Phillip encircled his shaft, surrendering to the mounting waves of ecstasy that enveloped him, until his body was left limp on the sandy shoals of sleep.

Waking in the early morning, Phillip saw that Brian was still on his back, sound asleep. He tossed the blanket over him and rose from the bed, bidding Cerberus follow him upstairs.

Wednesday AM

Brian awoke to a scraping metal sound outside his door. He looked around the shadowy room, recollecting his strange new world, as though in a dream.

"Who is it?" he asked, as if he didn't know. He wished he didn't.

"Phillip," came the muffled voice.

What choice did he have? "Come in."

"I will as soon as you open the door."

Brian was surprised Phillip couldn't let himself in. Did that mean the door also locked from the inside? He fumbled along the wall next to the door, searching for the light switch. When the light came on, he saw there was no push-lock in the doorknob. Hesitating only a moment, he swung the door open.

There stood Phillip in a black bathrobe with red piping along the edges, a perfect match to the bedspread. Right behind him was Cerberus, spittle hanging from his black-rimmed mouth. A common-place light bulb shone down on them from a ceiling socket outside the door. It highlighted the empty space above Phillip's upper lip. His mustache was gone. Brian thought he remembered that from last night, but there were so many other intruding images, whether from dreams or reality, Brian couldn't tell.

"What happened to your mustache?" Brian asked, avoiding his fear of Cerberus.

"What a way to greet a guy who's bringing you the best damn breakfast you'll probably ever eat. But to answer your question, I shaved it off. It was beginning to bother me. Let's try again."

"Good morning," said Phillip cheerfully, while Cerberus wagged his stub of a tail. "And thank you. I unbolted the door with the edge of the tray, but I couldn't turn the knob since my hands weren't free. I forgot to place a small table out there. Did you have a good night's sleep?"

"Yes, I guess so. What time is it?" There was no clock in the room and no windows, so Brian couldn't tell if it was night or day.

"Time for all good sailors to hit the poop deck. I've brought our breakfasts, Matey. You slept through your late dinner last night. Now stand aside while I deliver."

Phillip's mimicking voice changed. "Actually it would be best for you to get back under the covers while I bring this in."

"Yes sir," said Brian, remembering his instructions once again, fear mounting in the pit of his stomach. "As soon as I go to the restroom, sir."

When he returned, Brian climbed under the covers. Phillip had brought in a large serving tray, placing it on top of the chest of drawers. Brian could see a trail of drool Cerberus had left as he'd followed his master.

"OK, boy. Get set to feast on the Chef's best Shiitake mushroom omelet. Do you like mushrooms?"

"Yes sir. We pick a mess of mushrooms from the woods near our house every summer, but I've never heard of Shata..."

"No, of course you haven't. It's pronounced she-toc-kee, and spelled capital S-h-i-i-t-a-k-e. The Japanese cultivate them in young, green oak logs, boring holes and placing mushroom spores in them, then watering them down. Now tell me how it's spelled, and how they're grown."

Brian grew even more afraid. Was he going to be tested all the time, and what were the consequences if he got something wrong? Maybe he wouldn't get to eat. Swallowing hard, he said, "It's spelled S-h-i-t-a-k-e, and the way the Japs grow them is to get a whole bunch of oak logs, bore holes, and then sprinkle them with spores."

"That's just about right. You left one of the 'i's out of Shiitake.' And the Japanese people are never to be called Japs. You must have heard that from your grandparent's generation. Prejudiced remnants of the Second World War and the Kamikaze pilots, who were pictured in our newsreels in their suicidal bombers, leering at American plane pilots like devils. As though we could have photographed them inside their cockpits. Stay tuned. You'll learn much more about American political propaganda."

Phillip stood near the edge of the bed, continuing his exposition as though he was lecturing to a classroom. "And speaking of 'mushrooms,' which we were - in retaliation, we chose to annihilate two of Japan's biggest cities, Hiroshima and Nagasaki, with our 'mushroom cloud' A bombs. The bombs, nicknamed 'Little Boy' and 'Fat Man,' - how cute - killed 120,000 citizens outright, while at least another 100,000 died from the after-effects of radiation sickness. Thanks to the genius of physicists like J. Robert Oppenheimer. Later Oppenheimer quoted from the Bhagavad Gita, "Now I am become Death, the destroyer of worlds."

"Son, the Japanese are from an ancient civilization. They are very learned, cultured people and should be treated as such. These are the kinds of things you will learn from me." He moved to the chest of drawers, retrieving the trays he'd placed there, setting them on the wide headboard that extended to the wall. "Ah, but our breakfast grows cold."

Next, Brian saw him go to the wall closet, bringing back some black corduroy bolsters. "OK, pay attention. Sit up against one of these, and put this tray over your thighs. I know you're not used to eating breakfast in bed yet, but you'll learn." Then Phillip arranged an omelet dish, a bowl of fresh fruit, a goblet of what looked like orange juice, the cutlery, a linen napkin and a bud vase with a single rose in it, first on Brian's tray, then repeated the sequence on his own tray.

Plumping the extra set of pillows, Phillip slipped in under the covers. As he did, his mind flashed on Brian's partial, hidden erection of last night. He could scarcely suppress his fantasies of seeing it in the buff, but it was too soon, and he needed to attend to things at hand. Patting the bed beside him, Cerberus hopped up, nestling down next to him, his eyes trained on Brian.

"I didn't bring you coffee, because you haven't told me if you prefer regular or decaffeinated. Or tea. Regular or herbal. But we can decide on that later." He touched Brian lightly on the arm, causing him to flinch.

"No need to be so jumpy. Here, I fixed you a mimosa. That should settle your nerves. Do you know what a mimosa is?"

"Yeah, it's a tree with leaves that shrivel up when you touch them... sir," he quickly added.

"You're right. Sort of like you just did when I touched you. Yes, it's a tree, but it's also a champagne cocktail. Orange juice and champagne. A delightful way to begin a Sunday morning, which is generally when I serve them. But this is a special occasion. How do you usually begin your Sunday mornings?"

Finally he was allowed to speak of something familiar and safe. "My parents, my sister, Lauren, and I, take turns cooking breakfast for the other three. That way we all learn to cook, and then we put on our good clothes and go to church together."

"I like the family cooking part, but as for the other drivel, 'The family that prays together, stays together,'...I'm afraid that Sunday dogma is outlawed here. How is your omelet?"

"It's delicious."

"Yes. Too bad I can't instruct you in its subtle art, but you won't be allowed in the kitchen."

"Where will I be allowed?"

"At first, only in your room. Then, when you've earned it, the swimming pool, and the gym. But never out of the basement."

"Until when?"

"That you'll find out when the time comes. You'll be happily surprised when that occurs. My other boys always have been."

That was startling. But also comforting to know that Brian was in the emotional company of other frightened guys, even if they were ghosts. "Other boys? How many?"

"I don't count when it comes to people's happiness. It's a matter of quality, not quantity."

Brian felt the acidity of fear rising in his throat. "If you don't mind my asking, where do they go when they leave here?"

"That depends."

"On what? I mean, I want to do the best thing possible to achieve the best possible results...for both of us."

Phillip chuckled. "Boy, who says the Ohio briers don't know how to put a spin on things? You might just wind up being a politician. Would you like that?"

"Yes sir. I mean, no sir. I don't want to be a politician."

"What would you like to be?"

"I really don't know yet, sir. I mean, I guess I'd most like to go to college and study... oh, I'm not sure what, but become a track and field star. Maybe even go to the Olympics. But I don't think I'll ever do that if I have to stay in this room very long."

"You'd be amazed at what you can realize in this room. Microcosms become macrocosms. Energy doesn't dissipate, it simply converts. Einstein knew that. Now it's up to you to discover."

Phillip reached under the covers and patted Brian's thigh. Again, he felt him flinch. It would take a little more time to let things settle, but Philip thought he could practice patience. Although thinking about the treasure in store, made him impatient.

He withdrew his hand and said, "You never did tell me how you'd like to cap off your breakfast. Cafe con leche? Te?"

"What I'd really like is hot chocolate. Sir."

"Well, I'll be damned. Oddly enough, I've never had anyone ask me for hot chocolate before. I don't have the ingredients. But I'll be going shopping tomorrow, and I'll see what I can find. I want you to know Brian, that although this might seem like a jail to you today, soon it will not be. Good things will come to pass. And one of them will be that I can learn from youth. I mean 'you,' as readily as you learn from me. If it's hot chocolate you want, it's hot chocolate I shall learn to make."

"If it wouldn't be too much to ask, sir, could you get the kind that comes in a packet with mini-marshmallows in it?"

"Oh, you know how to work a guy, don't you, boy. But if you continue this good behavior, marshmallows you shall have. Isn't that right, Cerberus?"

Cerberus pulled his black muzzle back, exposing pink gums. "Good boy," said Phillip. "See, he's smiling at you, Brian."

Chapter 8
Dave

When he'd found an inexpensive *Days Inn* on the west side of Baltimore, Dave had taken a calculated risk and rented it for a week, making it even cheaper. Its best feature was a small refrigerator where he could store milk, juice, deli meats and left-over fast foods. He decided not to take advantage of the even lower monthly rate, because he didn't plan to stay that long. So far, that appeared to be wishful thinking.

One frustration was yesterday's phone conversation with Chief Compton, describing his difficulties in gaining the full cooperation of the Baltimore Police Department, which meant they had yet to relinquish the list of registered child molesters and their current addresses. The only tracking procedure Dave had open to him was to try and find the names of customers who had purchased 760i's in the past several years.

Feeling guilty about defacing property, he'd torn the page of dealerships that sold BMWs, out of the *Yellow Pages*. After visiting three within a forty mile radius, he was scoring zip when it came to knowing the identity of any customers who had bought one.

For instance, the guy named Chadwick who was waiting on him today. The name turned Dave off, right away. If his parents had been thoughtless enough to stick a young kid with the name Chadwick, why didn't the guy have the sense to call himself Chad? Probably because 'Chadwick' sounded better, linked with BMWs? Maybe they hired him for the name. Or asked him to change his. Anyway, Dave refused to call him 'Chadwick,' and let him know that every time he got a chance.

After sensing from two salesmen that he wasn't taken seriously as a buyer, he'd stopped at a hair-styling shop for men. Coming away with a sleek haircut, it made him want to run his fingers through it, messing it up. He even wore his suit to the dealerships, trying for the look of a businessman on his lunch break, but something was wrong with his impersonations. Maybe he had a southern Ohio accent he couldn't detect, or maybe his new haircut exposed his weathered red neck above his collar. It certainly wasn't from lack of knowledge about the cars, as he'd read as much as he could on the Internet before he approached the salesmen. Anyway, he couldn't help but rib Chad a bit, although the guy didn't seem to realize that's what was happening.

"Well, Chad, I'd like to find out more about your navigation system, as I'm buying this for my wife, who never knows where she's going. She doesn't have any metal filings in her brain."

Chad looked confused.

"You know, like birds have in their brains...like little magnetic compasses."

"Oh yes sir, we can equip your model with an added GPS system, an electronic navigating system that will guide her, either with audio instructions, or on an easy-to-read screen map." He hesitated. "Beyond that our new 760i's have..."

"Actually, I'm familiar with them, because my uncle has one. Maybe you could save us both time by just giving me an information booklet. And your business card, so I can contact you...if, and when."

"Of course, David."

It grated on him when salesmen kept repeating his name, particularly when he'd repeatedly introduced himself as 'Dave.' Maybe the guy was toying with him as well, but he wasn't going to let him know that he'd gotten to him.

"And may I ask if your uncle purchased his here?"

"Uh, no. My uncle lives in Chicago. But say, how many 760i's do you think you've sold in the past year? I mean, the whole dealership?"

"I'd estimate no more than a dozen. At most. They're our priciest car. Not that they're not worth every penny, but I do have a new..."

"No, I'm not interested in any other car. Could you tell me how many of the dozen BMWs you sold were black? For some reason my wife's hung up on getting a black one."

"Well David, again, I'd have to check to make certain, but I will say that these days, black is not our most popular color. Maybe a couple. Our customers usually go for the lighter colors. They don't have to buff them as much."

Leaving with yet another glossy booklet about the car's features, Dave didn't even ask Chadwick if he would release the name of someone who had purchased one in the past year, so he would chat with them about how they liked their car. The other salesmen had made it clear they protected their customers' privacy.

He supposed his next best option was to check out the registered child molesters. But he didn't have the list, and even if he did, he doubted that a guy driving a BMW would be registered. In fact, the thought was ludicrous. It seemed like any path that opened up to him, wound up in a blind alley. It reminded him of the video games Brian played, where brick walls went up, trap doors opened, and arrows rained down on the hero trying to get to the Holy Grail, or whatever it was he was seeking. It was all so discouraging. Dave felt like someone was coloring him gray, starting at his feet and slowly working their way up his body, until soon his brain wasn't going to be able to see through the fog. It occurred to him that he needed to take a break. Stop at a bar, have a few beers, and talk to someone about anything other than his obsession.

It was dusk and it had started to drizzle. His car windows were fogged over and Dave couldn't see well enough to check out the fronts of bars. More brick walls. And here he was in his suit, which would look ridiculous when it came to sitting on bar-stools, and he was too far from his motel to change. But wait, that was his gray thinking. Try something else.

Here he was in this nice business suit, near downtown Baltimore. He could look for a high-end bar, and strike up a conversation with someone who might give him a different view of things. After all, he was looking for someone who owned a BMW, not a Ford pickup. And come to think of it, this was only the second real day of his search. Between the ride to Maryland, his disheartening talks with Peggy, searching for new connections, and his heightening anxiety, it seemed more like a year. Of course, he hadn't accomplished anything yet. What did he expect?

He drove in squares on one-way streets, finally seeing through the drizzle what looked to be a warm inviting tavern with curtains opened to the street, the bar on one side, and tables for two running along the wall. It looked classy. Knowing he'd never find on-the-street parking, he looked for the closest parking lot. He found one, cursing his luck, since it cost him as much to park as an entire good meal at *Jack's Diner* would, if he were back home. Not only that, but he had to walk a block in the rain, to the bar.

Entering the dimly lit entryway, he shook off his suit jacket, hanging it on a row of brass coat hooks near the door. He ran his fingers through his new haircut, wondering if he had messed up the effect the obviously gay hairdresser had tried to achieve. It had been unnerving to have him touch his hair. Dave had almost asked him if he knew a twelve-year-old boy named Brian. But hell, hair no longer mattered. Whoever was there would have to take him, as is.

Choosing a seat at the bar, the first thing he noticed was that there wasn't the usual loud talk he associated with evenings in Digby, at the *Dry Gulch Saloon*. In fact, although there were customers seated at the tables, it was extremely quiet.

The bartender looked up from toweling the bar, smiled and said, "Good evening, sir. Is there anything I can get for you?," at the same time that he pushed a basket of cashews toward him. Dave noticed that he wore a white long-sleeved shirt with rolled-up sleeves, under a black satin vest. He guessed he'd picked the right place for high rollers. The only other customer at the bar, a man sitting two stools away, had distinguished gray hair and a large signet ring, surrounded by what must have been diamonds.

"Yes, thanks. I'd like a Guinness Stout." He'd never had one, but somehow it seemed like the right thing to order.

"Certainly, sir," said the bartender, as he carefully emptied the contents of the pint into a stein, pouring it down the side, to keep the suds low. "Would you like me to keep a running tab, or would you prefer to pay now?"

"I'll pay now."

"That will be six dollars, sir."

"Six dollars!" said Dave, practically whistling in astonishment.

The man with the ring turned toward the bartender and said, "Thanks, Tim, I'll have the same, and put the gentleman's Guinness on my tab. It's always good to see a new face.

Particularly that of a man who has impeccable taste in beer." He reached across the intervening seat to shake hands with Dave. "My name's Dave Hopkins. You look like you're new to this area. In any case, welcome."

"Thanks Dave. Just so happens my name's Dave, too. Dave Brefort. And you're right. This is the first time I've been in Baltimore. I'm from southern Ohio, and here on business."

"What sort of business?"

Dave blanched. "Actually it's a personal matter."

"Enough said. What do you think of our fair city?"

"It's big. The city closest to where I'm from is Dayton, and Baltimore looks to be, maybe three, four times as big. It's easy to get lost here."

"Oh, you'll get the hang of it soon enough....although that's easy for me to say, since I was born and raised here. How long you planning on staying?"

"As long as it takes me to do what I came for. I'm not sure how long that will be."

"Well, don't know what your goals are, but if they have anything to do with construction, buildings, or city planning, then maybe I can help you. I'm on the City Planning Commission and have my finger in a lot of groundbreaking works here. Right now, I'm whiling away some time until my wife joins me for the opening night of a Mozart series at the Philharmonic."

Within a half hour Baltimore Dave had moved over one stool and ordered more beers for the two of them. In spite of trying to avoid the subject, Dave told his new companion the real reason he had come to Maryland. He hadn't intended to, and it seemed brash, but maybe this guy could actually help him.

"I'm afraid I'm hard put to imagine how any man can kidnap a youth, particularly when ransom money isn't the motive," Hopkins said.

"To tell you the truth, I don't think the man's money has

anything to do with it. Plain and simple, I think the guy's a sex maniac. I can feel it in my bones," Dave said. He was surprised at what he was revealing, figuring it must be the beers. But he had enough sense not to get into the Holy Spirit that was leading him, because he knew a fellow evangelical when he met one, and Dave decidedly rode the secular train.

"It's just so inconceivable to me how a man can..."

"I know. Me too," said Dave, pushing his beer toward the back rim of the bar's counter.

"Say, Ed Malrooney's the Chief of the Baltimore Police Force, and a good friend of mine. I'll have to give him a nudge to release some info that might give you something to go on."

"God, that would be great." For the first time in a week, Dave smiled. It felt as though a dried clay mask had cracked open.

"But," cautioned Baltimore Dave, "it's important not to overstep any limits he imposes on what you can do, or else you'll find each other more of a hindrance than a help. The politics of interstate police work can be a sticky wicket. Particularly when you throw in an understandably emotional father." Both his gaze and his thick graying eyebrows rose, as he looked toward the entrance.

"I'm afraid I'll have to talk to you further about this on another occasion. My better half approaches."

"Look, here's my business card," he said, pushing it across to Dave. "And remind me of the name of your motel. I'll give you a ring tomorrow. If you don't hear from me within twenty-four hours, don't hesitate to call me."

"I'm staying at the *Days Inn,*" said Dave. "On the west side of town."

"Yes, of course. Great meeting you. Although I wish the circumstances were other than they are. But I'm certain I can help in some way."

"I could sure use it," said Dave, looking up to see Hopkins' wife wave to her husband from the entrance. Stopping under a lighted wall fixture and removing her rain hat, she ran her fingers through her shoulder-length hair, apparently trying to restore its volume. Dave was surprised to see that her hair was the same shade of red as Brian's. He watched as Hopkins joined his wife, putting his arm around her protectively. God, he missed Peg. But she'd be happy to hear that he'd finally made a good contact. Hopkins sounded like a man of resources. Exactly what he'd been looking for.

Dave's belly felt warm with beer and good will. It had worked. If he thought positively, positive things came his way. God's grace came to those who sought it. Getting up from his stool, he left a three-dollar tip for the bartender. He had never tipped one before.

Friday, April 5

The morning after he met Baltimore Dave, Brefort received a call from him in his motel room. He and his wife, Shirley, wanted Dave to have dinner with them at their house, that evening. Dave was hard-put to understand why they were being so hospitable to him, but how could he refuse? Certainly not for reasons of a full social agenda.

He wrote down the address, asked if he could bring anything, and was told, "No, just yourself. And dress casually."

Dave was pleased with their invitation and could think of nothing to demonstrate that, except to bring a bottle of wine. Stopping at the nearest state liquor store, he asked the clerk what she would suggest.

"Do you know if they're serving red or white meat?" she asked.

"I have no idea. I didn't think to ask."

She took down a bottle from a shelf in back of her. "Here's one of my favorites. A simple Chardonnay that goes with most any meal. "It's a medium-priced wine. That OK, Hon?"

"Fine. Thanks for the tip."

The clerk was a middle-aged bleached blond, wearing heavy eye makeup. She winked at him and said, "Hey, if you find you like it, come see me again. I have lots of hot tips."

Maybe she just acted that way to attract more customers, Dave thought. He was having a hard time with the recognition that since he'd been on the road, a lot of female service people seemed seductive. He was used to Digby, where everyone knew he was strongly attached to his wife and family. This flirtation must be what females commonly complained about when they said they were treated as 'sex objects.' But from what he'd sampled on his trip, many of them invited it.

He smiled at the clerk, saying, "Thanks," and left, carrying the customary brown bag tucked under his arm.

Following Hopkins' directions, he soon found himself in a more exclusive residential section of the city than he had yet seen. Checking the address three times from the car, he launched himself up the long brick walk leading to their front door, amazed that the bricks were all level. 'How could that be?'

He was surprised again, to see that there was no trace of crabgrass or dandelions coming up between the bricks, although it was a bit early for them. But come to think of it, they probably wouldn't ever come up here, as the grass was undoubtedly sprayed with chemicals. He had difficulty understanding why people would want to suppress nature with expensive weed killers, polluting the environment. And then he thought of the anhydrous ammonia that Forrest sprayed his fields with, and how it always choked Dave's family up when the wind blew their way. He'd forgotten that every man names his poison, calling it a friend, rather than an enemy.

Class distinctions melted away at the dinner table. Dave and Shirley made him feel very much at home, in spite of the sophisticated trappings of their house. Shirley even solved the problem of the Double-Daves.

"I've always preferred calling my husband by his proper name, 'David,' since all our friends call him Dave. That makes 'David' a special name, reserved just for me." She paused and then said, "Dave, I meant to have David ask you on the phone whether you're a vegetarian. Are you?"

"No, I'm a dyed-in-the-wool carnivore."

"Good. I could accommodate you if need be, but I made crab bisque for dinner. Do you like seafood?"

"Oh yes," said Dave, not lying about it, but wondering what the *bisque* part was. He was half-prepared not to like it from the sound of it, when Hopkins read his hesitation, saying, "Bisque, stew, whatever you call it, you can be sure it's the best when Shirley makes it." Dave was curious about how well Hopkins read his inner reactions, saying the right thing to put him at ease. It was quite an art.

After dinner, they retired to the family room, where Dave was shown photographs of the four Hopkins sons, each of them living away from home, either at college or in another city, where they were establishing their professional careers. They had recently learned that their second son would be making them grandparents. The Hopkins seemed to take every bit of their parental fortune for granted, not even aware how blessed their lives were, with all four sons just a phone call away. An exception to what he'd noted as Hopkin's sensitivity. He thought of showing them the photo with Brian, but no, not now. Dave tried to think of something pleasant to say about their sons, and finally landed on, "You must have had a full house when they were younger. Did you raise all of them here?"

"Yes, we did," said David. "Which leads us to an invitation we're happy to offer. Shirley and I would like you to stay in one of our three guest bedrooms while you're in Baltimore. The house is so empty these days that you'd be doing us a favor if you'll stay here, rather than in some dreary motel room. And then I can help you, give you some leads to important people who might have some inside information. What do you say, Dave?" he offered, as he poured him another glass of Chardonnay.

Dave didn't need to give the unexpected invitation a second thought. "That would be terrific. I'm overwhelmed with the hospitality you extend to a complete stranger." He laughed. "Not that it stops me from an immediate, 'Yes, I accept.'"

Within hours Dave had returned to the motel, packed up his belongings and settled into an old-fashioned, though luxurious bedroom, that he was told had been their oldest son's. Their continual ease with abundance had begun to irritate Dave. He doubted that it even occurred to them that his oldest son was his only son. Dave kept trying to reason out what it was that David and Shirley wanted from him in exchange for what they were giving. As far as he could see, he had nothing to offer them. And they didn't appear to have any religious convictions. Before eating, David simply said, "Salud." Surely they weren't as altruistic as they appeared.

He shared that thought with Peggy during their nightly call, and surprising him, she expressed the opposite opinion. "Hey, don't look at your Lotto ticket with crossed eyes and miss the winning number. They're the first people who've offered you hope."

"Oh Peg, forgive me. I'm just so scared about everything. I wish I could be in two places at once...be with you on Tuesday, as well as here. But as you say, I need to stick with this lead." There was silence.

"So it's all set up, and Sarah will go with you? And Lauren will stay with her friend, Winnie, for a few days. And you'll call and tell me the results as soon as you can, right?"

"Yes, dear. Everything's being taken care of here. You don't need to worry about us. I definitely think it's best that you remain there and take advantage of what appears to be God's plan for you finding Brian."

It was strange to hear his Doubting Thomas wife, switch sides. Dave needed her words of encouragement, yet he felt uncomfortable with her strength. It made him feel weak and vulnerable. He offered his wife a prayer for a positive outcome to her coming ordeal, although he still thought that his position was the hardest, because he was dealing with the unknown power of evil, whereas she had an army of good forces on her side.

"Let go and let God," Dave said to himself as his head sank into a memory foam pillow that first night in David and Shirley's house.

Chapter 9
Owen and Jane
Friday, April 5

What was going on? Owen was having a hard time believing in the chain of linked fortunes that began when he'd first met Jane on his way out of her apartment. Next he'd found the hash intact in his old rental, and then Jane's agreement to let him store it in her freezer, plus sleep over a few nights until he'd made a drug deal for cash, then extending the sleeping arrangement until Domino could come across with the cash, and now this. Once again, he spotted Phillip.

Since Friday was Jane's day off, Owen had cleared out of her apartment as soon as he woke, leaving her to her privacy and any plans she might have for visitors, particularly Danny. Owen knew she'd informed Danny of his temporary sleeping arrangements, and although he supposedly was alright with it, Owen tried to keep as low a profile as possible, not wanting to trigger any confrontations between the two lovers. He felt a sense of uneasiness about it on everyone's part, and wanted to get out as soon as Domino connected. Which Jane assured him could happen at any moment.

With no drug business to take care of, his old impulse to roam triggered Owen. Before he gave it a second thought, he'd found himself walking along the street bordering the 40 Expressway. It was like the old days when he used to hitchhike, playing the game that whatever the driver's destination was, he'd say that's where he was going. Just to see what shape would settle into his shapeless life. But this time he wasn't looking to go anywhere, except eventually back to Jane's, when a black BMW slowed down to turn onto the ramp headed north. Owen glanced up to see the driver. There was no mistaking him. It was Phillip.

Phillip's head was in profile from where Owen stood. He could tell *The Lizard* was looking for oncoming traffic, and his chance to merge onto I40. He hadn't changed much in ten years. As though evil blood was a preservative, Owen thought. He bent over and picked up a piece of paper, in case Phillip was looking in his rear view mirror. His only advantage was to see, but not be seen.

As he stooped down, he read the license plate, ODD 1317. That was easy enough. And strange too. Strange that someone as deviant as Phillip would have the word *ODD* on his license plate, although Owen remembered him as having a quirky sense of humor. Maybe he'd requested it. Perhaps in tandem with the odd numbers. He knew Phillip possessed a computer-like system of classifying things, storing them in the files and folders of his mind. Owen had learned that propensity from him, and it had served him well.

After Phillip's car disappeared in ongoing traffic, Owen headed down the slope that would take him back along Route 40, noticing some tender buds of grass making their way through the brown thatch of winter. Arising out of seeing him once again, the words of T. S. Elliot, Phillip's favorite poet, floated up: "April is the cruelest month…" Indeed it was, with its hope of spring and new life that poked its head above the ground, only to have it frozen off by a sudden drop in temperature.

But Owen would see that this human hope didn't die. He would take immediate action, hitchhiking or walking back to Jane's apartment where he would search her city directory, looking up the Bureau of Motor Vehicles. No way Phillip was going to elude him this time. He had him in the cross hairs of his rifle scope. Owen hadn't felt such a surge of elation since the last time he'd spotted Phillip. It was different than a drug high. The pure, natural endorphin release gave him the feeling of a bird in flight, finding a warm updraft and sailing along on its current, expending no energy to maintain its altered state of relaxed alertness.

Without thinking, he found himself in a drugstore, leafing through their phone directory. Much more efficient than returning to Jane's. He stabbed at a directory page with his forefinger. There was the address of the BMV. Only they called it the MVA here. He tore it out, noting the closest listed Bureau address was too far to walk. Not really, but his finding triggered impatience. Searching further, he found and tore out another page, this one listing cab services. No need to hitchhike or walk. Take a cab, stiff the cabbie. He hadn't lost his ability to run fast, dodge and dart, hiding from the tracker. Owen felt a puff of pride issuing from his finesse as an escape artist. Jane had recognized that.

OK, but there weren't any cabs cruising for customers in this area. The first thing he needed to do was to find a phone booth, dial the call from there, making himself untraceable. It was an exasperating and futile exercise. He searched the nearby streets and shops for fifteen minutes, only to return to the drugstore, telling the pharmacist an urgent situation had occurred, and could he please use his cell phone to call a cab.

The man behind the counter in his stiff white coat, looked

at Owen suspiciously, but didn't rebuff him. "OK, son, let me dial the number for you." He took the torn-out directory scrap, frowning at Owen, but dialed it, handing the phone to him. The cab company said it would be about ten minutes before they could dispatch someone to the drugstore address.

Owen ducked into the next-door *McDonald's* to wash up in their restroom. After registering the pharmacist's skepticism about his appearance, he didn't want to look like a complete deadbeat. Seeing his image in the bathroom mirror, he had to admit he looked pretty scruffy. Somehow it had felt like a further invasion of Jane's privacy to use her bathroom, other than the toilet, since she hadn't extended the offer, or a razor. As a result, he hadn't showered or shaved since he'd been given the boot from his apartment. His thick, nearly black hair made that readily apparent. Facial hair was beginning to creep down into his normally close-cropped jawline beard, and topping his lips were the beginnings of a scraggly mustache. Above his cheekbones he had dark circles under his eyes, nearly the same color as his brown eyes. The whites of his eyes seemed to glow. Overall, the effect was like the bandit mask of a raccoon.

A rodent. It was hard to imagine what Jane saw in him. As soon as he had the money, he'd have to go to the barbershop, get a trim. After that he'd make another trip to the Goodwill store and get himself some decent rags. He bent over the sink, scooping water into his hands and splashing it in his hair, raking his fingers through it. Standing, he shook his head like a dog coming in from the rain. Droplets ran down the mirror, reminding Owen of tears. How long had it been since he cried? A useless emotion as far as he was concerned. Self-pity was for losers.

Standing on the front curb, Owen saw a cab approaching. It was dingy and looked like an independent, although he'd called a cab company. He hailed it, and the driver made a hard turn toward him, screeching to a halt. Apparently the guy had been day-dreaming. As Owen opened the back door, the cabbie said, "Are you the one's going to the License Bureau?"

"Yes," said Owen, watching the driver crane his neck as he looked him over.

His appraisal was quick. "It's probably gonna run you around twenty dollars. You got the moola?"

That confirmed it. Owen pretty much knew this guy was an independent. He probably intercepted company calls and headed out on his own, beat them to the punch.

"Yep, right here," Owen said, flashing his last fiver in the air, crimping it in his fingers, as though there were more.

"OK then, off we go." The cabbie pulled down the metal arm on his taximeter, and it jumped quickly to five dollars. 'Just to get into the cab.' As the driver pulled into north-bound traffic, Owen saw a Yellow Cab headed in the opposite direction. It pulled over near *McDonald's*. So this guy was a pirate too. He hated to rip off a brother, but circumstances topped fraternal links.

The guy tried hard to start up a conversation, beginning with making eye contact in the rear view mirror. "So what's your name? Mine's Stuart. Spelled with a '*u*'. You know, like *Stuart Little*, the mouse in the kid's book." He guffawed, turning his head toward the backseat again. The tip of his nose and his cheeks were reddened. Most likely an alcoholic. Which was probably why he was a pirate. No cab company would hire an alkie.

He tried for conversation again. "So what's your name?"

"Jim. Just plain Jim," Owen said, remembering 'Just Plain Jane.' Like a period. No more information will be given. Owen turned his head and began to watch out the window.

Stuart waited for more, then said into the rear view mirror, "Oh, I see. You're the dark silent type. Well, I can live with that." He began whistling a tune that Owen recognized as the theme song from *Bridge on the River Kwai*. An old-timer. Owen knew more music from that era than he did current popular songs. Whenever he was in shelters, Owen searched for old movies, old music. They were the best. Current movies jarred him with unmitigated catastrophe, horror, and piercing music and vignettes.

The cabbie gave up on trying to converse, and they rode in silence, until Owen thought they must be getting close to their destination. He looked down at the scrap of paper with the written address. They were on the right street, and the numbers were diminishing toward the building he sought. Maybe only a mile or so to go.

They had slowed down to a crawl in the thick traffic. Just what he wanted. Owen began watching more intently, looking for an alley, or some other escape route. Before they got much closer to their destination, he spotted what was needed. Opening the back door, he tossed out the words, "Oops, I forgot something," as he hit the pavement running. He tore down an alley.

After he'd run until he was nearly out of breath, he became aware of a solid wood fence about chest high, that ran along his left flank. Backing up and running toward it full tilt, he reached out, grabbing its cap-rail with both hands, and vaulting it. 'Glory be to City Maintenance!,' it didn't even have any splinters. Nor anything but concrete on the other side. It could have been the 'Black Hole of Inner Baltimore,' and he could have been consumed in its depths, never to emerge again.

Ducking his head, in case the cabbie had made a U turn and headed down the alley, Owen continued running alongside the fence, becoming aware that it marked the backyard limits of a bank of run-down buildings. He saw a shadowy hole under a wooden staircase and headed for it. In it, there was an entrance to a locked basement door. Perfect. No one would see him there unless they were entering the basement. He sank into its protective darkness like an animal in its lair. It was dank and moldy.

How long should he wait before leaving for the BMV? He needed to make certain the cabbie hadn't loitered around, hoping to catch him. Owen had lost his watch two days ago. The fake leather band was so frayed, it had probably fallen off without his even noticing. Another item to replace when he hit payload. He wondered when Jane would close the deal. In the meantime, he calculated what he thought was about twenty minutes, figuring the cabbie wouldn't stick around longer than that, miss a paying customer.

Back on the street, at first he was cautious, scanning in all directions. You never knew, he might have screwed a hothead. He saw no sign of the cab, and for an instant felt sorry that he had beat the pirate at his own game. Then he reminded himself that guilt had no seat at the table of survival.

Entering the Bureau, he scanned the crowd to make sure the cabbie wasn't lying in wait. By the time he'd entered the only line with a female clerk, he felt like a caged cougar the zoo-keeper had forgotten to lock in. He found it difficult to stand still and contain the pent-up energy that ached for action. Picturing Phillip's face on the bulletin board in back of the clerk, he saw himself throwing a dart that struck the bulls-eye at the top of the bridge of his nose, where Phillip's eyebrows met.

"What can I do for you, sir?"

"Oh, I, uh..." Owen stammered, then collected himself. "Someone hit my car in the parking lot of a shopping mall, and sped away before I could talk to him. I got his license plate number and I'm trying to find out who he is, so I can file an insurance claim. I memorized the numbers. It's..."

"Sorry sir, we can't give out the names of license plate owners."

The clerk had a large chocolate brown mole above her left eyebrow. Why didn't people that could afford to, have things like that removed? It was ugly. "Why not? The accident was the other guy's fault and he didn't stop. How am I supposed to...?"

"Sorry sir, it's a state law. Part of the Privacy Act. Next please," she said, looking through Owen as though he wasn't there. She sniffled, and her mole jumped up and down. He wanted to rip it off.

Out on the street, Owen tried to locate where he was, and where he should go from there. The crazy state bureaucracy. Why the hell did they have people register their names and license plates, if no one could have the information? Except the police. The workings of a police state. And they were the ones that should have stopped *The Lizard's* unlawful activity. One more example of the upside-down morality of society. Protect the criminals, disinherit their victims from any remnants of power. Any form of anarchy would undoubtedly be more just than the prevailing government. There was an equalizing force in bare bones survival. Everyone had to depend on their own skills, their own wits. People like Owen would come out on top. He was doubting his luck, but not his ingenuity.

"I saw him again," said Owen in a tone that hovered uneasily between disappointment and excitement. He'd returned to Jane's apartment after what he calculated was a three-hour walk back, having decided not to press his luck by stiffing another cabbie.

"*The Lizard Man?*" said Jane, her back to Owen, as she rinsed their emptied soup bowls at the sink. Owen had passed Danny on the stairs, and was surprised that Danny was civil to him. The pair must have forged some trade-off.

"Yep, the *Lizard Man*. Same as ever."

"Considering how you feel about him, you seem amazingly calm. Where was it? Was it face to face this time?" she asked, as she dried her hands on a dish towel, sitting down across the table from Owen.

"No, if I'd seen him up close I wouldn't be here to tell the story. This time I was walking near a ramp onto....wherever, when he passed me. He's got a different car now. It's a BMW. I memorized his license plate and went to the License Bureau to find out his name. The frigging bureaucrats wouldn't give it up. Some shit about a Privacy Act."

"Yes, well it's there to protect the good guys as well as the bad. The law doesn't discriminate."

Owen took in Jane's appearance. She had on a navy blue pants suit. Her long blond hair licked at its darkness. "The hell it doesn't. What if both of us, dressed like we are, asked a policeman for help. Which one do you think he'd give his attention to?"

"Hopefully you, since you'd appear to need more help than I would."

"See there, you've made a judgment just like the policeman would. His might be the opposite of yours....in fact, I'm willing to bet my last dollar it would be. Nevertheless, he differentiates. Most likely on the basis of class."

"I get your point. And once again, I find it's oppositional to what I say. You play the Devil's Advocate well."

"I don't just play the Devil's Advocate. I'm the Devil himself," said Owen, a mischievous grin growing from his mouth to his eyes.

"OK, so how's the Devil going to find the *Lizard Man*?"

Owen's face collapsed. He looked out the kitchen window toward the darkening sky. "Good question. One I've been asking myself on my walk here. Got any ideas?" Before Jane answered, Owen continued. "I keep circling back to the bare bones of it. Which is that I need to walk the swanky neighborhoods around Baltimore until I spot him. Or his car parked in his driveway. At least I now know his new car, and its license plate. You got a street map of Baltimore and its outlying areas? That's a beginning."

"I do. Let's take a look," said Jane, riffling through a drawer under the kitchen counter. "Here it is," she said, hand-ironing the folds out of a map she'd laid on the table-top. "Do you think you can point out approximately where you were when you saw him?"

"Sure," said Owen, spiraling his finger atop a swirl of red and blue lines that marked the major highways crisscrossing the hub of Baltimore. "Ah, here it is. I'm pretty sure it was 140, headed out toward the northwestern neighborhoods. That's where I think his original house was. The one where he kept me. Did I tell you that I managed to make my way back there some six or seven years ago and found the house, but he no longer lived there?"

"Yes, you did, and how nothing came of it."

"Yeah, well it's about time I get real serious about this. Before *The Lizard* trashes more young guys. I need to buy me some wheels. An old beater will do. Then start a systematic search of the Baltimore mansions. *The Baltimore Mansions....* sounds like a new prime-time TV series. Don't you think?"

Owen looked Jane straight in the eye for the first time since he'd sat down. "Did Domino come through for me yet?"

"He's working on it. Says he's a little backed-up for cash, but that it should be only a day or two more. Though listening to you, I do have an idea. Like you don't have to wait 'til you have the cash to buy a car. I'd be glad to take you around the neighborhoods. Danny and I have plans for later this evening. But maybe early tomorrow afternoon?"

"That would be great. But I don't want to impose on you. Besides, you'll get bored with my schemes."

"Depends on what you're scheming. Like what would you do if you found him, see which house was his?" Jane fixed an unblinking gaze on Owen.

"To tell you the truth, I don't know. I honestly don't know." Owen was surprised to hear himself say that. He always thought of finding Phillip, facing him and telling him what an immoral bastard he was. And then? And then, Owen just thought of Phillip as obliterated. That once Phillip was faced with the truth, that the sheer force of it would cause him to implode. Owen now realized that he needed to think beyond some nebulous cosmic justice. Something far more was needed. What form that something would take, he didn't exactly know. But he had an idea.

Chapter 10
Phillip
Monday, April 8

Phillip found he was a tad nervous at the *Keep Our Children Safe* meeting. He had postponed it for nearly a week from his car's cell phone, because he knew he would not be prepared for it immediately after bringing Brian home. A sign of advancing age, he mused, since prior to this boy he'd always been fresh out of the starting gate the day after his return. As a reason for the postponement, he'd told his committee that he'd made a trip to Chicago to woo a philanthropist who was thinking of donating a significant sum to their cause. Now the four of them looked at him in anticipation of good news.

Phillip cleared his throat. "First of all, let me thank each of you for your flexibility in rearranging the date of this meeting. Gloria," he smiled at the organist of St. Matthew's Church, "and Dan, I know you have a very busy schedule these days," he said, giving deference to the *Ravens* assistant coach who had cut short a vacation specifically to attend the meeting. 'Or so he said.' "Not to omit Henry, whom we know has begun auditions for the new *Everymans Theater* production. And last, but not least, Keith, our Chairman Emeritus, who got us all off to such a fine start."

Damn, he still had a catch in his throat. Maybe he was coming down with a cold, though he hoped not, as he had big plans for his boy. Thinking of Brian's initiation only made matters worse. 'Focus on the meeting,' he told himself, bringing back a measure of his usual hard-headed concentration.

Phillip cleared his throat again. "Ah...hmm, I know that all five of us are looking for a boost in morale by securing our financial resources. So that we can stand on more solid ground after our reconfiguration of this committee." He paused. "I'm afraid I have some disappointing news, in that the party I visited in Chicago lost a great deal of his wealth in a hedge fund that went south on him. Quite out of the blue. In fact, that occurred between the time we set up our meeting and the day of my visit with him. The rumble was heard on Wall Street. So we're back to ground zero on that score."

"But I haven't forgotten that the major reason for this meeting is to come up with a plan for raising money to cover our annual expenses. Rent, utilities, office supplies, recruiting volunteers, their recognition banquet, advertising and other sundry expenses. I couldn't be more sorry about our disappointment. It was an old Harvard crony of mine, who I thought was quite solid. I must confess to feeling worse for our loss than for his, as he lacks the altruistic spirit we possess."

"I take it he was still planning to contribute to our cause before his castle crumbled," said Henry.

"Oh, no doubt about that. He wanted to help us, but it also meant a large deductible item on his tax return. You'll find, in general, that our average monetary contributor gives in order to make money elsewhere, whereas we contribute our time and energy knowing it has no payback, except that the cause we support gathers momentum. We can always trust those who give of themselves to causes such as ours."

"Which brings me to a sensitive subject. In spite of the fact that our organization has gained name recognition, I want to propose that we discuss the possibility of changing its name."

Gloria spoke up immediately. "That doesn't make sense. We have it printed on too many 'give-ways,'...whatever those are called...and on our official stationary. Why would we want to switch horses in midstream, when the horse is pulling his weight? "That doesn't make sense," she said again, followed by, "I already said that, but it bears repeating. What's wrong with *Keep Our Children Safe*? We all decided that was the best choice of names." She finished on an emphatic exhalation.

"Promotional items," said Henry.

"What?" said Gloria.

"Promotional items. That's the name of what you called 'give-aways.'"

"Well, whatever. My point is that we shouldn't change the name, because the community recognizes it."

The men looked down in embarrassment, Henry finally taking the lead by looking directly at Gloria. "It seemed a good name at the time, and still does, except for its acronym. We didn't consider that when we chose it."

Phillip felt certain that Gloria would now understand and yield to Henry's rationale, understated though it was.

"KOCS, what's the matter with...oh, how absurd. I never thought of it that way before, and I doubt if anyone does. Honestly, you men think with your..." Gloria couldn't suppress a laugh. "OK, I get it. It does call up the wrong image. For those who think that way. So, what do you have in mind, Phillip? I know you don't approach anything without a well-laid-out plan."

"Yes, thanks, Gloria. I've given it some thought and propose that we replace its present name with *Protect Our*

Children. Does anyone have any objections? If not, I'll go ahead and replace all items that have the old name on them. At my expense, of course. Is that agreeable to the board?"

"OK by me," said Henry.

"Aye," said Keith.

"Same here," mumbled Dan, casting his eyes down, as though he didn't wish to confront the situation.

"So, our new name is adopted: *Protect Our Children.* I'll see to changing the charter and other documents within the week, along with ordering new 'freebies.'"

"Hey, you forgot my vote," said Gloria. "If you're concerned about acronyms, POC calls to mind unpleasant images. Such as acne scars, distress marks on furniture."

"Whoever would think of that?" said Kevin.

"My point exactly. I never thought of anything from the acronym KOCS, except what it stood for. Male minds obviously operate differently. But I'm not going to fight about it. POC*s* it is. Though, hey, when I just said that, I'm reminded of 'Pox on you.' From the smallpox plague, I presume. You see, there's probably an unpleasant image for almost any acronym. If that's the track your mind follows. Really, I think the whole discussion is a non sequitur."

"OK, but we have a majority vote, so let's move on to more important matters," said Phillip. "We need to mount a money-making project."

"Well, bake sales are getting a little stale," said Keith, "as is my pun, but then so are marathons, be they biking, walking, or running. You must have given this some thought, Phillip. Any new, bright ideas?"

After hearing the word, 'bake,' Phillip thought of what sensual delicacy he was going to bake for Brian before the act of his physical seduction, finding it difficult to concentrate on the task at hand. He coughed several times, then answered, "Yes, I have given it some thought, and I agree with Kevin's assessment about 'the same old fund-raisers.' We need to come up with something for a *Ravens* half-time show that's child-focused, but appealing to adults. Something to win everyone's hearts. Like a vulnerable, talented young athlete who's had multiple congenital heart defects, and had something like six surgeries to correct them. Naturally he can't play tackle football. It just so happens that I know of one. So we show him catching and passing the football to...who else but our very own Super-Bowl MVP, Ray Lewis. And let's say that as a sponsor of our newly named *Protect Our Children,* we would get, say, one-quarter of the gate on that day. We would advertise our cause ahead of time, perhaps even increasing the sale of tickets so that the *Ravens* wouldn't lose much, but might attract more. We could even have this handicapped child punt the first ball. If he were capable."

"Well, I don't know about the punting part, Phillip," said Dan. "The commissioners might think that against the rules of the game. But it sounds like a good idea, even if it is unprecedented. I'm certainly willing to approach management about it. It might pack some wallop."

"Why not have it be an athletic female?" said Gloria. "There's plenty of them. Need I go beyond the Williams sisters and Kristi Yamaguchi, to name but a few."

'This token woman that Keith appointed to the board is really going beyond her realm of power,' Phillip thought. 'Perhaps I should speak to Keith after the meeting, and ask if he couldn't think of someone else to appoint in her place. We could can her and suffer no consequences, since it's an unpaid position.'

"Good for you for speaking up about possible discrimination against the 'fair sex'," said Phillip, "but the reason I think a male is more appropriate, is that professional football is an all-male sport. Plus the Williams sisters and Kristi are neither handicapped, nor children. Nor do I believe we can set up a tennis court or an ice-rink on the field. So do I have any other suggestions as to an appropriate poster child?

Beside the one I have in mind. It would, of course, need to be someone with a disability or handicap that he has struggled against the odds to overcome."

"If that's what you're looking for, then I think he should be someone like a kid with a severe learning disability or an autistic kid," said Gloria. "They're the most vulnerable children when it comes to being the target of child predators."

'No, Gloria, they're less likely to be, because an intelligent perpetrator is not going to abuse a kid who doesn't have enough sense to protect himself from dire consequences, by telling on his abuser,' Phillip thought. 'What would it take to shut this woman up?'

"Gloria, I appreciate your contributions to the discussion today, but I think it's important that this child we choose to represent POC be physically attractive and half-way intelligent to produce the proper image that would stimulate the donor's sympathy. We don't want the cameras zooming in on someone with ugly warts to hide, or the reporters trying to talk to someone who isn't capable of making articulate responses. Surely that wouldn't help our cause."

"So you want a nearly perfect child with a 'hidden handicap'?"

Phillip could tell his face was getting flushed with the effort needed to contain his anger.

Dan interrupted before he could speak again. "Listen, let's not quibble about details. Let me speak to management about this and get their permission, before we start recruiting our poster child."

"Good idea," said Phillip, happy to drop the subject.

"Just one more question before we leave the topic," said Gloria. "What exactly do we tell the public about what we do to protect our children?"

"I can speak to that," said Henry. "I sat in on a training session for one of our volunteers. Mainly the old school stuff about, 'Don't take candy from strangers,' 'Don't accept rides from strangers, no matter how friendly they seem'... you know, all that stuff. Every generation has to be taught the same old lures and come-ons that child abusers use."

Phillip felt himself heating up. "Listen, Gloria, I suggest you review the literature we use for our educational program, read the brochures and stay informed. The next time we meet, I'll ask you the same question and you should be able to answer it. I don't think you've been doing your homework."

'If there is a next time for her,' thought Phillip. 'And to think that I assumed Keith had chosen a soft-spoken church lady who wouldn't ignite any sparks. I'll see to it that we put out her fire.'

Chapter 11
Jane and Owen
Tuesday, April 9

Having worked the night shift at The Shelter, when Jane opened her apartment door on Tuesday morning, she saw that Owen was still there on her couch, although this was the third morning after they anticipated he would have the means to find his own place. It turned out that Domino had pancreatitis and was in the hospital. Aside from his not being able to help Owen, Jane was concerned about her old friend. Plus, she was irritated with Danny, as he wasn't demonstrating much tolerance for Owen's situation. Yesterday he'd begun suggesting that Jane was aiding and abetting a criminal, and stood to lose her job over it. She'd snapped at him, saying, "Does that mean you're going to report me?"

Danny hesitated. "Well, no. But I do think it should give you pause to think about the landslide you might set in motion."

"Meaning that you might slide away on it, never to be heard from again? Or that if I lost my job, you might have to support me? Just what do you mean, Danny? It sounds like a threat to me."

Danny winced, as though Jane had struck him. "No, Kitten, I'm not threatening you. Just trying to warn you not to climb too far out on the limb. You know, like the old nursery rhyme: 'When the bough breaks, the cradle will fall.'"

"Don't you worry about me. I've had plenty of experience at climbing out on limbs, and I've never had one break."

Danny came closer and kissed Jane on the cheek, his arms at his sides. "Whatever you say, whatever you say," he had muttered, as he exited into the outer hallway.

Sure enough, the mantel clock said 10:25, and Owen was still asleep. She'd let him stay that way a little longer. Hard to say what he'd been up to. Possibly even backslid into doing drugs again, although she was pretty sure he'd been honorable on that score since he'd been staying with her. At least there were no signs that he'd had other dopers in. If he ever crossed that line, he was out.

Keeping her red corduroy dress on, Jane settled down on top of her bedspread, pulling a comforter over her and leaving the bedroom door open. She fell asleep quickly and soundly. Later she awakened to the sounds of Owen in the kitchen. Her bedside clock said that it was close to noon.

Combing her hair with her fingers, Jane entered the kitchen. "Hola, mi amigo. Duerme bien?" It turned out that Owen knew a smattering of Spanish, as she did. She wasn't sure where he'd learned it. Probably had a Latino house-mate at some point. Or maybe Phillip had taught him.

"Si, duermo bien." He croaked a half-laugh as he said, "Hey, let's not go beyond that. It was hard enough to conjugate the verb. I think I got the wrong tense."

Apparently it was from Phillip. Most likely from one of his lessons, since Owen used the word 'conjugate'. It was amazing that he was able to retain as much as he did. Particularly since he'd told Jane he'd been stoned much of the time he was with Phillip, although he didn't even know what drugs his captor had fed him, just that it was part of his ritual. Once again, Jane felt a deep sadness in recognizing a native intelligence that was being wasted on the machinations of petty crime and drug dealings.

"Thanks for making the coffee. I need it," she said, joining him at the kitchen table.

He did not look at her as she addressed him. She raised the tone and volume of her voice, trying to capture his attention. "I have a good idea that might prove fruitful," she said, waiting until he looked up. "Do you want to hear it?"

"Sure. Lay it on me."

"Well, as you know, I'm a social worker. I've been in Baltimore's system of serving children for nearly ten years now. We have inter-agency dealings because of mutual clients, so I've been to a lot of meetings with professionals over the years. Last night it occurred to me that your kidnapper might be one of those people. Jaded as it sounds, pedophiles often position themselves where they're sure to have access to kids. And as a cover for their own activities," she said, eying him. "I need your help here. Can you give me a description of Phillip? If he actually goes by that name. You just saw him a few days ago, so you have a recent sighting. At least of his head."

Just say 'Phillip' and she had his rapt attention.

"Sure. He's probably close to fifty years old now. On the short side. Let's see...when I was with him, I was about five-foot-nine or so, and he was a shade shorter than me. Maybe five-foot-seven or eight. Small-boned, slight build. Maybe one hundred and fifty pounds, soaking wet. If that. Pasty complexion. Like he just crawled out from under a rock. Yeah, like a lizard."

"Go on."

"He has black hair, or as close as I've ever seen to black. Combed back, with a little wave in the front. I think it's still like that, from what I saw in the car the other day. And when he originally picked me up, he had a bristly black mustache, but I think it must have been fake, because it disappeared as soon as he had me caged. Looked kind of like Hitler's. Yeah, it did. Didn't look like he shaved the mustache off. I mean, it would be too apparent for ID purposes for him to grow it before he left, then shave it when he got back. The timing would be suspicious. I thought a lot about it and decided it must have been fake. But it looked real. Oh, and his eyes were dark brown. And, and…he had a mole on the back of his hand. Just above his right wrist."

"Any other distinguishing features you can remember? Although what you've said is a lot to go on."

"Yeah, he had a kind of…V in his hairline. Right in the middle of his forehead. I forget what they call those."

"Widow's peaks."

"Yeah, that's it. Goddamn. I can see that fucker plain as day. Even though it's been about ten years. I didn't even need the refresher course the other day. It's like somebody branded my brain with a photo of him. Comes to me sometimes when I close my eyes. Mostly at night."

In spite of herself, Jane smiled, wrapping herself around the warm nugget of her knowledge. Owen noticed. Having mastered body nuances in the game of survival, he could read interior landscapes on people's faces. "Hey, what's with you?"

"Well-ll," said Jane, drawing out his anticipation. "I think I know who your man is."

"You know him. Holy shit! Who is he? Who? Who?" said Owen, sounding like a night owl.

Jane gathered in Owen's excitement. She had never seen him so animated. But she knew she needed to be judicious about what she conveyed. It was too early to impart a name, or an address, even though she had gathered that information. Just yesterday she'd remembered Phillip Nottingham, the president of *Keep Our Children Safe*. As the Child Specialist at the shelter, she had been included in several city-wide youth welfare meetings, aimed at coordinating the efforts of all those who worked to keep 'at-risk children' safe.

She'd felt uneasy around Phillip. He didn't really have the feel of someone who would be interested in helping children. Call it intuition or, more likely, the years of experience she'd had with child-care workers. Phillip came off as arrogant, cocky, and not the sort who would choose to be involved with troubled children. Nor they with him. His position in the Baltimore world of child welfare seemed more likely to have been motivated by status and power. But if that were the case, surely he could have found a more prestigious director's board, rather than the lowest rung on the ladder, that of serving powerless children. On the wheel of of abuser-victim-rescuer, Phillip fit the profile of an abuser far more than that of a rescuer.

And now Jane knew he fit Owen's physical description of him exactly, displaying little change in his appearance in the decade that had elapsed. Even the widow's peak was still there, as his hairline hadn't begun to recede yet. She didn't, of course, know about the mole. But she had cross-checked his identification with the aid of the *Social Service Directory,* and through discreet inquiries at The Shelter. She had even found out that he drove a black BMW. In a world of underpaid social workers, wealthy patrons stood out. How much could she tell Owen? Not much. In her enthusiasm to help, she'd already mistakenly revealed too much to him.

The warmth of her knowledge was dispelled. "Owen, I'm sorry, but I can't release his name and address to you until I check some things out with my supervisor...and the possibly the police. You know about confidentiality, right?"

The fire in Owen's eyes turned to stone. "Yeah, right. I

know about confidentiality. Just like the License Bureau and the Privacy Act. We have to protect the privacy of child molesters. Very important."

Jane struggled to get back on top. "You know I want to help you. And I will. Just give me a week or so and I'll get this straightened out. We need to go about it cautiously. Stop and think Owen. You've waited ten years for this information. What's another week?"

"Yeah, right. What's another week in the life of a young guy who's getting all those good drugs, good food, and having his ears fucked off every night. Like I did. The kid should enjoy it while he can. Right?"

"Owen, please. I'm so sorry. I'll get on this immediately. I promise."

Owen stood up from the table, kicking its leg. She could see that his whole body was shaking with rage.

"Fuck you, Just Plain Jane. And fuck your promises. I'm outta here." He strode toward the apartment door, slamming it as he exited.

Jane knew that he'd be back. He'd left his hash in the refrigerator.

Chapter 12
Dave and Shirley
Tuesday

"Ductal carcinoma in situ," Dave said slowly, as he wrote it down. He would look it up on Hopkins' computer later. Now he needed to give his attention to Sarah McCammon, Forrest's wife, and Peggy's best friend. She had called him from the hospital, while his sweetheart was still in the recovery room.

"Yes, Dr. Vahi said to tell you that the results of the surgery were the best possible outcome. The tumor was malignant, as expected, but it was small, like under two centimeters, as I remember. They went ahead and removed a dozen lymph nodes, because the tumor sat right next to her armpit, where the lymph nodes are, I guess. Excuse me if I confuse you Dave, but all of this is pretty new language to me. You'll hear the exact description after Peggy talks to her oncologist. Anyway, it's my understanding that none of the lymph nodes were malignant. I know I got that part right, because it was the best news."

"Terrific. How long do they think she'll be in recovery? And what comes after that?"

"Peggy told me that she'll call you tomorrow, when she's rested and can talk straight. The doctor said she'll probably only have to spend a couple of days upstairs, at most, and that if everything goes as expected, she should be discharged after his rounds on Thursday morning."

"Terrific." Saying that for the second time, Dave noticed that in spite of its positive meaning, *terrific* came very close to *terrify*. "Did he tell you anything about the follow-up treatment?"

"He did, although he said that would be up to the oncologist, Dr. Simon, to inform you two. But he did say that normally with this diagnosis, Peggy could expect some radiation sessions to her left breast, probably followed by a course of some hormonal drug, called, oh...it sounded something like *Tampax*. Although I'm sure it wasn't," Sarah ended, her final tone conveying embarrassment.

"What about her heart?"

"Oh, there's nothing wrong with her heart. It's fine."

"No, I mean, in terms of radiation treatment. It sounds like they're going to be radiating her heart along with the breast tissue. I don't know how they could avoid it."

"Gosh, I don't know either, Dave. But I'm sure you'll get the answers to those kinds of questions from the oncologist after Peggy gets home."

"Of course, of course. Thank you so much, Sarah...for being by her side, transporting her...making sure Lauren's OK, and oh, a hundred kindnesses. I don't know how we'll ever repay you...and Forrest. But I'm sure the Good Lord has a special place in Heaven for the two of you."

Even though the news about Peggy was uplifting, soon after he hung up, Dave found himself wallowing in a trough of earlier dismal, disgusting images that clung to him like burrs to a sweater. Peg's breast cut open and bleeding, the malignant tumor somehow hairy, dark and menacing, the doctor actually stitching the wound shut, each stitch plunging deep into her sweet flesh. He was glad when his thoughts were interrupted by a call from downstairs.

"Dave, are you up there?" Hopkins called. Going to the second floor banister, Dave looked down. It must have been fifteen feet to the slate floor of the entrance hall. The late afternoon sun shone through the prisms of a crystal chandelier, casting a rainbow glow on a bald spot in the center of Hopkins' head.

"Yes, thank the Lord, I wrapped things up for the day. Aren't you home a little early?"

"You betcha. Things fell in place like a row of dominoes. I called home and Shirley's whipped up some fettuccine Alfredo. Would you like to join us?"

"I sure would. I've had a miserable afternoon, and I definitely need a shot of optimism. And that, I've found, I can count on from the two of you."

"Great," said Hopkins, one hand on the railing, calling out to Shirley. "Hon, hold up, say, five, ten minutes on the meal. I have to talk to Dave about something."

Hopkins arrived at Dave's open door, huffing a bit from the climb. "I've got to get more exercise. Been thinking of setting up an exercise room in that area off the den. Never did figure out its purpose. But a home gym would be great there. Shirley agrees."

"Now, what is it my friend? You look discouraged. Let me guess. Could it possibly be trying to sell magazine subscriptions to registered child molesters? I thought that was a bad idea from the get-go, but your Chief Compton said it was a place to start, until they got some other connections going."

"Yeah, you're exactly right. I can't bring myself to continue doing it. Like today...this one guy came to the door bare-chested – he must have weighed well over two hundred pounds. And he had on these dirty, skanky sweatpants that looked like he'd rubbed axle grease on them. He didn't even seem embarrassed. He invited me in, then tried to share a beer with me, while I was describing the subscription plan. And he told me that even though he's on welfare since he'd lost his job, he wanted to buy a subscription because it's a worthy cause. Said he really wants to help the schoolchildren. Can you imagine the gall it takes to say that, when you've been in prison for molesting kids? It was all I could do to sit on his filthy couch and talk to him."

As Dave was telling this to Hopkins, he felt a sharp stab of remorse for not talking to the guy about Christ and forgiveness. He had missed a ripe chance to bring a sinner into the fold. Then he flashed back on the thoughts he'd had when he finally got away from the guy and into his car. Uncle Harry's face had appeared before him again, and he knew he didn't feel guilty anymore about being glad his uncle died when he did. That guilt had arisen from the mind of an innocent child. Now that he knew and understood what Uncle Harry had done, he wished him a fate worse than death. He wished his uncle had lived, and been charged and sentenced for his crime. God, he wished that Uncle Harry had served time like the vile man he'd just left. Dave knew what other inmates did to child molesters. And he understood why. They were reviled, even by the lowest of the low.

Hopkins clapped him on the shoulder, bringing him back to the present. "I can only imagine how miserable you must have felt. Well, my good man, no more of that low-life stuff. I finally have some good contacts for you. I'll tell you all about them at dinner. Come on down and we'll discuss them. Plus I have a favor to ask of you."

As usual, the mahogany dining room table was set with gold-rimmed plates, sterling silver spoons and forks, plus linen napkins. Shirley even lit some candles. Now that Dave had dumped his dismal feelings about the child-molester, the dinner felt almost celebratory. He had told David and Shirley about Peg's up-coming surgery, and now he was able to share her post-operative success story with them. They were genuinely happy for him, and spoke of Peggy as though she were a member of their family.

"This calls for that bottle of 1957 Pinot I've been saving for just such an occasion," said David. Shirley brought it in from the kitchen, and Hopkins proposed a toast.

"May all the connections we've made through bringing Dave into our lives, continue to grow and reap positive results. And may we soon find Brian, bringing him into this good fortune, too. Salud," Hopkins finished, raising his wine glass to clink it with Dave's and Shirley's.

The pasta dish was delicious. After that, Shirley set a dessert in front of Dave that looked like pink whipped cheesecake. He was afraid to ask what it was, and bravely took a bite. It went down easily. Finally, Hopkins introduced the topic he'd been waiting for.

"So...I've got a pretty busy schedule for you this coming week." He laid a typed document beside Dave's plate. "Lucinda, my secretary, typed it up after I personally made the contacts. It's got all the appointment times, places, directions on how to get there, contact people, and their phone numbers on it. I've introduced the first three on the list to your situation. They'll try to have some leads for you. Our Chief of Police, Ed Malrooney, has talked to them too. If nothing else, I'm sure you'll feel that you're in more competent hands than you have been this week."

"No doubt about it, this week has been tough. But thanks for all the help you two have given me."

Dave looked at Shirley, including her. "Could you give me a rundown on who these people are?"

"Sure." Hopkins pushed the list between the two of them. "The first one, Steve Landus, is the head administrator of *Child*

Protective Services. He's about my age and probably has thirty years or more with the agency. Started out as a caseworker, right out of college. He knows the ropes when it comes to where to look for child predators."

Dave felt himself flinch at the word, *predator*. Of course that's what Brian's kidnapper was. It was just that it sounded like he was an animal from the jungle. Which, of course, he was, in the sense that he had no moral compunctions about preying on the most vulnerable.

"Then comes Patsy Gelmini. She's the top person at the local branch of the *Federal Bureau of Missing Children*. Malrooney set her up to talk to you. She'll have her finger on a lot of buttons." Hopkins looked up. "Are you comfortable talking about this with women as well as men? She's a different breed, but she is a woman."

"No problem," said Dave. "I had a wonderful mother, who always encouraged me to talk to her. Unfortunately, she passed from cancer a couple of years ago."

"Sorry to hear you've lost your mother. Even though we're captains of our own ships now, it's hard not to have the navigator who charted our course. But it's clear she gave you the gift of knowing how to choose another good woman. As did my mother." He gave Dave a smile tinged with sadness.

"So, that's good. Because here comes another woman, Patrice Goodman. She's the Director of *Planned Parenthood*. It might seem a little strange to include her, but both Malrooney and I agree, that if anyone knows our youth, and where to look for stray ones, Patrice is the one. She used to be a missionary in the Congo. Helped to set up a clinic for children with AIDS."

Dave swallowed hard at the thought that his son might contract AIDS.

"And the fourth one on the list is…you know what? I'm going to scratch this one." Hopkins got out a pen and struck it through several lines on the paper. "He's had a very recent death in the family, and come to think of it, I believe he's on a leave of absence. They'll want him to rest and recuperate."

"Let's see...that leaves two more. Father O'Shea is a priest in the East End parish. He's run a wonderful youth group for as long as I can remember. Kids who need all kinds of rehabilitation – drugs, prostitution, mental health, poverty, neglect, special needs. Now that might sound a little far off from your son's predicament, but believe me, those kids have a wealth of information, and there's no one who has their trust more than Father O'Shea. Do you feel comfortable talking to a priest?"

"Of course. I'm not a Roman Catholic, but I'm a Christian. I don't split hairs when it comes to Christians helping each other."

"Good. That brings us to the last one on our list. His name is Phillip Nottingham, and he's the Chairman of the Board of a grassroots group called *Keep Our Children Safe*. He's independently wealthy, and may not be the easiest on the list to talk to, but he's a dedicated man when it comes to protecting children. He's run into a lot of hairy situations akin to yours, and he should be able to direct you to a lot of resources, if he can't directly help you himself. I haven't been in contact with him yet, but I'm certain he'll be open to talking to you, when I am."

For some reason, Dave felt the hairs on the back of his neck rise at the mention of Nottingham's name. 'Wait a minute. I'm not clairvoyant.' It was probably because of the mention of wealth and the equal sign between that and the kidnapping car being a BMW that brought up the creepy feeling he had. And then again, maybe God was speaking to him. It wouldn't be the first time. But for now, he needed to concentrate on what Hopkins was telling him.

"I just don't know how to thank you guys for all you're doing for me. Taking me in like this, doing all this..." Dave pointed to the list, then spread his arms expansively. "I don't begin to know how I'll ever repay you."

"Actually, I have an immediate repayment in mind," said Hopkins. He turned to his wife. "Shirley, I just received an emergency call that I have to act on tonight. Bob Dimitri is down with a miserable flu, and he called me right before I headed home. He asked – well, ordered me is more like it – to meet a lobbyist in D.C. at ten tomorrow morning. There's a bill that includes building regulations going before the House on Wednesday, and it's imperative that we talk to this guy. That means I have to get on the road right after dinner, and hope to find a room when I get there."

The light seemed to leave Shirley's eyes. Hopkins took in his wife's disappointment. "I'm sorry, darling. It's one of those obligatory things, and I know how much you dislike being in the house alone at night. But it doesn't make sense to drag you along on such short notice. Believe me, it's a no-fun trip."

He turned to Dave. "This is where you come in. If you don't have any plans for the evening, I'd consider it repayment for your entire stay if you'll keep Shirley company while I'm away. I'm sure she would feel a lot safer if there's a man that she trusts in the house. How does that work for the two of you?" He looked to his wife again.

She looked crestfallen. "It's unexpected, as most of your trips to D. C. are. But I can live with it. I'm sorry you have to be dragged into this stuff at the last minute, but I'm content to stay at home, if Dave will be here tonight. I wish I wasn't such a scaredy-cat, but, the fact is, I am. Will it work for you, Dave?"

"Couldn't be happier to oblige. Actually, I intended to stay here, and be close to my cell phone. I might even get a call from Peggy when the anesthesia wears off, although she told Sara...the friend who called... that it would probably be best if she waits until tomorrow to call. But, other than that, I was just planning to kick back and do some reading tonight anyway." He smiled at Hopkins, who nodded.

"But this scarcely can be considered repayment for all that the two of you have done for me, and my family. Unless we can count it as one payment on an installment plan."

"Believe me," said Shirley, "we'll be more than repaid when you find your Brian." She reached across the table and briefly cupped the top of Dave's hand in her palm, squeezing it.

"Exactly," said Hopkins. "Listen." All three of them stopped to hear the chatter of nuthatches at the bird feeder outside the window. "That's the sound of a good omen," said Hopkins, with conviction.

After Dave helped Shirley clean up the remains of dinner, he retreated to his room so Hopkins could ready his overnight bag for the impromptu trip. He had nearly fallen asleep over some brochures about the agencies he'd be visiting, when he heard a soft tapping on his door. Rising and opening it, he found Hopkins, looking nervously down the hall toward his bedroom. He appeared startled when the door opened, collected himself, and then whispered, "Can I come in?"

"Sure," Dave said, opening the door wider. Hopkins stepped in, closing it behind him like a thief.

"Listen, there's something I want to tell you about Shirley. I think you should know, since I've asked you to pinch-hit for me tonight." He cleared his throat in embarrassment. "You know, in terms of keeping her safe."

"Sure," Dave repeated, feeling awkward with Hopkins' discomfort.

"You see, Shirley is afraid – paranoid might be a better word for it – to stay alone at night because when she was a child..."

"I think I know what you're going to say," said Dave, surprised at what he'd said, as he'd never given it a thought before now. Again, there seemed to be these unconscious connections that didn't make rational sense.

"Yes, well, perhaps you sensed that Shirley..." he cleared his throat again, "that Shirley was abused by her father. In the middle of the night. She still has nightmares about it. And can't stand to stay alone in the house at night without someone here to protect her. I can't remember the last time I left home overnight without her. I just don't do it. But she trusts you. Do you understand?"

"Yes, of course. And I'm so sorry. But I'll watch over her."

"We knew we could count on you. Did you know, Dave – no, of course you didn't, because I haven't told you – that Shirley is the one who insisted that you stay with us. She feels so strongly that we should do everything we can to support you finding Brian. Obviously she identifies with your son in terms of the fearful state he's in. But, more than that, I believe you represent the rescuing father to her, rather than the abusive father she had. And even though we're not really religious, she prays for the two of you at night."

Dave felt tears welling up in his eyes. It was the second time he'd come this close to crying since the whole miserable mess had begun.

"I'm sorry," Hopkins said. "I didn't mean to upset you. Maybe there are certain things that should be left unsaid."

"No, that's OK. I'm glad you told me. It helps."

"So, I'll be on my way. I should be back by tomorrow night. I'll keep in touch with Shirley, and she'll let you know when. You don't have to worry about staying with her during the day. She'll be fine then. Thanks." He extended his hand to shake Dave's.

Dave hesitated and then said, "There's something I want to tell you that probably sounds disconnected, but...Brian has the same color hair as Shirley." What he said was only the surface of the thought. Shirley seemed like the sister he never had, and would never be able to protect from people like his uncle.

"No, Dave. Don't underestimate the power of these unspoken things that bring us together. We're all connected. Sometimes we just don't understand the connections."

Hopkins shook Dave's hand again, and then gave him a quick hug.

After Hopkins left, Dave went downstairs and watched some TV shows with Shirley, but for the life of him, he couldn't remember what they were, or what they said to each other. Mostly, he was watching her as though he were in a trance. Like he used to watch the snowman inside the heavy glass ball that he shook when he was a kid. The snow would swirl inside the ball, until it slowly settled into a motionless world again.

Eventually, it was time to go upstairs, and the two of them performed their nighttime ablutions down the hall from each other. Finally Dave heard silence from Shirley's end of the hall, and he knew that the snow had stopped swirling. He fell into a deep sleep. Sometime later, he awoke to the sound of sobbing outside his bedroom door.

The full moon gleamed through his window, reflecting on the brass doorknob. He opened it and Shirley fell into his arms, pressing her face into his chest where he felt her tears on his t-shirt. Like Peg had done the night before he left. And even though Shirley had put on a bathrobe over her nightwear, Dave was aware of her breasts pressing against his chest. She was taller than Peg. Although he felt awkward, he cradled her as he would his daughter, letting her cry it out until the last whimper and shudder left her silent.

He said simply, "You're safe now."

"Thank you. I know that," she murmured. "But not in my room. Things come out of the darkness there." She hesitated and then said, "Could you come and sit by my bed until I fall asleep?"

"Of course," Dave said, knowing what was expected of him, and that he couldn't say no.

Taking his hand lightly in hers, she led him down the hall to her bedroom. Moonlight was coming in the windows, casting shadows on two full-size beds. Shirley pushed a padded stool up to the one nearest the windows, then crawled in on the other side of the bed, pulling the sheets up to her neck.

Sitting down on the stool, Dave felt relieved with the distance between them. He didn't say anything, leaving it up to her to break the silence.

After a few minutes passed, Shirley moved the hand closest to Dave out from under the sheet, extending it toward him. "It would help if you could hold my hand until I fall asleep."

Dave placed her hand on his upturned palm, unconsciously stroking the length of her fingers with his other hand. He'd seen Peggy do that with Lauren. Slowly, the snow seemed to resettle in the glass orb, until a spasm gripped Shirley, and she cried out again.

"Oh, please," she sobbed. "Please hold me. I'm so afraid he's going to leave me."

That made no sense to Dave, in terms of what Hopkins had told him. But it wasn't up to him to make sense of things. Just be there for her, as asked of him. Still, he remained on the stool, hesitant to move up on the bed, which he would have to do in order to hold her.

Shirley could barely get her words out until the sobbing decreased, when she began to shudder. "It's my David. I know he sees another woman in Washington. I found out about her. But I can't talk to him about it, because…because I'm afraid he'd leave me."

Dave was shocked. Could she be imagining things? "He told me you were afraid to be left alone because your father…bothered you in the night, when you were a child."

"He did, but it's much more than that now." Shirley started crying again. "Oh, please hold me. Just for a little while. I'm so afraid. All I need is to be comforted. Please," she said, another sob escaping her.

Dave hesitated only a moment this time. He crawled onto the bed, lying beside her, while staying on top of the sheet. Even though the room was nearly dark, he felt exposed with just his T-shirt and cotton briefs on. Laying there on his back, he felt like an overturned turtle. He couldn't figure out what to do with his arms until Shirley gripped his farthest shoulder, gradually urging him to embrace her.

They still had the sheet and their bedclothes between them, but he began to feel her body heat transfer to his body. Although it was the first time he had lain with a woman other than Peggy in nearly twenty years, Dave was surprised that it didn't feel sexual. He felt like a mother bear with her cub, snuggling deep in the cave of winter to secure their survival. He remained that way for a length of time he couldn't measure, until Shirley's hand dropped from his shoulder, and he heard a light sound, like the buzzing of a bee, pass between her lips. Lifting her arm ever so slightly, he slid away from her, watching to see if it disturbed her state of peace. It didn't. He rolled over to the side of the bed, quietly retreating from the bedroom, leaving the door ajar.

In his own bed again, Dave had trouble getting back to sleep. For some reason he couldn't understand, without anything to substantiate it, he believed Shirley, but not Hopkins. Rage swept through him, as he thought of how David was betraying Shirley, when she was so deserving of his faithfulness. And how Hopkins had blatantly lied to him, knowing he could play on Dave's sympathy for sexually abused children, manipulating their friendship to cover for his own infidelity. But the worst part was that he, Dave Brefort, would also have to lie, concealing his knowledge from David, because he so desperately needed his help to find Brian.

Morning came too early. Dave awakened to muted kitchen sounds of breakfast being made. He dressed, brushed his teeth and went downstairs. Shirley looked up when she saw him enter, and then looked down at some invisible spot on her blouse, appearing like a shy schoolgirl as she said, "Thank you so much for making me feel safe...if only for a little while."

"I'm so glad I could. And I'm so sorry I can't do more than that to help you. But I can't."

Shirley raised her head, and without a word passing between them, there existed the promise that there was no reason to try and explain this to either David or Peggy. There was no guilt. Last night was something sacred between them that would always exist. Telling it would only create misunderstanding and corrupt its purity. They ate their scrambled eggs in silence, occasionally smiling at each other, until Shirley turned on the TV to hear the morning news. Dave decided to go to his room to call Peg. He could hardly wait to hear her familiar voice.

Chapter 13
Brian and Phillip
Wednesday, April 10

Brian woke up from an afternoon nap. Phillip had been away most of the day and said he'd join Brian at what he called their "evening repast." Brian knew it would be served on laptop meal trays. He wished they could eat off TV tables set at the side of the bed. He felt so awkward eating a meal without his feet on the floor, or on the rungs of a chair. Phillip told him that this evening they were having beef Wellington, emphasizing that 'beef' wasn't capitalized, whereas 'Wellington' was, for the Duke of Wellington. Whatever it was, with Phillip cooking, it was bound to be good. He'd never realized that men could be such good cooks. His dad couldn't manage much beyond breakfast. That was the thing about Phillip that constantly confused him. Although his captor felt foreign and fearful to Brian, he admired his competence and capabilities.

There was a stack of new DVDs sitting on his bedside table,

but Brian was beginning to feel restless again. God, what he wouldn't do to get outside, see the sun, breathe in fresh air and run down the road until his legs could no longer carry him. How many days had he been here? It felt like weeks. He'd lost his sense of time. Phillip wouldn't allow any calendars, clocks, or even live TV programs in his room. The weather, the wars, nothing entered his room, unless Phillip brought it to him.

Brian realized he could have kept track of the days, marking down the passage of time by how many breakfasts and dinners he'd had, except that his brain was often foggy and he'd forget to keep track. It seemed that way for all personal knowledge, and yet when it came to reading and preparing for his daily lessons, clarity returned. Most likely it was connected with the timing of the pills Phillip gave him. He'd noticed that the evening pills made him drowsy and unfocused, but the ones he had to take after breakfast made his heart and brain feel like they were on fast-forward. That was when he studied the lessons that Phillip set up for him. The books he brought ranged from dinosaurs to nuclear power, from Aristotle to somebody named Noam Chomsky, who was alive, and who seemed like a really radical guy. Phillip called him a "libertarian socialist." Brian wasn't sure just what that term meant, but he was pretty sure his dad would disapprove of him.

Nevertheless, in spite of his nightly stupors, he always Aced the tests Phillip gave him in the late afternoon, before dinner and his evening pills. He wondered if he would retain the lessons after he left Phillip's. If he ever did. That was the thing that worried him the most. Not knowing when he would "graduate," and if being released from captivity followed that event.

Then there were the movies that Phillip encouraged him to watch. Brian had popped in a few when Phillip wasn't around, but they were dirty. A lot of nudity, sex and smutty talk. He and Lauren weren't even allowed to watch PG 13 movies at home. He popped them out. Phillip tried to make him watch one with him, but Brian faked falling asleep. Still, he kept hearing slurpy sex sounds, and after a while he felt himself becoming stimulated, so he rolled over on his stomach. Phillip didn't disturb him.

Another time when he was alone all day without any homework assignments, he'd even found himself trying to count the number of stones in the walls, but his mind would wander off, never completely settling on any one thing, except the terror of the possibility that Phillip might never return.

It was the pills. He was pretty sure of that. When he went for very long without one he became nervous and twitchy. He'd listen for sounds indicating Phillip was upstairs. If he didn't hear him, he began worrying that he could have had a car accident, and Brian would be locked in this stone vault until he disintegrated, floating through space like the dust motes that drifted above his lamp. When he thought that way, he panicked. One time he even tried beating down the door with his bedside table. All that did was arouse Cerberus, who barked and snarled, lunging at the other side of the door. He was right there, waiting. There was no escape. When Phillip saw the damage he'd done to the door, he'd simply said that it was immature behavior, and it would cost Brian in terms of increased freedom that only responsible behavior could bring about.

Right behind his fear of being left to die, Brian feared he was becoming an addict. He no longer felt any sense of self-discipline or self-control. His bonds to his family, home and friends were melting away faster than a votive candle burning day and night. The only thing he thought about and longed for, was stimulation. The sound of Phillip's footsteps on the stairwell, his company, the meals he brought, the pills he gave him. Although he was still afraid of Phillip and giving up control to him, at the same time he felt thankful for his teachings. Those first days, 'or were they nights?', Brian argued with him whenever Phillip had encouraged him to massage himself in ways that brought him pleasure. Brian told him, "It says in the Bible story of Onan, that it's against God's teachings to 'spill your seed upon the ground.' And you know what happened to him."

"No, what?" said Phillip. "I seem to have forgotten that one."

"He died because he refused his obligation to his brother's widow."

"That came about because of the 'spilling of his seed on the ground?'"

"Don't you see? Because of Onan's practices, he didn't have any left to give her. And he paid dearly for it."

Phillip chuckled. "I'm afraid you fundamentalists take the Bible much too literally. It's all parables, allegories. The same as the Bhagavad-Gita, the Koran, the Tao-te-ching. All world religions are based on the precept that God, or whatever you name that universal force, is within us. And that as the Golden Rule says, we must love our neighbors as ourselves. But the first step is to love ourselves. And our bodies are the temples that house God. We must learn to cultivate and accept the God-given pleasures that arise from within."

"That can't be because, because…"

Phillip directed a level gaze at Brian. "Have you ever masturbated?"

Brian looked down.

"Be honest, Brian. That's the one thing I know I can always count on from you."

Slowly, Brian raised his eyelids. "Yes, sir, it's true. I've tried, but I can't really come yet."

"But did you enjoy it?"

Brian stifled a cough. "Yes, sir. At the time I did it. But that passed. Then I felt terrible. Full of sin and guilt."

"That's because you've been conditioned by your parents, your church and society to feel bad about it. If you, and other men, were to, as you say, 'spill your seed upon the ground,' continually, I might add, there would indeed be fewer sons to labor in the fields and train as warriors, fewer daughters to bear more children. It's a matter of economics and power. If we stop reproducing, then the coffers of nations and churches would diminish, and within two or three generations, there would be no power greater than the individual and the pure God-principle within him."

Phillip gave Brian a solemn smile. "I've thought about this and I have a plan. I believe that to continue creating life and the power of God within the human form, we must have designated breeders. These breeders would have to pass rigorous biological standards, and train to be exemplary parents."

Brian kept shifting his gaze, first to a space somewhere beyond Phillip's left shoulder, then to the right.

"Go ahead, Brian. I can see your skepticism. I encourage critical thinking. Say what you will."

"Well, sir, it sounds like that weird novel we just read in freshman English so we'd see how creepy a world like that would be. *Brave Worlds*, or something like that."

"Yes, *Brave New World* by Aldous Huxley. My model is much more humane. And founded on the principle that I spoke of originally. Self-love. You would do well to practice it every day, when I leave your room. Your goal is to enjoy the godhead in you, and to feel no guilt or shame. I suggest that the best way to start practicing is in the shower. I'm certain you'll find it the most pleasurable homework you've ever been assigned. I'll be checking with you."

As Brian thought about that conversation, he felt a sudden warmth spread through his groin, when he heard Phillip's footsteps coming down the stairs. Just as quickly, the warmth dissipated. He heard the clank of the bolt being unlocked, and the snuffle of Cerberus at Phillip's heels.

"How are you, young man? It appears you've spent a leisurely afternoon in your bed. You look well rested. How do you feel?"

An automatic, "Fine, sir," and then Brian decided to risk a request. "But I'm becoming restless, confined like I am in this room. I was wondering when I might be able to leave it."

"Already you grow weary of the diversions I provide. I expected that, but not quite so soon. Still I believe you are nearly ready to go on to the next step. You have told me you are learning to love yourself, and God within the body-temple. So tell me, what is the next step?"

"To love thy neighbor as thyself."

"And how do you propose to do that?"

"Well, I'm not quite sure, sir."

"I'll give you some time to think about it while I prepare our evening repast. Then after we share our meal, perhaps you can give me your answer. The right answer and following through on it will be the key that opens your door to the gym and the pool. Excuse me. Cerberus and I will return within the hour." The door closed quietly behind them.

Brian sat with his arms folded around his knees for some time, imagining the bounce of the trampoline, the pull of the weights on his biceps, and the satin flow of water caressing his body. He thought he knew how he could unlock the door.

Phillip felt certain this would be the night. He rarely missed when it came to knowing his boys and what they wanted. This one was taking too long for Phillip's anticipation, but he didn't want to go about Brian's initiation in a brutish fashion, although some of his boys had required that measure. He was certain that Brian would prove much more malleable, if he could remain patient for just a little while longer. And well worth the wait. Not just for the bodily pleasure. He'd already grown quite fond of the boy. Perhaps he was becoming sentimental in his advancing years.

After he put the fillet of beef on the rack for the roasting, Phillip jumped in the shower. Toweling off, he observed his body in the mirrored wall. He didn't fool himself about competing with youth, but he knew that for forty-six, he was in prime condition. The slight softening of his contours and a shade of paunch in his mid-section were offset by his overall slimness, and the magnificent thrust of his maleness. Even now his tumescence was rising with thoughts of what was to come.

Phillip threw on his red and black velvet bathrobe over his black silk Jockey briefs, and hurried to the kitchen. While the fillet cooled, he rolled out the puff pastry he'd refrigerated that morning, then prepared a Caesar salad. Checking his wine rack, he selected a vintage Merlot. Using a portion of it for the Bordelaise sauce, he set the remainder in the refrigerator to chill. Within twenty-five minutes, he had a sumptuous beef Wellington prepared. He doubted that Jacques Pepin himself could have done better in the allotted time.

Phillip positioned the large serving tray on the table he'd placed outside Brian's door. He unlocked the deadbolt. Brian was standing expectantly right inside the door.

"Good to see you're up and at 'em, kid. I bet your hunger helps. You won't be disappointed with what the Grand Chef prepared this evening. Help me set up."

"Yes, sir, that's what I intended to do."

Cerberus was on guard behavior, as Brian had never met them at the door before. Once again, he began sniffing at Brian's ankles, a muffled growl rising from the back of his throat. Brian immediately retreated to his bed, pulling the spread up to his shoulders.

"I'm afraid that's not enough to protect you, should Cerberus attack. You have yet to realize that he won't, unless he has orders from me. Relax. Both of you. Help me get set up here, Brian. Get the bed-trays and bolsters. Cerberus, guard the door."

Cerberus retreated to the door, lying down across the threshold, balefully eying Brian. "Good boy," said Phillip, ruffling his ear as he passed him. Brian went about the business assigned him, casting a vigilant glance at the dog every few seconds.

"You know, son, there's something you don't understand about Cerberus' behavior. You'll never be able to be friends with him. Not just because he's a trained guard dog under my command, but because he's exceedingly jealous of you. He doesn't like it one bit when I talk to you, feed you, or give you any kind of attention. When he and I are alone, he's my buddy, my lone companion. And if I gave him the order, there's nothing he'd rather do than rid his life of you. But you're perfectly safe when I'm with him. He takes his orders from me, and me alone. Just don't ever get yourself in the position of being alone with him without my orders to guard you. Hard to say what he'd do."

Phillip saw the expected shudder he hoped for, pass through Brian.

After they'd settled in, Phillip said, "It was good to see you waiting for us, moving about the cabin. 'Cabin', as in the nautical term. You should do more of that. So, what have you done today in terms of your reading? I commend you on your retention of the unit I gave you about Chinese culture yesterday. I daresay, if you were being graded in mass education, you'd have earned an A."

"Thank you, sir. I found it interesting, and helpful in some ways. The best part is Qigong. I practiced some this morning. It seems to clear my mind."

"Yes, and don't forget to say, 'All meridians open. Every cell is healthy.' But I think you're avoiding what I asked. What about the story I assigned you to read? How did you find it?"

"Well, sir, I started reading it, but I kept falling asleep. Can

I add it to tomorrow's assignment?"

"Hmph...I suppose you'll have to since I have plans for you after dinner. But I think you're resisting the reading because of all the sludge in your mind."

"Sludge, sir?"

"Brian, do you know what homophobia is?"

"Ah, not exactly. All I can think of is homo-sapiens."

"Yes, I like the way your mind works. Deductive reasoning. It does have to do with man. Only in this case, it's an irrational fear and hatred of homosexuality. That's what the story's wrapped around. How two cowboys fall in love with each other, and the price they have to pay. But perhaps it's best if you read it tomorrow," Phillip said, patting Brian's inner thigh affectionately. He felt the boy's muscles tense under his pajama bottoms. But no, he couldn't postpone it any longer. He would call on the pill he put in his bathrobe pocket.

"Now, we must eat, before our beef Wellington grows cold. But first I want you to wash down this pill with a sip of wine. It's a fine Merlot."

Brian took the proffered pill and swallowed from the wine glass. He made a face.

"Don't you like my choice of wines?"

"It tastes like cherries and olives mixed with vinegar."

Phillip laughed. "A superb description for your first taste. Maybe you should be a wine taster. Actually, it's fermented grapes from the Bordeaux region of France. You'll acquire a taste for it. Or at least, you should. It's good for your heart."

Phillip felt his own heart beating hard and fast. "Brian, have you ever heard of Roofies?"

"It sounds like a drug I've heard about. That and Ecstasy. I think I've heard of them connected with Raves. Or something like that. Mosh pits? But that's all stuff I heard about on talk shows. I mean, I've heard of them. That's all."

"So, R-rated news has even reached the Heartland." Phillip stroked his chin as though he had a beard. "Well, let me say,

Roofies are very smooth. Just a euphoric loss of inhibition. And a heightened sense of your hormones working. You'll enjoy it. It will start to take effect in about ten minutes. In the meantime, let's eat this wonderful dish I've prepared for you. And I know you'll feel more relaxed, and enjoy everything more, if you slip out of your PJs."

Phillip looked at Brian's face and saw that the boy looked as though he'd just jumped off a bridge, and there was nothing he could do about turning back. He imagined how it would feel to Brian if he just relaxed and enjoyed the feeling of falling through space.

"Eat up, boy. And drink your glass of wine."

Brian picked up his knife and fork, cutting through the pastry and into the juicy pink interior of the fillet. Then there was only the clicking of the utensils, the sough of their chewing and swallowing, and the sound of glass goblets being set on a hard surface, until Phillip said, "You know, I think we've had enough food. We don't need to be gluttons."

He stood and hastily removed their trays, placing them on the headboard's shelf that ran to the wall. He poured himself another glass of wine. "Here, try this again," he said, pouring one for Brian. "You'll like it better the second time around."

Phillip was conscious of his decision to stay with the glass wine goblets rather than substituting the plastic glasses. He had the plastic set in the headboard for occasions like this, because one boy – he recalled that it was Jared – had broken a glass after his first seduction, using it to try and slit his wrist. He hadn't given him enough drugs. What a mess that had been. Phillip still sported a scar on his left index finger from trying to retrieve the shard from the boy's grip. But Brian wasn't foolish and self-destructive like that. And besides, Phillip hated to drink fine wine from plastic. It robbed the occasion of elegance.

Brian drank his second glass obediently, even though his lips pulled back from the rim in a grimace. He gave Phillip a wan smile. Brian was trying so hard to please, even though he was scared to death. He struggled to remove his pajamas beneath the blanket.

"You're doing fine, buddy," said Phillip, relishing Brian's frightened acquiescence. The lad knew what was coming. Phillip was glad he'd waited for a willing partner. "Keep it up. Tomorrow you will have won pool privileges." Again, he patted the inside of Brian's thigh, lingering and trailing his fingers up to his groin. This time Brian didn't pull back.

Phillip motioned Cerberus off the bed and as soon as the mattress sprang back, Phillip rolled over on his stomach, stroking Brian's face. "Brian, do you remember what I read to you, and then demonstrated, about massage? About the chakras and pressure points?"

"Yes sir, I do," mumbled Brian, shifting to a more comfortable position on his back, then closing his eyes.

"Good retention. Yes, just close your eyes and relax. In fact, I have something that will help you." He reached into the headboard, retrieving a loose face mask made of miniature sand bags, settling them into the orbs of Brian's eye sockets. "There. Doesn't that feel good?"

"Yes, sir. It makes me feel like I'm drifting off...like I'm floating on a calm lake."

"That's good. Keep up the visualization like I've taught you. Just let yourself drift." Phillip got up quietly from the bed, removing his bathrobe and briefs. Climbing back, placing his body as close as he could get to Brian, he stroked himself until his body essence was dripping, transferring it to Brian, rubbing and stroking it until that young member began to grow in his hands. It looked so pink and healthy.

"Son, I'm going to roll you over until you're almost on your stomach. But I'll keep a hold on you."

Phillip gently pushed Brian's right shoulder, as he continued sliding his hand up and down Brian's elongating shaft, until he no longer could. Then rising to his knees, Phillip began to position himself between the orbs of Brian's cheeks. Reaching for the vessel of lubricant he'd brought, he slathered it on the two of them, returning to the warmth of their embrace. It had been so long. "Stay relaxed. This might hurt for a second, but soon you will feel better than you've ever felt in your life."

He thrust himself deep into Brian's moist warm cave. He'd barely pumped him four or five times, when he exploded like a volcano whose fire traveled from his groin, soaring through the top of his head, into the ether of infinite space. Phillip collapsed beside Brian, slowly becoming aware of more than winging through space. He pushed Brian softly, but the boy didn't respond. Phillip rolled him over onto his back. The sandbags had fallen off, but his eyes were closed. He felt for Brian's pulse. It was fine. Slow and steady.

Phillip had come too quickly. Still it was the first time, and he couldn't contain himself. He would work on slowing it down. My God, it felt good to be back inside a young male. Inside himself, really. It couldn't be beat. Not by his own hand, not by drugs, or vibrators, or even by sex with an adult male. It made him feel godlike. To find this boy, to bring him into his kingdom, to train him to the point where he enjoyed their lovemaking so much that he would beg for it. Slowly, he would reduce the amount of the drugs, until Brian was more physically responsive to Phillip himself, and could never get enough of him. He would become completely dependent on him for his sole source of stimulation and bliss.

It was hard to think about getting up and putting food away. He rolled over, reaching to the headboard for the last piece of beef on his plate. Cerberus raised his head, his nostrils flaring. Phillip tossed the scrap to him, listening to the sounds of his contented chewing. Perhaps Phillip would sleep here tonight. No. He must get up and shower, clean Brian up. But for now, he would rest.

Brian slept soundly that night, and yet had the most vivid dream he'd ever had. In fact, he wasn't at all sure it didn't actually happen, because he was both inside the dream and outside of it, observing it, at the same time that he dreamed it. He was back in the kitchen of their farmhouse. It was a Saturday in spring, and a feeling of Easter-time renewal was in the air. The whole family was gathered around the oak table that had been his grandmother's. They were eating scrambled eggs, and he and Lauren were fighting over the last scrap of bacon. She'd won, and Brian could tell his dad was trying to distract him from his loss, small though it was. He asked Brian to come out to the welding shop with him, that there was something he wanted to show him.

They were approaching the shop when Brian saw a big black dog slink away around the side of the building. He could hear the squeak of the shop door hinges as his dad went in, but Brian decided he'd try to see where the dog went. As he rounded the corner, he saw something hanging on the side wall of the shop. At first the sun glinted in his eyes and he couldn't make out what it was, but suddenly he saw everything in sharp detail.

It was a man nailed to a cross, much like the Crucifixion, but this man wasn't Jesus. It was Phillip. He had nails driven into his palms, with drops of blood dripping down, and he wore a crown of thorns. But these thorns were made of metal, as though they'd been fabricated in his dad's shop. The disappearing dog must be Cerberus. Finally he could show his dad proof of what was happening to him. A wave of relief swept through him. But how did Phillip wind up here? And why was he dead?

Just as Brian was about to call out to his dad, Phillip's loincloth came unwrapped, falling to the ground. He still appeared to be dead, but he had an enormous erection that was pulsating. Maybe they could take him down from the cross and bring him back to life. Brian ran to get his dad, screaming,

"Dad, Dad, come here."

His dad followed him on the run out of the shop to the east wall. "Look, Dad, look. There he is. Phillip! I don't think he's dead yet. Look how hard he is. No one can have a hard-on when they're dead, can they? Let's get a ladder, take him down. Maybe we can revive him. Or call 911."

His dad just stood there staring at the sidewall. "What are you talking about, son? There's nothing on this wall. It's empty."

"No, Dad, he's there, hanging on a cross. Can't you see him?"

"No, Brian. I don't see a thing. Just some gray flaking paint. But you're right. We do need a ladder. I have a scraper and some paint in the shop. You can get started on it today."

"Oh Dad, he's up there. And he's dying. What should we do? Please help me."

His dad beckoned to him. Brian went to him and his father enfolded him in his arms, hugging him so deeply, Brian could feel their two hearts beating as one.

Brian awoke, sobbing. Phillip and Cerberus were gone from the room, and once again he was all alone.

Chapter 14
Dave
Thursday, April 11

"Come in," said a bruised voice, followed by a deep cough that sounded to Dave like a 'bar voice,' marinated in whiskey and cigarette smoke. There was a partially open door between them with the lettering, *Federal Bureau of Missing Children–Coordinator, Patsy Gelmini*.

Her bandy-legged male secretary pushed the door inward, and as he stepped aside, all Dave could see was the standing figure of an aging iron-woman. Her hair sat like a white cap on her head, while her robust physique suggested a weight-lifter or a javelin-thrower. If she had breasts, they were swallowed up by the broadness of her chest.

"Mr. Brefort, I presume."

"Yes, Dave Brefort."

"It's good to meet you, although I can't for the life of me understand why Malgooney, or however the hell you say that

Irish name, via Mr. Hopkins, referred you to me. Sit down," she pointed toward a straight-backed chair next to her desk. "I prefer to stand. I'm not cut out to sit in chairs all day."

She watched Dave as he seated himself, scrutinizing him from head to toe. "Yes, you look like you're from Southern Ohio," she said summarily. "It's good you're on time, because I have a busy day ahead of me."

The room felt like a pressure cabin with the air being sucked out of it. Dave wanted out. He came right to the point. "Do you have any clues about the disappearance of my son?"

"No, I'm afraid I don't. This has been a botched case from start to finish. Although I realize you don't see it as finished. But it's all been handled in a highly irregular manner. You must realize, Mr. Brefort, that parents of missing children should not be chasing down phantom clues. Anymore than your town's Chief of Police should have waited twenty-four hours to report to our Federal Bureau. Apparently he is not aware that forty percent of children reported missing, if abducted by a stranger – forty percent, mind you, are dead within one hour. That goes up to seventy-five percent of them dead within three hours. Those are harsh realities to be sure, but it's important that you know what you're up against. If not your son himself, the trail is undoubtedly dead."

Dave sat staring at his folded hands. He noticed that he had a hangnail on his left thumb.

"OK, look, I hate to be so brutal, but Dave Hopkins and others like him are giving you false hope. Give it up and go home to the remainder of your family. If your son wasn't killed, he'll probably turn up in a child prostitution ring. We'll be watching for him. I understand he has red hair. If he is alive and in Baltimore, it shouldn't be long before a red-headed, twelve-year-old male surfaces."

Dave gripped the wooden arm rests of the chair, knotting the veins on the back of his hands and paling his knuckles. As though a ventriloquist was speaking, he heard his voice saying,

"I don't care what your statistics show. I know my son is alive. And I will find him." He pushed off the arms of the chair, feeling his knees wobble, afraid that he might collapse.

The next time Dave was aware of his body in space, he was fumbling for his car keys in the parking lot. He stood in front of the yellow '22,' spray-painted at the head of his parking space. That was the same number as Brian's track jersey. He had counted on it to bring him good luck.

As he turned the key in the ignition, Dave thought about returning to Hopkins' house, forgetting about his next appointment with 'somebody Goodman' at Planned Parenthood. He didn't want to go through any more discouragement. Yesterday's appointment with Steve Landus at *Child Protective Services* had yielded no clues either. In fact, Steve told him that in the case of missing children, he always turned to Patsy Gelmini, who Dave now thought of as Brunhilde. Steve said that she was the ultimate authority on kidnapped children. She seemed extremely pessimistic to Dave, but then again, perhaps she was just a realist. She did seem to know the business.

Although there was that twenty-five percent unaccounted for. He should have asked her about how many of those kids were eventually found. 'No, I didn't need statistics.' They were drawn from people he didn't know, and had never spoken to. Last night, Brian again talked to him in his dreams. He had stood there as plain as the red light Dave stopped in front of, saying, "Dad, Dad, please help me." That was what Dave believed in. He refused to give up his faith that God would lead him to his living son.

Sitting in the Planned Parenthood waiting room, Dave felt uncomfortable. No *Parents* magazines here, least of all a

Sports Illustrated. He resisted picking up one of the brochures on STDs or contraception, just to have something to read. Instead, he tried to look at pictures on the walls, rather than the young women seated around him. One of them reminded him of one of Brian's friends, Heather. Pretty young thing. He wondered what her problem was. And if her parents knew she was here.

He heard his name called, and looked up to see the receptionist crossing the room toward him. "Mr. Brefort," she said, "Come with me." He followed her down a narrow hall, where she opened a door with the name *Patrice Goodman* on it.

"Sorry, I didn't think of it sooner, but I imagine you were uncomfortable in the waiting room. You can wait here. Patrice is out on a business lunch, but she should be back any minute. "I'll let her know you're waiting."

Dave was settling in the uncomfortable chair that was available to him, when the desk phone rang.

An answering machine came on after three rings, and he heard a male voice saying, "Ms. Goodman, you know who I am. This is your second warning. After my daughter, Suzanne saw you, she went ahead and had an abortion. She'd promised us to carry full-term, and that we could take care of our grandchild until she finished college. If she had the abortion because of any advice you gave her, my wife and I intend to sue you. Just be forewarned." Click.

God. The receptionist screwed up. He never should have been privy to such private information.

So this was the kind of thing Planned Parenthood dealt with. What was he doing here? He was about to reconsider and leave, when the director came into her office.

"Mr. Brefort," she said, extending her hand. "I'm sorry for the wait, and the receptionist's error in letting you wait here in my office. For reasons of confidentiality and privacy, that's definitely against the rules. I'm afraid she was rather flustered, as she'd just received a call from her daughter's school saying that her child had been hurt on the playground. My apologies."

Dave felt his face flush, and searching for words, nearly stuttered. "I'm sorry I heard about her daughter...that is, the receptionist's, I mean." He licked his lips and forced a smile.

Ms. Goodman returned his smile in a way that suggested she understood more than he'd said, but continued, "I understand Dave Hopkins sent you our way. What a good man he is. Always trying to help out in...ah, social situations."

For a brief second, Dave thought of how Hopkins was trying to 'help out in the social situation' of the triangle in D.C., but quickly dismissed it as unhelpful. "Yes, he is, both a good man, and trying to help. But I've been thinking about it, and I doubt that you'd have any reason to be privy to information about my missing son. Am I correct?"

"Indeed, you are. You're a step ahead of me. I'm glad you understand that. But I've been thinking about your situation, and I have a suggestion to offer."

"Anything would be helpful at this point," he said. He was surprised that she was volunteering something.

"Well, Dave told me that the car the kidnapper was driving was a top-of-the-line BMW – with a Maryland license plate of course, which I understand is what led you here. Just on the off-chance that the kidnapper is a well-to-do Baltimore man, I've been thinking that the best sleuthing you could do would be to explore the mansions and driveways of some of the exclusive Northern neighborhoods. In, or around there. Of course, the tricky part would come if you found one...or more. What would you do then?"

"You're right. What should I do?"

"I suppose the next best step would be to notify the police, but I don't know that it would constitute cause for them to investigate. But it's worth doing a little sleuthing on your own. At least it might satisfy your need to leave no stone unturned. Although, I must admit that I wonder why what appears to be a sophisticated kidnapper would drive a car that is so conspicuous and traceable. It's all very odd."

"Yes, my thinking too, although you're the first one to point that out. But thanks so much. Your suggestion is the best tip I've had since I've been here." Dave rose.

"Oh, and Mr. Brefort, would it be alright with you, if I share what little we do know with a social worker who knows 'the Baltimore underground,' shall we call it, better than anyone I know, when it comes to the business of finding and protecting lost children? Her name is Jane, and she works as the Children's Specialist at a Woman's Shelter. She's completely trustworthy and confidential. Do I have your permission to talk it over with her, as she might have some 'inside' information?"

"Yes, of course. And thank you for thinking of another avenue to possibly secure help. Outside of Dave Hopkins, you're the first one who has offered support. If nothing else, it gives me a more positive outlook, which helps in what sometimes seems like an impossible search. Again, thanks for your courtesy."

"You're welcome. And please do give me a call…if anything turns up. I'd appreciate knowing."

"Will do," said Dave, tipping an invisible hat, then adding, "And God bless you."

"Thank you," she said, an immediate blush coming to her cheeks. She undoubtedly was unaccustomed to having anyone bless her in what appeared to Dave as a most unrewarding job.

On his way to the car, Dave thought how much more in tune he felt with Patrice Goodman than the other two referrals he'd talked to. She played hunches, believed in possibilities, was a positive thinker. She seemed like a Christian, but then again, why would she hold a job that frequently dealt with abortion, if so? He hated to think of the phone message she would listen to after he left her office. Why were some people so hell-bent on revenge? Then he felt a hard knot form in his chest. When he found him, what would he want to happen to the man who had kidnapped his son?

Dave spent the rest of the afternoon and evening searching the Northern suburbs. No, he corrected himself, the Northern 'neighborhoods.' That's what the natives called them. He spotted three black BMWs, but none of them checked out. The first driver was a woman, and Dave seriously doubted that a female would be so intimately connected with a homosexual kidnapper, that she would be driving his car. The second one was driven by a man with black hair, but the car had a Virginia license plate. He followed him for some time, but it became clear that he was headed back to Virginia, so Dave let that lead die. The third was a younger man who kept turning and talking to someone in the front passenger seat that Dave couldn't see. He purposely passed him on the right side. As he suspected, he saw that there was a child's car seat strapped in that position.

It was after midnight by the time Dave arrived in the Hopkins driveway. Always vigilant about his comings and goings, they'd left the front entrance lights on, as well as those in the upstairs hall. The rest of the house resided in the dark of an obscured moon. They were always so damn considerate. Somehow this added to Dave's weariness. He'd felt it down to the marrow of his bones, in spite of Patrice Goodman's temporary hopeful reprieve.

Trudging up the stairs, Dave slipped his shoes off at the edge of his bed and pulled the coverlet back. He crawled under it with his clothes on. The last thing he remembered thinking before he fell into a deep sleep was, "Oh ye of little faith. Why did you doubt me?" It was Jesus' rebuke of Peter when the Lord gave him the power to walk on water, and Peter had become afraid, thus losing that power, calling out to Jesus to save him. No matter what obstacles Dave endured, he must maintain his faith in God the father, and Jesus, his son.

Friday morning

Dave awoke with a start. His bedside clock said it was 6:32. It was Friday he reminded himself. Eleven days had passed since he had begun this sacred journey, and he had yet to find the trail of Brian's kidnapper. Remembering his thought upon falling asleep, he said a silent prayer for the strength to renew his faith.

Dave and Shirley weren't up yet. He crawled out of bed, determined to get a fresh start on his hunt before they awoke. He didn't want to discuss his search with them. A fast-food breakfast could come later. He didn't really feel hungry anyway. Just hollow. Not even brushing his teeth, he left a note on the downstairs hall table, telling them he'd be returning around dinner time. He left swiftly and noiselessly.

Dave scored a couple more misses, and then, mid-morning, he found himself in a neighborhood that announced itself on a discreet wood-burned sign, as Knollwood Heights. He saw no cars parked on the street or in the driveways. He traveled slowly, but saw nothing that aroused his suspicions. Only one car passed him - a moss green sports car. He didn't recognize the make or model. He wasn't well-versed in high-end models, which made him aware of the information gap compared to his younger days when he could identify nearly every car on the roads, like Forrest still did.

Knollwood Heights had wide curving roads dotted with palatial homes set well-back, each of them on what he estimated to be at least a half-acre of landscaped and well-tended lawns. Most of the homes had dense shrubs and trees planted along the street side, obscuring his view of them. Which, of course, was their purpose. He understood that credo. He, too, valued his privacy, but his buffer was tens of acres of farmland, dotted with natural wooded lots, surrounding his house and the shop. Whereas, here, evidence of how modern privacy could be erected, there were a number of homes with high brick walls that followed the curvature of the street. Dave admired the skill of the bricklayers, at odds with his frustration of not being able to see beyond their construction. Each of the walls was broken at some point by a large gate that opened onto a double-wide driveway, but a moving car passed by it too quickly to see much.

'Whoa' – he was too wrapped up in his thoughts and nearly lost sight of his mission. He was about to exit at the junction he'd turned into, when a black BMW approached from the southwest. Slowing down so the driver wouldn't notice him, he hung back as far as possible, as the car turned up the slow rise to the residences. He followed for about a mile, seeing the other car turn into a property, stopping in front of a gate.

Dave parked around a curve behind a double row of trees between his car and the gate, and then turned off his ignition. He got out on the passenger side, no small feat, as the foliage extended to the curb. Crouching forward, he stepped carefully, an act reminiscent of the days when he and his friends played 'Cowboys and Indians.' As an Indian, the main strategy was to sneak up on the Cowboy, soundlessly, never snapping a twig, or rustling any fallen leaves. His mounting excitement made deliberateness more difficult.

When the gate came into view, the car was out of his sight, although the gate was still open. Dave stood up, advancing slowly, trying to think of an excuse he could offer the owner of the car, should he be spotted. Staying within the tree line as best as he could, he saw the car parked beyond the open gate, with the owner walking toward the back of the house. From his vantage point, Dave had a three-quarters view of the man.

He had short black hair, although there was no mustache. Easy enough to shave it off, so he would appear different than any description of an eye witness. Once again Dave's intuitive fear sensors seemed to arouse his hair follicles. He felt like a dog with its hackles rising.

Dave froze where he was, peering through some branches to see what the man would do next. He had closed the gate with a remote control, then apparently opened a back door Dave couldn't see, patting a huge black dog that now danced along beside him. The man returned and reentered his car, then drove slowly down the long drive, out of Dave's sight, the dog trotting alongside the car. Dave strained to see beyond his camouflage, but couldn't, without exposing himself. He heard the dog bark, and then a door slam, making him decide it would be best to return to his car.

When he entered his car on the street side and sat down, closing the door as quietly as possible, Dave braced his hands on the steering wheel. They were shaking violently. He took four or five deep breaths, exhaling fully, dropping his hands to his sides. He mumbled a prayer. Then, starting the ignition, he crept slowly forward, watching to see if there were any signs of activity. There didn't appear to be. He glanced through the gate's black ironwork and saw a two-story brick mansion with turrets at its corners and stone urns at the front entrance. After the gate, the high brick wall cut off his view.

Wait a minute – what was the number on the house? Dave decided to chance driving around the circular road, going by the house once again. When he had circled about one hundred and eighty degrees, in back of where he thought the property lie, he saw dense pine woods that most likely ran up close to the back of the house. He wondered if there was some barricade fencing off the backyard that he was looking for. Probably. Completing the circle, he saw the brass house numbers running vertically down the brick wall where the iron fence was hinged. 1334. What was the name of the street?

He checked the wrought iron signpost at the end of the street. Argyle. That sounded familiar. Still driving, he unlatched his glove box and removed the contact sheet Hopkins had given him. The last name on the list was Phillip Nottingham, 1334 Argyle.

'Sweet Mary, mother of Jesus, this must be the man who kidnapped my son!' How could he have lost faith. God was still by his side. Dave began trembling uncontrollably. As soon as he exited Knollwood, he pulled into a parking place at a gas station, trying to collect himself. What should he do now? He must think it through carefully. He couldn't tell Hopkins, because David had spoken about this man as a business associate. Nottingham would be forewarned if Hopkins talked to him to schedule a meeting, as he said he would, because he'd undoubtedly give Nottingham his last name, which would immediately identify him as Brian's father. If Phillip had Brian in his house, God knows what he'd do with him. The same was true about notifying the police. If anyone put forewarning pressure on this awful man, they could trigger him to do something catastrophic.

The twig had snapped, the leaves already rustled. The only thing Dave could think of that he, and only he could do, was to somehow gain access to that house as quickly as possible. He knew Brian was in there. His son had been silently leading him to his side ever since Dave had felt the Holy Spirit enter his soul.

Back at the Hopkins' house, Dave found himself pacing his room, trying to settle the crazy charge of energy that made his brain feel like it was about to explode. He wanted to call Peggy and tell her about his discovery, but he knew he'd only pass his anxiety on to his already overwhelmed wife, who could do nothing to help. He was about to leave his room for outdoors, counting on the spring breeze to help clear his mind, when

Hopkins rapped on the door. Dave opened it reluctantly.

"Hi, how did it go yesterday?"

"You mean at Planned Parenthood?"

"Yes, particularly with Patrice. Did she have anything worthwhile to say? I mean, I already figured that you'd probably strike out with Gelmini. She's hard-core."

"You're right about Gelmini. But Patrice? No, nothing particularly worthwhile there, either. That is, she didn't know anything about…anything. But she did suggest…." Dave stopped himself from spilling the beans.

"Suggest what?"

'The hell with it.' He had to trust Hopkins when it came to helping him, even if he seemed to be untrustworthy in other areas. He was the only person he could rely on, when it came to rescuing Brian.

"Please keep what I'm going to tell you between the two of us."

"Of course. That's understood. Unless you've broken the law."

"No, I haven't. And I don't want to. Which is why I'm telling you. To stop myself from doing something crazy."

"What's going on?"

"Yesterday, Patrice suggested that since my only clue is the BMW, the best place to look for one might be in the Northern neighborhoods. So yesterday afternoon and evening, I went to that area and conducted an exhaustive search. Without any results. I went again this morning, and after more missteps, I finally saw a black BMW pull into a driveway. And I saw the man that kidnapped Brian. I'm certain of it. He fits the description exactly. And…" Again Dave teetered on the brink of telling, and then pulled back.

"And what? I can tell this is extremely hard for you, but you need to tell me. I can help you." Hopkins reached out and clapped his hand on Dave's shoulder.

The clap released his internal pressure. "OK," said Dave.

"As soon as I pulled away from the house, I looked on my contact sheet, and the address and name matched the last resource you have listed. Although I'm praying you haven't made contact with him yet...to set up an appointment. It's Phillip Nottingham."

"My God," said Hopkins. He moved to the side of the bed, sitting down. He braced his forehead between his clenched hands. "Hold on a minute. I need to think about this. Of course, he lives in Knollwood Heights, and has a black BMW. But it never entered my mind..."

"You told me you know him personally, and that you've done business with him. I know..."

"Yes, you're right. This is hard to think through. But just because all these clues fit together doesn't mean that Phillip is the kidnapper. It's important you keep that in mind." Hopkins pondered a minute.

"Still there are some odd things about him that I've wondered about for some time. Things that have made me feel uneasy."

"Like what?"

"For one thing, he seems to have no friends. I mean, he acts a gentleman, is very civic-minded, but he's, well...he's very distant and secretive. As much as I've rubbed elbows with him in terms of service projects, he's never invited me over. As far as I know, he's never had anyone over. He's like a hermit.

And the biggest thing I've had in the back of my mind for years now is that he built some rooms in his basement that always seemed...oh, I don't know...sort of suspicious."

"What do you mean, suspicious?"

"I have a friend on the City Council who was the building contractor for Phillip's basement remodeling. Oh, probably ten years ago. Joe said one of the guys on the work crew told him that although they built it to his specifications, there were a couple of 'hidden' rooms. Rooms you couldn't enter by ordinary means. Something weird. And the workmen were told, by Phillip, that the reason for the hidden rooms was that he was planning exclusive parties with 'girlie entertainment' in them, for the 'high rollers' around town. So, not to spread the word. Even gave each of them a cash bonus to keep it on the QT. To some extent, I can understand that, but what I don't understand is that I've never heard of anyone who's been invited to a party there."

"If that isn't damning evidence, I don't know what is," Dave said, his voice quavering.

"Now, wait a minute, my friend. That's all circumstantial evidence. I can't stress how important it is that you don't do anything rash. Hold on a minute...maybe we could put together a plan."

Dave looked at him skeptically.

"Wait. How about this? I still haven't contacted him to set up an appointment with you, so he doesn't know you're on his trail. Don't have any contact with him. Or do anything we haven't discussed. In the meantime, I'll talk to Joe, the contractor, in detail. He'll probably still have the floor plans for that job. I'll find out as much as I can beforehand. And hey, I could even set up an appointment for you to talk to Phillip, using a false last name. That's a good idea. And I could go with you. We'll plan what to say ahead of time. To keep you calm. That's what we need here, Dave...steady nerves. Right?"

"Right," said Dave, all the while screaming *Wrong* inside.

"OK, so we have a plan of action and a verbal contract. Agreed?" Hopkins extended his hand toward Dave.

"Agreed," Dave said, shaking it.

"Good. Sorry this has been such a rough day for you. But, as always, Shirley will have something fabulous for dinner in about half an hour. You'll join us, won't you?"

"Thanks. I'll try to be down about six. But if I'm not there, go ahead without me. I feel like I've just run ten miles, and I might drift off for a much needed nap."

"Understood," said Hopkins, mustering a stiff smile.

Dave closed the door softly behind him. Turning his back to it, he slid down its length until he was sitting on the floor in a muddled heap.

Chapter 15
Phillip
Friday, April 12

Phillip looked at the caller ID. Dave Hopkins. Why would he be calling? They'd wrapped up the Kiwanis Club food drive more than a month ago. He sighed, picking up the receiver. "Yes, Dave."

"Hi, Phillip. Wondering if you could help me out with something. There's this guy I met from Ohio, Dick Durbin, whose teenage son ran away from home, and when last heard from, was here in Baltimore. He's desperate to try and find him, and I'm hoping that you might be able to give him some guidance...."

'It must be Brian's father, and Dave was putting up a front... how had he come this close? My God, it must be the car. Some Ohio neighbor must have spotted my car and the Maryland license, bringing the father forward. And I thought I was being crafty enough by having unregistered plates, simply because it had worked well in the past. I should have changed to the Pennsylvania plate earlier in the game. This is what comes of my getting by with it for so long that I'd gotten cocky. Damn. Now I have to think my way out of this one. This is getting uncomfortably tight.'

Hopkin's voice continued. "...because I thought you might hear him out. Maybe even offer him some help finding his way through the underground tunnels of runaway children. Having to do with your organization, KOCs. I had you on a list of resource people, but couldn't get hold of you earlier in the week. But as they say, there's no time like the present. Durbin has already met with Dave Landus, Patsy Gelmini and some others, but I think you're the most important stone unturned. I hope you'll be able to accommodate him."

Phillip cleared his throat loudly. "Excuse me. I seem to have come down with a nasty cold." He fought to buy time to think through this abhorrent turn of events. "Actually we no longer call it KOCS. I changed the name to *Protect Our Children,* so the new acronym is *POC.*" He remembered that ridiculous woman's association to smallpox scars. "Now what did you say brought his gentleman to our area?"

"He's following a lead from a neighbor back in Ohio. The kid isn't old enough to drive, but some old geezer spotted a black BMW with a Maryland license plate driving away from the kid's jogging route on a country road, about the time he seemed to have disappeared, and ..."

'Yes, it was the car.' This time he really was challenged. The stakes were high, but he'd find his way through this brain labyrinth.

Hopkins continued on with his drivel. "Oh, and did I mention that the father is staying at our place until he's exhausted his search? It seemed like the best thing we could do for him."

"I'm confused, Dave. How in the world is this guy connected to you?"

"Just one of those strange encounters. I happened to meet him at the bar, over a week ago. He told me his situation and I really felt for the poor guy. Thought I might be able to help him out."

Phillip felt as though someone had put a stranglehold on his throat, making it hard for him to talk much above a whisper without having his voice crack. He cleared his throat again. "It's good of you to be so gracious to a stranger, Dave. I'm not sure what I can do to help, but I'm willing to talk to him."

Phillip broke into a coughing fit that lasted at least a minute. "You know what, Dave? This cold is really getting its claws into me. I think I should lay low for at least a few days to recuperate. How about Tuesday? Will he still be here then?"

"Yes, I'm rather certain he will. In fact, I'll insist that he do so. I appreciate it, Phillip. Shall I give him directions to your place, or will you meet him elsewhere?"

"Actually, I plan to be downtown in the AM that day. Why don't I just meet him at the *Algonquin* for lunch? Say, at noon?"

"Excellent. Call me if anything changes, and I'll do the same."

'Yes, a great deal will have changed before then,' Phillip thought.

There was a silence on the other end, and then Hopkins began laughing. "Hey, I just remembered that you have a black BMW. This poor guy is so desperate, he can't think straight. Do you have another car you could drive to the meeting?"

"Yes, of course. I have a run-about Toyota to do my grocery shopping. I'll drive that to our meeting. So he won't get unnecessarily alarmed." 'Good to know that Hopkins was as naive as ever. Or maybe he wasn't. He did shift his story from the boy being a runaway, to possibly being picked up by a black BMW.'

"Sounds good. I'll inform him of our plans. If nothing else, perhaps you can calm this guy down and give him some fruitful suggestions. I'm fresh out of them."

Phillip sat down heavily in his recliner as soon as he hung up. Nothing had ever gone so badly awry before. It was the lure, the damn *Beamer*, the riff-raff called them. He'd have to put together a new plan of operation. But more important, in the meantime he must think of a way to dispose of Brian before Tuesday.

Phillip walked to the corner cabinet in the kitchen where he kept his supply of meds and took two Xanax. Luckily, one of the 'retired' board members of KOCS was a young hot-shot pharmacist who passed out pills like candy, among his favored working cohorts. The guy wanted to run for a congressional seat in the next election, and knew how to count on votes.

Back in his recliner, Phillip closed his eyes and took a twenty-minute power nap. He'd worked on that for years and was adept at clearing his mind and going into a trance-like state, awakening alert and active.

The passing of some clouds flooded his study with sunlight. He opened his eyes to see that the mantel clock said 10:10. Brian had yet to have his breakfast. As Phillip prepared some eggs and toast, it became clear to him what he must do. He didn't know what had pushed him into such a panic. Yes, he did. He flashed back to that horrific encounter when that one foolish boy – William was his name – had assaulted him in the basement room and Cerberus had mauled him so badly that Phillip had to shoot the lad with his pistol. Chaining Cerberus indoors in the basement, Phillip had put the boy in a garment bag and dug a deep grave for him, under the dog's outdoor kennel. He'd kept Cerberus indoors for several days while he arranged to have some workmen come and pour a concrete slab over the leveled area, where he'd deposited an extra truckload of fresh dirt. With the new hard surface, he could "hose down Cerberus' accidents," he'd told them.

He most certainly didn't want the Brian chapter to end that way. He wanted to keep him alive. It angered him that Brian's father had been stupid enough to play with his son's fate in this manner. The turn of events caused Phillip to think through 'close calls,' and how he'd handled them. The only other one – Tommy was his name – was the guy who'd broke down the basement door in his old house and escaped, the day he'd taken Cerberus the First to the vet. What a horrible day. He remembered holding the dear dog's head and talking to him as the vet put him down. He'd sobbed. Such a deep loss. His dutiful companion gone. Returning home to find Tommy had escaped had been the last straw.

Then he'd had to vacate the house, in case Tommy should find his way back. As a remedy to help him through his grief, he'd taken that trip to Italy where he'd purchased Cerberus the Second and brought him home. The airlines had caged him and put him in with the baggage. So inhumane. Instead, they should have caged those squalling children who disturbed everyone's in-flight comfort.

When he had returned home, he'd quickly and efficiently sold the house where Tommy had stayed. Another member of his board was a Realtor, and had found the best possible buyer, a rich widow with Alzheimer's, who'd had live-in caretakers. Phillip never had to deal with her face-to-face. An attorney signed at the closing. Clean negotiations, and then the basement renovation was contracted out in his new home. He'd been wanting to expand and improve the boy's quarters anyway.

As to what had happened to that idiot boy, Tommy, after he'd broken out, he had no idea. Most likely he'd been absorbed into the street drug-culture. God knows he'd had to give that one a continuing stream of drugs, as he was never cooperative without them. Or maybe he'd just turned tail and fled the city. Gone back to where he came from. Gary, Indiana, as he recalled. Miserable place. Phillip watched for him in the neighborhood and on the streets, but by now, over ten years had passed, and clearly nothing would come of it. 'The boy was a has-been.' But at least he'd served as a hard-earned lesson, which was never to pick up a boy who had sexually matured. It turned out that Tommy had been nearly sixteen when he kidnapped him, and if he didn't drug him to the gills, the kid was obstinate and scrappy as hell.

So where did this leave him with regard to Brian? He had time on his side. If he left in the middle of the night within a day or two, he would do everything in reverse, just as he did when he returned the other boys. How many enlightened boys had he educated and groomed by now? He'd lost count. It reflected his state of confusion, as he'd always remembered before. He knew it was well over fifteen.

So...he would drug Brian early and sufficiently enough that he'd be sound asleep in the car, and then he would drive him somewhere. Maybe western Pennsylvania this time. Then leave him at a deserted roadside park, or some pull-off where Brian would eventually wake and find his way back home. Of course, he'd put at least one hundred in twenties, not all from the same series, in the lad's pocket.

Phillip was sorry it had to end so soon. He was growing fond of Brian, and considered him highly trainable. The worst of it was that he'd waited too long, in deference to Brian's mental and physical virginity. If only he'd begun earlier. He felt robbed. Ah, but right now the boy needed to be fed.

He spent only fifteen minutes in the kitchen, fixing Brian's favorite breakfast. Hesitating outside his door, he savored the arousing wisps of body memories from last night. At least the intervening predicaments hadn't destroyed that.

Phillip had to rap on the door three times before Brian finally answered. His hair was tousled, his eyelids heavy. All in all, he still appeared under the influence. He probably didn't even know what had happened last night.

"Hey, rise and shine, Buttercup."

Brian scratched his head and shuffled back to his bed.

"Look," said Phillip, I brought your favorite – scrambled eggs with bacon crumbled in it."

"Thanks. I guess I'll eat it, even though I'm not hungry. I'm just so tired, I can hardly keep my eyes open. And I had a very strange dream."

"To hell with dreams. Let's get you back in the real world. This will help perk you up. This and a robust cup of coffee. I did give you a sedative last night, because you seemed unusually antsy. Maybe I gave you a tad too much. Do you remember taking it?"

"No, I don't remember a thing. Except eating something good, I think. Did we eat in bed?"

"Yes, and I gave you a massage. Do you remember that?"

"No...like I said, I don't remember much of anything. Actually, the first thing I remember is you coming in just now, and that strange dream. I must have slept really hard."

"I guess you did." Phillip was so relieved that it was all he could do to keep from hugging Brian. The Rofynol had worked better on him than any of his other boys. Brian wouldn't even remember that Phillip had promised him pool privileges. That was excellent because the less he saw of the house, the less he could describe later.

"Excuse me, sir, but I need to use the bathroom," Brian said, rising from his side of the bed. Within minutes he'd returned, looking perplexed. "It hurts to go poop," Brian said, "and I looked in the stool and saw some blood."

"Gosh, you're rather young to be bothered by hemorrhoids, but that's likely what it is. I'll get you some stool softener. That should do the trick. But if it continues, let me know. I have some other medication that'll fix you up in no time."

He certainly didn't want to send Brian home with evidence of – 'Whoa, wait a minute Phillip. You're getting much too relaxed about this.' Brian's father was obviously certain his son's kidnapper lived in Baltimore, and that he drove a black BMW. As things were now, Phillip was going to talk to this man, face-to-face, about those suspicions. Letting Brian return home was not the answer. Among other things, he knew Phillip's first name, could describe his physical characteristics down to the fact that normally he was clean-shaven, and didn't have a mustache. Plus the timing of the boy turning up at home soon after his father had come that close, would look highly suspicious. 'I'm losing my edge. That's what happens when I allow sentimentality to cloud my thinking.' There was a far better way to deal with this dilemma. Brian drizzled coffee down his chin. Phillip took his napkin and tenderly wiped the corners of his mouth.

He was going to miss him. "There," he said. "Don't want anything messing up your pretty face. You're a handsome young man, you know."

"Thanks," said Brian, and smiled.

Phillip couldn't sleep that night. His brain was in high gear and he couldn't slow it down. Getting up, he put on his bathrobe and walked downstairs to his study. He thought about taking a sleeping pill and resting on the couch, where he'd likely fall asleep, but no. He needed to stay alert and think the Brian situation through until he came to a sound solution. One thing for certain was that I'll have to get rid of Brian. 'Hell, quit dodging the word – I'll have to kill him.'

The odd thing was that he wasn't a killer. That time with William happened only because he had to put the poor lad out of his misery. He would have died anyway from the mauling he took. William never should have assaulted him with Cerberus standing guard. I'd had warned him a number of times. Poor dumb boy. Brian was a lot more intelligent than William was…had been.

As for the Sheriff's Deputy who had stopped him on that dark wooded road...well, she should have known better too. She'd approached a car with an unregistered out-of-state license plate in a desolate area at night, without even drawing her pistol. How had she even earned her badge?

But what to do this time? Whatever it was, it needed to be swift and sure, with no traces left. Brian's father was breathing down his neck. How the hell had he closed in on me anyway? And how could he have known to contact Dave Hopkins? Oh, that's right, Dave said he met him in a downtown pub. An unlikely coincidence if ever I've heard one.

Apparently Dave was the one who had pointed the way. But then, why would Dave be suspicious of him? Possibly one of the basement crew told Dave about Phillip's hidden 'entertainment' rooms. But even so, he would have been led to believe that Phillip had them built to cover up some of the debauchery of the city's movers and shakers.

'Enough!' It did no good to think of how this turn of events had come to pass. *What I need to think about is a good plan for getting rid of Brian. By the day after tomorrow, at the latest. Maybe even by tomorrow night. I've already kept him one day too long. Fortunately, that day had at least brought him the ultimate prize.* Thinking about it brought about another erection.

'Damn, Phillip, keep your mind on how to get out of this mess.' On the basis of his suspicions, Brian's father might jump the gun and not wait until their planned meeting time on Tuesday. He'd have to get rid of Brian before then. And, after he'd killed Brian, he would still be left with getting rid of the body, and cleaning up any forensic evidence that might be left in the room: fingerprints, hair, anything with Brian's DNA stamp on it. All the details that were usually a killer's undoing.

Actually, the murder itself will be the easiest part. I certainly don't want to hurt Brian, so an overdose was the cleanest, no-pain method. Brian was accustomed to taking his drugs by now, so he won't balk. I can give him just enough to make him nearly unconscious, and then finish the act by injecting him with an overdose of insulin. There was some left over from a bout when the vet had thought Cerberus the First would need more than pills for his creeping diabetes. Although with my diligent oversight, it proved to be controllable through dietary changes.' But he'd checked into it and knew that insulin was nearly untraceable in a corpse. Not that it mattered. They would never find the body.

Now, how to dispose of the body? His preference was always incineration. Cremation, the euphemists preferred to call it, when it came to human remains. If he had a choice in the matter, Phillip knew he'd like his body to be immolated in a funeral pyre, then have his ashes scattered in the Chesapeake Bay. Which was a poor substitute for the Ganges, but it would do. Of course cremation was out of the question for Brian. Phillip had no means for such a disposal. Burial it would have to be. 'Where?' His original thought was the woods near an abandoned farm he'd driven past many times, ten minutes or so from the city limits. But that was too close. It should be across the state line, in Pennsylvania. He thought of some state parks in the Alleghenies. No, that was too far. I'll need to do it during the night – maybe tomorrow night – and return home to sanitize the room on Sunday, so that my absence won't be apparent in terms of appointments I'll have to keep. The contacts would provide a time-line alibi, if it should come to that. Surely it wouldn't.

His mind rambled over the land, the roads, the parks he'd passed through in his searches for boys over the years. 'Ah, just the place! A Pennsylvania state park with a large lake, no more than an hour and a half from here.' He couldn't remember the name of it, but he knew how to get there. Then he would have the choice of digging a grave deep in the woods, or dumping the body in the lake. The ground had softened considerably since the pith of winter had passed. Still he remembered how exhausting it had been to dig William's grave in Cerberus' pen. And dirty. He'd had to burn the clothes he'd worn, and then scrub his hands with lemon juice to get all the grime out from under his fingernails. 'Like a common laborer.'

Thinking about it, he realized there were insurmountable problems with dumping the body in the lake. It would have to be away from the shallow water near the shore, which meant he would need a boat of some nature, and that would require rental. Easy to trace, aside from the chore of heaving a dead weight out of the boat, into the water. With his diminishing strength and the difficulties of maneuvering the whole business in the dark, he'd likely fall into the water himself. 'Burial it would have to be.'

'Think.' He would serve Brian breakfast in the morning, go about preparing the drug dosage to be administered at their evening meal, get all his tools together, and make his run-about car ready, checking the tires and making certain all maintenance was up to snuff so he wouldn't require any automotive rescues. The car trunk had always locked securely, and …what can I use for a body bag? He'd used a garment bag with William, but that was possible because he only had to drag the mangled body out of the house across fifteen yards or so, to the dog pen. Outside of digging the grave, it had been the cleanup afterward that was the hardest. 'At least there should be no blood with Brian.'

Suddenly, he visualized the perfect body bag. After his father had died, Phillip had kept a few useless but somehow sentimental mementos from his affects. One of them was an intact, khaki Army-issued sleeping bag that his father had brought back from his combat days in WWII. 'Perfect!' Designedly body-sized, with tough canvas straps sewn into the bag, which would be excellent for picking up and maneuvering Brian into his grave.

After all the hard work was done, with the ground leveled

and then strewn with pine needles and forest roughage, Phillip imagined himself standing over the grave-site, holding his hat to his heart and saying, 'Goodnight, Sweet Prince.' 'A fitting eulogy to a sweet lad. I will miss him. My boy, Brian, feels like the closest thing I'd ever had to a son.'

'But there's no time to get sappy about this. First I must sleep, and then tomorrow will dawn and I'll go about the nasty business of ending yet another life, when all I want to do is to be a benefactor. Society skewed my motives, making it appear that I'm the evil-doer by putting me in a position where I had no option other than to kill or be killed. I'm a Darwinian. It's a topsy-turvy world I have to tolerate. Particularly when the power-mongers, crime syndicates and corrupt politicos all over the world, who killed on a whim, were seldom brought to justice for their deeds.' With that comforting comparison, Phillip fell into a deep sleep.

Chapter 16
Patrice, Hopkins and Jane
Friday, April 12

Patrice Goodman was glad that she had thought to obtain permission from Dave Brefort to exchange information about his son's kidnapping with her friend and fellow social worker, Jane. It had been an intuitive hunch, and now it appeared that it might prove to be a valuable one. It had come about in a most unexpected and bizarre manner.

Years ago she had been at a boring evening social event, sponsored by the City Commissioners, and had met Dave Hopkins, who had flagrantly flirted with her, although she had not encouraged his attention or intentions. Patrice was single, and knew he was not, so she was turned off by his attempts to get her to leave the party and go to a 'night spot,' as he called it. She wound up leaving the party early, and thought that would be the end of it.

Then, several years later, Hopkins unexpectedly called her

at her office, about a business matter. It was, in fact, a real business matter, she being the Director of Planned Parenthood and the business being the lease on the city-owned building they occupied. Hopkins remembered first meeting her on the occasion of the party, and apologized profusely, saying that he had had too many 'Bloody Mary's.' She accepted his apology and they managed to deal fruitfully with the matter at hand.

That was then. Yesterday Hopkins had called her at her agency, and apprised her of the kidnapping of Dave Brefort's son, which she informed him she had foreknowledge of, as Brefort himself had approached her through Hopkin's referral. Yes, he realized that, but he wanted to clarify "smoky trails," because now he needed her help to establish, or rule out, the possibility that a prominent professional member of intersecting agency paths, might be the kidnapper of Brefort's son. He didn't want to discuss it over the phone, and could he please meet with her in her office as soon as possible.

Hopkins was there within the hour, and although both of them were intimidated by the potential sound waves created by their situation, they immediately got down to business.

"Who is this prominent person you believe might have kidnapped Brefort's son, and why do you believe that's possible?" asked Patrice, pouring Dave a cup of coffee, and pushing a packet of powdered creamer his way.

"Well, I hate to be so abrupt, but I need to tackle this head-on and not waste vital time. The person I suspect is Phillip Nottingham, the head of KOCS, or *Keep Our Children Safe*. Unbelievable as that seems. Which, also, I understand, has recently had a name change because of the unfortunate acronym. I believe it's now, POC, or *Protect Our Children*." He glanced up from stirring his coffee to catch Patrice's reaction. None was apparent. Just a nod.

"And why do you suspect Mr. Nottingham?"

"Well...or not so well, it begins with the fact that the kidnapper's car was spotted on a rural road in Ohio where the unfortunate victim was picked up, as you know. The car was identified as a high-end black BMW with a Maryland license, which Nottingham has. Along with a general description of the prominent facial characteristics, from a neighboring farmer who saw him pass by. Which, by a chance meeting, led the father to our doorstep, seeking his son's captor, finally honing in on him through an extensive search, interviewing resources I suggested, until he found a black BMW in Nottingham's driveway, and got a good look at him exiting his car, which doesn't sound like much in the way of identification, but…

"Yes, I'm aware of Mr. Brefort's mode of narrowing his search to the driveways of upper class residences, since I was the one who suggested that to him. Prior to that he had been looking in all the wrong places, following false leads the police gave him….like interviewing released child molesters."

Hopkins pulled back and arched his eyebrows, displaying surprise and admiration. "That, most certainly, was the coup de grace leading to Nottingham's identification." He gathered himself. "Although it was I who referred the boy's father to you as the most effective agent when it comes to tracking lost children." He nodded self-approval. "But there's more relevant information about him that brought me to hopefully collaborate with you in terms of reporting this to the proper authorities, although I'm not certain just how to go about that."

"Please go on…you have my full attention."

"Well, about ten years or so ago, Phillip Nottingham left his old mansion – I'm not sure just where it was, but he purchased a newer one in Knollwood Heights. At the time I was on a committee with the man who designed and oversaw modifications of his new place…it was Joe Brooks. I don't know if you've ever had occasion to meet him…"

"No, but please continue…"

"Well, Joe told me that Phillip had him oversee the construction of some sub-level rooms that were hidden in some way, and could only be entered through the elaborate basement gym and indoor pool that were part of the lower floor plan. And that Phillip told Joe he'd had them concealed, because he planned on having 'girlie entertainment' there for some of his cronies, and he wanted it to have the feeling of an old 'speak-easy,' privacy and concealment being the top considerations. And yet, I have never heard of any of the men who were likely to be invited, ever going there. And that's what's highly suspicious to me."

"So-oo, if that's the case, what is being done about it? Anything?"

"Well, not exactly, as there are further complications. As you know, Brefort is staying with us, and after some of his sleuthing, when he returned from seeing Nottingham get out of the identified car, and checked my 'resource list' that I'd compiled for him, he saw that Phillip was on it as the Chairman of KOCS, formerly that is. KOCS, not Phillip. Sorry if I keep repeating myself, but all of this doubling back has me in a state of confusion. But the foremost thing I'm certain of, is that someone needs to get to Phillip before he does something drastic to the boy. Brian is his name. The reason for that is that I contacted Nottingham, told him that Brefort – I gave a false name – Dick Durbin, as I remember, is staying with me and that he wants to meet with Phillip as the Chairman of, the now, POC, in the hopes that he might be of some assistance to Dave in searching the 'underground' for his son, whom I described as a 'runaway' youngster from Ohio."

"Phillip was taken aback by the suggestion, begged for time, as he said he'd developed a nasty cold, but through me, finally arranged a meeting with the boy's father for Tuesday, noon, at the *Algonquin*. I conveyed this to Brefort, and he agreed not to take any action before the scheduled meeting with Nottingham."

"And...?" Patrice said.

"Wait, there's more about the father. He supposedly agreed

with me about waiting until Tuesday to talk with Nottingham, but I sense that he's so emotionally overwhelmed and vulnerable, fearing that Phillip might do something irreversible with his son...if he is indeed holding him captive, which appears more and more likely..."

Hopkins stopped, sucked in a huge breath, then let it out explosively. "I don't know what to do. Which is why I'm here. I know you're as well-informed about the situation as any of those having knowledge of the kidnapping are, and beyond a doubt, in my opinion, are the most sensible and pragmatic, so that I'm seeking your opinion before going any further."

Patrice was silent for a long moment, and then said, "You flatter me, Mr. Hopkins, but in spite of the time imperatives, I need to give this some uninterrupted thought and check with a non-legal resourceful person I know about the risks and ramifications of involving the police. Realizing full-well that time is of the essence, I don't want to 'jump the gun'.... so to speak. And be assured that confidentiality will be maintained. I won't give actual names when I discuss it with this, ah, person. And in spite of the gravity of the situation, before I consult my source, I do need to get back to an important matter I have coming up, before I take the next step in this strange scenario. As you know I'm not accustomed to getting involved in matters of crime, which this has definitely become."

"Of course. And thanks for reshuffling your schedule, but I obviously felt that it was important to check with you before taking any abrupt action. You will get back to me as soon as you're able?"

"Of course, and hopefully that will be by tomorrow before noon. Although if I don't have a definitive answer by then, I assume you will precede to take a judicious course of action. Please do trust in your own acumen of experience, and your intelligence. I respect them, as you apparently do mine."

Patrice rose from her desk chair, shaking Hopkins hand. He gave her a wan smile and exited.

Saturday

Patrice was sitting with her friend, Jane, in their favorite lunch spot that they'd frequented over the years of their intersecting work association, and long friendship. At one point they had even entertained the idea of joining forces and work interests, by starting their own foster-care service agency.

Today, recognizing the need for privacy, Patrice had chosen an isolated table in back of the self-service food bar. "So that about sums up what Hopkins informed me of. And he is expecting to hear from me after I talk to you. Not that I identified who I was going to confer with about it."

"Well, it is a huge ball of wax," Jane said, "and I'm terribly uneasy about how to go about the melting process. I do think everyone needs to be very careful not to bring on further catastrophe. And for that reason I don't advise summoning 'police intervention' at this stage. Although how to intervene without them, in order to reduce the risk to the young boy, I don't know…"

Jane looked down, appearing in deep thought, so Patrice held back on interrupting.

She was right. After allowing a moment of silence, Jane nearly exploded. "Wait, there's more that I haven't disclosed to anyone, until now. I know that Phillip Nottingham is the pedophiliac kidnapper, because of a young man by the name of Owen, whom I have been helping out – much to the chagrin of Danny. Although Danny is the one who initially brought him, plus a couple of other guys, to my apartment one evening, before I left for my night shift. Owen wound up leaving my place when I was coming up the stairs in the morning… oh, I think it must have been Monday morning. He'd slept over because he was homeless, and Danny had left my place early, the evening before, having forgotten to lock up his own place. I gave Danny hell about his negligence, and we're still out-ofsorts, because I wound up letting Owen sleep overnight on my couch, on nights when I'm not there, clearing out before I returned home from work... or being with Danny."

Jane continued, nearly stuttering with chagrin, knowing she was lying about Owen's sleeping over on several nights when she wasn't at work. "So..., I got to talking to Owen on a couple of occasions when we crossed paths, as he was leaving and I was coming home, and as usual, I was a sucker for listening to the story of a 'down-and-outer.' Strange as this all seems, it turns out that Owen was kidnapped by Phillip about ten years earlier, when he was about fifteen."

Patrice covered her mouth in an attempt to silence a gasp. "Excuse me. Go on."

"Turns out Owen had escaped, busting down the door to his room one day when Phillip had taken his guard-dog to the vet. Heavily drugged by Phillip, Tommy - that was his real name at the time – wound up blacking out on the streets and being taken to the hospital, where he began the long road back to recovery. Although he never really recovered from his drug addictions. He couldn't remember where Phillip had lived when he was his captive, but as I now know, from Hopkins, Phillip had moved, and had his new place in Knollwood Heights renovated, adding some 'hidden rooms' on the basement level, which he told the building contractor were for 'girlie entertainment' for his male cohorts. Hopkins apparently has been suspicious about those rooms for some time, as he'd never heard of any known 'work-buddies' who had been invited to them in the past ten years or so, since they were installed."

Patrice kept shaking her head, and finally said, "There doesn't appear to be any harmless route to take in terms of rescuing the poor boy, so that police intervention appears imperative, though dangerous. How old did you say the boy is?"

"I believe he's twelve."

"What a horrendous situation to be in. It most assuredly calls for a rescue team of some nature, but who, and how?"

"Yes, indeed, those are the questions. And you understand the gravity of it. What do you propose?"

Patrice appeared deep in thought for several minutes. "Oh dear friend, I'm afraid I have no immediate plan in mind, and this does call for quick action. It occurs to me that perhaps the best thing would be to go to the records and intervention manual at The Shelter, and see what they've done in situations where the safety of the child is at stake from the mother's abuser. But I'm sure you've thought of that."

"Yes, I checked that out, and believe it or not, that's never occurred since...oh, forever. Because most often the abuser has fled, or is under tight surveillance, is being held by the police, or has already been incarcerated," Jane ended on a note of exhaustion.

"Listen, I'll get right on this, and get back to you with more information and some sort of plan that doesn't threaten this poor boy's life. Within twenty-four hours, hopefully less. I promise you, Jane."

"Oh, thank you, dear friend. I'm fresh out of protective ideas, and I knew I could call on you."

"Well, no promises of solid protection for the boy. But I'll give it everything I've got."

'That most likely won't be enough, or soon enough,' Jane thought. She'd been hoping for miracles from her friend, but unfortunately she was afraid she might be called upon to put a more radical plan in action.

Chapter 17
Owen
Saturday

Owen's rage toward Jane had obliterated three whole days. Trying to put out the ravenous fire, he'd made a drug contact and been in an opiate daze since he'd left her apartment on Tuesday. Now that he was sober, he knew he needed to find Phillip before Jane began to make inquiries that might send him into hiding. If she hadn't already. Just Plain Jane talked out of both sides of her mouth. Save the children, but wait, let's have tea and talk it over first. Meanwhile Phillip was going about the business of dooming yet another boy's soul to the eternal fires of hell. Owen knew that as sure as he stood outside Jane's apartment door, Phillip was up to the same old game.

Using the extra key she'd given him, he opened the apartment door. The bedroom door was closed. Behind it Jane was undoubtedly enjoying the peaceful sleep of those who believed themselves to be innocent. Let her be. He needed to get his hash from the freezer and figure out where to go after that.

Tiptoeing to the refrigerator, Owen saw the coveted journal that Jane ordinarily kept within her reach, there on the kitchen table. Maybe she'd written something about Phillip. Opening it, the first thing Owen came to was an entry about himself. It questioned why Jane had bothered to connect with him in the first place. 'Good question.' Flipping through to the last entry, Owen saw an address: Phillip Nottingham – 1334 Argyle Ave. 'Jesus Cristo! Could this possibly be?'

Remembering the map drawer, Owen laid the city map out on the table, looking on the street index for Argyle. There it was, with a red dot marking the street, smack-dab in the middle of a red-circled neighborhood named Knollwood Heights. One of the names that was above the exit ramp Phillip took when Owen had spotted him last week. The McMansion part of town.

Returning to the map drawer, Owen saw a key chain with a little globe of the world on it, lying in the drawer. That was Jane's car key. 'Hold on – this must be intentional. First the journal with Phillip's address, then the map with his street circled, now the car key. Jane wants me to go to Phillip's. She just doesn't want to be responsible for my actions. This is as simple as the childhood game, *'Simon Says.'* All I have to do is find Jane's car.' He knew where she usually parked it.

Grabbing the map, Owen fled the apartment, knowing he wasn't really stealing her car, just borrowing it. He must hurry to get it back in time for her to use that night. She was probably going out with Danny. 'Forget the hash. I'll deal with that later.'

When he got into Jane's car and turned on the ignition, her GPS lit up with the address 1334 Argyle, and an active map, displaying the route he should take. 'My God, she'd taken care of everything.' Good that she had, since in his hyper state, he might be able to find his way around stellar space, though certainly not anything so concrete and particular as Baltimore streets.

Owen pulled out from the curb to hear the screeching of brakes as a Jeep swerved out around him, the irate driver honking his horn and shaking an upraised fist as he raced to the corner. Owen hadn't checked his rear-view mirror. He needed to pay close attention. Driving in city traffic was a lost art. 'How long since I've been behind the wheel? A least a year.'

He needed something to help him concentrate intensely. Suddenly he remembered the packet of bath salts he'd been carrying in his jeans pocket since he'd started his search for 'uppers'. Someone in Chino's had given it to him, saying, "Try this when you need a stimulant. It's wacky, but it works." Owen had almost thrown it away, because he knew it was an amphetamine-based concoction and he didn't like their results. But this seemed like an ideal situation to use something that would give him a giant push toward needed action.

Owen pulled into a side street, tearing open the packet that was labeled, *"Unfit for Human Consumption."* He didn't know how many milligrams the packet held, or what was considered a decent dose. 'What the hell, this calls for drastic action.' He didn't really have anything to snort with, so he tipped the envelope into his mouth and swallowed. It tasted nasty, making him afraid he might throw up, but he spotted a plastic water bottle that Jane had left behind. He took a big swallow, chasing the salts down, then rinsed his mouth of the nasty after-taste, opening the door and spitting in the street.

'There, that should do the trick.' He couldn't feel anything immediately, but he was sure he would before long. He hoped he didn't turn into a zombie. He'd heard some strange stories about the stuff. People going psycho, and becoming cannibalistic and shit. 'Nah, I didn't take that much.'

As he headed north along the beltway, Owen thought about coming face-to-face with Phillip. 'What do I want to happen?'

That part was simple. Let Phillip know how he'd destroyed young boy's lives. Make sure he understood how hokey his Renaissance teacher bullshit was. That it was just mental acrobatics to justify his perverted soul. 'Yes, make him grovel,' as he'd made Owen do.

He began to feel the effects of the salts. His heart was beating double-time. And he was seeing strange creatures in the play of light and shadow on his windshield. 'Think. What do I want to do to Phillip? I want to obliterate him. How can I do that?' He would stub him out, much like he would a cigarette. Crush him, extinguish his fire, watch the thin white skin of him peal open, squiggles of his innards fall out, until the physical form of Phillip was no more.

'But what about the guard dog?' In order to get to Phillip, he'd have to get past the dog. He needed a gun. Oddly enough, something he'd never possessed. There were places that sold guns. But not tonight. No. He couldn't wait that long. It had to be now. He'd figure something out when he got to Phillip's and assessed the situation.

By the time Owen reached the Knollwood Heights exit, he was primed for action, feeling like a panther crouched low to the ground, approaching his prey. He got off the main thoroughfare as soon as he spotted the sweeping lawns and palatial homes of the wealthy. 'The fucking "leisure class," Thorsten Veblen called them. Another Phillip-taught lesson. Why do I remember all that rot?' The closer he got to Phillip, the more he remembered. Soon he would face him and stuff his words, his books, his food, his pills, down his throat. The mortician would be amazed at what he saw when they cut him open. But now he needed to watch for Argyle, and 1334.

Owen drove as though he was in a Salvador Dali painting, zipping along a series of winding streets, passing twisted clock faces, and upside-down horses galloping in the sky. He passed one mansion that he was certain must have been Phillip's old home. The one that he'd escaped from. It emanated loud sound waves that crackled with high voltage. Owen knew it came from an energy field his brain stored, that was like a divining rod, pointing him toward the ultimate source of evil. He stepped on the gas, screeching around a bend. Soon he would be in mortal combat with it.

Chapter 18
Dave
Saturday

Dave had scarcely slept a wink Friday night. Even though his own thinking, and Hopkins, advised him against taking matters into his own hands, every molecule of his being told him that's what was needed. There were those who had tried to help, but basically the offers had been inadequate, if not completely incompetent. The fact that he had come this close to the kidnapper was due to his own persistence in following through on intuition and hunches. And his faith in God. With the exception of Peggy, after she came around to embrace his own thinking, and his host, David Hopkins, until the action was this close to the finish line, nearly everyone had tried to dissuade him from following his gut reaction, saying it should be left in the hands of law enforcement. He heard his inner thoughts, realizing he was no longer calling it Divine Guidance, but 'gut reaction.' Oddly enough, he didn't see much difference between the two anymore. They both were based on faith, and possessed a sense of certainty.

And then there was Patrice, whose lead he was following. She was more like an Angel of Divine Guidance. But basically, law enforcers had done next to nothing, even when one of their own kin, Brunhilde, the head of the *Federal Bureau of Missing Children,* gave him the straight statistics on this type of case. She made it clear that they should have acted much sooner in order to track down the kidnapper, even if all they found at the end of the trail was a dead body. At least that would have allowed them to prosecute, keeping this monster from repeating his evil ways. And now it was too late to call on the police. If he did, it would highly increase the chances that Phillip would try to destroy the evidence – his son – before the meeting Hopkins had set up for Tuesday. Again, he, Dave, must take matters into his own hands. With the divine help of God's word, through the Holy Spirit.

Dave was sure Brian was being kept in the secret basement rooms that the contractor had told Hopkins about. But what was the best way to get to Brian without alarming Phillip Nottingham? Of course he'd brought his *Ruger Centerfire* for just such a case, but how would he even get close enough to threaten Phillip, so that he would release Brian? There was the brick wall, the locked gate, the huge attack dog, and the distinct possibility that Phillip might not be at home, or if he was, that he kept tight surveillance and wouldn't answer the door. If Dave could even get to the door.

'How can I gain access to the house?' There was the long shot of disguising himself as a serviceman of some sort, but there wasn't nearly enough time for that. If he could get on the grounds undetected and somehow get Phillip to come close to him, that was clearly the best plan. The only other way he could think of was to break in, but there were problems with that. Someone that rich must have an alarm system throughout the house, and if that went off, it was possible that the first thing Phillip would do was to snatch Brian, and use him as a human shield. What to do? Dave tried to think it through, but all he could come up with was the need to somehow survey the grounds for a possible entrance point, before deciding what his next step would be.

With that in mind, Dave drifted off to sleep for a short time, dreaming about running through a dense forest, the tree limbs snatching at him and lacerating his face. When he reached a clearing, by the light of a full moon, he could see his blood drops fallen on the pure white snow. Soon, they began to flow out of him, coursing back down the path he had made, the blood filling the trough of his booted footprints.

He awoke with a start, for an instant thinking that the first morning light he was seeing came from the forest. But no, it was filtering through the pink-tinged budding leaves of the maple tree outside the guest bedroom, where he had awakened every morning since he'd come to stay with the Hopkins. He looked at the green eye of the electric clock that Shirley had thoughtfully set on his bedside table. Five-fifty.

He would get up quietly, slip out of the house, leaving a note for David and Shirley, saying he had an errand to tend to and would see them later in the day. If need be, he would have breakfast at a fast food place. Right now his stomach felt hollow, yet he wasn't hungry.

Dave arrived at Knollwood Heights soon after sunrise. As he drove the circumference of the boulevard, he saw no other cars. That was good, as he didn't want anyone noticing him in his scruffy car, making it obvious he didn't belong here. As he slowly passed 1334 Argyle, he was not able to spot the dog. That was also good, although it didn't necessarily mean Nottingham was indoors. The second thing Dave noticed was a huge spruce behind the house. It must have stood at least five stories, and was considerably taller than any of the other trees around it. It provided a good landmark, as he had decided to try to approach the house from the back of the property, through the woods.

He parked his car on the street outside the development, and then walked toward the hill on the backside of Nottingham's place. There were no houses facing toward him, only woods. When he spotted the tall spruce, he looked around. Seeing no one walking their dog, or jogging, and not spotting any cars, he quietly entered the woods. He was surprised at how dense they were. Maybe they too had been left to grow wild for the seclusion-exclusion factor. Dave ducked under the low-hanging branches, watching his footing. He kept scanning the ground for any wire detectors that might trigger an alarm, although he doubted the presence of one, since it could be triggered by woodland animals. His clarity of thought surprised Dave, in that he was able to keep his wits about him, in spite of the basket of fears and doubts he carried in his mind.

As the trees began to thin, Dave could see the beginning green of a planted flower garden. It had freshly turned soil around the beds, which undoubtedly meant that Nottingham had a gardener. To the right of the garden, near the back of the house, there was a tall dog pen, enclosed with cyclone fencing. The fencing must have been nearly ten feet high, with a concrete slab running up to a large red doghouse topped by a shingled roof. The dog must be inside the house, as there was no activity in the pen, and Dave knew he was close enough that the dog would have heard him by now, if he were in his doghouse.

He stood behind the thick trunk of an oak tree for several minutes, surveying the back of the house. Clearly there was an entryway to some large room, which was either a utility area or a recreational room. Maybe both. Although it wasn't on a basement level, Dave judged that it was probably the closest room to the hidden rooms. But that didn't make it the most desirable entrance, since it meant that Brian might be brought forth more easily, as a hostage. There were enough windows that Dave was able to see that there was no one inside the area closest to the door. Another plus. God remained on his side.

Dave leaned against the tree for several minutes, thinking things through, finally deciding that knocking on the front door was the best way to bring Phillip to him. Even though the gates were locked, so clearly he would be an intruder, it should bring about a response, if Phillip were home. Or if he wasn't, the dog would undoubtedly be guarding the house and come rushing to the door. If that were the case, then Dave could force entry by breaking a window. It didn't matter if it set off the alarm system, as that would bring the police. Under the circumstances of responding to protect Phillip's property, they might be of service, whereas they probably would have dismissed Dave as a mental case if he had called them beforehand.

Dave crouched down as low as he could, approaching the back entrance, then stood and darted to the side of the house, slithering along the bricks with his back against them, so he couldn't be seen from a window. When he arrived at the front corner of the house, he realized he'd have to run up the porch's stone staircase before he reached the front door. That could prove problematic. Fortunately there was cement fretwork along the bottom of the porch, before he would come to the stairs. It was right above eye level for Dave, allowing him to stand on tiptoe and look through the wide openings in the patterns. He was unable to see very far up the front of the house, but at least high enough that he could tell no one was standing at the front windows.

Swallowing hard, he touched his hand to the cold metal of the gun in his pocket, and then made a mad dash up the porch steps. Before he expected to be there, Dave was standing in front of a solid mahogany door with a brass knocker on it. On either side of its colossal width, there were long panels of leaded glass, joined by lines of silver soldering. Afraid if he hesitated too long, he might turn to stone, like the gigantic urns on the ends of the porch balusters, Dave lifted the heavy knocker and struck it twice on its sounding board. Immediately he heard a low growl from behind the door. The dog must have heard him approaching. He knocked once more, and the dog began a deep-throated barking, jumping against the door and clawing its interior.

Dave heard the rasp of a lock being unbolted, and stepped back behind the hinges of the door, slipping his hand into his jacket pocket, pulling back the gun's safety lock and curling his index finger around the trigger. The door opened slowly, pushed by some invisible force.

A voice commanded, "Who is it?" Dave remained silent. The voice repeated in a more inviting tone, "Who is it, please?"

Dave attempted to throw his voice across space, as though it was coming from a different direction. "It's Dave. Mr. Hopkins friend."

This time the voice was hard, like the sound of a rock hit with a sledgehammer. "Attack, Cerberus. Attack!"

A huge black dog tore out of the opening, stopping for an instant to sniff the air. Then he saw the intruder and lunged toward him. Hand on the trigger, Dave instinctively raised his gun, aiming two shots through his pocket. For a split second, the dog seemed suspended in midair, and then dropped to the porch floor with the grim thud of over one hundred pounds of flesh hitting concrete. A spasmodic shudder passed down the dog's spine to his tail. Ripping the gun from his pocket, Dave shot him again, this time in the head.

Rushing to the edge of the door, while keeping his body behind it, Dave waved his gunless arm rapidly up and down the frame. There was no answering shot. No one grabbed at his arm. He opened the door wider, and still there was no counter move, no sound. Fearing that Phillip had fled the room, Dave flung the door wide open. Still no movement.

Becoming bolder, Dave stepped into the space, peering into the room. What he saw astounded him.

Chapter 19
Dave and Phillip
Saturday

In the middle of the night, Phillip had been aroused from his sleep with an uneasy feeling that he might need protection, should someone come to his door. With great difficulty, he'd removed the heavy steel shield from above the fireplace, leaning it against the wall by the front door, just in case. It was a custom-made heraldic shield with his family's coat of arms emblazoned on it.

When he heard Cerberus' harbinger growl, Phillip found it difficult to maneuver the shield away from the wall and squat down behind it, but a rush of adrenaline gave him strength he ordinarily didn't possess. 'God, I wish I'd thought to have a weapon on me.' But he never imagined he'd need more than his guard dog. Hearing the shots, when Cerberus didn't return, he knew he'd been killed. 'The rube killed my golden Cerberus.'

Phillip spoke from behind the shield. "Mr. Brefort, I presume?"

"Yes," said Dave. "Where is my son?"

"First things first. It was most uncivilized of you to shoot my life companion, Cerberus."

"You ordered him to attack, and he was attacking me, Mr. Nottingham."

"But of course. That is, or shall we say, was, his nature. He was born and bred to attack intruders. Which you are Mr. Brefort. I'll spare no words here."

"Nor will I. I'm here to get my son."

"Yes, of course. I know your mission. But before I lead you to him, you must lay down your gun and act like a gentleman, much as your son does. I am unarmed."

"No, the gun stays, and you come out from behind that shield, or I'll be forced to come and get you."

That was the last thing Phillip wanted. The image of Brian's father grappling with him, touching his skin, repulsed him.

"You realize that you should not harm me as I am the only one who can lead you to your son. There are many locks between here and where he stays. Comfortably, I might add."

"Cut the crap and put down the shield. Move."

Phillip realized he couldn't string Dave along much longer without risking harm to himself. At least he could rid himself of the heavy shield. He laid it down awkwardly, and straightened up to see just what Brian's father looked like. Aside from the lack of red hair, Brefort looked much like a larger, aging rendition of Brian. Actually, he was pretty rugged-looking. Country rugged. Like he might lift anvils, instead of gym weights. Not that he planned on getting in any physical encounters with Dave. Once again, he would have to rely on his wits. They'd never disappointed him before.

He saw that Brian's father was also scanning him, probably estimating his strength. "Yes," said Dave, "you look just like my neighbor described you, minus the mustache. You were seen, you know."

Phillip was terribly disappointed in himself. He had to be more careful about the car, about his appearance. The next time, he would have to use his old car, think of something beside a mustache. If there was a next time. It suddenly occurred to Phillip that this might spell the end of his pursuits. Unless he could outwit Dave. He knew he could.

Dave interrupted his thinking, saying, "OK, now, turn around and put your arms behind your back as though you were handcuffed."

'Good God, those were the same instructions I gave my boys in the act of kidnapping them.' Phillip couldn't help but appreciate the irony of it all. This was getting to be high theatrics.

Phillip followed Dave's bidding, turning and putting his hands behind his back. "You don't mind if I call you, Dave, do you? I feel as though I already know you on a first name basis. Brian talks about you a lot, and you could say that we already have a strong bond."

"I don't give a damn what you call me. Just get me to Brian."

"Of course. Follow me. I'll take you to your son," he said, all the while running through the opportunities he would have to turn the tables on Dave. 'First there's the rack of knives on the kitchen counter beside the door to the basement. But no, not enough time to grab one before Dave could shoot me. Then there's the steep stairs to the basement, but unfortunately I'll be leading, so I'm the one who could be pushed down them, not Dave. I could go the long way, through the gym and the poolroom. The gym has potential weapons in the form of my iron weights, but again, not enough time to beat out the swift impulse of a finger on a trigger.'

Phillip realized that he would have to depend on the heightened emotional state of Brefort, as he got closer to his son. He seemed fairly collected now, but Phillip knew the closer they got, the more overwhelmed Dave would become. He would become more emotional, easily distracted.

'There's the pool. I'll think of something to get Brefort close enough to the edge, to push him in. If that doesn't work, there's the poolroom door leading to the anteroom. Just inside it, there's that long-handled net I use to fish things out of the pool. I could easily topple it with my foot, causing a lot of confusion, possibly trip Brefort. But again, that's unreliable. I could still be shot in the process. God I wish Cerberus was here. Poor thing. Not being able to fulfill his in-bred duty to his master.'

Still, Phillip knew that if all else failed, he could always depend on the loaded gun, resting on the lintel above the door to Brian's room. 'I'll tell Brefort that the key to the door is there. Without turning on the overhead bulb, the room will be dark enough that drawing down the gun will go undetected. Until it's too late for Brefort.'

Again, the irritating, "Get moving," interrupted Phillip's thoughts. 'But that's good because it means Brefort is impatient, probably anxious. Of course that could work against me too. People do impulsive things when they get anxious.'

We were already at the door to the basement. I could tell from the sound of Brefort's footfall that he was staying back far enough that he wouldn't be taken by surprise, if I should turn around and rush at him.

Moving down the stairs, he had the advantage because he purposely didn't turn on the light, hoping Brefort might stumble. He didn't. Next they came to the shelving outside the door to the gym. Here was another possibility. "The key to the door is in a jar on the top shelf. I'll have to free my hands in order to get it. Do you want to take it down?"

"No, you do it. I have my gun cocked and aimed at your heart. No funny stuff."

'I said nearly the same thing to Brian in the car. This was

getting to be too much. Even though Brefort undoubtedly figured there's a chance I could throw the jar in his face, he's not about to be distracted from his target.' Phillip got the jar down, tipping the key into his hand. Then with his back to Dave, he punched in the combination to the lock, letting the key fall to the floor. Both of them ignored it, stepping into the gym. Like his son, Phillip knew this would boggle Brefort's mind.

"Put your hands back behind you," Dave said. Phillip glanced over his shoulder at Brefort's unwavering look directed at his back. 'What would it take?'

"Where is the next door," Brefort asked.

"On the other side of the gym," said Phillip.

"Go to it as directly as you can, but avoid the equipment."

'Damn, this guy is really digging into my mind.'

"You know Dave, you have a very intelligent son, and now I see where it comes from. One little tip from me. Forget the track stuff. Let Brian concentrate on his academics, so he can get a full scholarship to college." 'There, flattering him, assures him that we all have a future beyond this.'

"Don't tell me how to raise my son. Cut the bullshit and open the next door."

'Same stuff. But the pool will wow him, throw him off a bit.' Phillip came to the climbing wall and said, "I need to use my hands to open it."

"Go ahead," said Brefort, not even commenting on the fact that the climbing wall didn't appear to have a door in it. Given the circumstances, Phillip had to admire Brefort's tunnel vision.

Phillip found the receptacle key, turned it, and pulled on the climbing peg doorknob. The disguised door magically opened. 'If Dave only knew how long it had taken me to calculate and design that feature.' They stepped into the poolroom, which was quite dark. "I'll need to turn on the light switch."

"Do it."

Phillip clicked on the lights. They glimmered on the placid surface of the pool. He half expected Cerberus to come trotting out from behind him to gaze at his reflection. Putting his hands behind him again, Phillip proceeded around the end of the pool, hearing Brefort's footsteps on the tiles behind him.

"The next part is tricky," he said. "I have to push a button under the surface of the water to open the next door."

"I don't believe you," said Dave.

"Well, here. Stand right here and look down in the water. You'll see it."

"Stand on the edge of the pool? I don't think so. You go ahead and do it. I'm busy holding this gun."

Phillip cursed himself for having to carry through with his unsuccessful guise, reaching into the water, pretending to push a button, and then struggling to his feet, nearly slipping and falling into the pool. Retrieving his arm, water slid down his sleeve, dripping onto his best slacks. 'OK, so that too failed, but the last thing will surely work.' He walked to the door leading into the anteroom of Brian's chamber, quickly hitting the pool light switch, turning both rooms as black as a moonless night.

He immediately felt the barrel of Brefort's gun in his back.

"Turn that on immediately, or I'll shoot."

For the first time, Phillip felt strong fear. It climbed up his back like an electric eel that kept short-circuiting, making his eyelids and the corners of his mouth twitch. It occurred to him that even if he killed Brefort, he wouldn't know what to do next. There was Hopkins who would be missing him, and probably even knew where he was, right now. 'And even if I manage to kill Brefort, I would have to flee like a fugitive. Give up all of this.' He flipped the wall switch back on.

"OK, now push the door open slowly." A silence, and then, "Yes, we need that light on."

Brefort was right, of course, but there still wasn't enough

light to see all the way across the room to Brian's door. He crossed the room with Brefort behind him. He had broken out in such a profuse sweat, that he couldn't tell which was perspiration, and which was water from his fumbling attempt at poolside.

"Is this the door to Brian's room?" said Dave.

His voice sounded remarkably calm. Phillip felt some indescribable energy emanating from Brefort, and for the first time he realized that Brefort might actually beat him at his own game. He was amazed that someone who he thought was ignorant, could out-think him. The man had thought his way through the labyrinth, until he found his son. It must come from the kind of bond this man had with his son. The kind he never had with his father. The best part of it was that Phillip probably wouldn't have to kill Brian.

"Yes, this is your son's room."

"Brian, Brian! This is your dad. Are you in there?"

There was a hesitation and then Brian answered, "Yes, Dad, I'm in here. Is Phillip with you?"

'Now is the time.' While Brefort was distracted by hearing his son's voice, and before he answered him, Phillip said, "I have to get the key from the ledge above the door."

"Go ahead, and be quick about it."

Yes, he would. He reached above him to the door lintel, drawing down the gun, as he felt his chest implode, sending out concentric circles of the brightest light he had ever seen. He floated on its blood-red bed into outer space. He had a strong sense that he wanted to thank Dave, but he couldn't say it. For the first time in his life, and for the last chance he would have, words failed Phillip.

Chapter 20
Brian and Dave
Saturday

The shot rang out, striking Brian's ears like a clapper clanging against an iron bell. Its resonance continued to vibrate in the chambers of his ears for minutes, as though he'd been picked up from a sandy beach and hurled into a stormy sea, the waves striking his eardrums in an unremitting rhythm.

He listened for subtler sounds he might recognize, but heard nothing except the dreadful ringing. He sank back in his bed, writhing in mental anguish. Who fired the shot? His father? Phillip? Why didn't he hear Cerberus' bark? Was anyone out there? He tossed and rolled on his bed, pressing his hands against his ears, until he felt someone touch his leg and call his name.

Brian opened his eyes, expecting the worst, not even knowing what that would be. There stood his father, saying, "My son, my son..." Was this more of the dream he'd had about being home, with Phillip nailed to the side of his father's shop? Or maybe that was real, and this was the dream. The dream and the clamor melted away when his dad sat down on the bed beside his quieting body, stroking his arm and saying, "It's OK, Brian. It's Dad. I've come to take you home."

Brian sat up, still dazed, and his father put his arm around his shoulder, saying, "Do you need help getting up?"

"No, I'm OK. I ...I just don't understand what's happening. How did you get here? Did Phillip invite you? Where is he? And Cerberus? What was that shot I heard?"

"That's the worst of it, son. In order to get to you, I shot Phillip. I shot the dog too. I had to. Phillip sicced the dog on me, and I had to shoot him. He's dead on the front porch. Then Phillip led me here. But when he was about to open your door, he pulled a gun on me, and...and I had to shoot him too."

"Where is he, Dad?"

"His body is right outside the door. As to where his soul is, it's either on its way to heaven or to hell. Only God knows. He..."

"Oh, no, dad. You didn't kill him, did you?"

"I'm afraid I had to. I didn't shoot to kill, but that's what happened. He drew a gun on me. From above the door."

"Are you sure he's dead? You remember how he was when he was nailed to the shop wall. He still..." Brian stopped. He could see his father didn't understand. "We should call an ambulance. Maybe they can bring him back to life."

Brian looked at his father's expression and saw that he didn't want to help Phillip. His father thought he was a killer. Brian knew he wasn't. "Dad, we need to get to a phone. Call the emergency squad, or something. But I've never been out of my room. I don't know where the phone is."

"You've never been out of this room? What did you do in here all of this time? My God, Brian, it's been nearly two weeks since he stole you."

"Dad, that doesn't matter now." He stood up. "Take me to Phillip."

"He's dead, Brian. Goddamn it, he's dead." Brian had never heard his father use the name of the Lord in vain.

"Son, you've got to believe me. I felt his pulse. There is none. There's nothing we can do for him. For better or for worse, he's in the hands of God."

"I still want to see him."

"There, see for yourself," Dave said, pushing the bedroom door ajar. The ceiling light was turned on and Phillip was plainly visible from the threshold of Brian's room. His still body was lying on the basement floor, face up, his left arm and leg stretched out in a nearly ninety-degree angle from his shoulder and his hip, the position his dad had left him in when he dragged him away from the door. He was wearing Brian's favorite paisley vest over a maroon long-sleeved shirt. There was a pool of blood outside the bedroom door, and a streaked trail of it to his body.

Brian took several steps toward Phillip, stopping to check the soles of his slippers to see if he'd stepped in any of his blood. He had. Ripping the slippers off, he threw them against the wall. Barefooted, Brian continued on to Phillip's fallen body, crouching beside him, and whispering in his ear, "Don't give up. Help is coming."

Brian turned to his dad who stood as far away from the body as he could, his shoulders slumped, his chin nearly resting on his chest.

"Dad, Dad, don't just stand there. Do you have a cell phone on you?"

His dad barely moved his head from side to side.

"Hurry, let's go upstairs and find a phone. We have to call the medics. Do you know your way upstairs?"

His dad nodded.

"Then quick, show me."

His father led him back through the open doors to the swimming pool, and then the gym. When they got to the gym, Brian raced ahead of him, taking the stairs two at a time, stumbling several times. He spotted a cell phone on the kitchen counter. Grabbing it, he opened its case, looking helplessly at its face. He yelled, "Dad, do you know how to call EMR?" as his father emerged at the head of the stairs.

"No, I don't. Just dial 911." He sank down on a bar stool next to the counter, suddenly feeling the weight of all that had happened.

Brian punched in 911 as though the keys were resisting him. It rang only once, and then a woman's voice answered: "911. What is your emergency?"

Gasping, Brian answered, "Phillip's been shot."

"And what is the address of this emergency?"

Brian looked confused. "Ah, I don't know where it is. I just know there's a dying man here. He's been shot and he's bleeding." He looked helplessly at his dad. "Wait, maybe my dad can help you." He handed the phone to him. Brian watched him take it heavily in his hand, as though it weighed a hundred pounds.

Next he heard his dad give an address, adding, "There are heavy iron gates that open to the front of the property, but they are locked." There was a hesitation and then he said, "No I can't open them. I entered the property through the woods in back of the house." As though in a dream, Brian remembered the big gates and the woods from that first night.

Another hesitation in his dad's speech, then, "Yes, the property owner's name is Phillip Nottingham."

So Phillip's last name was Nottingham. Like the Sheriff of Nottingham in *Robin Hood*. Brian wondered how his dad knew his name.

His dad's voice again, low and contained. "Yes, I entered the house by the front door. I am not a thief. I shot him in self defense in the act of rescuing my son who was kidnapped from Ohio, and has been here nearly two weeks." A pause, and then, "Good, we'll be looking for the police and the medics within the next ten minutes. We'll be on the front porch. And yes, my gun will be exactly where I left it...on the basement floor. Thank you."

His dad placed the phone face down, on the counter. He looked like a ghost, almost as though the blood Brian saw on the basement floor had been drained out of him, rather than Phillip.

"Dad, you look awful. Are you OK?"

"Yes, I suppose I'll live through this, but..." Brian saw his eyes glisten with tears. "Son, I've been searching for you for so long and...I came here...my only intent was to rescue you."

"Dad, I don't know what to say. All I could think of when I saw the blood and Phillip's body...is that you might have killed him. Please don't let that be the truth."

Brian could tell his dad was as confused as he was. "I don't understand, Brian. Why did Phillip bring you here? Didn't he hurt you? I mean, why did he have to keep you locked up? If he was up to 'no good,' then why are you being so protective of him?"

Brian could already see that his dad, and maybe no one would ever understand how he could care about someone who had kidnapped him.

"It's so hard to explain. I'm not even sure I know myself, but it was sort of like I was the son he never had. Aside from keeping me locked in my room – actually I was working toward privileges in the gym and the pool – he was good to me. He fed me good food he cooked himself, and taught me about things in the world I never knew existed. Like the story of the Taj Mahal, the reason tsunamis happen...oh, a thousand things."

Brian was afraid to look at his dad, and when he did, he saw his father was openly crying. He'd never seen him cry before. His dad rose and tried to visibly shake it off, saying, "The medics and the police will be here shortly. We need to go out on the front porch where they can see us. God, I guess we'll have to raise our arms up in the air, wave a white flag or something. Like we're the criminals. We better get a move on. They should be here within five to ten minutes."

Brian followed his father, going through a series of rooms that he had never seen. The dining room had a crystal chandelier and dark green carpeting that was so soft it felt like his bare feet were sinking into a thick bed of moss. He tread lightly, hoping he didn't leave any traces of blood on Phillip's beautiful carpet. That would upset him. The living room had burnished cherry floorboards, partially covered with several large Oriental rugs. There were brocade sofas and chairs, a huge fireplace, and baby-blue velvet drapes, drawn shut. The walls were covered with tapestries and oil paintings. Lying beside the front door was a large stainless steel shield that seemed out of place, but there was no time to look around or inquire about what Brian saw.

His father flung open the massive front door. Brian recoiled from the radiance of the sun's light. Phillip's story about the men emerging from the cave and being blinded by the light, came to him. He felt himself getting heady with the open air, the greening trees and grass. Breathing in his first breath of fresh air since he had come here, he felt faint. He wobbled, and his dad drew closer, steadying him. Brian looked through the aura of his room at all that had been Phillip, and at the sun's blinding light, actually seeing his father for the first time. Their eyes met, Brian trembled, and said, "I'm sorry Dad. I'm really sorry."

"So am I, son. So am I." Side by side, they stood. Brian felt the solace of his dad's arm around his back, steadying him. Although in ways he'd never felt before, it seemed like he was steadying his dad.

Chapter 21
Owen, Dave and Brian
Saturday

The closer Owen got to where Jane's GPS was guiding him, the louder the sound of the sirens became. Owen knew they were heralding his arrival at the *Wicked One's Palace*. It didn't matter that Phillip must know that he, Owen, was closing in on him, because there was nothing Phillip could do to protect himself from the conquering rays that were emanating from Owen's brain. Owen became so concentrated on directing those rays, that he nearly crashed into a squad car in front of a towering metal gate. He stomped on the brakes and screeched to a halt, just in time to avoid a complete collision, his front fender banging into the side of a Maryland State police car. A uniformed policeman was standing on top of the cruiser, trying to vault the adjoining brick wall, while several others were ramming the lock on an iron gate with giant spears.

Owen leaped out of Jane's car, as the toppled policeman and two other officers dashed toward him, one twisting Owen's arms in back of him, while the second one locked steel handcuffs on his wrists. He fought senselessly, as there was little he could do. Trying to kick them only threw him off-balance, the handcuffs grating into his wrists.

"What the fuck are you doing?" screamed Owen.

"No, it's what the fuck are you doing?" said one of the officers. "There's been a murder here."

Owen continued twisting and screaming, "I know that. I killed Phillip and I've come to rescue the boy that's locked in the basement."

One officer cocked his eyebrows at a second, whispering, "How the hell does he know that?" The third placed his knuckles under Owen's chin, raising it. "Look up at the front porch. See the pair up there? They're father and son. The boy has been rescued by his dad, who claims to have killed Phillip with his gun. Several officers gained entrance through the woods in back, and we're in the process of investigation. We've found the dead guard-dog that the father killed before entering the house, and then, Nottingham's corpse in the basement, where the dad says he shot him with the gun we now have in our possession. How in the world could you have killed him?"

"It was me. I killed him. Shot him before the dad arrived. He was mine. I killed him!"

"This makes no sense," said the first officer. "How do you even know Phillip?"

"He kidnapped me. Turned me into his sex slave. Like he did this kid. Ten years ago. But he moved, and I've been trying to find him, stop him from his evil ways. And I have! Vengeance is mine!" With that Owen let out another banshee scream, turning and trying to bite the officer who was restraining him.

"Grab a hank of his miserable hair, and put him in the car, Kevin."

"Listen, you idiot, you're just making it harder on yourself. If we don't charge you with homicide, like you say we should, then we'll get you on assault and resisting arrest."

"I did kill him. I said I did. You can have me. Just let the boy and his dad go. They didn't do anything."

The policemen ignored Owen, one of them pulling him by the hair toward the Sheriff's car. Owen let out a blood-curdling scream, shouting, "You sons of whores, mother-fucking cretins!"

The youngest officer went to a cruiser, returning with a sock and a roll of duct tape. Another officer grabbed Owen's handcuffed arms from behind, while the third ducked under his fellow officer, getting on his knees in back of Owen. He hugged Owen's legs to his chest, while the one with the sock tried to stuff it in his mouth. Owen clenched his mouth shut. The officer stomped on his foot, and when Owen screamed, he jammed the sock in his mouth, slapping a piece of duct tape over it. "There, that should do it," he said.

"Kevin, take him to the cruiser and stay with him, while Paul and I go up to the house as soon as we break into the gate. See what's what, here. No...wait a minute...as soon as we break open the gate, we need to escort this dude to the porch, where the other suspect is. You can bring him up the driveway in the cruiser. After we complete our search, and shake-down - I estimate that'll be fifteen minutes, give or take five - then we'll be out of here, take all three of these guys into the station. We'll be going to *Metro Transition*. They have the personnel we'll need in order to book the two adults and the boy into the system."

"Do I have to stay...," said Kevin, disappointment swimming behind his unsaid words.

"Don't worry, you'll get your turn. You're still wet behind the ears. If you lack for entertainment, just rip the tape off that Yo-Yo's mouth. Tom started to grin, then shifted gears. "No, on second thought, don't."

Chapter 22
Dave
Saturday

It was all a blur as Dave tried to adjust to the sudden reality that Brian had been rescued, and that he was intact, though not the same Brian he had known less than two weeks ago. And that indeed, Dave himself was a criminal. Before he even had time to process the jarring changes, Dave found himself in the back of a police car, unlike any he'd ever seen. There was no backseat in this one. Instead, there was a plastic slope with its high point where the top of the back seat ought to be, angling down to the floor in back of the front seat. When two policemen grabbed him by the shoulder and thigh, thrusting him into the cruiser, he'd managed to arrive in a somewhat upright position with his back against the plastic slope, making the steel handcuffs dig into his wrists. Contorting his torso to relieve the pressure of the cuffs, his upper body began to slide toward the floor, and soon he found himself helplessly wedged in the vertex of the plastic triangle.

He considered a plea for assistance, but realized the two policemen riding in front could care less about his comfort. Their only job was to transport him to jail. He tried wiggling around to keep the cuffs from cutting into his wrists, but that only made matters worse. Finally he relaxed, finding some relief, remembering that knowing when to fade was a vital technique in the marital arts.

Being captive triggered a boyhood memory of the time he had been accidentally locked in a closet, while playing hide and seek. He remembered how scary it felt to be trapped with no way out. The other kids ran helter-skelter outside, and it was a long time before anyone heard his cries for help. My God, that was like Brian's situation had been. For weeks. Dave felt a swift, awful sinking, as though he were in an elevator that had fallen ten stories.

Yet Brian never expressed relief or gratitude when he was rescued. His main focus had been Phillip's welfare. For the life of him, Dave couldn't understand his son's feelings. He tried to veer away from thinking about it by looking out the window at the moving scenery, about an arm's length above his feet. Hopefully Brian was riding in a cruiser with back seats. At least he would be moving and seeing different things, after being cooped up in that small room for so long.

Dave pictured the room. Without the overwhelming emotions of those few minutes before they'd left the room, he became aware of how luxurious his son's accommodations had been. The whole house was that way. And Brian had said something about earning "gym and pool privileges." Maybe he was treated well, and that had something to do with his feelings of not wanting Phillip to be dead. Maybe he even preferred to be stay there. 'No!' Dave couldn't believe that. It was too shattering.

Up front the two cops were telling each other 'What's-the-difference-between' jokes. The one he heard was about the position '69'. He didn't want to hear the crude punch line, so he interrupted them.

"Where are you taking me?" As though he didn't know.

"We're taking you to the police station to be booked," said the one riding shoot-gun. "It just so happens it's also the state penitentiary." He grinned, thinking it payment for this guy taking the law into his own hands.

"Will my son be taken there too?" Dave asked, trying to keep his tone civil.

The driver said to his companion, "Go easy, Sean. This guy's worried about his son. How do you think you'd feel if it were your Patrick who was kidnapped?"

'Oh, the 'Good cop, Bad cop' scenario,' thought Dave.

Then the driver said to Dave, "In answer to your question, your son will be taken by the squad car he's in, to the same facility. He'll be held there and questioned, separately…just until it's established that he had nothing to do with the murder. Then he'll be released to his mother. I thought I heard them say she's back in Ohio."

"Yes, she is. Will she be able to pick him up at the prison, or will he be taken home?"

"Whatever the system allows. I'm not sure about the judicial part. Seems that she'll most likely come to pick him up. Probably after the arraignment, which usually happens in two, three days."

After their exchange, Dave shut down, watching the buildings diminish and more trees and sky flash by. As the squad car slowed down, he saw the profile of gray, flat buildings. They passed a guardhouse, and then electronically controlled gates, finally reaching the prison itself. It was surrounded by high fences that Dave could see were topped with razor wire. This was not a movie. This was the real thing. He'd seen these fences from a distance, but never this close. It made him feel physically vulnerable, somehow creating the feeling that his muscles were bulging.

Both policemen had to help Dave out of the car, then stand him on his feet. It was humiliating. Inside, he had to stand in front of a white wall while they frisked him again, one officer running his hands around his groin area, as though he could carry a concealed weapon there. Then they took mug-shots, full face and profile. After that came the identifying information about him at the front desk, given by his escort police, making feel even more infantile. Next they told him they were taking him to an interrogation room inside the prison.

On the way through the corridors, Dave witnessed an unanticipated flurry of activities. Armed police officers were everywhere. Walking from office to office, escorting handcuffed prisoners and talking to each other in cop lingo. Some of them, whom he assumed were undercover officers, wore face masks. In the hallway, approaching the interrogation room, he saw an inmate on his knees in an orange jumpsuit, scrubbing the floor with a brush.

Inside the interrogation room, everything turned quiet, as though he was in a soundproof recording studio. At least they'd removed his handcuffs before he'd entered the room. Still, Dave found himself seated rigidly on the edge of his chair, once again not sure of what to expect.

Surprisingly, a woman entered the room to question him. She was a strikingly beautiful, young, black woman, and introduced herself as Keisha Morgan. Dave thought that she was bold to give a supposed criminal her name, although she might have made it up. She sat in a chair directly across from him.

Dave was intimidated by her appearance after receiving such rough treatment from the officers, but listened attentively to her reading of his Miranda warnings. Knowing she was recording his speech, after her recital, he told her that he had already admitted culpability for the murder of Phillip Nottingham on his 911 call, and that he needed to have an attorney appointed, as he could not afford one. Then he signed a waiver of rights, noticing that his hand trembled when he wrote his signature.

As soon as he signed, he said, "I know you're the questioner, but I'd like to begin by asking a couple of questions of my own."

"So long as you're cooperative, I'll answer the questions you have, if I can."

"Thanks. I'll get them out of the way. Actually I have three questions, come to think of it. One is whether or not my son will be held beyond the questioning of the two of us. I am one hundred percent certain he had nothing to do with the murder of Phillip Nottingham." God, he hated to keep saying his proper name. He wanted to call him 'Scumbag.'

"Two is whether or not I am allowed to make one phone call before I am held here. I'd like to call my wife. And three, if I'm jailed until a trial is held, or whatever comes next, whether or not I will be allowed visitors."

"Well-stated, Mr. Brefort. I'll do what I can to answer your questions. To the first, no, your son will not be held after questioning, if it is determined that he is not a suspect. I'm not sure how it will be arranged, but he will be allowed to return home. How soon, I don't know."

"As for your second question, yes, after this, you will be allowed one phone call. And seeing as how you will leave it up to the court to appoint an attorney, your one call can be to your wife, or whatever close relative you wish to call."

"Third, no one can answer your question about visitors until your arraignment, which should be timely. The judge will set the conditions at that time. Does that satisfy your questions?"

"Yes, thank you."

"OK then, let's proceed. I want to remind you that you have been read your Miranda Rights, have signed a waiver, and know our conversation is being recorded." Dave nodded.

"Speak up Mr. Brefort. The machine cannot record body language."

"Yes...to all you just said." Dave was aware of how hard he was trying to be polite and agreeable, knowing that if his interrogator had been a man, his attitude and speech would have been far more negative. 'Maybe that's why they sent in an attractive, positive female,' Dave thought.

"OK, said Keisha, "let's cut to the chase. You've already admitted that you killed Phillip Nottingham, and from all that we know, so far it appears that your son was kidnapped and held captive by the same said man. The biggest question that remains is whether or not you went to rescue your son with the intent of killing Phillip."

'Wait a minute.' The attractive questioner was going beyond what he'd assumed her job was. But that didn't change his response. "Absolutely not. I had no intention of killing Phillip Nottingham."

"There are two contradictory facts that weigh against that, Mr. Brefort. One, that you went there armed with a pistol, and two, that you did not call the police to intervene when you apparently suspected your son was being held captive there."

Dave thought a minute before answering. "I too will 'cut to the chase.' I went to Nottingham's to find out beyond a shadow of a doubt whether my son was being held captive there. There were many previous clues that he was the kidnapper, including a description of his car and his appearance on that April day, April first, when he picked my son up on a country road near our home in Ohio. He and his car were seen and described by a neighbor. The police work was very slow, and so understandably..."

Dave looked up from his folded hands. "Do you have any children, Miss Morgan?" He had decided 'Miss' was the most polite way to address her, since she wore no ring on her wedding finger. And she didn't correct him.

"No, I don't Mr. Brefort. But that is irrelevant."

"Not in my book, it's not. Unless you're a parent, I can't expect that you would appreciate how deep the bond is that drives a parent to try and rescue his child when the child's life is endangered."

"Yes, I understand that is the case from many previous examples, but go on with your response to the questions asked."

'Just the facts,' thought Dave. 'That's all she wants to hear. So I best stick to them.' "The police weren't coming up with anything to go on, so after twenty-four hours, I decided to..."

"Twenty-four hours, Mr. Brefort? How did you expect police results in that short of a time? Your appearance here demonstrates that it took you well over a week to come up with Mr. Nottingham's identity and location."

"That's not the point. Did you know that over forty percent of missing children are killed within the first hour of their abduction?" 'Brunhilde was good for something, after all.'

"Yes, I'm aware of that statistic. But I would hope that you understand that our legal system is in place so we don't resort to 'an eye for an eye' type of justice."

"I repeat, Ms. Morgan, I was not seeking retribution. I was seeking my son, who I believed was alive and being held captive in Nottingham's house. Which indeed, he was."

"So we're back to where we started. Then why would you come armed with a gun?"

"First of all, I drove by his residence on Argyle several times and knew that he had a huge attack dog. And I also knew he had a brick wall and locked iron gates along the front and sides of his property, so that I needed to gain access to it from the woods in back of his house. I was not attempting to 'break and enter.' I wanted to get to his front door. And I was afraid the dog was on the grounds, so I brought the gun to protect myself, should I be attacked. As a matter of fact, that is what happened when I went to the door. As I'm sure your records show."

"So they do. At least that you shot the dog on the front porch. You don't appear to have any wounds or scratches. Go on."

'If she only knew how hard it is to chronologically reconstruct the events that led up to this interrogation.' His mind was abuzz with anxieties, anger and confusion. The only thing he knew for certain was that he needed to concentrate and keep the facts straight. It was being recorded and he didn't want to give contradictory information in future questionings. He was sure there would be more. This was just the beginning.

"First of all, I drove by the residence on Argyle several times and knew that he had a huge black attack dog. And I..."

"Hold on, Mr. Brefort. How did you know where Mr. Nottingham resided?"

"I was given his name and address as a potential source of information by Dave Hopkins, the city planner who was acting as my host and trying to supply resources. He told me that Nottingham was the head of a grass-roots organization called KOCS, which I believe stood for *Keep Our Children Safe*. The irony didn't escape me."

He glanced up at Keisha's face and once again realized it was in his best interest to stick to the facts. "So since I knew about the brick walls and locked iron gates, I investigated, and found I could only enter from the woods at the back of the property. I was not attempting to 'break and enter.' I wanted to get to his front door. And since I was afraid that the dog was on the grounds, I took my gun to protect myself, should I be attacked. I have a permit for the handgun. And as you know, I shot and killed the dog." He hesitated, wondering how much she wanted to know. He was aware that he was repeating himself. It was almost as though he had to convince himself that he didn't go there with the intent to kill.

"Please continue."

"So even though I had an appointment with Mr. Nottingham for next Tuesday – arranged by Mr. Hopkins – I didn't want to wait that long because, through Hopkins setting up the 'interview,' we'll call it, the kidnapper knew I was Brian's father, just from my surname, which is rather unusual. My reasoning was that if the man was crazy enough to kidnap and keep a boy in a hidden room, he's crazy enough to kill him and destroy the evidence, so he doesn't get caught with 'the goods.' I felt I had to take action. If I had called the police and told them about what I was nearly certain of, they'd probably have locked me up as a 'looney.' Or they might have told Nottingham without really investigating first, so that again, seeking outside help only increased the chances of him destroying the evidence. The evidence being my son, keep in mind."

Ms. Morgan didn't respond, so Dave went on. "I'm well aware of the respect Mr. Nottingham has...had...in the community through his organization. A 'wolf in sheep's clothing' as the saying goes. Always the best place for psychos to hide."

Dave was immediately sorry he'd made that remark. It was his opinion, not the facts. And it was now recorded. "That's about all I have to say on the matter."

"That's about all I have to cover," she said, picking up the papers she needed, indicating that the interview was over. Making a swift turn on her black patten leather heels at the door, she said, "Thank you, Mr. Brefort. Please wait here. I'll ask the Chief if you can make your phone call home, now."

"Thanks," he said, folding his hands again on the cool Formica surface of what he now thought of as 'The Inquisition Table.' After the tension of the interview, he went limp with waiting, dropping his head to the table. He quickly lifted it when he smelled the caustic odor of bleach. The Formica was swabbed down after each interview, no doubt, to rid the room of the germs the 'defectives' might leave behind.

Dave felt a ball of bitterness in his stomach, rising to his throat. The law now viewed him as the criminal, rather than the wronged. It felt like they were protecting that son-of-a-bitch, Nottingham. Or at least, his reputation.

Prayers were in order, but somehow Dave couldn't bring himself to ask for guidance. This was no place for God. The meaning of 'God-forsaken' came to mind. It described exactly how he had felt since he was transported to this God-forsaken place.

He dropped to the floor and did some push-ups, then rose and did some 'jumping jacks.' He needed something vigorous to clear the smog from his brain. Soon he would be talking to Peggy, and he must keep it succinct and optimistic. He was thinking of how to phrase the most important information he needed to convey, when Keisha again entered the room, this time with an old rotary phone in her hand, which she plugged into a jack. She positioned the phone in front of him. Alongside it, she placed a timer. As she came close to Dave, the musky odor of her perfume filled the air. In spite of the morass of heavy issues Dave had on his plate, he suddenly and unexpectedly had an erotic image of a voluptuous Keisha lying naked on a bed, her brown skin glowing as she beckoned him toward her. He felt an instant stab of shame, and glanced at his lap to see if his partial erection was visible.

Keisha hovered over him a few more seconds, telling him he had only five minutes to talk, that she would dial the number, that his conversation would be listened to, and she would set the timer as soon as he connected with his party.

She turned the phone toward her and dialed the number Dave gave her, waiting a few seconds, and then saying, "Mrs. Brefort, this is Keisha Morgan, Maryland State Correctional Officer, placing a call on behalf of your husband, Dave Brefort." A pause, and then, "Yes, I have him with me. Here he is..."

'My God, what an introduction,' thought Dave. 'What can I say to reassure her that everything is alright, even though it isn't.'

"Peg...I'm here at the jail, and Brian is safely here too. He can't talk to you right away, but he will as soon as they allow him. He's absolutely fine." That was the biggest lie Dave had ever uttered. "And darling" - 'no,' he told himself, 'this is not the place for endearing phrases'... "even though these circumstances are quite extreme, I have only five minutes to talk to you. There's a timer in front of me, and I will tell you when we are down to one minute."

"My God, Dave," Peggy said. "I don't know what to say, what to ask. I had no idea. Except I'm so thankful the two of you are okay. Why don't you do the talking and if I have a question, I'll interrupt."

That was his sweet, sensible Peg. 'God, how I miss her. How could I have had a sexual thought about another woman?'

"This is awful hard to say in five minutes, so I'll have to be…stark. I'm here because I went to the kidnapper's house to rescue Brian. When the front door opened, on command, a huge attack dog jumped at me. I was prepared for that possibility, so I shot and killed him." 'God, I'm getting so tired of repeating the whole awful mess, but I have to keep to the same account of things, because once again, I'm being recorded.'

"Then I turned the gun on the kidnapper so that he would lead me to the hidden room where he'd kept Brian all this time… in his basement. I figured all this out from things that Dave Hopkins told me about the man and his house. And I didn't call the police because I was afraid they'd tip off the guy – his name is Phillip. He led me to a secret room, and as we were about to go into this room, where he kept Brian, he reached for a hidden gun, to shoot me. So I shot him first. I killed him. After I made sure Brian was okay, we called the police and they brought us here for questioning. And… and…what else would you like to know? 'Like to know….what a strange way of putting it.'

"Oh, darling, that the two of you are okay, is about all I can take in. Praise the Lord."

'God, I'm glad to hear her give homage to our Creator.' Maybe she would finally leave her skepticism behind, as he was becoming more skeptical. It seemed like anytime they were in crisis, they seemed to shift roles. Eventually they would come into balance. Maybe that was the ultimate reason for their realignments.

Dave suddenly remembered her surgery. "Are you OK, Peg? How are you healing?"

"I'm fine. Don't give it a second thought. Listen, can Lauren and I leave immediately and come to you? Will they hold you much longer? What about Brian?"

"I think they'll probably keep me here until my arraignment. I'll probably plead 'guilty' to the murder on the grounds of self-defense. Then I think they'll assign me a Public Defender. I don't know when any of this will happen."

Dave was surprised that he knew as much as he did about procedures no one had specifically informed him about. That is, no one but the crime shows he watched on TV, never guessing he would meet circumstances calling on that information. "They should release Brian as soon as they finish questioning him. He's in a separate room. I don't know if they'll let him call you."

Now he felt the black pit of his lack of knowledge. "Peg...I don't know much of anything yet. I don't know how often I can contact you, or anything. Wait, I have an idea. I think the best thing for you to do is to keep in contact with Dave and Shirley Hopkins. Anyway, you have their number. I'm sure they'll stay on top of the information as it becomes available."

He hoped that was true. He didn't think Hopkins would desert him in his hour of need, because he hadn't heeded his warnings.

"What about bail, Dave? Can't you be released on bail?"

"I'm not sure. I do know I've committed a felony, so bail will probably be set really high, if at all. We wouldn't be able to afford it, and I don't dare ask Hopkins for another thing. He's already done more than his share. He and Shirley."

'Shirley again. Yes, she counted.'

"What about asking them to recommend a good lawyer? Do you think we can trust in a 'pig in a poke' Public Defender?"

"I'm afraid we'll have to, Peg. Listen, time's running out. Let me assure you that aside from this awful mess we find ourselves in, Brian and I are fine…physically. Neither of us were injured." He recalled the time on the floor of the police car. "And Brian looks healthy. Apparently he was well fed, even though he was locked in a room the whole time. The thing that confuses me is that he seems grief-stricken over his kidnapper being killed. Maybe the guy actually treated him well. I don't know. It doesn't make any sense to me."

"He's probably in shock, Dave. Particularly since he knows that you're going to be tried for murder. I know it scares the hell out of me."

"Of course… that makes sense. But I'm sure I'll be exonerated. It's just a matter of time. And our time's running…" Dave heard the phone go dead, followed a second later by the timer's ding. It made a hollow sound in his head. It was the most deafening silence Dave had ever experienced. He hung up the receiver and laid his head back down on the table. He couldn't even smell the awful odor anymore. When Keisha entered the room to retrieve the phone, he didn't even look up.

Chapter 23
Owen
Saturday

Owen had gone to jail in a police cruiser before, but this time he was sliding down the crest of the bath salts, which made it far more interesting. It was like having his private peep show on the world.

Along with surfing a wave of triumph about the fact that *The Lizard* was dead. And he had killed him. The father of the kidnapped boy had simply wounded Phillip. *The Lizard* was still moving when Owen's magic rays finished him off.

Owen wiggled on the plastic slope to ease the pinch of the handcuffs. It occurred to him that Jane might never see her car again, but she wouldn't mind sacrificing it for the death of *The Lizard*. She wanted to exorcise him from Owen's mind, and it was done. She'd be proud of him. Maybe even visit him in prison. Bring him some dope. Yeah, she liked to fulfill other's needs. He'd let her know. And he wouldn't let the police know that she was a co-conspirator in the crime. He certainly wouldn't tell them that she'd left him the GPS directions to Phillip's house. He'd say that he broken into her apartment and stolen her car keys. Maybe they'd even see to it that the car was returned.

In the midst of his exhilaration it struck him that he'd feel bad if Jane lost her car because of him, but that the same weights and measures didn't apply to his killing Phillip. That was because Jane was a good person, and *The Lizard* was evil. Owen had done the world a service by ridding it of Phillip. No more tormented boys. This boy would not land on the street like Owen had. The reason he knew it would be different, was that the boy's father had rescued him.

Owen tried thinking about his father. The only thing he remembered was the big snowstorm the day his father had left home. His dad had made huge footprints in the snow going down the front walk. Owen had sat by the window all day and watched the hollow imprints slowly fill up with snowflakes, until there was no longer any trace of them. From that day on Owen thought of his father as *Big Foot,* the hairy monster that was said to inhabit the mountains of the Pacific Northwest. There had been sightings of his footprints that measured as long as two feet. He wondered if his dad was still alive, and if so, if they'd ever catch him.

"You sure have quieted down," said Kevin, the rookie patrolman driving the squad car. He couldn't see Owen in his rear view mirror, but he could talk to him through the heavy wire screen between them.

"Nothing left to say," said Owen. "I've got a movie going on inside."

"Yeah, it must be rough to come up with anything after you've killed a guy. If it really was you who killed him." Kevin was hoping to get more information out of this kook than the others had, so he could bring him in with something to report and win his colleagues respect.

The salts bubbled up and exploded. "It was me. Fuckin' me who did it."

"OK, if you say so. I just don't understand why you'd take the blame when the father said he did it. I heard him say so. You don't have to take the rap. The dad will get off real easy, because it was self-defense."

"Yeah, well I want him free to go home with his son. I don't have anyone to go home to. In fact, I don't have a home. Prison sounds just fine to me. Three squares, a warm bed, and a pot to piss in."

"Well, if that's the way you want it. It's just hard for me to imagine giving up my freedom for some person I don't even know."

"I gave up my freedom a long time ago. Prison will make the path of no escape simpler. Kind of like Buddhist monks meditating in a cave. Only they don't have drugs in their caves. I'll score some. Make some connections. Then I'll be set for the rest of my life."

"I hope it works out for you. You know I'm not supposed to be talking to you about this shit. It's just that I feel bad about putting that sock in your mouth. But I have to do what my supers tell me. I'm the rookie."

"I know that. Just so you know – it wasn't putting the sock in my mouth, it was ripping the duct tape off that was the hard part."

"I'm sorry. I'm really sorry. That must have been bad."

"No, don't go doubting your line of work. Some things choose you, rather than the other way around. You look like the straight and narrow is good for you. As for me, I'm glad I'm an outlaw. Hey, isn't that the Big Pen comin' up?"

"Yeah, that's it. It's a pretty dismal looking place, isn't it?"

"Not at all. It looks like 'Home Sweet Home' to me. It's all in how you think of it."

Chapter 24
Jane
Saturday

Jane awoke from her 'catnap,' removing her earplugs. As soon as she entered the kitchen, she knew that Owen had followed her flagrant trail of clues. Her journal was open to Phillip's address, the city map still laid out on the table, and her car keys gone. She looked out the window, and yes, her car was gone too.

'Good God! What had she been thinking?' Of course he would follow through on any lead that took him to Phillip. Was this her 'planned protective intervention,' instead of going to the 'rescue manual' at the Shelter, as Patrice had suggested. Clearly she was losing her mind, as well as deceiving her best friend. For what? So Owen could finally confront his abuser and save the boy? What a high-stakes gamble. The more likely outcome was that Owen would be killed by Phillip. Along with the evidence, the boy. Danny was right about going too far out on a limb.

And now she had no way of knowing what the immediate outcome was. She had figured he'd be back later to return the car, and yes, she'd checked, and his hash was still here. But if he'd taken any action at Phillip's home, he'd undoubtedly be arrested.

'Hold on. The five o'clock news is coming up.' Nottingham was a prominent citizen, and if there had been anything like a B & E, it would probably make the news. Jane had made certain Owen didn't possess a gun before she'd left the clues, and since the hash was still here, he undoubtedly didn't have the means to acquire one. Unless he'd connected with a buddy who had one, or he stole one. Jane knew that wasn't beyond his field of endeavor, given all the other means she'd supplied him. If there was any crime, she certainly would be named as an accomplice. Whatever demon had possessed her, was one she'd never encountered before.

Jane turned on her old TV, fumbling with the dials and the 'rabbit-car' antennae, trying to clear up the reception. She really needed to get a flat screen TV and cable, but it was low on her list of buying priorities. Except for moments like this. All she could hear was the end of the weather report and how little precipitation they'd had in the past year, and if it didn't increase, the farmers were afraid it would drastically reduce crop yields, that would be passed on to the consumers in the form of higher prices. 'Yes, it was hard being at the end of a food chain that was at the mercy of the whims of nature. But then again, if that wasn't her position, she'd probably become some larger animal's dinner.'

Jane's attention lingered on the screen, with background awareness that she was distracting herself from her real worries, until there was a special news flash. A familiar reporter came on expressing more than his usual amount of excitement about a prominent Baltimore man who was found dead from gunshot wounds, in his home. His name had not yet been released until the next of kin was notified, but there was some video footage of the police and medics milling about, around Dave Brefort and a younger-looking version of him. And yes, she was relieved to see Owen there too. All three of them were handcuffed. They stood on a wide Victorian-looking front porch with two-story columns and huge stone urns topping its flight of stairs. The reporter announced that the two unrelated suspects had both confessed to the shooting. They were being held in custody, along with the adolescent boy who was alleged to have been kept prisoner in the murdered man's house for an unknown period of time.

It was back to the weather with updated versions of the news story, as it unwound. Her brain in a whirl, Jane thought that the first thing she needed to do was call into the Woman's Shelter and let them know she couldn't make it to work this evening because her car had been stolen. 'No...this is Saturday, my day off.' My thinking is so scattered. 'What to do?'

She had no car to begin to investigate the chain of events. The police had undoubtedly impounded her car since Owen drove it there, so that was the logical place to begin - contact the police. In the process, perhaps she could gain access to Owen and talk to him. She would say she'd had contact with him as a social worker. And that she knew he had a sister, and she, Jane, would search for her, possibly helping to shed some light on matters, if indeed Owen had shot Phillip Nottingham. Strange as it seemed, given the depths of his psychotic hatred of *The Lizard,* Jane had more and more doubt of what she had formerly feared.

Jane wouldn't tell them that Owen had once been kidnapped by Phillip himself, unless it was already known through Owen. He probably was shouting that from the rooftops. He had no sense of discretion or self-protection. Clearly she needed to get Tina's full name from Owen, and try to find her. That would be the lynch-pin to helping Owen. And she was responsible for helping him, much as she was responsible for his appearance at the scene of the murder.

Flipping open her cell phone, Jane looked at the blank screen, not certain where to start with her search. 'Wait...a text message is coming in.' She opened it to read: Proverbs 27.6: "Wounds from a friend can be trusted, but an enemy multiplies kisses." Do your work. I understand, Patrice.

Jane's heart sank with the knowledge that her dear friend recognized her betrayal of trust, but just as quickly, it bobbed to the surface with Patrice's message of forgiveness. Just as she had never lied to Patrice before, she had never known her friend to quote the Bible. Clearly these were unprecedented times for everyone involved.

Chapter 25
Brian
Saturday

"What do you mean, I have to be examined by a doctor for sexual abuse? I told you he never touched me that way. Just the massage and stuff like that," Brian said, finding himself getting angrier and angrier at the two detectives questioning him.

The one with the spiked hair did most of the talking. The other one sat back and played with a key ring he held in his right hand. That irritated Brian too. Along with the fact that he'd been taken to the youth correctional facility, while his dad was in the prison. Even though he blamed his dad for killing Phillip, he didn't like being separated from him so soon after they'd just seen each other for the first time in weeks. He felt at the mercy of the system he was in, and once again, helpless. When Phillip first kidnapped him he'd felt that way, although he'd come to see he really wasn't a victim. As Phillip frequently reminded him, he was the "co-creator" of his own destiny. For if he cooperated and met his goals, he would earn more privileges and increasing freedom.

He wasn't sure what was going on with him. He figured he should be happy that his dad rescued him, and soon he would be free to go home. Isn't that what he'd wished for? It wasn't just that Phillip was dead, and his dad was being held for his murder, although god knows that was more than enough for one day. It was his nerves. They were all standing up straight. It felt like someone was combing them in the wrong direction with a wire brush.

The spiked-hair guy spoke up. "Nevertheless, you'll need to be examined. In fact that will take place this afternoon, soon after this interview. We have a highly qualified MD, who just so happens to be here today, making rounds. He'll give you a general physical, a rectal exam, and take some blood, see just what concoctions this Phillip put in your body. That'll save your parents the expense of paying for it privately. This one's on the state."

"Don't I have any rights here?" Can't I refuse to have the...rectal part."

"No, not really. Sorry Brian, but you're a minor. Your dad has to sign for it, and I'm sure he will, if he hasn't already. It's part of the evidence that will be needed for this case. And your welfare. Who knows, you might have contracted AIDS from your guy, Phillip."

Brian rose from his examining chair, thrusting his chest and chin forward. "Fuck you guys. Just plain fuck you! You never knew Phillip. He was the cleanest guy in the world. He even washed his hands before and after he brought me my meals. And he didn't touch me that way. How many times do I have to tell you that!"

"Take it easy, Brian," said the key ring guy. He put both of his hands on Brian's shoulders and gently pushed him down into a seated position again. For a second, Brian felt like turning his head toward the guy's hand and biting him. He wanted to draw blood.

"You know what I think's wrong with you?" the bristle-haired guy ventured.

"No, tell me, please do," said Brian. "I suppose you have a psychology degree.."

"No, no degrees, but plenty of experience. And what I'm seeing is a kid who's strung out on drugs. Going through withdrawal, actually. You told us Phillip frequently gave you pills, and you didn't know what they were. Just that they made you feel drowsy sometimes, giddy, other times. 'Giddy-up' is probably more like it. And you said that happened every day. More than once a day. Do you remember when the last time was that he gave you a 'so-called pill?'"

Maybe the guy had something there. The last time Brian remembered his body feeling this way was the day Phillip fed him breakfast early and was gone all day. Probably into the night, although Brian had no way to calculate that. Just that it was a long time, and that he felt like he did now. Brian opened his mouth to say something, although he hated to give this creep any credit. It trickled out slowly. "Maybe you're right. I think it's been since before dinner yesterday. Since I've had any of my medicine."

"Medicine," the key ring guy scoffed. "Well, the doctor will take some blood and a urine sample to find out what kind of 'medicine' you've been receiving from your good friend. Don't you get it? Anything we find that's a wrongdoing on the part of your 'friend,' will be on the positive side of the ledger for your dad's case."

"Hey, let up on the poor kid, Frank. He's been through a lot in the past few weeks. Plus today for a capper. Keep in mind he's been a prisoner. No choice. No freedom."

"Sure, sounds like he's had it almost as tough as the kids in Auswitz. Difference being that their showers weren't wet."

There was a rap on the door and Frank said, "Come in."

A gray-haired woman poked her head around the door frame, saying, The doctor's ready for the exam. He'll see him in room 12."

"OK, we're on our way," said the spiked-hair guy. He waved his hand at Brian, signaling him to rise and follow him. Brian didn't rise immediately and he said, "Do we need to put the handcuffs back on you?"

"No," said Brian, instantly rising. He hated those things. He followed him down the hall, scuffing his feet, concentrating on every stride his gray Pumas made, now that he was shod. He didn't want to look to the right or left, because every sight and sound made the hair rise along the nape of his neck. Even his hair follicles grated on his nerves.

They entered the doctor's office by a back entrance, taking them directly to an exam room. Frank knocked on a door that was opened by a man in a white coat with a stethoscope dangling from his neck, like some bizarre necklace. Brian's doctor always took his out of a drawer. This doctor looked directly at Brian, then stepped forward to shake his hand.

"Hi. You must be Brian Brefort. Sorry for the circumstances of our meeting, but I am Dr. Forsythe."

Brian dipped his head in recognition. Dr. Forsythe dismissed the interrogators, and motioned Brian toward the examining table. In spite of the circumstances and the clinical aspects of the room, Brian didn't feel intimidated by the doctor. His manner was casual as he said, "Here, sit up there, and we'll begin your exam. You'll find it routine. I'm sure you've had a number of physicals over the past few years. Probably sports physicals most recently. Am I right?"

Again, Brian nodded.

"Umh, let me guess. Track and field, right?"

"You're right," said Brian. "How could you tell?"

"Primarily your lean build and estimated BMI. You look pretty darn good for a young man who's been held indoors for weeks. How did you manage that?"

"Well, I'd run in place in the corner of the room, do push-ups on the floor, things like that."

"Good for you. Whenever we find ourselves in adverse conditions, it's essential to try and maintain our body health. Even in state prisons, the inmates have access to the outdoors and opportunities to exercise away from their cells."

"Yeah, I was close to earning privileges to Phillip's gym and the swimming pool," Brian was surprised to hear himself say.

"I see. What did you have to do to earn them?" At the same time that he was talking to him, the doctor was examining Brian's eyes, ears, mouth, and then pressing and rubbing on sections of his upper body. Brian scarcely noticed because he kept talking to him like he used to talk to Phillip when he was being massaged.

"Not much, really. Just be polite, and learn my lessons. Eat the foods he fixed for me. He was a great cook." Brian's small Adam's apple bobbed as he swallowed hard, noticing that he was already talking about Phillip in the past tense.

"Yes, you certainly don't look undernourished," Dr. Forsythe said as he listened to Brian's heart and lungs. "What kinds of lessons did you have to learn?"

"Oh, a lot of things about history, geography, art, that kind of stuff. It was more than I learned in a year of middle school." Brian blanched as he thought about the lesson he didn't read. The one about the two cowboys.

"I see, and did he test you on it?"

"Kind of. We always talked about it."

The doctor stood back, returning the stethoscope to its dangling position. "Well, the major part of the exam is over. And I must say, you're in excellent health. Ready to get back into running when you get home?"

"Yeah, I guess so. I've missed out on some of the conditioning, but I think I can make it up. When do I get to go home?"

"I'm afraid that's not up to me. But I suspect it won't be

too long. As for now Brian, there's still a part of the testing left. A nurse will come to draw some blood samples, and you'll have to give us a urine sample. Have you gone to the bathroom lately?"

"Not for a while."

"Good. In the meantime, there's only one small part of my physical exam left. When I leave the room, you need to take off your clothes from the waist down, and put on a hospital gown. Leave it open in the back. I have to do a rectal exam. It's required."

"But..."

"No 'buts' about it," said Dr. Forsythe. "And no pun intended." He smiled. "Don't worry about it Brian. I'll be gentle and it will be over in a minute or two." He left the room.

Brian took off his clothes and put on the ridiculous gown as though he were in a trance. He hadn't even tied the closures in the back, when the nurse came in. He sat down on the exam table, keeping his back turned away from her.

"OK, here to draw some blood. You'll need to sit in that chair over there," she indicated a chair that reminded him of study hall chairs, with an extended arm section for writing, but narrower. Brian transferred to the chair, clutching the back of his gown as he moved.

"OK now, make a fist. Clench it real hard. That's a boy." She smacked the inside of his wrist sharply with her three middle fingers. "Hmm, good veins. A small stick, and then I only need three vials of blood."

Brian watched, fascinated, as rich, red blood filled the tubes. It had been a long time since he'd seen any evidence of what lie inside his body. Except for pee and poop, but those were things that his body needed to get rid of, whereas this was a vital fluid that made his body run.

"Hey, hit a gusher," said the nurse. "You might have broken a speed record," she said, taking off the last tube and tapping the cap on it. She briskly extracted the needle from his arm, slapped a band-aid on it, and exited with her wire carrier of vials. As soon as the door closed behind her, it opened again, and the doctor reappeared.

"Brian, I need you to get up on the examining table. Just sitting this time."

Brian stood up from the chair and crossed to the table, again, clutching his untied gown shut.

"Son, I can see all this questioning, sticking and probing has been hard on you, so I'm going to give you something that will help you relax. It's just a sedative, but I'm going to give it to you intravenously so it will act quickly. All you need to do is hold out your right arm, open and close your fist a couple of times, and leave the rest up to me."

The doctor had his back toward Brian and after several minutes, he turned around, a hypodermic needle in his hand. His stick was even easier than the nurse's, and soon Brian felt warmth radiate throughout his body.

"OK now?" the doctor said, and Brian nodded. "This is a simple procedure. I'll have you lie on your side, and I'm going to insert a small instrument in your rectum to examine it. It's called an endoscope, and it won't hurt as long as you relax and don't move around. It's got a light in a long flexible tube, and I look through it and examine the inner tissue to see if there are any injuries, bleeding, things of that sort. Got it?"

Brian suddenly thought about the blood in his stool, and how Phillip assured him all would be well. "Yes, but I..."

"No arguments, Brian. This has to be done. Tell me this – did you empty your bowels during the night, or before you arrived here this morning?"

"Yes," said Brian.

"OK, that's good to know." Brian heard the snap of the doctor's latex gloves, the oily feeling of something being rubbed in, a parting of his cheeks, and then the slow insertion of something in his anus. It felt like a snake slithering up him, but the snake didn't bite. He felt the instrument being withdrawn, which made him feel like he needed to go to the bathroom, but he checked the impulse, and soon found himself sitting up, facing Dr. Forsythe.

"Well, Brian, contrary to your recollections, or lack of them, your anal canal was penetrated sometime within the last twenty-four hours. There are signs of recent penetration and injured tissue, but I'll be unable to procure a semen sample because of the time lag, and the fact that you evacuated your bowels this morning."

"I don't understand. Phillip never did anything like that to me. It must have been that thing you put up me that did it."

"Don't argue with me, son. It's not the instrument. All that does is examine the damage done. Now get your street clothes back on, and come out whenever you're done. I've finished my part. Good luck with whatever comes next," the doctor said, as he exited the examining room.

Brian sat on the exam table for a few minutes, dazed and disoriented. It was all too much. He'd awakened this morning in familiar surroundings, expecting to eat his breakfast, when he heard the shots, then his dad entered his room, Phillip lay dead on the basement floor, the police arrested him, handcuffed him, brought him to prison, the detectives had questioned him, brought him to the doctor who examined him.

'No, he just couldn't make sense of it all. It was like that artist's school Phillip had taught him about. Yes, that explained it. He was caught in the middle of a *surreal* picture that was being painted around him. None of this was really happening.'

Chapter 26
Dave
Saturday

Dave was behind bars. And even though he'd taken matters in his own hands, shot and killed his son's kidnapper, somehow he'd never expected this. He came from a middle-class, Christian, law-abiding family. Hell, he'd never even had a parking ticket before. His only previous encounter with prison had been in high school, when the Preacher's Choir was bussed once a month on Sunday afternoons, to sing hymns to the inmates. The choirmaster had always counted on Dave's deep voice to carry the altos, since many of the other boys' voices hadn't changed pitch yet, and they still sang in the girl's section.

They'd sung in the prison chapel where a carved wooden crucifix hung to the left of them, while on their right side, there'd been a stained glass window that became a prism when the sun shone through it. It had always been an inspirational event, and Dave had felt an outpouring of love toward the miserable souls they'd sung to.

There was nothing inspirational about his jail cell. Just cold hard steel everywhere he turned. His house was a cell that was smaller than their family bathroom, the one everyone complained about because the tub took up half the floor space. But this was his bathroom, his bedroom, his everything. And everything was hard and cold and metal. The bars clanged whenever a door was opened, or a jailer's key raked them. His bed was a steel slab anchored to the wall, covered by a two-inch lumpy mattress. Even his quarter-size sink, and his toilet with no lid. Everything was metal. He wondered who the contractor was, and how they'd bid on it. He must have made a fortune.

'Oh, hell, there were so many units, they'd probably been produced on an assembly line. The Feds never gave small businessmen any contracts. They just incarcerated them for doing the work the police should have done. My god, I'm getting cynical.' Switching sides with Peggy once again.

Dave sat on the edge of his bed, his elbows propped on his knees. Their bony knobs dug into his skin. He concentrated on the discomfort, because it helped him realize that he was still alive. Everything else in the universe was either gone or disappearing, as though it was being sucked into a black hole. When he was taken to his cell, he'd been told that Brian would be going to a youth correctional facility, and that Peggy and Lauren would be coming to pick up Brian, but he had no idea when, or if he'd be allowed to see them. Having lost his normally acute sense of time, Dave sat on his bed for what could have been minutes, or hours, until a guard called in a gruff voice, "Hey, it's supper-time. Come and get your grub."

Looking up, Dave saw that a formerly solid steel section of his cell door opened, then slid down and forward to make a horizontal slab for a food tray. He stood, his legs from the knees down, partially numb from lack of circulation, making him shuffle to the door like an old man.

"Hey, you hurt, or somethin'?"

"No," said Dave. "I'm fine. Just stiff."

"Say, aren't you the guy that's been brought in for shooting your son's kidnapper? It's all over TV."

"Yes," said Dave. "That's me. I've done a lot of other things in my life, but I s'pose that's the one I'll be remembered for."

"Hell, I don't blame you. I'd done the same thing. Except you did it to a BMAB – *Big Man Around Baltimore*. And the law in these parts don't go for vigilantes. But at least you picked a good night to get here. It's our primo meal. Crispy fired chicken, just like *KFC*. Even some mashed potatoes and gravy, applesauce to boot. There's a plastic spoon for the gloopy stuff. No metal utensils allowed. But you can pick your chicken up with your fingers. My mother taught me that. She said Emily Post says so. Just so's you keep your pinkie cocked like this." The guard demonstrated, his little finger raised in the air, guffawing at his imitation of etiquette.

Apparently it amused him to have a new prisoner. Dave could almost understand. It must be a pretty crummy job, pushing one to look for diversions. On the other hand, why would anyone ever apply for such miserable work? He couldn't help but think that if the guard had a family to return to, they must be embarrassed when people asked what their father did. And wouldn't there be a stale prison odor about him as he embraced his wife, when he arrived home? Maybe he was a bachelor.

Good lord, why was he bothering to think of such pitiful things. Probably because he felt helpless and hopeless. Even the chicken didn't help, although it was the first solid food he'd seen since last night. But it was greasy, the potatoes were lumpy, and the gravy was a thin grayish-brown. He didn't touch the food, thinking of last night's meal at Dave and Shirley's, and of Peggy's delicious fried chicken, baked after frying, in order to evaporate the grease. Thoughts of good food and the dinner table made him sink even further into an abyss of loneliness.

'If only I'd listened to Hopkins about going to Phillip's. If only…if only, if only. No, I did the right thing. If I hadn't acted as quickly as I did, Brian wouldn't be in this safe place. Strange to think of incarceration in this light, but actually Brian was safe for the first time since he'd left home. And he wouldn't be thrown in with adult criminals, just wayward youth.' With that dark, though comforting thought, Dave put his tray back on the metal slab, and the guard appeared like the genie in the lamp.

"Hey, buddy, you barely touched your home-cooked meal. Guess you're one of those who don't like good meat when you see it. A veggie-tarian, huh? Or maybe our four star accommodations don't suit you, huh?" He grabbed the chicken and took a huge bite of it, grease sluicing off his chin. As he held the chicken, he raised his little finger, waggling it at Dave. "See you tomorrow," he said.

Dave knew the guard shouldn't be acting in such an offensive manner, but what was he going to do, report him to the warden? He retreated to his bed, feeling a strange need for privacy, not even taking off his Levis. He punched the pillow, in an attempt to plump it, pulling up the lone scratchy blanket, barely saying a silent prayer for his family before he surrendered to a state of exhaustion.

Sunday, April 14

Dave awoke the next morning to a different guard, who didn't make small talk. He just grunted as he pushed the morning food tray through the steel contraption. Dave threw back his blanket, surprised to see that he was in the exact position he'd fallen asleep in, and that he'd never risen to use the toilet. That was a first. But then so was everything else he'd done in the past two days. As soon as the guard passed his cell, he rose, and turning his back, used the toilet. It had a floor pedal to flush it. He felt himself fascinated by the silvery whirlpool that circled the bowl, feeling as though he was being sucked out of his cell into the unknown ether beyond.

For a moment, he felt a sense of freedom. Brian was safe and would soon be returning home with Peggy and Lauren. It wasn't too late for Brian to get back into the swing of things before the school year ended, which come to think of it would be in a little more than a month. And given the circumstances, they would probably waive a lot of the schoolwork Brian had missed, pass him on with his class, and maybe have him make up some of it over the summer. Then, once his son was freed from being held in a cage like a lamb for slaughter, he'd get back into his conditioning routine of running, lifting weights, along with practicing with his new track team, so he could start the season in the fall. 'Or would he? Something in his son had radically changed.' Something told Dave that Brian might have a great deal of difficulty returning to his former outgoing self.

'What about me?' They'd indicated that since he'd committed the crime in the state of Maryland, he couldn't be released to the state of Ohio until…until when? He'd heard the next step was arraignment, but he didn't know how far off that was, or what followed. As long as he was here, he couldn't get back to work and support his family. He wasn't sure how much of their savings Peggy must have spent to cover home expenses, but he hadn't used nearly as much of it as he'd anticipated, all because of the kindness of Dave and Shirley. He wondered what they thought of all this. He hadn't heard from them. But then, what did he expect? There were no private telephones in their cells.

'Well, at least lodging here won't cost me anything either,' he smiled grimly to himself. But Peggy couldn't go on without income. She hadn't worked a paying job since the kids were born, when she'd been a cashier at Tom's Market. Maybe she could do that again, but with the summer coming up there was going to be a lot of hardships for them in the days ahead. Peggy was their rock.

He thought of the smooth gray rock he'd brought home when he was a kid, and how his dad encouraged him to crack it open, because, he'd said, it was a geode. Dave hammered away at it until it cleaved in two, and inside he found sparkling crystals that looked like a colony of lavender church spires. Peggy was like that rock to him. She appeared ordinary on the outside, but internally her strength and beauty could make a blind man see. He prayed that they wouldn't refuse to let him see her when she came to pick up Brian.

Dave was in a momentary reverie, his head leaning against the bars, when yet another guard approached. "Dave Brefort," he announced, "you have a visitor."

"Yes, that's me." 'My god, could my prayers have been answered so soon?'

"The State's Attorney is here to see you. Step out of your cell, please," the guard said as he unlocked the door, swinging it open. "We need to put your cuffs back on. It's routine when you're seeing someone in an open visiting room." Finally someone had given him an explanation of what they were going to do, before doing it. It must be because of the hierarchy of the visitor. Dave stepped out of his cell, and in a practiced way, put his hands behind him, feeling the pinch and snap of cold metal again.

"Follow me," said the guard. Dave had been the sole occupant in a small cubicle of four holding cells, each like the other, but the guard opened a door that led into a long corridor braced by scores of cells like his, broken only with a staircase that led to an upper level. Feeling the prisoner's eyes following him, he forced himself not to stare back, instinctively knowing it would arose something in both them and him. Most likely fear on his part. He wasn't sure what they felt. Maybe envy, since he wasn't wearing prison clothes. Dave was not yet a member of their fraternity. He followed the guard to the far end of the corridor where a heavy metal door was emblazoned with red block letters, proclaiming, DO NOT ENTER. The guard chose the longest key on a giant ring attached to his belt, inserting it in the keyhole and pulling on the thick heavy door that yielded after an arthritic series of creaks and groans.

It took Dave a moment to adjust to the natural light that flowed into the room from a horizontal series of windows that were laced with diamond-shaped, black iron-webbed screens. The room was bare, except for a long, heavy wooden table, with four card table chairs scattered around it. On one sat a slight blond-haired woman dressed in a severely cut black suit. 'Surely this couldn't be the attorney,' Dave thought.

The woman rose and walked toward him with an extended hand. "It's good to meet you, Mr. Brefort. Oh, that's right, they put handcuffs on you. Guard, remove them, please."

The guard looked startled, then looked down at the floor, making no move to remove the cuffs.

"You were going to stand guard here anyway, right?," she said to him.

"Yes," he said, "that's required."

"Well then, stand guard, but remove the handcuffs. Don't worry. If there's an incident, I'll be the one to answer for the irregularity. But I can see at a glance that Mr. Brefort is an honest man, a gentleman. And if he's treated as one, he'll measure up, won't you, Mr. Brefort?"

"Yes, of course," said Dave. The guard stepped forward and sprung the handcuffs, taking them with him, retreating to the far side of the room.

Dave rubbed his right wrist. "Dave Brefort," he said, as he extended his right hand.

"Karen Falstaff," she said. "Sit," she said, waving her hand at a chair facing the one she'd risen from. "For beginner's, you know that I am the State's Attorney, right?"

"I do now," said Dave, somewhat taken aback by the swift direct energy issuing from such a small package. 'Minus her brown leather heels, she couldn't be more than five feet tall. Maybe she'd sought high status to overcome her short form,' Dave thought.

"Which means of course that I have been appointed by the state to ascertain whether or not there is enough evidence to prosecute you for the murder of Phillip Nottingham. In actuality, the judge will decide that, but after talking to you and other interested parties, plus reviewing the evidence, I will present to him, or her, a plea that I think will be in the best interests of the State of Maryland. I've already read as much information as the police have been able to gather about you, before I came here today. Whereas, you know nothing about me. Correct?'

"So far, yes."

"A 'yes' will be sufficient at this point. Now I'll ask you some questions, and then we can get into some mitigating circumstances you might care to interject."

Dave nodded, still rather dazed at the attorney's demeanor. She looked as though she wasn't old enough to have graduated from law school.

"Now before I get to the first question, I do want to state that as a human being and a single mother, I have the utmost admiration for your act of saving your son, but as a lawyer, I must lay those feelings aside and be as objective as possible. Maintaining that objectivity is my main job. So you know where I'm coming from, yes?"

"Yes," answered Dave, once more amazed that this woman was not only a lawyer, but a single mother to boot. 'Although I knew it was out of the question, somehow I want her to whip out a picture of her child and tell me the story of how she had managed it all. Maybe she could talk to Peg and coach her on how to hold a job, while taking care of the kids at the same time. I completely trusted that Karen Falstaff's child was well cared for. Although it could be a trusted grandmother or a highly paid child-care person. Resources we don't have.'

"So, where I will start is to question you about why you felt compelled to seek out this person yourself, instead of requesting police intervention. Please stop and think before answering this, and my other questions. Respond as briefly as possible, because I'm afraid I only have fifteen minutes with you."

Dave liked her combination of boilerplate and 'I trust you' approach. It was the language often spoken in the trades.

"Adding together some original clues from Ohio and information Dave Hopkins, my Baltimore host, gave me, I was almost certain my son was being held captive in Mr. Nottingham's basement."

'For some reason, I felt it was important to maintain a detached formal tone when talking about the man I'd killed. Even though every time I said Phillip's name, I wanted to spit.'

"And that no police action was being taken about him being held prisoner," Dave continued, "so, as you put it, I felt 'compelled' to act on my own, in order to save my son's life."

"And did you not approach Phillip Nottingham's property in an act of trespassing?"

"Yes, I was aware that was what I was doing, but I had no safe alternative, considering my son's captivity. The front sides of Phillip's property were impenetrable, so I snuck up through the woods in the back. But I did not break in. I went to the front door and knocked, knowing full well that my appearance would alert the kidnapper, as I was an uninvited person."

"And why were you carrying a gun?"

"Because I knew how dangerous the situation was. I had driven by the property several times beforehand, and knew he had a monstrous guard dog. I assumed if I made it into the house, I would have to deal with the dog, and he would undoubtedly attack me."

"Was Phillip unarmed when he led you to the basement room where your son was being held?"

"Yes, as far as I knew. I assume that was so because he was counting on his dog to disable me. He ordered the dog to attack me when he opened the front door. I shot the dog as he was lunging at me. Then after Phillip acknowledged he had my son, I ordered him to take me to him, walking behind him through the house with a gun pointed at his back. I had no intentions of shooting him until he reached for a hidden gun on a shelf outside my son's room, and I heard him cock it. That's when I shot him."

"You did an excellent job, you know. You shot him directly in the heart. The coroner says he died instantly."

Dave felt like a robot when he spoke. "I'm glad. It was not my intent to cause him pain. My only mission was to rescue my son. And in order to do that, I had to kill Phillip."

"As it should be for a self-defense case. But there are some legal obstacles. In Maryland you can use self-help to retrieve property that has been taken, but must do so without violence. Here we're dealing with quite a bit more than property, and quite a bit more than peaceful retrieval. Which may put the judge in a quandary. Aside from the fact that another man claims to have been the murderer. I..."

Dave interrupted, saying, "I know he claims to, but..."

Ms. Falstaff held up her hand, signaling she did not want him to complete his sentence. "That will be up to the judge to rule on. It occurs to me that you could even enter a plea of *Not Guilty* at the arraignment. That said, I'll allow you one question to close with."

Dave had numerous burning questions, but he knew Karen Falstaff wouldn't put up with anything other than what she had stipulated. He asked the one question that made every other one pale in significance. "Will Brian be released, and when his mother comes to get him, will I be allowed to visit with her?"

"That's two questions Mr. Brefort. And two that I do not know the exact answers to since the judge makes those rulings, but I'll do what I can on your behalf. In the event that the judge decides to hear the charges, even though I am not your defense attorney, you can count on me to see that the letter of the law is acted upon." With that, she rose and turned on her heels, nodding to the guard.

"I'll come back for you," he said to Dave as the door clanged shut.

Dave watched Karen Falstaff's tidy black suit diminish down the corridor, but this time it seemed to have robbed the windows of some of their light, which now appeared as a shimmering aura around her vanishing figure.

Chapter 27
Tina
Monday, April 15

Tina Longworth was twenty-two years old, and this was the first time she had ever flown in an airplane. It made her anxious. Her daughter, Tomena, was almost five, and although this was her first time, too, she possessed the air of a veteran flier. She sat on her mother's lap with her nose pressed against the window.

"Look, Mommy, cotton candy."

Tina relished the release of laughter at yet another of her daughter's discoveries. "Yes, the clouds look like the cotton candy you had at the carnival last week."

When the plane had taken off, pushing them back in their seats, Tina gripped the armrests, while Tomena giggled, saying, "It's like when you push me high in the swing."

After the takeoff, she was allowed to sit in her mother's lap, where she immediately kept watch on the disappearing sights of the ground, accompanied by her breathless chatter. "It's like the town under our Christmas tree. There's a church. And a swimming pool. Some are round and some are long. They're that pretty blue color. Now the people look like ants...now they're gone. There's big blobs of green and brown. Getting little and more little. Now they're gone too. Just blue sky. I didn't know it was so blue from down there."

She sighed and settled back in her mother's lap. "I like flying in the big bird. When I grow up I want to fly one. What's the name of that man who flies us?"

"A pilot."

"Yes, I want to be a pilot," Tomena said, resolutely. She nestled back in her mother's arms and promptly fell asleep. Tina stroked her daughter's smooth forehead, treasuring her innocence. Tomena was told they were flying to meet her uncle in a place he had to stay for a while. This was her only uncle, the man who her mother had named her after. Once her Tommy, now a man named Owen, Tina had been informed through the TV news.

As a child, Tomena did not grasp the significance of the volcano that had erupted in her mother's life, even though she was following Tina's footsteps into the caldera. The tremors began two nights ago when Tina was watching TV in a woman's shelter in Gary, Indiana, where she and Tomena had been for two months. They sought refuge there because her husband was a junkie, and when he couldn't get his fix, he resorted to bullying his wife and daughter. A policeman took them to the shelter. Tina took only her purse and Tomena, but for the first time in a long time, she felt safe.

That evening in the shelter, Tomena stretched out on the couch, her head resting on her mother's thigh. Tina was nearly nodding off to sleep when she saw her brother in the video of a crime scene, somewhere in Baltimore. It was eerie, but she instantly knew it was him. There was a certain way he carried himself, the cock of his head, and the way he thrust his chin out when he spoke to the policeman that hadn't changed in the ten years since she had followed him around so closely that his pals had begun calling her 'Tomcat.' The sight of her brother alive and moving made Tina ache with longing to be with him. He'd always been such a good big brother to her. Then one day he just disappeared from their lives, and they never heard from him again. Just like she'd heard her father had disappeared, right after she was born.

Before her mother had died she'd told Tina, "Give it up girl. Your brother's never coming back. He's probably dead and buried years ago. I'm soon to die and you'll be on your own. Unless you marry that punk who's kid you're carrying. Even though he's a deadbeat, at least you can give your kid a legal name, and have some place to call home. And if he skips out on you, like your dad did, at least if you're married, they'll be after him for child support. Then if they don't catch him, you can still sign up for welfare." Her mother's benediction.

After seeing Tommy, Tina was glued to the newscasts for the next twenty-four hours. It turned out that he was a suspect in the murder of some wealthy man in Baltimore. They gave his name as Owen, but Tina knew better. That was her Tommy. She explained the situation to the Director of the Shelter where they were staying, and Doris helped her get in touch with the Baltimore police.

Through a series of calls, they put her in touch with a woman named Jane, who was looking for Owen's lost sister. Jane told her how thrilled she was to have found the two of them, and immediately invited her and Tomena to transfer to the Baltimore Women's Shelter, where she worked. Jane reassured Tina that she'd see to it that the plane fare for the two of them would be covered, her flight scheduled, and she herself would meet mother and daughter in the Baltimore terminal.

But much more than taking care of the travel plans, Jane explained to Tina in a calm manner the story of Tommy's life since he'd left his sister, ten years earlier. Although it was in no way a pleasing story, as Jane didn't skip over the gritty parts, she'd emphasized how resourceful Tommy had been, and how he had emerged a resilient survivor.

She told Tina about how she'd met 'Owen,' how it was that he'd changed his name, and how difficult it was for him to get back on the right track, because he became so obsessed with finding Phillip. Tommy's mission was to keep Phillip from harming other young boys, as he had him. She said that the day of the murder, Tommy had just found out where Phillip was living, borrowed her car and gone to Phillip's new home to confront him, without a gun. "Which was a foolish thing to do," Jane added, knowing full well that she was continuing her lie. "But that's what he did," she continued. "And he got there just after the father of the kidnapped boy that Phillip was holding in his basement, had shot and killed Phillip, then rescued his son."

Jane emphasized that the father was certain that he'd killed Phillip with just one shot, but after he called the police and he and his son were standing on the front porch, waiting for them, Tommy had arrived outside the big iron gate, insisting that he'd killed him. Jane shared how difficult it had been to piece together the story, but she'd been able to, with the help of the police and what she knew about Tommy.

Tina followed the complex story well in spite of Jane's confusion about Owen's name, sometimes calling him Owen, sometimes Tommy. But when Jane got to the part where Owen insisted to the police that he'd killed Phillip, Tina broke down, sobbing. "I don't understand. Why is Tommy doing this? Phillip was killed just like he wanted, the boy is free, and Tommy could be free too. Why does he insist on being the killer when he wasn't? I could help him get back on his feet. And he could help Tomena and me. I can't make any sense of his lying."

"Sweetheart, settle down and listen to me," Jane said over the phone. "You can't make any sense of it, because it really doesn't make much sense to anyone but Owen. Owen, excuse me, Tommy, is terribly emotional about all this and wants to feel that he has rid the world of Phillip, and that the good father he never had – that would be Dave, the man who actually killed Phillip – can be free to go home to be with his son, and the rest of his family. And besides, Tommy never really had a home since he left you, and probably feels a sense of relief that he doesn't have to worry about providing for himself anymore, since the state will take care of that. Now that his mission is accomplished and Phillip is dead, he really doesn't have anything outside of the jail to live for anymore. And that's where you and Tomena come in. You will give him something to live for. Do you understand?"

There were sniffles at the other end of the line, a long silence, and then, "Yes, I think I understand now. But how will I know who you are when we get off the plane?"

"I'll hold up a sign that will tell you," Jane assured her.

As they pulled up to the prison gate, the first question Tomena asked was, "Why are there knives on the fence for?"

'Leave this to me,' Jane signaled to Tina. Tina nodded.

"They put those there so bad guys can't get in and hurt the people inside. It's for their protection. They're keeping your Uncle Tommy safe until we can find him a good home to move to. It's going to take a while, but we'll do everything we can to fix it so that he can come out and be with you. In the meantime, the policemen that protect your uncle and others like him, won't let children inside to visit. You have to be at least twelve years old. So you'll have to wait out here with me until Mommy gets to see Uncle Tommy. She can even take a picture of him on my Ipod and bring it back to you, so you can see what he looks like. Your Mommy tells me he looks a lot like you."

"Not fair," said Tomena, her head down, twisting her left thumb with her other hand. "I wanna go too."

"Yes, you're right," said Jane. "It's not fair, but those are the rules. And we can't argue with those big molice-pans."

"Those are not what you said. Those are policemans."

"You're right again. But I said that funny word from a silly poem I know. I bet I could teach it to you. Mom, go ahead, and by the time you get back, we'll have a silly poem for you to hear. And maybe even a special picture I brought for Tomena to color."

Before Tomena even had time to protest, Tina slid out of the car, and Jane started in, "Once a big policeman saw a little bum, sitting on the curbstone, chewing bubble gum. Said the big policeman to the little bum, "Give me some."

"What's a bum?

"Oh, someone who doesn't have any money. But this is a little bum."

"She does too have money. She bought some bubble gum."

"Gosh, you're awful smart to figure that out. But she spent it all. So now she's a little bum. Do you want to hear the silly part of the poem?"

"I guess. Will Mommy be back by then?"

"Maybe by the time you learn how to say it to her... OK, here goes. 'Once a big molicepan saw a bittle um, siting on the surb-cone chewing gubber um. Said the big molicepan to the bittle um – sim me gum."

"That's the same, only all messed up."

"Yep, you got it. Now let's see if you can learn it the funny messed up way. We can record it on my phone, and the next time your Mom can play your silly poem for Uncle Tommy."

"OK, but my mommy better be back by the time I know it."

"She will Darlin'. She will."

Chapter 28
Owen and Tina
Monday

Tina laced her fingers together, tightening them to keep from trembling. Something must be wrong. There was a score of visitors seated at intervals along the Formica counter, already speaking to their loved ones through voice-vents in the safety glass barrier that kept visitors from touching the inmates. Or passing contraband. Tina was familiar with prison safety features, having visited Tomena's father when he was in on drug charges.

'Where was Tommy? They must have told him she was here and brought him down from his cell. Was he ill? Didn't he want to see her?' She was about to leave the visiting room and make inquiries from the outer guard, when the back entrance to the inmate's enclosure burst open, and she caught sight of a guard grappling with a handcuffed man. At first all she could see of the prisoner was his back. He had a midweight physique and long stringy black hair. 'It could be –' she returned to her seat, waiting to see.

Finally the guard pulled the man around and pointed toward Tina. 'Yes, it was her Tommy, but a hammered-down, much harder rendition of him. "How long had it been?" This man, Owen, he called himself, could be mistaken for a man of her father's generation. Hard times were etched on his face.

Owen's jaw dropped when he first saw her. It was his Tina, all grown up and even more beautiful than he remembered. 'Why didn't they tell me it was my sister?' They simply said it was a woman, and he couldn't imagine any, other than Jane, who would be visiting. He didn't want to see her and talk about all that had come down. He was growing confused about his part in it, and didn't think he could face her probing in tender spots. None of that applied to his baby sister.

Owen turned to the guard, said something, and the guard immediately removed his handcuffs. He strode toward the bolted-down chair across from Tina, finding it hard to check his impulse to reach out and touch her. Instead he placed the palm of his hand on the window and spoke through the vent.

"Good lord, Tina – they didn't tell me it was you. I wasted precious moments fighting them. How did you find me? How did you get here? Where did you come from?" Owen felt as though he would implode from containing a decade of pent-up emotions.

Tina was slower to respond. When last she was with her brother, she'd been a young girl, innocent and naive, looking up to him to meet all of her nurturing needs, since her father was long gone, and her mother rarely at home. The man she saw in front of her did not match the image of who she thought her big brother would be, even though she was informed of the circumstances that brought him to this place.

She blushed, and Owen said, "You used to do that when you were a little girl. Good lord, I can't believe it's you – after all these years. I've thought about you, dreamed about you, and how beautiful you are. You look just like I thought you would. Tell me what you've been doing."

A smile flickered on Tina's face, but disappeared when she looked into Owen's eyes. "Where have *you* been all these years? Why didn't you call, or write, and tell me where you were? I still lived at the same address for at least six years after you left. I didn't even know if you were dead or alive...I cried myself to sleep for years before Mom finally convinced me that you were dead. Did you know she died? About four years ago. Right after my daughter, Tomena was born. I named her after you. Why didn't you come home, Tommy?"

"Tina, my sweet little Tina...I'm so damn sorry. Let me try to explain." Owen looked down, rubbing his head with both of his hands as though he could extract his story from an oven between his ears. "At first I was kidnapped by an evil man, and when I escaped I was so pitiful, I couldn't stand the thought of you seeing me that way. I thought I'd be rehabilitated and then come to you, but instead I got further into drugs and crime. And I didn't want to come to you like that. I was so ashamed."

"I know about all that history, Tommy. Jane told me. She's the one who arranged for me and Tomena to come here."

"Oh, Tina, I'm so sorry. I can't begin to tell you how sorry I am. But if there is any way I can make it up to you, I will. Please tell me how."

Tommy's dark brown eyes had softened until they reminded Tina of the fawn she once fell in love with, in that petting zoo. She wanted to take him home, and Tommy even tried to buy him from the zoo, promising to build a backyard pen for him, but of course the zoo-keeper informed them that the animals were never for sale. Tina had been broken-hearted, and Tommy promised her he would never disappoint her like that again. And he had.

"Yes, Tommy – you don't mind if I still call you Tommy, do you? I know you changed your name to Owen, but you'll always be Tommy to me."

"Yes, call me Tommy. I consider it an honor. Owen is not a person you would ever want to know, and I hope you never do."

"OK, Tommy. I know we're short on time, so here are some of my answers to your questions. I was in a Battered Woman's Shelter in Gary with my daughter, Tomena. She's your niece, Tommy. I named her after you. She's almost five, and bright as a new penny. She's my whole world. I left her father, who's a drug addict. He's done time for possession and resisting arrest. Plus he abused me. That's how I wound up in the shelter with Tomena. And that's where I first saw you on TV, made some calls, and finally got in touch with Jane, who knew you. Tomena and I both need you. But not as you are. Jane says the two of us can stay at the Shelter, or with her, for as long as it takes you to get out of here. She says she's willing to watch over us until you get out, get straight…and then she'll help you get a job. And she says I might be able to work at the Shelter. I can't tell you how helpful she's been to us. I don't understand why she's so good to strangers, but I sure do need her help. And she's just great with Tomena…I'm afraid Tee's gonna throw me over and want Jane as her mom."

Finally Tina's words ran down, as she paused and took a deep breath.

"You're right about Jane. She's a good woman. I'm so glad she found you. I hope I can measure up to what she expects of me. For starters I'll have to beat the rap that I admitted to. That's murder, you know. Plain and simple. I really didn't kill that horrible man, but I arrived at his house to find a young boy that he'd kidnapped and abused, as he did me. His father had just killed the asshole – excuse my French – trying to rescue his own son. I wanted the father to be free to take his son home. At the time, I was in an altered state – drugs I never should have taken – and I really thought I'd killed the guy because of the death rays I was sending into his body."

Owen stopped as he looked up at the guard whose stance

had changed, signifying their time was about up. "But none of that matters now. We probably only have about five minutes left 'til visiting hour is over. It's really not an hour. More like fifteen minutes. But quick, tell me what you can about Tomena. My niece. I can hardly believe it."

Tina rummaged in her purse and fished out Tomena's picture from her wallet. She rubbed the front of it on her shirt, as though polishing it, then pressed it down on the countertop, sliding in under the thin opening where the glass met the counter. The guard immediately stepped forward, pulling the picture back and inspecting it closely with a flashlight. Apparently satisfied, he slid it back toward Owen. Although only a small photo, Owen held it between both thumbs and index fingers, staring at it so fixedly, that it seemed as though the photo would ignite from his penetrating gaze.

"I don't understand," he said, holding the photo. "She looks more like me...as I used to be, than you."

This time Tina's smile was wide, displaying the dimple above the corner of her mouth. "Of course, Tommy. It happens all the time in family trees. You're probably not into studying them, but sometimes a grandson resembles his grandmother, two cousins look more alike than they look like their parents. Genes have a way of jumping around. Tomena's chose to resemble you, and I'm glad of it. Thinking I had lost you, it was a way of keeping your memory alive. Wait 'til you see her in person. Beside your dark eyes and hair, she has your wicked sense of humor."

"Now just a minute. You told me she's not yet five. And she has a 'wicked sense of humor'? How does that happen?"

"Sometimes I wonder myself. It's been like that from the beginning. She's been like an old soul born into a baby's body. I can't explain it, but when you're around her, you'll know what I mean. I was going to take a picture and show it to her, but maybe next time, after you've cleaned up a little." Tina blushed with embarrassment at her frankness.

"Thanks for the reprieve. And yes, I'll clean up my act. Not just the surface, but every little crevice. The inside too. Now that I have a reason to, I'll do my damnest, to look and smell, think and talk like a preacher's son."

He cast an eye on the guard. "They're coming to get me now, Tina, but the next time you see me you won't be able to believe your eyes. I'll be able to talk the talk and walk the walk with the straightest and holiest of them."

"That's good, Tommy. Just don't rub all the wicked away. I want to be able to recognize my Tommy when I see him. There's nothing wrong with *him*. Bring my brother back to me."

Chapter 29
Brian, Peggy and Lauren
Monday, April 15

Brian felt awkward hugging his mother, and then Lauren. Somehow it didn't feel right. It was something he'd done almost everyday at home, which wasn't that long ago, but it didn't feel at all natural. Maybe it was because his dad wasn't here with them. That didn't seem right either. After all, he'd rescued Brian and Brian had seen him, but he hadn't been with the rest of the family for two weeks, they'd told him. And the visiting room seemed almost as drab as the holding cell they'd put him in at the juvenile detention center. Nothing seemed to prepare him for these new beginnings of his old life.

His mom stepped away from the hug, her hands still embracing his shoulders. Brian could see the glossy path of a tear on her cheek. Lauren had her usual lips-shut smile, trying to hide her braces. His mom gave him her inspection look, scanning him from head to toe. Her assessment was favorable.

"You're a little pale from being shut in, but all in all, you look pretty healthy. How do you feel?"

"Well, I'm nervous about all this," said Brian, looking for a place to sit. There was a long narrow table with three chairs, apparently set up for them. He walked toward it, his mom and Lauren following.

"But of course you are. Anyone in your place, would be," said Peggy. "This isn't exactly the Ritz." She gave a nervous laugh that seemed to ricochet off the metal bars. "But soon it will all be over," she continued, easing into her maternal comforting tone.

"Did they tell you that your dad's arraignment will be on Tuesday, and..." Peggy saw the puzzled look on Brian's face. "You don't know what day this is, do you?"

"No, I don't."

"It's Monday, April fifteenth, so the arraignment is just two days away. Then I can take you home. I don't understand why, but you need to go back to your cell after our visit, and then when the arraignment's over...and you can come to it...then we can take you home."

"What about Dad? Will he be coming home too?"

"Maybe, but we don't know yet. They have stuff they have to go over in court with him here, but he should be released soon after that. Even if he's not released, he wants us to take you home. Get you back in school. Get things back to normal."

"Yeah, Brian, I'm going to have a surprise welcome home...oops, sorry. I guess it isn't a surprise anymore. I never was any good at keeping secrets. But you know that," said Lauren.

Brian pulled back in his chair. "Mom, Lauren – I don't want any parties. You know...or anything like that. I just want...I'm not sure what I want, except I don't want anything to be different than when I left home. Like maybe have lasagna for dinner." He looked to his mother for her consent. "I guess I said lasagna because I remember that's the supper you were making that night. You know, the night I didn't come home."

"Oh, Sweetheart, I don't know what to say," said Peggy, taking out a hankie and dabbing at her nose.

"Me neither," said Brian. "How's Heather? He winced at the thought of greeting Heather. It had something to do with Phillip. Everything had something to do with Phillip.

"Oh, she calls almost every day, asking if there's any news of you," said Peggy as Lauren began picking imaginary lint off her blue sweater. "She wanted to come with us, but of course they don't allow...gosh darn, this just doesn't work."

There was an awkward silence and then Peggy's face lit up. "Listen, Dad's arraignment is in, oh, I told you that. Well, come to think of it, you probably don't know what an arraignment is, but I asked and they told me that it's where the judge sets bail, and – oh, you probably don't know what bail is. Hmm, it's kinda like the 'Get Out of Jail Free' card in Monopoly, except you have to pay someone, or I mean, they have to pay the court, and..."

Peggy stopped suddenly, and then, starting with suppressed laughter, her hand over her mouth, the three of them heard it build to a crescendo.

Brian didn't see what was so funny. It was an entirely different kind of humor than Phillip's. It seemed like child's play. But it continued, and before long Lauren joined in, her arms crossed, holding her sides. His mom reached into her jacket pocket and began dabbing at her tears of laughter. Brian couldn't help himself. He began laughing too. At first it felt artificial, as though he was forcing it from inside, but before long it just slipped out and filled the pit in his stomach that had been hollow for so long.

Just as suddenly as she'd started, Peggy stopped laughing, and began crying again. "Oh Brian, I'm so sorry. There's nothing funny about this, but I just don't know what to say to bring back the Brian we all knew. Tell us what we can do." Peggy dropped her hands to her side in an expression of helplessness.

Brian had stopped laughing, and gave a deep shuddering sigh. "I really don't know myself." That wasn't exactly how he meant it, but it said everything he couldn't say. He no longer knew himself.

Lauren interrupted a long silence, saying, "Let's say the Lord's Prayer together. That's something we all know. I think it will help."

She looked to her mother, as Peggy began, "Our Father, who art in heaven, hallowed be thy name..." Lauren and Brian joined in, and when they got to "For thine is the kingdom, the power and the glory...," Peggy asked them to repeat the whole prayer, over and over.

Brian lost count, but by the time they had said it repeatedly, ending with "Amen," he felt a radiance that seemed to issue from within the three small bodies that huddled around the table, holding hands, almost as though they were in a sacred place.

Chapter 30
Dave and David
Monday, April 15

It was the second morning that Dave arose to the sound of clanging metal, as the guard opened the feed bay and slid a bowl of what appeared to be oatmeal, along with a carton of milk and a cup of coffee, into his cell. Dave made the mistake of pouring the milk on his cereal before testing it, only to find that it didn't need cooling down, but warming up. It scarcely mattered. He was famished.

Finishing the gruel, he found the coffee was still steaming hot, so he poured the remainder of his milk in it, stirring it with the lone spoon. The mixture in his cup resembled a muddy sea, while the chunks of oatmeal that dropped from his spoon became floating islands. It was amazing the mundane things that caught his attention when there was sensory deprivation. No wonder some prisoners became artists, some writers, some turning to religion, while serving time.

Although he had no standard to measure from, Dave was fairly certain that if he had to stay confined much longer, he would surely hallucinate.

How had Brian managed to maintain his sanity confined in one small room for weeks? But perhaps he hadn't. Dave realized he might never know what his son had experienced. It could remain a gulf they would never cross.

The guard appeared again, and after removing his tray, said, "Mr. Brefort, you have another visitor. Sorry, but I'll have to handcuff you again."

Dave automatically turned his back, thrusting his wrists behind him. He wondered why the courtesy on the part of the guard. Maybe it was his defense attorney that the court appointed. Again, the long trip through the cell block to the holding cell visitor's room. This time he thought he heard a few jeers from the inmates. They probably didn't approve of his separate status.

Arriving in the room where he met with the prosecuting attorney, he was startled to see Dave Hopkins rise from one of the card table chairs. This time the guard removed his handcuffs without being asked. Hopkins rose and gave Dave a hug. Dave left his hands at his side, afraid of how the guard might react if he reciprocated. His assessment proved right, as the guard stepped forward, saying, "Excuse me, Mr. Hopkins, but you are not allowed to have physical contact with the prisoner."

"Sorry," said Hopkins to the guard, then turning to Dave, said, "Man, it's good to see you. It's a damn shame to have to visit you here, but bad as it might seem, I'm just glad to see you alive. And your son too. You were exactly right not to listen to me. Knowing what we do now, if you had followed my advice, Brian probably wouldn't be alive to tell his story. Illegal as it was, you did the right thing."

Dave immediately thought of Hopkins betrayal to his wife, but just as quickly, buried it. In this situation, he believed and trusted his host. "There was no other way," Dave said, "once I realized that Phillip knew who I was. I wanted to abide by the law and your advice, but that was overturned by the risk of losing Brian, when I was so close."

"Of course. I understand that now. But I came here today to discuss some positive directions for your family's future. Actually I guess you could say that I'm a stand-in for your attorney, Mark Close, who is out-of-state and couldn't get back in time to talk to you. But he'll be well-prepared with reports via phone and emails. And he'll be present at the arraignment, which is tomorrow afternoon. Then you'll find out about the actual charges, bail, next court date, and all that."

"So the state has chosen a defense attorney to represent me. That's good. Do you know anything about this guy, Mark? Perhaps by reputation?"

"Yes, I know a great deal about Mark Close, and he's the best damn lawyer we could get. And he's not from the Legal Aide department. I chose him, and he's happy to accept a high profile case like this. He'll see that you get the best representation possible. And that justice is done."

Again, Dave's betrayal of Shirley flickered across his mind. He'd thought he'd put it to bed. "Gosh, Dave, I don't know how I'll be able to afford him. Even on a time payment basis, if he'd allow that. I've got two kids to put through college coming up. I don't even see where the daily costs of living are going to come from, if my sentence is very long."

"Don't you worry about a thing. It will be taken care of. What you don't know, and I've been privy to, is a wealth of information about Phillip Nottingham that has a number of influential folks in the city all abuzz. It will definitely impact your case, It might even elevate you to the role of hero."

"I'm not sure what you're referring to," said Dave.

"Of course not. You've been locked in a cell and don't know what's going on in the outside world, but believe me, it's been all over TV. With photos of Phillip Nottingham. Wouldn't you know that no less than three men have called in, recognizing him, and stating that similar things happened to them, at the hands of the same man...when they were youths. It appears Phillip was a serial kidnapper and pedophile going back, at least twenty years ago. God only knows how many more are out there that we may never hear from."

No flicker of recognition crossed Dave's face, so Hopkins continued. "And listen to this! It turns out that the crazy bloke shot and killed a female deputy sheriff in Pennsylvania, the night he left your area, on his way home, with your son in the car. Does your son even remember? Apparently not. Why? Because Phillip kept those young boys he kidnapped, drugged to the gills. They never even knew what state they were in, let alone a street address. Because when he'd finish with them, he'd drug them into oblivion on their way back, then drop then off within twenty miles or so of the neighborhood where he'd picked them up. So they had no means of ever identifying him, or where he came from."

He paused for a minute, but Dave looked stunned, so Hopkins continued. "Dave, I'm so deeply sorry you had to go through all this to rid our city of such a depraved individual. He had us completely deluded about what he was. *Keep Our Children Safe*! Ha! When what we should have been doing is to keep our children away from the likes of him."

He paused again, looking for a response, but Dave was still speechless. "Sorry for going on so, but I couldn't get over the depths of his depravity and how he had so many honest men, and women, helping him go about his dirty business, right under our noses."

Hopkins removed a tissue from his pants pocket, wiping some sweat off his brow. "Sorry," he repeated. "I see, I've got myself all worked up." He took a long slow breath and continued. "But what I came to tell you is that a substantial group of our city planners, plus the board of *Keep Our Children Safe,* will see to it that you get the best lawyer, and will put up whatever bail is asked for at your arraignment. You won't have to pay a red cent. We'll see to it that you and your family are taken care of. And we'll arrange for whatever treatment your family needs in the aftermath. Back in Ohio, I mean."

Dave tried to take it all in, but still remained nearly paralyzed with disbelief. He kept lowering his head and shaking it. Hopkins supported his silence, not interrupting it.

Finally Dave said, "I don't know what to say. My poor son. And Phillip's 'other boys.' Now I fully realize that Owen was one of those, and look what a mess his life is. No wonder he wanted vengeance. But the lawyer, the bail, help beyond that...it's all too much for you to do for my family. We'll have to work out some way for me to repay you."

Hopkins glanced at the guard, who seemed to be preoccupied with a magazine near the exit door, nevertheless, he dropped his voice. "But that's what I've been trying to tell you, Dave. You've already repaid us by killing the son-of-a-bitch. Think of all the money that would have been wasted on his trial, incarceration, appeals, because he probably would have gotten life without parole...oh, it's endless. You've saved our Great State of Maryland, millions of dollars. The least we can do for you, is pay for whatever your needs are to get through this travesty."

"Again, I don't know what to say. Except that it will be so wonderful to get out of here, get on with my life and try to make things as normal as possible for my family. Especially Brian. Get him back into school and running track again. Back to church. I'm sure he'll heal a lot faster than someone like Owen, who must have been treated a lot worse, for a lot longer. And then, no one to support him afterward."

Dave paused, running his hand over his mouth, almost as though releasing the word he wanted to speak. "I mean, Brian speaks well of Phillip, so I guess Phillip must have been kinder to him. Actually I don't understand it, but Brian seems to have a...oh, I don't know...almost a reverence for Phillip. I hate to admit this Dave, but I know Brian's deeply upset about the fact that I killed Phillip. You know, I wouldn't have, except it was the only way I could save my son's life."

Hopkins started to move toward Dave to comfort him when he remembered the guard's warning about physical contact, and stepped back. The guard looked up from his reading, saying, "You'll need to finish up your business. I have to escort the prisoner back to his cell in three minutes."

Hopkins visibly shuddered, saying, "My god, Dave, how can you stand it? To be called one, and treated as a prisoner. Well, hopefully you won't have to put up with it much longer. We think that there's a good chance that Mark will be able to get you the shortest sentence possible for 'Justifiable Homicide," which I understand will be less than six months. And Mark hopes the judge will set bail for you, so you can return home after the arraignment…as soon as possible."

"Oh, and one last thing that's a partial answer to your concern about Brian's feeling toward Phillip. Shirley's pitched in and spoken to a lot of people, rallying support for you. One of them is Jane, a social worker, who somehow managed to locate Owen's younger sister and brought her here, and…no time to go into that, but through Jane, Shirley got an explanation of what you're witnessing in your son. She says that aside from *Post Traumatic Stress Disorder,* that Brian will undoubtedly experience, that he will need to be treated for *Stockholm Syndrome.* You're probably too young to remember Patty Hearst, the granddaughter of William Randolph Hearst, the newspaper scion, but…"

"No, I do remember reading about the case years later when her daughter got married. About that radical group she was mixed up with, and the bank robbery that she was involved in," said Dave. He paused thoughtfully. "But I don't see the parallels."

"Yes, well she was pardoned from prison on the basis of the fact that she was kidnapped and identified so strongly with her captors that it led her to partake in serious crimes that were not in her nature. As I understand it, it's rather like bonding with someone who has you in their thrall, out of deep fear. That is, if you don't comply, your life is at risk. Even though Brian's captivity was much shorter, thank God. But it still applies."

Dave sat down at the table, and the guard left the corner of the room, coming toward him with the handcuffs. "I think I begin to understand, but I'm not sure what I can do about it."

Hopkins watched the guard, as Dave stood, and the handcuffs were replaced. "I don't think there's much you can do about it, except be there for your son. And leave the rest to the professionals, and time. Listen, I'll see you on Tuesday at the arraignment. Shirley and I will be there, but more importantly, your whole family. If things go well, you might be able to leave with your wife, your son, and your daughter, soon after the arraignment. And return to Ohio until the trial. What a blessing that will be for you."

"Yes it will. And I have you and Shirley, and a whole host of others to thank for it," said Dave, walking ahead of the guard toward the iron gate.

"And don't forget your Higher Power," said Hopkins. "Never used to be a believer, but your strength in the face of adversity has converted me. No more trips to Washington, leaving Shirley alone. And when you get settled back in Ohio, Shirley and I would like to visit you. Maybe see Brian in a track meet, and go to church with your family."

"Hallelujah, Brother," said Dave.

"Hallelujah," said Hopkins.

Chapter 31
Dave, Peggy, Brian and Lauren
Tuesday, April 16

Dave was behind the wheel after the arraignment, leaving Baltimore, driving his family back home. He knew he'd have to return for the preliminary hearing, but for now, he felt good. For the first time in a long time, he felt in control of his life. Peggy was in the front seat, beside him. She was unusually quiet, but kept reaching over with her left hand, patting his thigh. Looking out the window, she broke her silence, saying to no one in particular, "Baltimore is really an ugly city, don't you think?"

Dave answered, "Yes, I think so too, but that's probably because of our experience here. Actually I remember liking the section where Dave and Shirley live."

"Probably because that section was positively reinforcing for you," said Lauren. "We're studying that sort of stuff in the psychology section of our science course now. Actually I find it pretty interesting. The city, I mean. What do you think, Brian?"

"What did you say?"

"I asked you what you thought of Baltimore. Pretty? Ugly? Or pretty ugly?"

"I don't have an opinion yet. I've never seen it before."

It was like that now. Brian would put a stop to whatever they were talking about, because he would inevitably make a comment that would remind them that he had traveled other roads than they had. It almost seemed like he was a hitchhiker they had picked up, rather than a member of the family.

Lauren couldn't hold her tongue any longer. "Brian, can you try a little harder not to be such a party-pooper. I mean, Dad just got out of jail – at least for a while – you got out of your prison, we're together again, going home, and...there's lots of reasons to celebrate. Come on."

"Lauren, this is your father speaking. Rest easy. Brian, do you need any of your anti-anxiety medication that the psychiatrist prescribed for you? He said you could take it up to three times a day."

"No, Dad, I don't need any pills like that. Now or ever again. I'm just sad that I'm leaving and I'll never be able to come back again. Never see Phillip again. It doesn't feel right to be going home and not really be able to speak about this, because no one will understand."

"Son, you'll be able to speak about your experience with someone who will understand what you've been through. Dave Hopkins and that social worker, Jane, as I recall, saw to it that you'll have immediate access to a counselor as soon as we get home. You can see him alone when you want, and he will also meet with our whole family on occasion, so we can better understand each other. Do you think that will help?"

"Maybe, some. But I can't really talk to anyone about Phillip, when they never even knew him. They're going to think bad things about him because that's what everyone else is saying, when he wasn't ever mean to me."

"No, Brian, I don't think that's where this counselor will be coming from. He won't think badly of Phillip. He'll be more interested in what you think of him and why."

Peggy began to cry. "Brian, I'm sorry I'm not able to share your grief, but there's some things you need to know about Phillip."

Dave was having a hard time concentrating on his driving. "Peggy, you need to hold your tongue. It's up to the counselor to deal with these things. Please."

"No, I won't be quiet this time. Brian needs to face some hard-to-hear facts about Mr. Nottingham. Brian, older men have come forward, saying that Phillip kidnapped them as teenagers, and that he drugged them and forced them to have sex with him. And the police report says that on the way to his house, when you were drugged in his car, he shot and killed a female police officer. Brian, you need to know that no matter how well he treated you, Phillip Nottingham is an evil man."

Lauren gasped. Dave was having trouble getting over into the right lane for the exit ramp, so he could stop some place before he had an accident. There was a long silence as everyone tried to collect themselves, and then Brian said in a soft, breaking voice: "Mom, why do you think Phillip was an evil man?"

"I just told you. Because he killed someone in cold blood. I'm sorry, I shouldn't have said that. But you need to know."

Dave managed to get off at an exit ramp, and pulled into the first thing he saw. A McDonald's. His tires screeched as he made a sharp right hand turn into their parking lot. As he brought the car to rest in a parking space, he heard Brian say: "So then my father is an evil man because he killed somebody in cold blood."

Dave got out of the driver's seat, closing his door, as he opened Brian's door, directly behind the driver's seat. Brian stumbled out, his knees buckling as he fell, sobbing, into his father's chest. Dave wrapped his arms around him, then smoothed his hair back from his forehead as though he were a baby.

"It's OK, Son. It's OK. It's gonna be rough sailing here for a while, but we'll bring this boat into calm waters again. We're good sailors. We'll show the ladies how it's done. Right? You gonna be my buddy? I can't do it alone."

Brian looked through his tears into his father's eyes. "Yes, Dad, I'll be your buddy. I hope we can do it together. I can't make it alone either."

Dave imagined Brian someday holding his own son like this, consoling him, offering him support. Hopefully it would not be over a catastrophic event such as this generation of his family was going through, but there would be something hard. Something that would break people apart, bring them together again. There would always be something.

About Atmosphere Press

Atmosphere Press is an independent, full-service publisher for excellent books in all genres and for all audiences. Learn more about what we do at atmospherepress.com.

We encourage you to check out some of Atmosphere's latest releases, which are available at Amazon.com and via order from your local bookstore:

New Shores, a novel by Ciaran McLarnon

Murder at the Olympiad, a novel by James Gilbert

The World Turned Upside Down, a novel by Steven Mendel

Dolly: The Reno Story, a novel by Fern Hammer

Moments of Truth, a novel by Stewart Bellus

ReStart: Stories of the Cairn Age, by Scott Bollens

A Strand of Gold, a novel by Elisabeth Conway

Welcome Home, a novel by Michael O'Brien

Comfrey, Wyoming: Marcela's Army, a novel by Daphne Birkmyer

Reunion of the Good Weather Suicide Cult, a novel by Kyle McCord

About the Author

Although the characters in *Bone Deep Bonds* are fictitious, they are based on the author's thirty-five years as a licensed professional clinical counselor, where she worked with families of incest and other sexual abusers and victims. Participants find that recovery is a lifelong process, but through the years it brings health and healing not only to themselves, but to their families, friends, and communities, creating a more charitable world for all.

CPSIA information can be obtained
at www.ICGtesting.com
Printed in the USA
LVHW040006261022
731534LV00002B/226